THE HISTORY OF ARCADIA

THE
LIZARD
PRINCESS

The Lizard Princess and the Princess Lizard

THE HISTORY OF ARCADIA

THE LIZARD PRINCESS

TOD DAVIES

ILLUSTRATIONS BY
MIKE MADRID

EXTERMINATING ANGEL
PRESS

EXTERMINATING ANGEL PRESS
"Creative Solutions for Practical Idealists"
Visit *www.exterminatingangel.com* to join the conversation
info@exterminatingangel.com

Exterminating Angel Press book design by Mike Madrid
Layout and typesetting by John Sutherland

ISBN: 978-1-935259-29-9
eBook ISBN: 978-1-935259-30-5
Library of Congress Control Number: 2015905429
Distributed by Consortium Book Sales & Distribution
(800) 283-3572
www.cbsd.com

PRINTED IN THE UNITED STATES OF AMERICA

 **CONTENTS**

Editor's Note
A Letter from Dr. Alan Fallaize   i
The Beginning   1

    I. The Lizard Princess   5
   II. Through the Enchanted Wood   33
  III. In the Bower of Bliss   56
  IV. Conor Barr   68
   V. The Centaur and the Mermaids   85
  VI. In the Dead Wood   99
 VII. On the Ruined Surface   109
VIII. Susan   128
  IX. Rowena   148
   X. To the Moons   172
  XI. Livia   197
 XII. The Moon Itself   215
XIII. On the Road of the Dead   229
XIV. In the Domain of Life   247
 XV. Sophia the Wise   253

Afterword by Shanti Vale   270

Three Young Women and Death: 274
An Arcadian Fairy Tale

EDITOR'S NOTE

*T*he *Lizard Princess* is the third book in the History of Arcadia, the latest that Arcadia sent us from their world. And I think I see the pattern that these books are meant to form.

The first, *Snotty Saves the Day,* was a story for 'children'. Although the footnotes by an Arcadian physicist hinted at something more. That book came by air.

The second, *Lily the Silent,* was obviously meant for an older reader, what we would call a 'young adult'. For it was a more romantic story than the first. That book floated to me on a mountain lake. By water.

The book you're holding now, *The Lizard Princess,* came by fire. Through a mirror reflecting the last of a blazing sunset, all red and gold and green and violet around the edges. I was pleased to find that communication with Arcadia flows much easier now. For when the light is right, I can see through that mirror into Arcadia.

When the sun sends out one last ray, I can see Arcadia through the tawny shadows in the mirror—the forests and the rivers, the green and gold fields. I can make out dim figures of people I've come to know from its history. I can see these people at different times in their stories, which confirms what I suspected: Arcadian time doesn't march with ours. It spins in the same space as our own, at a different rate of speed. And we can enter its present, its past, or even in its future, depending on luck and the physics of the place.

I think I see now what Arcadia itself is trying to get through to our world. Although only time will tell if I have it right.

If *Snotty Saves the Day* was a book for children, and *Lily the Silent* one for young adults, who is meant to read *The Lizard Princess?*

I always thought there were two kinds of truth in the world: truths of reasoning and truths of fact. But the Lizard Princess proposes a third: truths of imagination. I think the book you hold now is meant for those who believe that kind of truth has the potential to show us new ways of seeing, and with them, new ways of being. I think that is what Arcadia is trying to say.

I believe Sophia when she says she learned that truth in her days as the Lizard Princess. She says it takes a lizard, an angel, and a girl to make a great queen. All three together made Sophia the Wise.

And I look, hopeful, into the mirror in my room waiting to see what next missing piece of the story—of the History of Arcadia—will emerge from the golden shadows there.

Tod Davies
The Colestin Valley, Oregon
Spring 2015

Dear Editor,

Much has happened to Arcadia in the days since Queen
Sophia set down the story of the Lizard Princess. You
know some of it from the works we've managed to send
to you from our world, happily with increasing ease.
But it's only recently we've discovered this text,
which our queen meant for us to find, along with
Snotty Saves the Day and Lily the Silent.

I completely understand why Queen Sophia kept these
tales to herself all these years. She was right: we
wouldn't have understood their meaning before now.
We barely yet have come to grips with the undeniable
physical fact that it is symbols joined with energy
that form the stories making up the reality of our

every day (or, as the equation has it, $\odot + \text{⌇⌇⌇} = \maltese$).
Even more astonishing is the fact that stories change
as the symbols appear, grow, die, and are replaced by
new ones.

These are truths that Professor Aspern Grayling and
his Megalopolitan backers (for I can call them nothing less) challenge and attempt to suppress—with
contempt to start with, and then, when that doesn't
work, with violent control. "Childish" is what they
call the History of Arcadia. "Works of imagination,"
they scoff—as if works of imagination are not the ba-

sis of our past and the hope of our future.

"Unproved by science."

But in that, at least, they've been proved wrong. For
the fact that our reality is formed by our symbols is
proved by Arcadian scientists, in every branch of our
science, every day.

The work of all the great natural scientists is not
mere fact collection. It is also theoretical, and that
means constructive, work. This spontaneity and pro-
ductivity is the very center of all human activity:
humanity's highest power. At the same time, it de-
lineates the natural boundary of our human world. In
language, in religion, in art, in science, human beings can do no more than build up their own universe,
one that enables them to understand and interpret, to
articulate and organize, to synthesize and universal-
ize our human experience.

It is in this deeply satisfying activity that I have
found my life's work. I, along with so many others, was led in this by our late colleague, Professor
Devindra Vale, she who Professor Grayling professes so
loudly to despise. Would that Devindra, who would have
found so much to study and ponder in this text, were
here with me now! For those of us who knew her best,
the years since her death have only served to illus-
trate her uniqueness, and to deepen her memory. They
have made us feel how much our research has suffered
from losing her sense of humorous adventure, sympathetic fellowship, and deep delight.

Yet much remains that we will share, as long as we are able, with your world.

First Queen Sophia, and then Professor Vale, left us to continue alone, to fight our battles with Megalopolis as well as we might, with little but these texts as our guide. For the Key has once again been hidden, or has hidden itself, as happened in the past after the death of Queen Lily the Silent. The civil war rages on, with Aspern Grayling at its head. He holds that it is ridiculous of Arcadia, if not actually insane, to resist the greater power of Megalopolis, rather than joining with it. 'Joining' here means 'being swallowed by', and we hold that our own rooted experience, lived day by day in Arcadia, is worth any amount of promised Megalopolitan power.

But whether the smaller, kinder, nimbler, and—I would argue—wiser land that is Arcadia can survive, thrive, and live to encourage others is another question altogether.

It's this question that has led to our great experiment: sending word of our history and our plight to other worlds, to uncover what solutions might be found there. Our first attempts have been stories of Arcadia, as we found these were the only words capable of breaching the barrier between worlds. But further work leads us to hope that works of other types, differently illustrative of our situation, may be able to follow. We plan to send you next the recently discovered Report to Megalopolis, written by Professor Grayling, with my annotations meant to counter certain twisted facts and outright falsehoods therein.

Our thanks to you in sharing this work in your world. I'd also like to thank Shiva Vale and Walter Todhunter for the tact and energy they have shown in readying these texts to be sent across the barrier.

Most of all, I salute our late queen, Sophia the Wise, she who was the Lizard Princess, for grasping the Key and showing us the way. In doing so, I defy Megalopolis and my former mentor Professor Aspern Grayling to do their worst. For if truth exists, one can hide it from oneself. But it can never be destroyed. Sooner or later, it will find us all out.

With faith and hope, for your world and for Arcadia, that the truth will find us before it is too late,

Alan Fallaize

RESIST

For Lanny

" 'Where shall wisdom be found and where is the place of under-standing?'. . .'Under an apple-tree, by pure meditation, on a Friday evening, in the season of apples, when the moon is full.' "

—Robert Graves, *The White Goddess*

The Beginning.

There are stories you tell because you can, and there are stories you tell because you must. This is one of the latter. A life is a story after all, a story filled with symbols, or, more precisely, a story made of symbols: symbols married to the actions we take and the wisdom we bring. Do we know our own lives? Not directly, I have found. We know them through the stories we tell. And the images in those stories. They come to life, join, divide, multiply...and when they are done, they fall back, letting other symbols, other stories, rise up from them. That is the trajectory of all things human, for it's humans who are made of stories.

What else am I but that?

I dreamt last night there were no symbols left. They had all moved out of that land to the North, where they're born into a phantom existence on the Crossroads of the Road of the Dead, passing through the Wall of Fire, coming down over the Samanthan Mountains into Arcadia, their outlines getting sharper, their persons more colorful and solid with every step. Singing and picking flowers as they came—it was spring, in my dream, and the wildflowers and the dogwood were everywhere, even though, in the slim, half spring that we, poor humans, can only manage to see, they bloom at different times. In this Spring, the whole of the mountain was in bloom, and the air filled with deep smells that were like food. With every scent those walking, strolling, hiking symbols breathed in deeply, greedily, the more they were nourished, the brighter they stood out against the greens of the meadows and the forests they passed. The greens were greener than any I have ever seen before; the pale green at the ends of the newly unfurled leaves more silver, trembling in a light I knew, in the dream, that I had seen before, maybe before I was born, a light clearer than any seen in any of the worlds where human sight is still too dim to bear it. One that touches the viewer until she can feel it all the way through to her heart.

That light both showed the symbols as they came to life, and fed them, encouraging them to step out of the phantom land where they lay, heaped, until...until when? Do I think it was me who timidly opened the door in the wall to the Domain of Life beyond, letting, without even knowing the good of what I did, some light, some small part of that greater light, in to make them stir and feel themselves vaguely, and groggily half wake, shambling out through to the green light of our world?

I did think it, in my dream. I greeted them as they came down the mountainside into Arcadia, greeted them as a true queen—not the silly, trivial and vain, gilded doll some of my own people would have me be, but a real queen, one who is free in herself, and in the help she gives when she can to others around her to be free in themselves. Because what does it mean to be queen, if it doesn't mean that the world will be lighter and brighter and larger and more joyful than it was the day that the princess was born?

Hasn't that always been what I thought? More than what I thought, what I felt? And wasn't it those feelings that led me to those symbols, that led me, shyly, to greet them and suggest that they might want to step outside, come over the desert, come over the sea, come over the chasm, come over the mountains, through the dense wood, and down the foothills until they reached Arcadia? Wasn't it those feelings that formed the possibilities that rose to meet them, and greet them at our door, as it were, and love them and mate with them and have new symbols as their children, living symbols that I will never live to see?

Wasn't it my feelings that told me that life is a river running into a sea coming up into clouds, falling down like rain and making a river again.... and that no moment lasts, but every moment moves as part of one great whole?

It was. It may have been my thought that led me on, and taught me the ways to get on, and terrified me, too, at the perception that there are no guarantees. But it was my feelings that urged me to act, and, reckless, led me to that place of symbols, even while they told me, laughing a little as

2

they did, that when I had held open the door and emptied the room filled with my own possibilities, then it would be time for me to go. Go where? My feelings didn't answer that when I asked, and my thoughts tried out many answers, not one of which they could vouch for with any certainty. But my feelings surged up again, with sorrow, and then with joy, then with sorrow again, until I saw that joy was too small a word for what the combination of joy and sorrow can bring. Which is renewal. Which is Spring, indeed.

My own symbols have played themselves out, have spent themselves on the world, and I know what that means. It means I don't have that much time left. Having done my job, I can dust off my hands, and sit down, tired in that good way you feel at the end of a long, productive day. And then... then I believe what will happen then is the arrival of another exuberant symbol cut off from the others, tumbling down the mountainside after them, asking anxiously about my whereabouts. Its job: in gratitude to bear me up and away, and back to everyone and thing I have ever loved. For I have found in my own time, that the symbols we release into the world help us in their turn. Unless we have done badly, and crippled or enslaved them. Or, worse, turned them to evil and squalid ends.

There are no symbols left, no dead possibilities, none in my life, none left by my hand. I can say that. There are no symbols left where I am now. They have all come to life.

A glass filled full takes one more drop and overflows.

All my symbols have come to life.

Part I: THE LIZARD PRINCESS

I was born in the winter, in a cave in the snow, with only women and children and animals looking on. This was in the Ceres Mountains, which run across the southern border of Arcadia, butting into the dry, high Calandals to the east, and running to join the evergreen-covered Donatees at the west. The sacred mountains, we call them, though by the time of my mother, Queen Lily the Silent, people had begun to forget what that meant. My mother came down out of the winter mountains where she had led the refugees from the disasters of Megalopolis—the Great Flood, caused, our scientists say, by the insatiable demand for growth and power that the Empire had laid on a groaning earth. And by the time she appeared, at the start of spring, holding me in her arms, accompanied by the hardy women who had made it over the range—by that time Arcadia itself was exhausted. Years of occupation and enslavement had drained our land of its original charm.

My mother's adventures had been as harsh as Arcadia's—kidnapped by Megalopolis at the start of the Occupation, forced to work in the Children's Mine in the Donatees, then saved by my father, a prince of Megalopolis, and taken to live as a passionately loved slave (for that's what she was) in the Villa in East New York where his mother Livia reigned. And then, losing my father to the rich beautiful young woman he had always planned to marry. Tearing herself away from him to seek out her own home before it was too late, walking wearily over the cold mountains, pregnant, leading a band of trusting women. And she was only sixteen.

But she never lost her charm, which was light and joyful (if tinged with unspoken sadness, the way true joy always is), utterly female and strong. All mothers are endowed, in their children's eyes, with a certain glamour, and then, of course, I lost her early, which just enriched her mystery, her loveable enigma. When I think of her (and she was so young! So much younger than I am now! Will she recognize the little daughter she left behind when I find her at the end of my own last journey on the Road of the Dead?) I remember her great beauty, the lushness of her gold-tinged black hair, the slimness of her ankles and wrists and hands (the right one showing her one flaw, that strangely missing finger), the pale coffee sheen of her skin, and, most beautiful of all, the soft, silent, searching, loving gaze of her dark green-brown eyes. Those eyes were like a forest to me, a friendly forest, where there was much that was unexplained and hidden, but all of it—all!—wishing heartily for the good of whoever walked there.

My mother had a great capacity for love. That was both her strength and her weakness. I, who have a less single-minded nature, find much to envy in that, though I know her road was much rougher than my own. The upheavals that Arcadia saw in her early life were missing in mine. And, I, and all of Arcadia, have her to thank for that. She did what she could to restore Arcadia to what it had been before the horrors of the Occupation. But it was a task that would have been beyond anybody, let alone a young woman who undertook it out of a sense of duty, rather than love—even though love was always the strongest current in her life. Let Aspern Grayling say what he likes. Let pompous old Michaeli, her Lord High Chancellor and then mine, Goddess help me, think what he likes, and mutter to himself about how it would have been far more sensible to entrust the guidance of Arcadia to him and his descendants. Let them all fantasize and second guess as much as they please about how things might have been different. It's a waste of time, of course, that kind of petulant muttering—to say 'what if?' when you should be concentrating on the far more interesting and necessary 'what next?' I don't have a lot of patience with it. And when I sift through what I know and what I've learned, I realize that my mother was called to do what she did because only she could do it. No one else could have done the same, or better.

I can't do better. Although, Goddess knows, it's not for lack of trying! Or for lack of a proper education, because she gave me that, too. She and Devindra, companion of my mother as she walked over the mountains from Megalopolis to Arcadia the winter I was born. Professor Devindra Vale, founder of our Arcadian Otterbridge University, her closest friend and confidante, who fearlessly waded in to a corrupted Arcadia, straightening out its laws and organizing its educational system to a simpler, more useful, more poetical (more useful because more poetical, she says) form.

Devindra, mother of Merope, who hates me. Who can say why? Who can say why she hates her own mother, who everyone else but Aspern Grayling admires and loves? I often meditate on Merope, as if finding an answer to such questions would also answer the questions facing me now as ruler of Arcadia. Both our mothers came over the mountains bearing us, leaving our fathers behind. Both of us had the same beginnings. My mother hated being queen, and wanted to restore the magistracy that governed Arcadia before the Occupation; that was what she and Devindra trained me for, to help bring the land back to where it was when she was young. Impossible hope, but she wasn't to know that before she died. She never meant for me to be queen; she planned on abdicating, but was murdered before that momentous move. Devindra told me later she wanted nothing more than to go back with me over the mountains to the inland sea that had been Megalopolis, and find a ship to take us up to the False Moon, where she had heard that my father's family now lived. She wanted to find my father. She never wanted to be queen. She never queened it over anyone, let alone Merope, and Merope had everything anyone could want, as Devindra's daughter.

But Merope was sullen as a child, secretive, resentful and envious (of what? what could there have been for her to envy?). I know Merope well; she is my cradle companion, which in our Arcadia is the closest relationship we can have, after our own blood and the one we choose as our mate. The cradle companion is the person of your own sex who is child of the closest friend of your parent of the same sex. So for a girl, as I was, the cradle companion would be the girl child of my mother's closest woman friend. This is a sacred tie, in our land, as much as anything can be sacred anymore, now that the light from the older symbols has sputtered out and died, and I have tried to be true to it in the old way. But Merope makes that hard. More than hard, impossible. Which, strangely enough, is the good of her. She makes me know, over and over, in a hard, practical way, the lesson that I had to learn on my own, since it was the one truth my powerful mother shrank from knowing: that Love is not enough. It has never been enough. Not enough for my mother, for Lily. Not enough for me. More importantly, not enough for Arcadia.

Still, I can't fault my dauntless mother for the passion she brought to the task of proving it was. Of showing everyone that a land could be ruled mildly and collectively, that might wasn't right, that Power ended by consuming itself, while Love created the only true life, which was one of joy. That was her mission, the quest that she passed down to me. And I, the Lizard Princess, discovered for myself (and that was my mission), that this was impossible, a phantom invented by a desperate yearning for a happier age, when the only technology to achieve that age was made, inadequately and even dangerously, by the Old Symbols. The Old Stories. And that to make the world my mother envisioned, a world where we were restored to our rightful place, a garden, those Old Symbols needed to pass away. And be replaced by new ones. A new story, one that hadn't yet been born when she died.

But the energy she brought to her own vision, the energy, the commitment, the creativity, the passion—all these were of a beauty I can not only appreciate, but learn from, lean on…use as a walking staff on the steep road of my life. For I know that it was her energy that brought the symbol of the Lizard Princess to life. Her energy and her wisdom gave birth to our stories. Which is well for a queen.

As queen after her, I have done what I could with what I had. What I had, she gave me, she and the other much-loved women in my life. This was all treasure. But I also found treasure for myself in other places, like bits of gold and jewel I found in strange lands. One of those treasures came from the lowliest of places (and didn't I learn from my mother's example to look for them there?), from a dirty, greedy traveling circus, what was left of Megalopolis's great zoo, after the Great Flood had swept most of it away. It wandered here and there, around the edges of the mountains, picking up what pennies it could to survive. And in its travels, it came across Arcadia regularly, although it had a hard time finding an audience there. Even now, in our fallen state, we don't, as a people, like to see animals and performers abused; there's no pleasure in it for us. Instead, my fellows have a tendency to uneasily reach in their pockets and buy what animals they can back from the villainous owners of the caravan, and then release them or find them homes. That was how Leef came to me. I had been looking for a gift for Michaeli's oldest daughter, Faustina, and I found him, one market day in Walton, a frightened lemur clinging to the back of his cage. I bought him for her, but he refused to leave me. He would wait patiently at every closed door in the beautiful house that passes for our palace in Mumford, on the edge of the Juliet River, and the moment the door opened, he would rush forward, not stopping till he found me. He had a genius for evading those in my household who would contain him—my nurse Kim the Kind, for example. Leef drove her mad. "Scoot, scoot, oh, the dirty thing!" she would say, exasperated, as she tried to drive him away from my door with the end of a broom. But he wasn't dirty, and she isn't called 'the Kind' for nothing, and he won her over by the sheer intensity of his personality and his need, until he was allowed in and out of my study first, and then my bedroom. Where he would sleep curled up on the pillow beside my head.

One night I lay in the tower, the Moon Itself shining through windows

I would never curtain. These windows are my delight, looking out over the Juliet River to the south, and past her, to the Ceres Mountains where I was born. I was turning a problem concerning Merope over in my head: should I tell her mother that she had been seen sitting adoringly at Aspern Grayling's feet? A small voice whispered to me, "Devindra will never believe any evil of Merope. Better to keep still and keep watch." Only half-startled—for some reason that voice seemed entirely natural—I turned my head to see Leef's eyes staring at me in the moonlight. He closed them almost at once and, sighing, put his head back down on his paws, pretending to sleep. "I'm not fooled, you know," I whispered softly, gently putting my hand on his black and gray-brown head. His only answer was an even deeper sigh, one of such contentment that I smiled in spite of myself, and went off to sleep knowing, even in my dreams, that I had found a counselor, a guardian, and a friend. And those are valuable treasures indeed for a princess who is trying to be a queen.

My mother had a guardian, too—much grander, much graver than my own dear, antic Leef, as befitted her needs. That was Star, the Angel, who was with her always, up till the moment of her death. I could see Star clearly as she stood by my mother whenever there was a decision to be made. As a child, I knew Star was inside Lily even when she couldn't be seen.

I tried, years later, to bring Star into my government as a minister of state, but Aspern Grayling would have none of it. His argument was that angels don't exist, which was ridiculous, since there she was. In fact, he argued that she didn't exist while she was standing there patiently by one of the delicate pillars that hold up the ceiling of the Round Hall, where meetings of state take place. It is always a wonder to me that people find it so easy to deny the evidence of their own senses when it goes against what they imagine to be their own interests. I found this astonishing and irritating, but of course, no one likes to admit being wrong, even when their lives depend on it. So it is with Aspern, and that, combined with his undoubted charisma, brilliance, and strength of personality, makes him a dangerous opponent indeed. He leads people into error so easily. And this is because he believes in the error with every fiber of his being, though he thinks it cleverer to pretend he's a cynic about belief of any kind. Dangerous, as I said. The most dangerous people are the ones who fool themselves.

Aspern was there the autumn when everything changed, for both Arcadia and me. I was six years old, looking forward to my seventh birthday, which in our land is the time when children are expected to stand on their own. It would mean I would stop sleeping in the trundle bed next to my mother's, in her room in the Queen's Tower (the room and bed that are now my own, and the trundle bed where Shanti, Devindra's great-grandchild, sleeps now on the nights I have the care of her). I knew it meant a change, but like a healthy, happy child, rather than fearing it, I looked forward to it as a new adventure. I thought it would be the beginning of the time where I could be a help to my mother. For my mother needed help.

The six years since I'd been born had been busy years for her and Devindra. In Arcadia, there is a strong feeling that it was some kind of magic that Lily brought with her from the mountains that made the people rise up and proclaim her queen, even against her will. And it's true that she had the Key, which the ignorant think of as magic, not understanding that magic is just another name for a new reality not clearly seen.

It wouldn't have taken any magic to urge Arcadians to make her queen. The country was exhausted and enervated by the occupation. The old ways, the magistracy that had competently, and largely harmoniously, administered Arcadia, had all been forgotten, based as they were on values it had been hard to maintain through harder times. People were looking for a leader; they were used to being led by now, and were afraid to lead themselves. They were looking for someone to take responsibility.

Aspern Grayling would have taken it gladly. But my fellow citizens have a healthy fear of anyone who too nakedly wants power. And of course, Aspern thinks this is the only reason anyone would want to rule; he despises those he believes are too sentimental to face that fact head on.

In any case, it wasn't much of a choice. There was Lily, young and beautiful, with a distinguished lineage: her mother was Mae the Magistrate, and her stepfather Alan had been greatly admired by Arcadians for his strength of personality and gentle, affectionate nature. Her famous step-grandmother, Maud the Freedom Fighter, had led the successful fight against Megalopolis at the time of the First Invasion. So there was that.

Then there was her obvious power, her talents, her competence. She had led all those women and children to safety out of Megalopolis into the mountains, right before the explosion and Great Disaster that caused the Great Flood. She, along with Devindra, had kept them alive, most of them, and led them to Arcadia. It was obvious she was born to lead, and so the Arcadians chose her to lead them. She could keep her own counsel. Wasn't she called Lily the Silent, after all?

So the years just after I was born were busy years. With Devindra, she began restructuring the legal system, with the intent of restoring the magistracy and stepping down. The Constitution, in fact, was completed in the month before her murder, and was shelved in the confusion after. I take it out regularly and ponder it, its beauty, idealism, and thorough impracticality. Still, there is something in it, as there is in all fully, deeply felt art, and I draw inspiration from reading it.

They were all full of idealism: Lily, Devindra, my nurse Kim the Kind who had come with Lily over the mountains. And Clare, my dear friend we call 'Clare the Rider' for her genius with horses, who had lost her mother that harsh winter, and who was there when I was born. Even though she was only ten years old, she set to work with the rest of them; there was so much to be done. They all worked like the horses Clare loved so much. Devindra drew around her a group of young intellectuals who enthusiastically embraced what they called 'The New Subjectivity' or 'The New Idealism'…much to Aspern Grayling's vocal disgust. Those were exciting times. And Merope was born at the height of the excitement.

Was that where all her secret, winding hatreds began? Did she hate sharing her mother with the nation? Did she loathe the University that Devindra so lovingly fashioned, nurtured, administered with the care a mother usually reserves for a daughter?

There was so much to be done, and that was the cause of the first great error of Lily's reign. Michaeli suggested that he take over administration of the government as the Lord High Chancellor, and Lily, grateful, accepted his suggestion. Pompous old Michaeli had owned a sweet shop in Cockaigne in Lily's childhood, and she, with her usual optimism, was prejudiced in his favor for just that reason: the clannish intellectual families of Paloma who assumed their superiority over the farmers and small business owners of the other towns made her suspicious. She wanted someone by her side from a class she trusted. She was right about that, but she was wrong about Michaeli. It was many years before I knew for certain what I had long suspected, that Michaeli had got by during the Occupation by collaborating, and in sly ways, so that he could turn his coat at any moment and pretend innocence and true patriotism. Men and women like that often rise to the top, and once they are at the top they are nearly impossible to dislodge. Still, as I have also learned, it's always better to keep someone like that under your eye, dependent on the honors and prestige you supply them, rather than letting them search for a more generous master.

The second error of Lily's reign was that since she cared little for honors or prestige herself (and why would she, being so busy with the actual business of governing?), she was almost diabolically insensitive to other people's deep desire for these. All unknowing, she made enemies. Sometimes it was the person she was kindest to who schemed against her the most: Aspern Grayling was a case in point. Admiring him, and sorrowing for the losses he had suffered in the Occupation (he had witnessed his entire family wiped out by Megalopolitan forces), she offered him the running of a college in Otterbridge. But this offer was fatally misunderstood. It was Yuan Mei Agricultural College, in Ventis. To Lily, this was a grand offer;

for her, agriculture and farmers were the backbone of a living Arcadia. But to Aspern Grayling, farmers were, literally, dirt. Farmers were what he had come from; his mother was a Dawkins, and the Dawkinses had been farmers outside of Eopolis for as long as anyone could remember. He had been born Andy Dawkins—a name he couldn't wait to change. Aspern knew farmers, and despised them, and because he was capable of mocking others, he assumed Lily mocked him. He refused, to her great surprise, and hated her all the more when she, perplexed, made no effort to win him over by offering him something grander. For Lily, there was nothing grander. Her great project, the year before she died, was to put into place a support network for small farmers. This turned out a tremendous success, and Arcadia's working middle class was greatly strengthened. That was the class she trusted most, and they have been the class I have always counted on for support.

I, more cynical than my idealistic mother, hand out honors with both hands, the more meaningless and glittering the better. But I have learned never, ever to trust those I give the honors to. The more medals clanking on the chest, the more parchment covered with calligraphy and framed on a wall, the more you can be sure that person has never enjoyed the confidence of Sophia, surnamed the Wise.

Those I have trusted most have been these: two old women and one young. An animal. An angel. A loving couple. And the murderer of my own mother.

For that, Aspern Grayling calls me criminal. Worse than criminal: a fool. But he is wrong about that, as about so much else.

"Check."

My forehead creases in concentration, furrows as I look over the marble pieces on the chessboard I inherited from my mother—some rosy, some veined with verdigris. It had been a gift from Michaeli, to celebrate the first year of my mother's reign. But she never used it. Lily had little use for games.

Was I in danger, I wondered that day, staring hard at the position of the queen, of the single knight that remained, and of my pawns. Was there a way out? Careful now, I thought to myself. Not too fast. Sometimes you go too fast, Sophy, leaping when you should be looking, and then you miss the hidden gate that leads to the one creative solution. Go too fast, and not only is the game over, but you miss gaining another…tool, another arrow in your quiver. This is your school, Sophy. Even Otterbridge University hasn't taught you so much.

This is what I'm saying to myself as I sit at the game, facing my opponent. I am fifteen years old. The man across from me killed my mother more than eight years before. I have played chess with him every Tuesday since I was twelve years old. There was a ruckus about that when I announced my intention, of course. But I was a strong-willed child—it was that or go under, given the circumstances—and the end result was never in any doubt.

I still remember (it makes me smile even now) how surprised Will was to see me that first time, the heavy board under my arm, the pieces in a silk bag slung over my shoulder. He was sitting by the window in his Tower, the one that looks out over the Samanthan foothills, smoking one of his endless cigarettes. Brooding and silent, according to Kim the Kind, who was responsible for his food and his linen. "Ah, why wouldn't 'e be silent!" my nurse cried. "Him that murdered the best woman 'oo ever lived!"

She had been there when Lily died. Not only was Kim my own dear nurse, but she was my mother's own dear friend, and where Lily was, I was, and where I was, Kim was. We were all there in the Great Hall that day, for Lily was planning a special Feast to celebrate the success of the year's harvest. My mother never cooked, herself—I've always thought it was because her own mother was a renowned cook, and Lily didn't want to compete, though of course everyone in the court took it as a matter of course that a queen would stay out of the kitchens—but she delighted in giving others the opportunity to share what they'd prepared. It was a special joy for her to plan a party, and she took great pleasure in every bit of it.

There was a glow about her that day. Everyone remarked on it. "She'd heard your dad was lookin' for 'er," Kim still says sadly when she remembers. "The Mushroom Women said they'd seen 'im in their fires at night, yer know, Soph, the ones where they see ever-thing. Yer ma always believed 'em, and they said yer dad was lookin' for 'er."

So when a strange man, wrapped in rags and bits of fur up to his eyes, with heavy worn boots on his feet, came into the room with the late autumn sunlight streaming in behind him, she thought it was my father. Warm as it was around the Queen's House, in its protected gardens by the Juliet River, the mountains would have been cold and hard to cross at this time of year when it was easy to be caught by an early snow. She had been lying awake at nights, worrying about my father Conor Barr, worrying that he would catch cold and wouldn't have anything good to eat. "Because, Snow," I remember her whispering to me one night, one of the last I was to sleep in the trundle bed beside her own (and 'Snow' was her private name for me), "he was raised to be a prince in Megalopolis, and they don't learn what we do—they don't learn how to care for themselves, they make others do things for them. Alone in the mountains, he's helpless, do you see?" I did see. I saw I would have to learn not to be helpless myself. But I also saw something strange: that she didn't mind the idea of his helplessness. She liked the thought that she could care for him better than he could care for himself.

She missed him. And she missed caring for him.

Lily must have turned over in her mind many times all the things she would do for Conor when he finally came, walking over the mountains, to find her. She would make him sit, she would rub his back, she would bring him hot wine and fresh bread and good things to eat. All of this must have been on her mind, because she didn't wait to see who it was who stood there, framed in the door, startling the women inside. She just flew at him, a smile of pure joy on her face lighting the room even more vividly than the late afternoon sun.

She ran to him, but he wasn't her Love. He was Will the Murderer, half-starved, half-crazy, who shouted, "Death to Tyrants!", that old, hackneyed phrase that has covered so many inadequacies and insufficiencies and left so much agony behind it so many times in so many worlds. There was a flash in the sunlight as he raised his arm. The flash came down in an arc, and my mother fell. He had been lucky with his knife's aim. It was the only thing he ever was lucky in, poor Will.

"Check," he said again, this time more insistently. It was the only word he ever did say, ever had said, all the years we'd played the game together. It hadn't been much longer after my mother died that he realized his mistake, his enormous error—realized he'd been a pawn in a game he hadn't understood, realized (and this would have been the harshest penalty anyone could have devised, the biggest torture) that what he had thought was heroism was villainy, what he had thought was grandeur and transcendence was meanness and vanity.

Aspern had been for killing him right away. "Hang him up on the front gate of the palace," he said grimly. "Do the usual. Cut his head off and put it on a stake. Give his eyes to the crows, it's what a traitor's head is meant for." He didn't say this because he had loved my mother, but because he thought it right to brutally punish any who dared to violently question the state. It was Devindra who stopped him. Lily's will was clear: Devindra was to rule as regent after her, in the event of her early death. And Devindra refused to change Arcadian law, which was even clearer on the subject of capital crime. "There is no such thing in Arcadia," she said flatly, and as Arcadia's foremost legal scholar (she had, after all, written most of the laws herself), she had the force to back up her statement. So Will was hustled off to a half-finished tower, opposite Lily's own—there was so little crime in Arcadia then that there was nowhere else to put him. The Tower was too far up for him to escape through the window, and the staircase was easily guarded.

It wasn't much longer before it was apparent to everyone, even to Aspern, how deep Will's remorse was, how innumerable his contrition, how unremitting his suffering. So he stayed in his Tower staring out that window that looked north to the Samanthans, and he never said a word, until the first day I arrived there to play chess. "Check," he said then, at the end of our game. And then, "Checkmate." I was too young and foolish to give him much of a challenge then.

That changed over the years. Of course it did. That was my goal from the start.

"Why do yer do it?" Kim asked me shyly. She had become shy with me as I grew older, around when I turned twelve. Later, when I asked her about this change, she said, "It was you who changed, weren't it? Something in the eye. Yer weren't a little girl no more, ye were…well, ye were my queen. I felt all funny trying to question ye or boss ye around, it just didn't seem right anymore." I laughed when she told me this, and kissed her, and said I didn't believe her—she'd never stop bullying me, no, not if we both lived to be a hundred. "Don't know about that," she murmured, but she smiled too. Didn't I know, though? Didn't I know that she was never as comfortable around me as she had been around Lily? Loyal, yes. And affectionate—well, Kim could hardly be otherwise. But not comfortable. I was an unknown quantity to Kim, which was a sorrow to me when I was younger, but which really couldn't have been otherwise. Lily's silence was one thing; Kim had known her from the start of it. But my silence was more ominous: darker and deeper and impossible to understand. It came from what I could see that was invisible to almost everyone else.

What I had seen when Will's arm flashed up and down, when Lily crumpled to the floor like the rejected draft of a difficult poem, was this: the Angel Star flew out of her where she lay, and flew directly into Will. I remember running to him, throwing my arms around him in protection, and refusing to let him go. Did I think my mother's soul had entered his body? No, for I knew Star. I had met her many times in my mother's rooms, at night. We had held conversations, Star and I. Did I think that Star meant to protect Will, and Star's duty was my own, as well as I could manage it? And my duty came out of my love for my mother—so now, more than ever, I owed it to her to be true?

Whatever I thought in that moment, I still remember the feeling: compelling, direct, irresistible. I did what it told me to do. I clung to Will and refused to let go, until the wailing died down, and the shouting had stopped, and I was sure that Devindra had won out over Aspern, even if only for a time. When I was sure of that, I dropped, exhausted, from where I had clung to his leg; he himself had strangely never tried to shake me off, but had sunk, quiescent, to the floor where he sat in passive surprise, as if the whole of his own fatal action had been unexpected to him. We sat there together, me holding on grimly, until I knew he was safe, and then I let go. Kim carried me to my mother's room, and I slept there, for the first time, in her bed alone. I had no dreams. I have always been one who dreams vividly, even violently, each night, but that night I slept the sleep of the dead. I remember that clearly, even though it was so long ago, and I was only a child.

"Check," Will said that autumn day of my fifteenth year. And then he squinted at me uneasily, sharply, as if he suspected what was coming, what was going to happen next. He rolled another cigarette.

I looked down at the board, a harassed expression on my face. I meant to fool him, but of course I didn't. Will and I had been playing this game every week since I was twelve years old, since the year I started my silent investigations into our land's archives, trying to piece together my mother's history, and through her, my own and that of Arcadia. I wanted...I needed...to find out who I was and what it was I was meant to do. This is true of girls my age everywhere. How much more when your mother is a queen, and you are expected to take her place!

An instinct led me to Will, irresistible as the one that made me cling to his pant leg like a foxtail the day he killed my mother. In all those years, I was the only one who spoke in that room, and that very little. He would only say 'Check.' And then, with relish (for he always won, every single time), 'Checkmate.'

You might be surprised at how much you can learn from a person when you sit with them in silence, week after week, year after year, watching closely the actions, the moves, that are the promptings of a deeper spirit they try to hide. You cannot hide when you act. Not if the person watching you knows how to look, how to read, how to understand. I was teaching myself to do all three; I know that now. I was educating myself to be a queen in the only way I knew how.

"Check," he said again while I hesitated. He stared at me out of those hawk eyes of his, gray in a lined white and red face, his black hair overlong and straight, so it had to be impatiently pushed back from his eyes. He brushed it back now and held it on the top of his skull with the long white fingers of his left hand, as if pressing down on his head would somehow compress his thoughts, direct them, so that he could understand the mystery of what was before him.

For I had, in that moment, become a mystery. As I stared down at the board, and tried to look as confused as I had at one time felt, I saw his mistake. It was clear. Suddenly the game resolved itself under my look, and it became a very simple matter to see how he had ignored a pawn and a knight, whose sacrifice would open up a clear opportunity for my queen. He had missed it because of the grander, more tempting option of sweeping the board of a bishop and a castle. Missed it. Still couldn't see. The chance was hidden behind a thicket of artifice and convention.

I don't know if it's possible to grow up all in a moment, but if it is, that was the moment for me. It may be that we move from stage to stage, gathering further information and further desires, until they mass together in a furious ball and explode—and move us to another place, one we never could have predicted.

For years, I had been losing the game we played together, Will and I. But recently, I had started to understand why—and I think he had spotted this, judging from the strange, alert look he began to have. When you know why you miss your chance, why you lose out to a more skilled and ruthless opponent, when you can see that clear, that is when you can start to win. Or choose to walk away from the game, and use your knowledge for other things.

I was a dreamy child…or at least, a little too dreamy for a child meant to be a queen, that's the truth of it. When Devindra would try to teach me my duty, with that anxious look on her face I knew so well, I would smile and drift off into my own thoughts. This worried her. "The Key," she would say urgently, for I understood that the Key was what I was meant to recover for Arcadia. "Nothing has been the same in Arcadia since we lost the Key."

The Key was kept by my mother, Lily the Silent, and how she found it in the Mermaids' Deep has been told by me elsewhere. She held it, though Aspern Grayling demanded it be given up to an elected council headed by himself. But Lily, serene and silent as ever, had her own way, and the Key stayed under her care. I remember her giving it to me to play with in her room, much as I now give it to Shanti when I take care of her, and she plays with it in the same room, which is now my own.

It disappeared at Lily's death. No one could find it, though the whole of the Queen's House—what Aspern and Michaeli call the Palace—was searched from top to bottom.

"Your job is to find it," Devindra would say, trying her best to sound severe, she who was the kindest of teachers. And perhaps it was her lack of severity that let me drift along in a youthful daydream about my own vague triumphs to come. Perhaps she should have been more severe: harsh, even. For it was Will the Murderer who finally pushed me, fledged abruptly from the nest. I was doubtful I could fly. But there was no choice. It was time to go.

It had been a while now that I had grown to understand why I lost the game. With each game, I added a little onto my map, my vision. Each time I moved forward an inch and pretended I hadn't, hoping to lull my opponent into thinking I was still the same heedless, impulsive child he had dealt with up till now.

I had become canny. I had yet to become wise, but now I could see the path to a larger wisdom, and that was a magnificent gain—it almost took my breath away to see it. I had difficulty restraining the sign of my excitement. Leef felt it. He was always curled at my feet, or at the foot of the rose-colored chair where I sat. I knew he felt my excitement, because the tenser I felt, as if I were a bow being drawn back, the more languidly he lounged. The more I sprawled in my chair, the more he stretched out and yawned.

Probably it was this mild conspiracy that alerted Will that something was up. There was a little too much emphasis on innocence, if you know what I mean—I've seen it myself in others, and when I do I'm immediately on guard. Will knew something was up that day, and he, too, was on guard. Though against what, I was still too inexperienced to understand.

I could see it. I could just reach out my hand, move a pawn in one direction, then the knight in another, and then put Will's king in checkmate with my queen. Three smooth moves, and my apprenticeship was over. I sat back in the chair, which rocked contentedly with my secret knowledge, and savored the moment. On this side of the moment, I was a child. On the other side, a full person. Or so I felt.

Then came the fear. I can admit this now, so many years later, for it takes many years not just to admit fears like these, but to recognize them at all. I certainly couldn't admit to myself then how frightened I was of the years to come, how inadequate I felt, how certain I was that every other fifteen-year-old child would have faced the doorway to adulthood with far more bravery and competence than I could ever hope to muster.

How could I admit to myself that I was afraid of what lay ahead? I was the daughter of Lily the Silent. I was expected to lead a whole people. I

How could I admit to myself that I was afraid of what lay ahead?

was expected to know what I was doing—so I thought. More than that: I was expected to find the Key. What would happen when the whole world knew what I suspected: that I wasn't up to the job?

The fear was like a sneaker wave from the sea, which, true to its name, comes up behind you and sweeps you away before you even know it's there. And so I dealt with it the way any inexperienced, arrogant, frightened human would: I pretended I had meant to be swept away, and I pretended to swim. And I felt contempt for all those unworthy people left safely on the shore.

I would be magnanimous, I thought grandly to myself. What did Will have after all? He never spoke, except those two words he said to me each week. Years before, he had written his confession, and since then had never communicated beyond those words. It was an honor I was giving him, I reasoned, letting him beat me at chess on my own mother's royal chessboard week after week, year after year. It was the generosity of kings I was showing him. Why would I end that largesse, that two-handed freedom that added so much to my honor as a princess?

Hah! I thought to myself in the shallows of my mind, ignoring the dark shadows swimming below. Why should I humiliate this man, the least of my subjects? Wasn't it incumbent on me, soon to ascend the throne as the second Queen of Arcadia, to let those lesser than myself go triumphantly before?

At this, Leef stopped his lounging. He sat up and looked at me hard. I can still hear his faint protest: "Cree…cree…cree…" He knew what he was about. Will knew too. Only I was blind, deaf, and dumb to my own nature, to Reality itself, in that fatal moment.

I didn't listen. I paid no attention to a warning look, and a gathering storm, in Will's creased face, the skin crisscrossed with a thousand lines of mastered pain. I paid no attention to the warnings of my betters. Those warnings then were beyond me. They were on the other side of the moment. And I was about to cross over.

Instead of moving the pawn, I pretended to be flustered. I let my shaggy red hair fall down over my face as I hunched toward the board, hiding my eyes. With overly exaggerated gestures I mimed uncertainty. This piece? Move this? Move that? What to do? Where to go when faced with such a clever opponent? I pretended to a brave decision to go forward in the face of the knowledge that it was, once again, inevitably all over for white, the side I always took. Another hesitation of my hand as it wavered over the board. And then, as if I decided in an instant to plunge ahead or die, my fingers swooped down over my queen and moved her into exactly the wrong place, the trap that had been laid for her by black, as it moved in, gloating, to win.

I sat back and held my breath.

But Will didn't move his hand. Black didn't move, gloating or otherwise. Black had, in Will's hands, made its last move.

Instead, he stared at the board as if he couldn't believe his gray hawk eyes. Stared and stared, as his expression, pointed, grew more and more appalled. Appalled. I saw that, and I was afraid. What was it I had done to appall him? What had I done to provoke his growing rage?

He raised his eyes, now darting with more life and fury than I had seen in them for years. And he raised his finger. The whole of his arm trembled as he pointed at me. And then he spoke.

"You!" he said hoarsely, as if the word was the start of a flow of water from a rusty tap. Instinctively, I shrank back, swinging my feet onto the floor. Leef ran onto them, wringing his paws, crying softly, "Cree…cree… cree…."

"Sophia!" Will said, clearing his throat as if to make space for the words, the curse, coming up from within. "You let me win."

In a flash of insight, I saw my error. Horrified, I leapt to my feet. But it was too late. I hadn't realized…I hadn't known…I hadn't understood…

This was how Will had kept himself alive through all those years. This was how he had devised, in himself, his own redemption. He would teach the daughter of the woman he had murdered how to be a queen.

And she, the daughter—pathetic creature!—had failed her lesson.

This had been the moment he had been waiting for, when he would have completed the first part of his penance. He had planned for this moment, led me step by step to knowledge, to a sight of the road to wisdom. And I had turned away to go up my arrogant little by-way.

The years of disappointment, of self-control, of secret, infinitely hopeful art welled up in Will; I could see them rise like a tornado into his eyes, only to be forced back down to his arm, to his outstretched finger. I winced as I watched him gather all his forces into one immeasurably powerful curse, throwing behind it all his hopes and tragic disappointment, watched his shaking finger, watched as the curse came at me, fast and hard and gray as metal.

I felt it hit me, right in the center of my breastbone. Gasped. And felt it seep through my veins like a quick-acting poison.

Leef wrung his paws. "Cree, cree, cree…" he cried in distress as he scampered off my feet, which changed, metamorphosed as I stood there.

In terror I fled out the door, down the winding stair, into the great hall at the bottom where my court had gathered in preparation for a meeting about my coming of age. I stood there, looking wildly about, thrashing my tail this way and that in my agitation.

My tail. Did I have a tail? I didn't remember having a tail.

There was a strange silence in the hall. Everyone there stood absolutely still, staring at me in fascinated horror. Leef, who had followed me down the winding stairs, ducked to avoid the lashings of the large, thick, green scaly thing that was—there was no doubt about it now—my tail. I looked down at my feet. Feet no longer; they had lengthened and hardened into bony claws. My legs, grayish green stumps, were covered with dry, loose-fitting skin that felt like paper. From my hips up, I was still Sophy. From my hips down, I had become the Lizard Princess.

They say, in the legends (and I have repeated this when I thought it made for a better story) that I made a joke of my new and astonishing situation, that I was insouciant, courageous, high-hearted and eager for adventure. And I'm sure I pretended to be all these things. But in truth, I was terrified. In my terror, I acted in the only way my now lizard nature knew how. I fled. Ran for the door, parting the crowd of my courtiers, my tail lashing angrily left and right. And Leef ran after me.

I wish I could say that I knew I was running to my destiny. That I set off, determined, a dreamy child no longer, to find the Key that had been lost to Arcadia. But I was terrified at the change in myself, and in my panic, I had only one thought: to get to my grandmother Livia. She would be able to undo the spell.

I was still a child. I was still looking for others to do what I needed to do for myself.

My grandmother was a famous witch, loathed in Arcadia, feared in Megalopolis. That much I knew from the stories told me from childhood. Livia, who ruled Megalopolis through the weaker men she appeared to serve. Livia, the mother of my father, Conor Barr. Livia, who ruled over the False Moon, which Megalopolis had built to challenge the supremacy of the Moon Itself.

I would go to my grandmother, I thought as I ran…or, rather, what went through me was not even a thought. It was a feeling, an instinct, a desperate bid to have things return to the way they were. My grandmother, the witch, would know how to undo the spell. I would go to her.

I ran clumsily, learning as I went to keep my tail out of my way. Leef ran beside me, neatly avoiding it as it slashed this way and that.

What I know now is that spells can never be undone. They can only be unpicked, and the pieces need to be sewn together in a new way. A spell is a call to a new way, like it or not.

I could feel the new way, or at least its current. I went to the stables and saddled Grete, the second swiftest horse in Arcadia, bred and trained by Clare the Rider, who is famous in all the worlds for her horses, which she will not sell to just anyone. Clare had raised Grete for me, training both of us until we rode together as one. Grete would help me, I felt in my panic. Grete would take me to my grandmother, the witch.

That I thought this means that in my terror I forgot two things: that there are no horses on the Moon, not the False Moon or the Moon Itself. And I forgot that Grete might not see me now as the same person she had known and trusted, now that I was the Lizard Princess.

I remember the feeling of being the Lizard Princess. As if two kinds of blood, one hot and one cold, met at my waist in a kind of shock. There were two different halves of me now, and they were fighting. No more was there the complacent unity of my childhood; my body had turned against itself.

And yet, in that battle, while there was fear, there was an exhilaration I had never known before. Excitement and terror urged me on. They got me on Grete's back, even though she reared up at first on smelling me, hitting her hooves against the stall walls. Who was I? It would take my Grete a few moments of gentle handling to understand, and it was just those few minutes that I didn't have. For the first time in our life together, I was brutal to Grete, rather than coaxing. I forced her through sheer will to calm down, take the saddle and the bit, take me, the Lizard Princess, with my scaly legs and sharpened nails and heavy tail that lay coiled on Grete's rump. Leef jumped up behind me, clutching onto my leather jerkin, and, using the newfound spurs of my lizard feet, I kicked Grete forward and out of the stable door.

She flies, Grete. We were long gone before anyone could come after us. But long gone where? Which way was the False Moon?

"Which way? Which way?" Leef whispered in my ear from my shoulder, where I could feel his claws dig through the leather as he hung on. We were already outside of Mumford heading east toward the Juliet River. On the far side were the high Calandals, on whose snowy tops I could see the reflection of the setting sun. I knew from my studies that Megalopolis had reclaimed land from the Great Flood on the other side of those dry mountains, and that this was where they kept their ships that sailed up to the False Moon, beside the Moon Itself. I would go over the Calandals, I thought. I would cross the Mum Ford.

But when I got to the Ford, the bridge was closed. No one was there. Not the tollgate keeper, none of the dozens of people usually waiting to cross over to Eopolis or Mumford. Closed and barred with an iron gate, one I didn't recognize or remember.

Dusk was falling. I reined Grete in. She was sweating, more with fear and confusion than with fatigue, but I had no time to spend in soothing her. She reared up again, and I saw, at her feet, a marching regiment of ants, big ones, a long snaking line that vanished into the distance on our right, and to our left disappeared into the Samanthan foothills. Grete had been wiser than I. Ants are sacred in Arcadia, or they were in the days when we still believed in the sacred. I had been raised in the old ways by Devindra and Kim, and for me, trampling a legion of ants going about its business would have been sacrilege.

So I backed Grete away, and we headed south, to cross the Otter Bridge to Walton.

The strange line of ants snaked that far back. There must have been hundreds of thousands of them. Where had they come from? What were they doing? Where were they going? The odd thing was that I didn't even wonder. I had other things on my mind. I simply accepted that I couldn't cross that marching line, and headed west for the Donatees, toward the setting sun. I knew the sea was on the other side, and I think I had some idea of hiring a boat and getting it to sail me around to the east. But what would I hire it with? I'm afraid that didn't occur to me either. I had, as a princess, only the haziest idea of economics, and the idea that I might need money never crossed my mind.

Again, it was strange, but I saw no one. The fields between Mumford and Amaurote should have been full—it was harvest season, after all. But there was nothing on the road west but a light wind. That and, of course, the inexorable marching column of ants. It was as if, being half-girl and half-lizard, I was half in my old world and half out.

As I was to learn, that wasn't half-wrong.

Sunset now. The sky was streaked green and blue and gray and rose. I didn't know where I was going, I didn't know who I was. I didn't know anything, except that I needed to go forward. But forward to what?

I had fledged, all right. Pushed out of the nest by Will the Murderer.

To my left streamed that long regimented line of ants. Grete and I were careful not to get too close to them as we ran in the opposite direction. As the sun fell suddenly down below the mountains, and the shadows lengthened, I half saw the line of ants end as it marched away toward the east. At that, I pulled Grete up. We could cross the Juliet now and go south. South was the direction I knew best. South was the Ceres Mountains, where I was born, where I had spent much of my childhood exploring and learning, for Devindra had strong feelings about children learning from Nature rather than about it.

But as I hesitated, the light wind ruffling my hair, and considered what direction to take, Leef tapped me on the ear. "Look," he said quietly. "Over there."

I looked. We weren't alone. What seemed, in the dusk, to be a round sack of black rags sitting by the road moved. In its depths, I could see a pair of bright eyes sparkle. They sparkled and darted and shone. There was no one else on the road but us and…whoever this was. We were miles from the nearest towns, from Ventis or Amaurote. If this…whatever, whoever it was…was on foot, they were far from any shelter for the night. And of course, whoever it might be was my responsibility, as the princess of Arcadia.

It never occurred to me that it could be a fellow Arcadian. No Arcadian would have been sitting alone like that at dusk, far out in the fields. Surely this was a stranger, a beggar—we got them from time to time, straggling over the mountains. And we always took them in. At least, we did in the old days.

"Can I help?" I said. And the eyes sparkled even more brilliantly as if in amusement. "Are you…?" I started, and then I stopped. For the rags stood up, and most of them fell away from a face so round and rosy and jolly and modest and…useful…that I couldn't think of another word to say.

She—for I could tell now the bundle was, in fact, a 'she'—stood up, creaking a little in a good humored way, so I knew she was old. She had black hair piled high on her head, streaked with white that began to glimmer now as the moons rose in the sky. She walked toward me slowly, an amused expression on her face. It was all so odd that I might have ridden away in fright or confusion, except that Grete stood perfectly still, as if through courtesy, and Leef breathed one word into my ear. "She," he said simply. I didn't know what he meant by that. But I knew it did mean I needed to keep still. And learn.

I began to dismount rather clumsily, because I was still unused to my new feet and tail. But she made a kind-hearted gesture that was unmistakable; she wanted me to stay where I was. So I did. She came closer and looked up at me, and the Moon Itself shone on her face as if it was the only thing on the earth the moon wanted to shine upon.

Looking down at her round face was like looking at the moon's reflection in water. And I knew, looking at her, that it was she who would help me, rather than the other way around.

"Are you lost?" she said in a sympathetic voice, and as she did, I knew that it was true. I was. So I nodded.

"Go North," she said. And she nodded again, her face shining and dimpling, silver and white. "Definitely North." Then she smiled—a brilliant smile!—turned away and went back to her spot by the road.

"But," I said. "But." Leef put his paw over my mouth. Grete gave a small snort. I moved her closer to the side of the road to ask a question of the woman, but she was no longer there. Or, if it was she, she was now only a milestone, telling the amount of distance from there to Ventis. And the milestone was covered with busy ants.

We were silent: Grete, Leef, my newfound lizard nature, and me. But I don't think there was any doubt. She was the Moon Itself, who had just spoken to me there on the empty dusky road, and to ignore her counsel was the act of a fool or a criminal. So, silently, Grete, Leef and I turned North. And rode toward the Samanthan Mountains, which had been the last place I had thought to go, past which no Arcadian had ever ventured, or if they had, from which they had never returned.

We rode hard and fast, and made good time—though good time to where? I didn't ask myself that question. Soon enough we were in the foothills, and as the Moon Itself moved in an arc overhead, with the False Moon following arrogantly behind, we were in the mountains themselves, away over a ridge, out of sight of Arcadia, looking at the greater mountains ahead. We would need help from this new half-world I found myself in if we were to go on any farther. I could see that.

And as so often happens, when I needed help, help came.

Part II: THROUGH THE ENCHANTED WOOD

If we had turned to the south, or the east, or the west, Time would have continued as I knew it in the Queen's House in Mumford. There would have been no strange eliding of time the way there was that night. Grete flew, as if she was in truth the Pegasus that Aspern tries to create in a test tube in his laboratory. Leef clung to my shoulder. And I laughed out loud as my horse's stride ate up the miles it would have taken her days, perhaps, to overcome without the help of the Moon Itself. I saw the vineyards on the foothills flash past, and then the scrub oaks, and then the pines and the fir trees as we ran higher and higher…and then the first of the mountain passes. In a moment we were over it and heading down into an alpine valley that was flooded with the light of the moons. We could see boulders dotting a meadow that stretched out in front of us for miles. We could see streambeds waiting for the snowmelt of spring. We could see the beginnings of another dark mountain forest, and above it the dry gold mountain grasses.

We plunged on. Grete wasn't pushing herself, and this—to my surprise— didn't surprise me. She wasn't lathered, or labored. She ran as if she was made for it, and I sat her lightly, with my tail coiled on her rump, as if a half-half-lizard, half-half-girl was made for it as well.

We had come far. Farther than was possible in Everyday Time.

This has only happened twice in my life, that Time worked for me,

33

for ends we both served. We worked in partnership now, rather than my serving Time at her will. It was as if she whispered in my ear, "Go on, you'll make good Time tonight." Taking her at her word, I did.

Stars wheeled overhead. The Moon Itself, and its follower moon, crossed the sky. We slowed to a trot on a meadow, in sight of the edge of the forest. There the road petered out beside a disused hut, half-overgrown with vines, where hunters must have slept long ago.

The wood loomed ahead, dark and impenetrable. I pulled Grete into a walk, and as I did, the Moon Itself slipped under the opposite horizon. I knew our run was over, and I knew that it had taken us many, many, many miles away from home.

It was too dark now to continue, even if I had known where we were heading. My main goal had been to get as far away from the court as I possibly could, and that goal had certainly been reached. So I pulled Grete up, and carefully dismounted, swinging one lizard leg over her back and stepping down to the ground. The small of my spine ached. Apparently, I thought wryly to myself, the transformation into a lizard had done nothing to improve my stamina on horseback.

And I was hungry, too.

There was a small, active spring by the hut that nourished a still-green patch of clover and wild mint and lemon balm. I took Grete's saddle and halter off, and let her trot to the patch, where she put her head down and shook it luxuriously, snorting as she fed. I would have rubbed her down, but her flanks (I stroked her side as she hurried past) were strangely dry and sleek as satin, even after the miles we had come. Leef gave a sleepy squeak and headed for the spring, where he ducked his head and washed, then looked about expectantly, trying to make out what we would have for our dinner.

I stood there for a moment, staring up at the stars, relishing the quiet of the night.

Until a loud rattle came from the dark woods around. The long, drawn-out rattle made all of us freeze where we stood. Grete let loose a terrified neigh.

Now Grete was a strong horse, bred from the wild horses that live in the ravines of the Donatee Mountains. She still had the instincts of her kind. None of that fearful shrinking from the unknown of the spoiled stable thoroughbred, not from a horse raised by Clare the Rider. Grete knew in her bones and sinews what to do in a mountain fight. And it was a mountain fight Leef and I knew she was prepared for now.

"I know what that rustle means," Grete's dark mahogany eyes said to us, rolling back to show their whites. "Snakes."

Of all the creatures of the mountains, snakes are the ones most hated and feared by the wild horse. This enmity reaches back beyond what any horse can remember. All mountain foals are taught at their mother's side, early on, to trample any snake before it can strike.

There was silence then. Whatever we had heard must have taken alarm and fallen still.

The trees seemed to march up from the forest and cover the meadow, letting starlight shine through their tense branches. There was a faint rustle of leaves, as if a slight wind had risen up. But there was no wind that night in the forest on the far slope of the Samanthan Mountains. Leef's nose twitched, and the fur on the back of his ears stood up. Grete's great front hoof pawed at the earth, till a quiet word from me stopped her.

Another rustle, this time from farther inside the encroaching wood. My tail twitched in involuntary alarm, and my grip on Leef tightened. We slowly turned to face the rustle, which trailed off and disappeared.

We waited.

Leef climbed up my arm, one paw on my shoulder, and, head extended, sniffed the air.

He shuddered. There was a dank scent in the night air, almost too faint for my own senses. Grete's fine nostrils widened, her highbred ears pricked up, her beautiful copper-colored neck arched in the moonlight. Leef saw these signs and was satisfied.

Grete shifted her weight restlessly. She seemed to measure the distance between herself and the rustling in the woods.

There it was again, that sound, but now from the opposite side of the hut. Leef frowned. No snake that he had ever known could move as quickly as that. "More than one?" he murmured, before shaking his head. The rustle, faint as it was, had a definite sound; it belonged to the same animal moving around us. But for it to move so fast it would have to be enormous. The biggest snake anyone ever saw.

He shuddered again. Leef didn't like snakes, not even small ones. No lemur does. He hid his head in my neck, and then, ashamed of himself, looked up at my face.

But to his—and my—surprise, I stared straight into the trees, and said softly, "Come out. Don't be afraid."

"It's not a puppy," Leef sputtered, in spite of himself.

I laughed. "No. But I don't think it means us any harm." I moved confidently toward the bushes where we had heard the last rustle.

Leef, vastly less confident than I was, leapt out of my arms and ran lightly up a tree at the edge of the clearing. There was an ominous rattling noise below, while I walked forward with strange confidence, and a huge, dark, slithering thing with long, skittery legs and scaly clawed feet came out from the bushes toward me. As Leef watched in horror, it uncoiled and uncoiled, and uncoiled—seemingly without end. He began to call out in distress, "Creeeeeee! Creeeeee! Creeeeeee!"

Grete moved forward with a high-pitched whinny. The thing crawled up to my feet, and Leef gave another tortured "CREEEEE!", as horse and lemur rushed to my side. But I, concentrating on the strange creature writhing on the ground before me, hardly noticed this uproar until Grete was almost upon us, rearing back, readying her hooves to come down on the ghastly monster lying there in the moonlight.

"No, wait," I said, in such a thoughtful voice that we shook all our heads simultaneously, as if a tossed bucket of ice water had caught us unawares.

All might have been well then, but for the creature. It lay there glistening with dark green slime, and moaned. It lifted its front up painfully by its spindly little legs, and a long flickering red tongue shot out. "Ssssssssssss… ssssiiiiiissssstttttt…" it said. Behind the coils and coils and coils of its body, its tail rose up and sounded a long, loud rattle.

"Ssssss…sssiiiiisssssttttt…," I said, encouraging. I held out a hand to take the bony finger extended toward me—I knew, just knew, it was a supplication, not a threat—and all would have been fine except for that rattle.

For a wild mountain horse, a rattle of any kind is just about the most terrifying sound it can hear. It has no control once it's heard that rattle. All it knows is that the Rattle Means Death. There was no turning back now. Grete made a wild, dizzying shriek, and dashed herself forward onto the creature. Grete was a mountain horse, bred to protect herself and her grazing mates from harm, and there was no stopping her from trampling the creature until it was bloody and dead.

She would have done it, too, except for Leef. Quicker than Grete could move, he was between me and the Thing and Grete, swarming up her neck with a cry of anguish, for if Grete went on, she would mow me down too. "Cree! Cree! Cree!"

The Creature reared up on its spindly hind legs, its fore claws scratching at the air, and grabbed me around the neck. "Cree! Cree! Cree!" Leef cried, clinging helplessly to Grete's neck as she reared up, foaming, coming down hard on the single figure that was now the Creature grasping me to its chest. She came down and trampled it, hitting the Creature's back over and over, and Leef saw she had to be stopped before she trampled me down, too. Jumping to the ground, he dove under the great horse's hooves, nipping at her heels to turn her, and, when that had minimal effect, he leapt at her head in desperation, clinging to her forelock, covering her eyes, and murmuring in her ears the special language they shared, until she calmed and backed away. She was lathered and confused, but controllable once more.

He spoke to her in a voice that was soft and stern, though a bit shaky, and in a moment she was, if not calm, at least obedient. Her eyes had lost that blank and furious look, and Leef jumped down and ran back to where I lay, wrapped in the arms of the Creature. The Creature's back was bleeding, but Leef couldn't see how deep the injuries were. Worse, he couldn't tell whether I'd been hurt as well.

"Creee! Creee! Crreee!" he called out mournfully and scampered to my face that lay there, crushed under the scaly cheek of the Creature. He reached out to touch my cheek, and then gave a startled jump backward.

"CREEE! CREEE! CREEE!" he called out again, this time in panicked surprise. The noise woke me, and I sat up, still held by the Creature's bony claws, but having enough possession of myself to give Grete a quiet order to stand.

I looked down at the Thing then, my free hand at my mouth. As Leef and I watched, the Creature faded away, like a painting left too long in the sun. It turned pale and then it began to disappear, from its edges in. As if it were a painting to whose surface someone now carefully applied turpentine and other tools of the restorer's trade, the Creature faded and disappeared, revealing a boy my own age, skinny, pale-faced, with wide, protruding ears. His mouth opened slackly, and his breath was labored. Blood ran down his back. But he held one of my hands tight, and now it was plain to even Leef that he had meant not to attack but to protect, and that I would have been safe wrapped in his arms.

Something else was clear—whatever curse afflicted me, it lay on the boy, too. Because curled underneath our feet was my tail, and wrapped carelessly around it was his, its mirror image.

"Joe?"

Silence. But no sound, in the dark, of even breathing. He was awake then.

"You're mad at me, aren't you?"

Still no answer. Leef crept up from my side where he lay, and nuzzled the base of my neck for comfort.

"Joe, I didn't mean what you thought I meant, really. Honest."

Still silence. Then a small snort. That made me smile. I knew him well enough by now, even though this was our first night lying together in the Enchanted Wood, to know what a snort of his was likely to mean. I could tell he wasn't a boy…a man…who could stay angry long. Quick temper, hasty tongue, impulsive hand—but no meanness in him. Not a single drop.

"Come on then," I said coaxingly, though I didn't move from where I lay; that would have been cheating. Even then I knew it was cheating to use the magical thing that had sprung up (though little did we know the magic was of the same kind that made the sun rise in the morning, and the dew drop from the trees to the grass below) to get something I wanted. That thing—I didn't know what else to call it then—was sacred. We both felt it, all the way through our shy, adolescent being. I know it was the realest thing I had felt up till then, lying together with Joe on the springy fall turf of the forest.

"When I said I was surprised that you didn't know how to make a fire, what I meant…"

"Stop! Just stop right there!" I could feel the whoosh of air as Joe's long skinny frame bounced up beside me. "I do know how to make a fire, I just don't do it the way you want me to, it's not like you know it all, you know. I'd have made the fire all right." Pause. "If you'd let me." Pause. A sniff. "If I didn't want to let you do it your way, anyway." Pause. "Because I like you."

"Do you like me then, Joe?" I said with pretended diffidence, but my heart filled with an enchantment I can still feel and be warmed by, all these years later. I remember the endearingly shy look on his face as he peered down to see if his tail showed, and then showed his worry that I had seen it and found it ugly.

"You don't…you don't mind it?" he said, pointing. It was almost the first words between us.

"Of course not, look!" I said, lashing my own tail gaily, which made him laugh, and then wince at the pain of his wounds. At that I jumped up, full of concern and a strong feeling that I was responsible for his well-being—this stranger who was so immediately known. Because he was known to me. A shared curse is a kind of bond, I thought, and I ordered him to lie still, and hurried to get leaves from the plantain I'd seen growing by the spring, which I knew from my lessons with Devindra would soothe the hurt.

I made him lie still as I chewed them—although that was always tough, getting Joe to be still; he was the most mercurial being I was ever to meet, in any of the countries, and in any of the worlds. Death herself found him so, and who am I to argue with Death?

For now, though, Death was far away from us both, although she is probably much closer to Young First Love than is commonly imagined. But I wasn't thinking about her then; we had scarcely met at that time, Death and I, not in a way I could call up her image at any time, not the way it's possible for me now. Then all I could see was Love and Life springing up around me, all around us. Even though it was autumn in the mountains, the world seemed to be drenched in spring. So I chewed the plantain leaves and laughed, and laid them gently on his wounds and coaxed him to lie still, for coaxing always worked better than ordering with Joe. (And with everyone else, too, come to think of it, which is why it is said that Love is the first School of Wisdom for queens and kings.)

Fortunately the wounds weren't very deep. Foraging around in the starlight to cover his embarrassment at being nursed, he uncovered a threadbare quilt left in the wreckage of the old hut, and we wrapped ourselves in it, Joe wincing a little from the pain and trying to hide it from me who pretended not to see. I was so charmed I forgot to be hungry, and Grete and Leef sighed, fending for themselves with whatever herbs they could find in the wood.

We lay there, Joe and I, staring up at the stars, and I told him what their names were, and he corrected me.

"That's not Lydia. That's not a star's name at all. That's 'MR7 dash dot dash CORMET,' of course." This with a kind of affectionately patronizing arrogance that I couldn't help but find both aggravating and attractive. (How annoying and endearing men are when they are sure the story they know is the only one! There have been times when I've been led into error with Aspern Grayling just because I couldn't help but grin at one of his pronouncements, as if he meant it as a very good joke between us.)

"Why can't it be Lydia, too?" I said, trying not to laugh and hurt his feelings. Lydia is one of my favorite stars, and the idea of calling her by a number was just too funny for words.

"Because you can't be right all the time," he said in the dark.

He punched me on the arm and lay back with a sigh, shifting over to his side, and casually throwing an arm over my stomach. We lay there for a while like that, me trying not to giggle as he pretended to have an itch he had to scratch, and in doing so, wriggled even closer.

The fire I had built died down. I hadn't dared stoke it, worried it would hurt his feelings if I did. I had been so relieved when he found that blanket. It took the worry off me that he might not like me for knowing something more than he did.

He did like me. He moved a little closer to me. And I to him.

The stars wheeled. Lydia (or MR7 dash dot dash CORMET) smiled down at us as she crossed the sky. And then Joe said, "Sophy?" For I had told him that was my name.

"Are you cold?" he whispered.

I considered this. I suppose I could have been annoyed at the question, given how we'd let the fire I'd made go out. But somehow I wasn't annoyed at all.

There are other kinds of fire, when you're young.

"Yes," I said finally. "Are you?"

More pause.

"Yes," he said. "Very cold."

Grete snorted. Leef gave a resigned cheep and a sigh, and moved over to a clump of grass by the spring, where he curled up with his paws over his eyes.

"Well then," I said. I moved even closer to him, squiggling on the ground under the blanket until our bodies touched and made a boundary of warmth.

"Better?" I said.

"Much," he agreed.

His breath was on my face, and mine was on his. He pulled the blanket tighter around us both.

And the night spilled open like spring spilling into summer, even though it was fall. And we were both warm, as if we would never be cold again, as if the fire lit between us would burn forever.

So it was I met Joe. The first and only love of my life. The kind of love of which there are not many examples even in the luckiest draws of fortune. I, at least, have no reason to complain of mine.

At first I'd thought he was one of us, an Arcadian, partly because his ears stuck out, and his nose listed to the side, and his teeth were crooked, and his hair stood straight up in an endearing cowlick. Although when we foraged for breakfast the next morning, and he looked at me as if expecting I would find it for him, I had my doubts. For the young men of Megalopolis, unlike those of Arcadia, are raised to have others do for them. To give him credit, the moment he saw his new circumstances, he plunged in as enthusiastically as I could wish. Even if the mess of greens he proudly brought back were, in the main, inedible. I hurried them away to Grete, who was glad to have them and thanked him for her breakfast prettily. This pleased him, I could see.

Indeed, he was from Megalopolis, that vast empire that surrounded us, far away on the other side of the mountains.

In Megalopolis, at this time, the idea of designer children had so taken hold of all classes, and was so inexpensive and easy to achieve, that it was difficult to imagine a Megalopolitan child, not absolutely dirt poor, who could look like Joe. And so many of these children had lost what souls they were born with—those souls whose existence Aspern Grayling stoutly denies, in defiance of common sense and all evidence. These children were crushed and mangled by childrearing practices we Arcadians regard as no better than torture. Megalopolitan education prizes constant activity, bright lights, loud noises, lack of common space and access to nature, along with the aid—if it can be called that—of an astonishing variety of drugs administered at the slightest sign of a child's disability, no matter how small. Where these obstacles are to us in Arcadia the signs of a soul's attempt to reach a freer space, in Megalopolis they are cause for hurried intervention. But the idea of interfering in any way, let alone chemically, with an individual soul's quest horrifies any true Arcadian.

Joe had a soul, all right. There was no doubt about that. You could see it in his face, his affectionate, eager, questing face. That face was, by common standards, funny-looking and loveable, and I loved him immediately, taking to him as kin, and warming myself in the glow of energy that constantly surrounded him.

I loved him. And he loved me back. Like all true lovers, at all times and places and worlds, I wanted to know everything about him. And like all truly loved men, at all times and places and worlds, all Joe wanted was to be asked.

He was from a princely family in Megalopolis, he told me that first day as we walked together in the woods—only they don't call them that there. "We have to pretend we're all equal," he said as we, or rather I, cleared our little camp. "But I don't know who believes that anymore."

This meant that he should have been sculpted and medicated within an inch of his life, trying to reach that fake perfection Megalopolitans prefer to the real, the kind of glossy look that makes any decent Arcadian shudder. So how had he escaped? How had Joe ended up with those endearing mismatched ears and that outdoor broom hair that pointed toward the sky?

Two things. One: "My mother and father hated each other. Still do, or they would if they were in the same room together. He ran off years ago. Can't blame him, really. My mother is a nightmare. Center of the universe. Spends all her time shopping, or at the surgeon's, or at her mirror, or she did till she ran her health into the ground, all that stuff she takes to keep her looks. She drove him out, frankly. The fights they used to have were unbelievable.

"They fought all the time. I never remember a time when we were happy together, when we were happy as a family." And since his mother was loud in her grievances, real or imagined, Joe grew up familiar with the story as she told it, venomously, aggrievedly, finally destructively.

"He'd loved some other woman, a girl, I think, before my mother, and would have stayed with her if she hadn't disappeared on her own. Mama never forgave him that. Or her—the other girl. I probably know every insulting adjective you can use to label some girl, since Mama would spew them at breakfast, during luncheon, over dinner…all day long." Joe sighed and shrugged. I put my arms around him and my head on his shoulder and thought about my own much-loved mother— how kind she was, how silent except when need demanded. How conciliatory. All of these things Aspern Grayling calls weak, and dull— mediocre, earthbound—but as the child who grew up in the warmth of her unquestioning affection, I know I prefer her way to any other. As I lay there with Joe, I remembered my childish wish for a father. But if a father and mother together were the way he described them, how much better not to have a father at all.

Did I suspect the truth then? I don't know.

He sighed again and continued.

"They had me almost exactly nine months after they were married. Big wedding, huge production, everyone still talks about it back home." He paused there. "I don't think you'd like my home, Sophy. It's not really the kind of place you'd want to be." His arm circled my shoulder and held me tightly as we walked in the woods and the birds sang. I knew what he meant: the island of privilege where he had lived, the wretched crowds outside his door, the noise and grayness of it all. "And then the False Moon," he said, his voice trailing off as he shuddered at the thought of it.

"So," he said, more quiet now, "she must have hated him from the beginning. I don't think he hated her—my father is way too easygoing to hate anyone—but he didn't like her much, that's for sure. How could he, with her nagging at him all the time, and her plotting to get back at him for not loving her the way she figured she deserved?

"I guess I was the first thing she used for revenge. Do you know about the pills they feed rich women in Megalopolis, Sophy?"

"You mean the ones to keep them from crying? I've heard about those." I had indeed. They, and mood alterers like them, are banned in Arcadia. (A law Aspern Grayling never ceases to protest, which is, of course, consistent with his belief that Nature is an enemy, a thing to be contained, modified, fought and defeated—Aspern is nothing if not consistent.)

"No, not those," Joe answered in his most serious voice. "Mama always took those. She still does, as far as I know. No, when I was born, scientists were experimenting with pills you could take when you were going to have a baby, pills to help you choose its sex, but not just that, the way it would look, its features, talents, and goals. The more complete the set, the cooler the goals, the more expensive the pills. So not just anyone could do it like that. My grandmother—that would be my dad's mother—got together the most expensive set of all. That set of pills was supposed to make me, oh, I don't know, about seven feet tall, with copper-colored hair and steel-blue eyes, strong as a rocket, cool, calm, collected…"

Here Joe laughed and laughed, and I did too, the description being about as far from my Loved One as could be imagined. Good thing, too.

"I don't think I would have liked that," I whispered, and there was a moment of quiet while we smiled at each other, filled with our new happiness. "What happened then?"

"She flushed them," Joe said flatly, and then he went off laughing again. "Pure spite. She told me later, 'Why should they have the perfect child they all wanted? Did they deserve it? Why didn't anyone think about me for a change?'"

"She said that to you?" I was amused and horrified in equal parts. Impossible to imagine an Arcadian mother speaking to her child like that.

He laughed again, and—this was one of the most endearing things about my Joe—it was a true laugh, one that accepted everything that came to him, even if in a rueful spirit, a laugh that had no self-pity in it. Joe's laugh was the outward sign of a soul that rested easily in the world, that took what the world was willing to give thankfully, without a quarrel.

"Oh, Sophy, you wouldn't believe the things she would say, I really think she hated me. I know I hated her. She knew it, too. That just made things worse between us, if they could get worse. I used to throw these huge tantrums when I was small; the whole house would be in an upset…"

He stopped then, worried, I think, I would recoil from this picture of him as like his mother. Because he must have inherited her stubbornness and her intense desire for revenge. It was a battle between them, from the moment he was born, and where else, I wondered later, did that battle go on?

"She used to screech at me that I wouldn't do one thing she wanted, not one. And it was true. If she wanted me to eat an apple, I'd eat an orange."

A handful, my Joe. Did I realize it then? Would I have cared if I had?

But what I did have to thank for it was the second reason Joe was the lovely, untouched boy that he was. He was born as stubborn as his mother. And he wouldn't let anyone interfere with who and what he was. No one.

"I wouldn't go to the surgeon's. I wouldn't even go to the doctor. I wouldn't swallow any pills—I'd seen enough of that with her. Wouldn't pay any mind to anyone I didn't like. If I took against some teacher, if I didn't like the look of them—and my parents got me the best, so my mother never tired of telling me—, or if they even looked at me some way I didn't like, I'd down tools. Just refuse to do any work at all. And nothing anyone could do would make me change my mind."

His father, good-natured and weak as he was, had said to his mother,

"Let the boy go his own way."

"I don't think he was particularly interested in me, not till I got a little older, to be honest, though I know he always tried to do his best. He pretty much left me alone. And he tried his best to get her to do that, too."

Joe's mother, though, never tired of attempting to force him to her will. She would scream and rant and whine and rave, and the more she assailed him, the stronger he became. "It was weird, really," he said. "It was like she was doing me this huge favor. She didn't love me, so I didn't love her. I didn't have to do a single thing she asked—there was no reason for it. It was like I was free. Like she freed me."

"But how could you be free?" I objected. "I mean, if you had to oppose her in everything? How could that be called 'free'?"

At that he gave a whoop, my Joe, and, throwing both arms around me, hugged me so tight my shoulder blades gave a crack. And he said, for the first time, but not the last by any means, "Oh, Sophy, how I love you. You are my favorite being in all the worlds."

I shivered with happiness at this, and would have assured him again in the ways we had newly discovered, that he was mine as well. Except that we were in an Enchanted Forest, and it was a different kind of enchantment that took charge now.

An Enchanted Wood, of course, is a more serious proposition than your usual magic that's found in almost every forest. All woods have these effects, this magic. I am unsure of the science involved, Devindra would have to explain it to me again. While there are magical beings who do indeed live in trees, in the woods of all worlds, I don't think they are solely responsible for what happens there. And besides, in so many woods, they have been chased away, by violence or the milder, but perhaps no less painful, effects of indifference. There are so many woods—I've been in them myself, in Megalopolis, and, alas, in my own Arcadia—where the dryads and other tree spirits have simply abandoned their homes and migrated far away.

But the trees themselves still live, and still have a magic of their own. It might be slow magic, but it's sure. And the main point about the living magic of trees is that it amplifies other effects: that is its charm and its usefulness for humans. If there is any other magic about, the presence of trees will enlarge it, intensify it, make it more visible to anyone who has the eyes to see, or the ears to hear. And humans, even the ones who don't believe in magic, at certain times in their lives are helpless to evade it. Very small children can perceive it, before they acquire the ability to manipulate speech. So do very old people, on the verge of passing over, accompanied by Death. And, of course, so do young lovers, who have entered into real love for the first time.

This was Joe's and my secret, why the Enchanted Wood invited and protected us, displaying its magic the way a great actor might display her gifts, informally, for pleasure's sake rather than utility's—and nothing even close to what she might do when she really took the stage.

We didn't notice at first. We didn't hear the rumblings that would have told us of the approach of magic. We went on ambling in the sunlight, arms around each other, talking of ourselves and our delight in our newfound love.

Of course I was curious: how had Joe become a snake? Not that I cared one way or another, it was just another aspect of him that fascinated me, the way a lover is fascinated by every aspect of the loved one, no matter how tiny. But when I asked him, he stunned me. "What are you talking about?" he said, laughing. "What tail?"

I blinked. And shook my head as if to loosen the feelings churning around inside. "Don't you remember?" I said. I pointed down to his tail. "That. Don't you see?"

"Oh," he said, bashful, "you mean my feet. They are pretty big, aren't they? Do you mind that?" And he looked at me so anxiously that I reassured him, no, of course not, I loved his feet. "I'm so glad you don't mind," he said simply.

Of course I didn't. What I minded was that he didn't know he had a tail. When I cautiously reminded him that he had asked me last night if I minded something about him, he said of course he meant his elbows; he'd always worried they stuck out too much, that no girl would ever like them.

He had forgotten entirely that he had a tail. More. He couldn't see it now. But why?

Then I was saved from worrying about it anymore, at least for a time. Because the little ruined hut we had lain beside that first enchanted night suddenly asserted the magic that was latent in it, and showed it had an enchanted mind of its own. Now it creaked and cracked, moving sideways on its boards, swaying, even though it was a windless day. And Joe, Leef, I, and even Grete looked up at it, startled, as it shuddered and tore itself from the ground, standing now, eight feet or more above us, shaking dust off itself like a duck shaking off water. Or, rather, like a chicken shaking off the dirt of the farmyard, it stood up teetering on skinny chicken legs.

Grete backed up slowly in amazement. Leef ran up my arm onto my shoulder, and kept a wary eye on the moving hut, intent on protecting me from any unforeseen bad magic.

Somehow, though, the magic didn't feel bad. Not to any of us.

"Wow," Joe breathed. Then, "Cool."

Enthralled, I agreed, and we watched as skinny-feathered wings burst through the sides of the hut. It preened itself, and then with a ponderous clucking started off into the forest. mowing down trees in passing as if they were blades of grass.

Joe tugged at my shirt, his eyes gleaming. One thought leapt from me to him.

"Adventure." There was no question but that we would follow it. For we were young and in love, and when has it ever been otherwise for young lovers?

I hurried to saddle Grete, leaping up with Leef clinging to my leather shoulder, tucking my tail off to the side in order to make room for Joe. I held a hand out to him.

He hesitated, though. Ride like that? he was obviously thinking. Behind a girl? On her horse? For a second, I thought he'd balk, and I was hurt. I thought I'd have to get down, and let him get up and take the reins, and then climb up behind him, clutching him around the waist instead of vice versa. I resented this. I was prepared to sulk. Although I will say in my favor that I was not prepared to just hang around arguing about it; it never occurred to me to follow any other course of action than just getting after that enchanted hut on its tall chicken legs, come what may. Still, I was a little hurt, a little resentful, a little confused, and all this might not have had a good outcome, when intuition overcame vanity, love overcame pride, and Joe leapt up behind me, our tails curling together, twined for added stability.

Did he feel it? Did he see? There was no time to worry about that now.

I kicked Grete up with a whoop, and we rode, hell for leather, down the clearing left by those enchanted, awkward feet as they loped along, cutting a swath down the mountainside, deeper and deeper still into the forest.

We rode on, down into tangled berry-vined valleys that the hut on its chicken legs simply cut across, and up onto ever higher peaks from which we could see peaks ahead that were higher still.

We rode and rode and rode. The valleys began to be shallower, the mountains higher. The air thinned so that the forest scents came through ever more sharp, more clear, more intoxicating, like a piney green wine. We had already traveled farther north than any explorer could have gone without magic. This, along with the air, made me giddy with expectation and delight.

The Hut stumbled at the foot of the last, the tallest peak that we—that I—could see, and then picked itself up and began the steep climb to the top, swerving here to avoid a rock outcropping, and there to miss a stand of trees bent by a wind sweeping down from the arctic heights.

The sun dropped behind the mountains to the west. The sky began to darken, and even though our blood was running hot, we felt the cold. Leef shivered against my chest.

"Too high!" Joe murmured in my ear. His arms tightened around my waist, and my tail lashed, curling around him, pulling us together. "If we go much farther it'll be too far to turn back to shelter by night."

"Do you want me to stop?" I shouted back over my shoulder. He just laughed in return, my Joe. His tail flicked up and chucked me under the chin, and I was sad for a moment to think he didn't know it had done this. I was about to turn around to say something cheerful and encouraging when Grete stumbled, and I concentrated on pulling her head up and steadying her. I scanned the slope ahead: I saw nothing but the upper reaches of the mountains, above the treeline, fantastic wastelands, and to the side of us, down steep mountain drops, the silver shimmer of faraway mountain lakes. I shivered. I was a little sad, but I was not unhappy. I felt as if I were going toward, rather than running away, and that gave me heart.

I laughed now, pushing away any dark feeling, and, Grete steady, settled back again in my seat and looked up into the sky.

That was when I saw her.

Star.

The Angel.

My guardian, as she had been my mother's before me.

She rose in the west out of the dying light of the sun. As the Hut blindly plunged upward, and dusk began to fall, a light rose up like a planet in the evening sky, but much more swiftly than a planet ever could. Her light was gold at the heart, surrounded by a circle of silver, and as she flew closer, I could see the gold was herself, and the silver the quickly moving white of her wings. Her black hair streamed out behind her, as if she swam through water rather than air. We neared her as Grete, laboring now, ran dutifully on. I could see her eyes shine.

In one hand, she held a flaming torch, or sword, I couldn't tell which. It was red gold at the heart, surrounded by more silver.

"Star," I murmured to myself, and Leef, peeking out from my waistcoat, saw her too, and gave a faint, encouraging 'cheep'.

"The evening star," Joe said into my ear. "That means luck, Sophy. You know it's a planet, don't you?"

I was startled, but wary now. Star was close enough to us now that Joe should have been able to make her out, see her outline at least. The dark feelings nipped at my heels, and I kicked Grete on.

The sun slipped down behind the mountains. A thin crescent of the Moon Itself rose up into the pale green and gray and rose and violet sky, beside the always full False one. Star hovered above the peak of the mountain we climbed, waiting patiently for us to arrive, and the lumbering Hut disappeared up and over as we followed.

"Almost there," I muttered, teeth clenched against the cold and with determination not to fall back now, now that I'd seen my Star. "Almost…"

We swerved to avoid a clutch of boulders, and charged upward.

In the twilight, the land around us was treeless tundra, windswept and ancient. Lonely. Far from the haunts of women and men. There was no sign of the Enchanted Hut, though its chicken feet left enormous tracks in the ancient dust before us.

We crested the top of the mountain, and I drew Grete up with a gasp.

There it was before us.

The End of the Earth.

As for how I knew it was the end, that was simple.

The mountain we stood on now sloped downward, more gently than had been the climb on its southern side. Farther down the slope, in the twilight lit by the stars and that tiny, shiny sliver of a moon (and the blaring fullness of its false neighbor), you could see trees of all kinds sprouting up, decorating the lower slopes until it came to a sheltered valley, its dark gray-green hinting at a meadow, and a clear silver lake which reflected the moon. But not the False Moon. Never when we lived in the Bower of Bliss—for that was what I knew it was, the moment I saw it—never did I see the False Moon's reflection in that lake.

It was beside the lake that the Hut stood. As we watched, it sunk to its knees and drank. As it drank, its tall skinny legs shrank, disappeared, until it was a hut again. No, not a hut. Tidier than a hut, warmer and more welcoming, too. A cottage. A bower. It shone with a golden light from within, which soon enough we were to learn was a welcoming fire in a stone hearth, burning fragrant wood given us from the trees that surrounded the valley. As we watched, a garden formed around the little house, welcoming and warm and pleasant. I could feel the Bower calling us, inviting us, bestowing on us all the charms and graces of its joy.

I could see all of that. Even in the dark, lit only by the crescent moon, the dim False Moon, and the stars. Because on the far side of the little valley, tall and impenetrable, and stretching as far east and west as the eye could see, was a Wall of Fire. And standing in front of the Wall was Star, where she alighted. She held a Sword of Fire in her hand, guarding a Door in the Wall, a stern expression on her face, so stern that I could feel it—it was too far to see—even from where we stood in the cold tundra's wind.

Joe whistled. "Look at that. What a piece of luck."

I turned and looked at him questioningly. My tail, circling his back, lashed a little and moved him forward with a jolt. The whole of my body was tensed in awe at the sight of Star guarding the Fire. Sacred awe. The kind that fills your heart with a white light.

But Joe saw none of it. I realized that at once. He whistled lightheartedly at what he clearly thought was the end of this part of the adventure.

He kissed my neck with relief. "Look there, a little house. Maybe someone there will take us in. And we can explore the forest on the other side tomorrow."

"What forest?" I said. Joe laughed. He kissed my neck again. "Well," he said. "It's late. And we've ridden far enough tonight. Let's go down and see if the people in that house might give us some dinner. I'm starved, aren't you?"

We rode down the mountainside in the starlight, navigating by the glow from the Wall of Fire. Joe didn't seem to find it at all strange that Grete and I could make our way to the little house without a misstep. He just slid with a sigh of relief to the ground inside of a little wooden fence parted by a little carved wooden gate. He rubbed the small of his back.

"Ooof," he said. "That's better." He looked around with interest, and I, dismounting, and pulling off Grete's reins so that she could help herself to grass and water, watched him covertly to see if he noticed that Wall of Fire not a hundred steps from him to the north. With an Angel staring at him from her place before its Door.

"Nice trees," he said approvingly. "I like a house in the trees. Hey, let's see who lives there."

Of course I knew then. No one lived there. It was the Hut, waiting for us in this Bower of Bliss. I knew we'd come to the End of the Earth, the place my nurse, Kim, had described to me in bedtime stories when I was young.

I took his hand. "Joe," I said. I pointed to where Star stood. "What's over there? I can't quite make it out."

He cheerfully turned and looked where I pointed. Looked right at Star, who glowed gold and silver in the night.

"Hmmm," he said. "Not sure. Looks like some kind of weird tree, covered with bright orange fruit—which is strange for this altitude. We'll have to take a look in the morning." And then he drew me up to the wooden door and gave a knock. The door swung open to show an inviting interior: a table laden with food and drink, a warm fire, and, beyond that, a big white-sheeted bed covered with a thick coverlet. And no one inside. Of course not. It was our house, waiting for us, made for us. It was our house on the edge of the Domain of Life. But Joe did not know it. Did not know it, couldn't see it, and wouldn't know it no matter what I said.

That realization was the start of what real wisdom I now possess. The knowledge that you cannot make a dearly loved one see what you do unless they are able. And to become able is a journey they have to take alone. No matter how much you love them and want to go along. No matter how much they yearn to go along with you.

How much less, then, is it possible to tell others anything they don't want to know or aren't able to see themselves? How much less?

Part III: In The Bower Of Bliss

So began the happiest days of my life.

We could have stayed there forever, I think, as far as we both were concerned. Enveloped in that bliss that comes with the first physical expressions of love. The old story. So it was a blessing that Nature herself, in one of her many guises, prodded us on, the way Nature always does. For Nature is another name for Fate.

I often bring out the memories of those days with Joe in the Bower of Bliss and sort them, as it were, in small piles on the floor, picking them up, smiling, putting them down, rearranging them—comforting myself with the sight of them. I do this in the room in the Tower that was my mother's before me, when I wake in the early hours and nothing is awake around me but the stars and the crescent moon, while I ignore the full False Moon that shines so balefully down.

It was the happiest time of my life. I learned about Joe, and what gives more delight than the first forays into the heart of a loved one?

"What if this is all a dream? Maybe I am only dreaming that I rode into the Dead Wood, that I jumped down from the dead tree, and I'll wake when I hit the Dead Ground," he would muse, and I would say, "What Dead Wood? What Dead Ground?" But he would fall quiet, remembering something he hugged to himself, so instead I would hug his ribcage tightly, and press my cheek against his bony shoulder in the candlelight.

He was on a Quest, he told me one night as we lay together in the big wide bed next to the embers dying in the woodstove. He was the hope of his family. "And I never wanted to be," he said earnestly. His eyes shone in the dark. "Until I learned about the Key."

The Key. What Key? Vaguely, some memory stirred in me. I turned over on my side, my head on his shoulder, and pushed my scaly lizard leg up against his boyish one. His tail stirred, and I smiled.

Then I frowned. A memory flashed past, my mother, in the Room in the Tower, brushing her long black hair as I sat on the rug beside her in the dying firelight, playing with a large rose-gold Key. As I played with it—was this imagination? The fantasy of a child turned into memory?— I could hear the animals outside in the night speak to each other; I could hear the wind and understand what it said; I could see the stars, and they leaned toward me and spoke.

My mother smiled down at me sadly. "It will be yours to hold some day, Snow."

I pondered. But Joe went on with his own story, intent now on telling me what he hadn't dared to before.

Our world, he told me—his world and mine, inhabited by the ruined Megalopolis of his birth, and my green and pleasant Arcadia—was in great trouble. This much I knew as well, at least as it concerned Arcadia. Wasn't Megalopolis, that huge, wretched Empire that surrounded her, our chief worry? How could we be Arcadia when a larger, stronger, more ruthless enemy surrounded it on almost all sides?

"We're running out of…things," Joe said earnestly, his eyes shining in the dying firelight. "We grow and we grow and we grow…endless growth—it's no good, but try telling my folks that. We invent, and we plan, and everywhere we turn it's like we're stuck. We know more than any people ever before us, we Megalopolitans, we tell ourselves that over and over. We've achieved astonishing stuff, success beyond any in history. But there is nowhere for us to go."

"You've gone, so I've heard," I said cautiously, "to the Moon. And conquered it, and created a False Moon to live on by its side. Yes?"

He fell silent. Megalopolis was proud of its False Moon, but I suspected he felt differently, my Joe. And that he knew that we in Arcadia didn't think so much of it as all that.

"Yes," he said slowly. "And the False Moon has every delight a man could want—that's what they teach us in school, Sophy. But it isn't true. You can't breathe on the False Moon. Oh, I don't mean you can't take breath; we've solved that problem; there's oxygen there recirculating all the time. But it's not like here." He turned his face toward mine, and his eyes glistened. "It's not like lying here by the fire with you, with Leef on the rug there, with Grete outside breathing the same air." He sighed. "We can breathe here. And the promise is that when we find the Key that has been lost, we'll be able to breathe there again, the way we could on our own world, and we'll be able to jump up into other worlds and breathe there, the way we were meant to."

I was silent. I knew it was the same Key my mother had given to me to hold, and that disappeared when she was killed. And he was on a Quest to find it, too. I had stopped him on his Quest. This Bower of Bliss, I suddenly understood, was to my own dear Joe an uneasy obstacle to the completion of his own Fate.

A horrid pang went through me. My lizard tail twitched and I buried my head in his shoulder.

"My family was told we'd be the ones to find it—the Key." He was drowsy now, falling asleep even as he told me the most important words, the closest to his heart. "That's the legend. At my parents' wedding, a Fortune Teller said that my father's son would find the Key." He gave the sigh that meant he was about to drop from wakefulness into sleep. "He said: 'Conor Barr's child will restore the Key. Conor Barr's child will rule over all.' What a lot of pressure, eh? But I mean to do it…I mean to…not rule over all, that's stupid. But find the Key. Find it and find out the better way…there has to be a better way, don't you think, Sophy?" He dropped off to sleep.

An electric surge, uncomfortable, startling, was going through me, as I forced myself to lie still, so as not to disturb my sleeping love. Conor Barr's child? I was Conor Barr's child. And suddenly, it was as if I remembered a task given me in a dream. I was to find the Key I had played with as a child. That was the secret of Will's curse, of my own quest. I was to find the Key.

And I knew it, too.

Strangely, it bothered me not at all that I lay now in the arms of my own brother. There was no horror attached to that realization; it seemed, to tell the truth, the most natural thing in the world. Though I was careful not to mention this truth to Joe, just in case he wouldn't see things in quite the same light.

Firelight, I thought drowsily to myself, even though I had meant to stay awake and plan. Firelight...bed...warm...tea...heart...hearth...heat... beat...feat...we...key...

I slept.

And I dreamed. The night was still, except for the hooting of a lone owl, and I dreamed. I still remember that dream, so vivid was it, and so strange.

I was in a great gray city, half-ruined, with torn streets and crumbling buildings. A baby cried forlornly from a cellar below the street, the entrance blocked by fallen bricks. Panic possessed me, and I hurried to the pile, throwing the bricks aside in a frenzy to get to the crying child. "Don't worry, baby," I crooned. "I'm coming, I'm coming." My hands bled, and I wiped them impatiently on my legs—which were my own, in this dream, lizard no longer, but wholly Sophy's—and dug and dug. The baby's cries changed from forlorn to terrified, and I threw myself at the bricks, until I saw a chink of light, and diving there, dug and dug and dug, and threw away the last brick.

Breaking through, I saw the scene change. Instead of the dank cellar I had expected, I stepped onto a gentle green meadow, not unlike the one surrounding the Bower Joe and I had found—but longer, thinner, and more cultivated, as if it had been in place and tended by humans a very long time.

At the end of the meadow was an enormous tree, and under the tree was a naked baby lying on its back, not crying any longer, but crooning, looking up into the sun shining through the tree's full leaves, so full it must have been high summer there. I went to the child and scooped him up, and he was warm from the sun, and as I looked up, I saw the tree was actually two trees growing side by side, their leaves twining together.

Still holding the child, I turned and looked back the way I had come. No cellar was there, no pile of bricks, no gray ruined city, but a small house, neatly built in the style of an Arcadian farm cottage, airy and snug. Before it was a long table with benches on either side. A middle-aged couple sat there, side by side, holding hands and talking seriously to each other.

To my surprise, I recognized them: Francis Flight and Amalia Todhunter, a cultivated man and woman who live in a small community at the foot of the Donatees, near Ventis, where the Agricultural College was established in my mother's day. They had been favorites of my mother's (she had, Devindra tells me, the most hope for the well-read, healthy inhabitants of the villages of Arcadia), and I remembered them coming to court when I was a child, bringing me honey and almonds from their farm. Though I hadn't seen them now in many years, I knew where they lived, and where they lived looked nothing like this house in my dream.

As I puzzled over this, a traveler approached, and Amalia and Francis stood, still holding hands. As he came nearer and stopped, his back to me, wrapped in a long topaz and gray traveling cloak, they bowed deeply.

The baby sat up in my arms and stared. And in my dream, I knew the stranger was a god. What god? I wondered fretfully to myself. I wanted to call out to him, but something restrained me, and I clung to the baby more tightly.

He turned and looked at me, and I saw his face. It filled me with a sadness I couldn't name. I clutched at the baby, but to my grief, I now clutched nothing but air…the baby was gone. I held only a sheet and blanket…

I woke. It was morning, and I could hear Joe making tea by the woodstove. Leef sat on the pillow next to my head cleaning his paws. Grete snorted happily outside, which meant Joe had already piled some grass for her to eat. It was morning in the Bower of Bliss, next to the Wall of Fire, the normal waking world, the world I was used to.

But what god had I seen?

"Morning, Soph," Joe said, grinning, holding two mugs of steaming tea as he climbed awkwardly back into bed, hauling his tail in behind him. Leef leapt neatly away from Joe's pillow and curled up onto mine. I took my tea and thanked Joe, sipping it, smelling the good morning air, as he nuzzled at my neck, holding his tea aloft to keep it from spilling. It was another beautiful morning; the mornings, here in the Bower of Bliss, seemed to have no end.

That was wrong, of course. Everything ends.

But what god?

It was a good thing we had come to an Enchanted Valley, a Bower of Bliss, a Horn of Plenty. For Joe had very little practical knowledge, which came from having been raised an aristocrat in Megalopolis, where to be practical is to be a servant. He didn't know how to cook (except for tea), or clean, or hammer, or even forage. So it was lucky that in that Enchanted Bower, food and drink were magically plentiful, at least to a certain extent. And past that extent, I was quite competent myself to deal. Devindra and my nurse, Kim the Kind, had seen to that. They'd made sure I was able to keep house, to tend to myself and others. Because that is one of the things that, in Arcadia, it means to be a queen.

Those skills came in handy now, what with Joe and me setting up household. And any signs of the housewifely on my part enchanted him. Well, maybe not at first. At first, to my chagrin, he took for granted that it was I who swept the floor, and I who smoothed out the bed when we woke in the morning. But like all true lovers—I remark wryly—we had our share of sharply spoken words, maybe even a pot or two thrown against a wall, followed by bashful apologies, kisses, lessons learned and acted on the next time. He learned to appreciate what I had to give. And I learned the same about him.

In fact, I learned more from those months with Joe in the Garden than in all my years of being princess, or later on when I was queen. This kind of education, of what you might say is two people joined together, rubbing the rough edges off each other in delight and in anger, is undervalued, or even scorned. Yet two people together can find a third wisdom greater than either of them alone could have known. What they make together, every day, in each action and interaction, is as real as any child they might make together in moments of passion. And has as much effect on the world in the years to come. More, maybe.

Be careful then, oh be careful! in how you live with each other, and love each other, and quarrel and learn from the quarrel and move on. Don't yearn for endings in your ignorance, the way I sometimes did in the early days, when I thought Joe too full of himself, too regardless of me; little did I know then how short and sweet those days, even the moments of quarreling, would seem now.

For it was short, that time. It was only a year. Only one dear year. Or, at least, it was only a year to us, there in the Bower of Bliss.

Yes, it was a year, and in all its seasons, too. I know from experience that it's wrong to think that Paradise is only spring, or high summer, or harvest season. It is all these times, and it's winter, too, when everything seems dead and frozen as if it will never come back to life. All of these are Paradise, for without one of them none of the others would live. Paradise lives in the changes around us, in the exuberant changes in our bodies and our minds and our souls, which make one deep and steady pulse in the world.

We both were that pulse together, which is the kind of joy that True Love brings, through all kinds of weather, in every season. Making a home in the Enchanted Hut, setting up our own place, with spots by the fire for him and for me, a pillow for Leef beside mine, where he curled up in the evening while we made the last meal of the day. Putting up stores against the winter, stores of the food that appeared like magic around us, both wild, growing in the forest at the edges of our meadow and around our lake, and in the cupboards of the little house. Winter with the snow banked up against the windows, and the woodpile appearing in a little shed beside the door, to be gathered in armloads and brought inside. That winter was the sixteenth since my birth.

Then spring, when the snow disappeared, leaving a marshland in the meadow outside, and streams running here and there, digging furrows through it, some mornings rime-covered, then fewer and fewer of those, until the sun warmed and came up earlier and earlier, as we rose earlier and earlier, and the meadow dried, and was covered with a soft green sheen, and flowers sprang up, first the white, then the purple, then the yellow and blue. Joe had his birthday then.

Then summer, and the sun stood high in the sky till late at night, and we spent long hours outside warming ourselves. Then fall, when the wild things were the most awake getting ready for winter, and we, wild things too, got ourselves ready, thinking the years would go on and on like this, but knowing that they wouldn't, not really.

So as the autumn came in that year, we were sad and silent, though happy, too, which I think is a secret that only people truly in love who have lived together know. For we had come to know each other over that year, as true joy and true sorrow (two sides of the same coin) teach knowledge of the loved one, and wisdom too. We had come to know that we were both alike and different, and that this was the way it needed to be.

We shared the same religion, if I can call it that, even though Joe, like all Megalopolitans, scorned the idea of religion, or even the sacred. But nevertheless, I knew that we both believed the world outside our Bower could be a better place than it was. And that was why our sojourn in the Bower of Bliss could only be temporary, a way station. We had both set out on our adventures to try and find a better way. To find it just for us two was a blessing and a treasure. But it wasn't what either of us was meant for. To find what we were meant for, we would have to be apart.

I began to understand this, as that second autumn drew on. When the days shortened, I would ride Grete farther and farther afield in search of wild berries and mushrooms, for one more ramble in the warm fall air, that air that changes so quickly into a rush of cold current from the north. I often rode alone, around the edges of our world. Joe was not a good rider, or a very interested one; he had, like all the princes of Megalopolis, preferred to drive a machine that had been given him on his thirteenth birthday, which he had left behind on his quest into the mountains.

So my offer to let him ride Grete was always declined. And I would ride out every afternoon, or sometimes in the early morning, me and Leef and Grete. We would explore the edges of the Wall of Fire, which burned brightly without consuming anything that could be seen within. I know this, because Joe only saw, to the north, an impenetrable forest that stretched as far as his eye could see. He described it to me when I asked, with feigned casualness, why he never went that direction in his rambles. "Too thick," he explained. "All underbrush." No way through, and nothing, apparently, of interest there.

What did I see? That wall of flame that warmed, but never burned, as I held a hand out near it. A wall twice as tall as I was, a wall guarded by an angel. Star. All that year, she stood there, a flaming sword in one hand, and her other held up, forefinger at her mouth, in the universal sign of silence. She was silent, that year. I knew enough not to try to get her to break her silence; I knew…I was afraid…it would happen soon enough.

I knew…I was afraid…it would happen that autumn. I knew when I saw the cobwebs at the end of the meadow.

"Do you see that?" I asked one afternoon as Joe applied himself happily to his newfound skill of splitting wood for the winter. I began to suspect this was wood we would never need. But I stayed silent.

"What?" he said, wiping his forehead, his hair sticking up even more than usual. He followed my look, and my finger that pointed to the western end of our meadow, where the sun was already beginning to sink below the trees. "No, I don't see anything. What is it?"

"Nothing," I said. But it was something. It was cobwebs, appearing first fragilely, then thick and strong, in the trees there hedging the meadow. They multiplied as I watched. Leef watched, too. He looked at me, and I knew he saw as well as I did.

"No," Joe said, "but...!" The excitement in his voice made me whip round to see what he meant. He looked in a different direction than I did, to the south, to the crest of the steep mountain there. "Look there, Sophy. Look!"

I followed his finger. I could see nothing.

"Look! There's a man there, standing at the top of the path we came down. Can't you see him, Sophy?"

It was no good. All I saw was a ridge and some trees.

"He's coming down the mountain," Joe said, dropping his maul. "Slowly. He's leaning on a staff, so he must be old...go on, Soph, you must be able to see him!"

No. I couldn't see him. I looked anxiously back to the west. The cobwebs had grown stronger, and they now stretched from the trees out to the edges of the meadow.

"He's dressed like no one I've ever seen, in a long orange coat. He's... you must see him now!"

Still nothing. The cobwebs stretched out toward us. Star burned ever more brightly, and her expression settled into one even sterner than before. Stern and beautiful.

"I think...no, it...Sophy! It is...!" Joe threw down the wood splitter and raced across the meadow to the foot of the mountain, shouting as he ran.

It was then that my vision cleared just enough for me to see Joe leap across a boulder and run to a tall man, hunched with age or pain or both. The man stood perfectly still as Joe came toward him, and in that moment, the sun broke through the tops of some trees to the west and lit his face. It

It was Joe's father. It was my father, too.

was then I recognized him. It was the god of my dreams, the god who was the guest of Amalia Todhunter and Francis Flight.

"Father!" Joe yelled out in a voice of sheer joy. "Father, father, father!"

It was the god. It was Joe's father. It was my father, too.

And it was the end, I knew, for us together, me and Joe, for in our time here in the Bower of Bliss. I had thought it was the happy ending. But it really was only the beginning.

Part IV: CONOR BARR

I don't know how, over that whole year's idyll, we never conceived a child. It must have been the magic of the place, that knew the right time of things, and the right ways to nurture what needed to be born. Joe and I never thought of it. Each moment had stretched out in all directions to Eternity, so that we moved effortlessly through Time in all her directions. Having a child then would have anchored us to one point in that golden flow of Time, as I was anchored later, when it was right that I be so.

But not yet. Not then, during the halcyon days of our own paradise. There was no generation there because there was no duration. No Time. No potential to become actual—it was all actual, everything, in every direction. So we lived our days, one golden hour flowing into the next, until the god came.

He was an old god. An ancient god. Battered and beaten, his bright blue eyes showing, rheumy, in his deeply lined face. Joe led him toward me, and I knew him for who he was, my father, the god, the old man, the young man who had loved my mother, the man my mother had waited for and never found again, the young vain hero of his family, and now this bent, tired, sorrowful god who walked toward me with a limping tread. I could see all of these figures, all of his history, as if it flowed out of him in a series of shadows, all the people he had been in all the many places of his life.

And he was blind. He walked sightlessly forward, holding out his arms, and Joe led him tenderly, whispering in his ear.

All Joe saw, I was sure, was his father, his dear father, who had left many years before but was still recognizable by his dearly loved face. But I saw who Conor Barr really was, who he had made himself into. He had wrestled with the world and lost, but salvaged godhood from the match all the same.

And he had become blind to the world. To all except his memories and his inner landscape. He had become wise. But at what a cost.

As they both stopped a few feet away from me, I saw Conor Barr did not know me, could never know me. My heart felt heavy in my chest as he greeted me gravely, greeted me as his son's wife.

"My dear," he said. He held a hand out in blessing. I went forward and knelt before him and let him place his palm on my head. "I am so glad," he said simply. "So very glad."

"Three years I've been searching for you, Joe," he said gently, motioning to Joe to help him sit on a bench we had left out on the late fall yellow grass. "I went back for you and found you gone. Three long years they've waited for you to come home."

I looked at him, eyes open wide. Three years? It had been three years? Startled, I looked at Joe, but he, gathering an armload of wood to take into the house, seemed not to have heard. I thought about it. Three years. Yes. It could have been thirty, and without the arrival of the god, I would never have known.

"But leave that for now," the god sighed, leaning back and shivering as the sun dipped behind the trees. "Forgive me, but I'm tired and cold, and I wonder if I might trespass on your hospitality for a while, sit by your fire, tell you why I've come, hear your stories, perhaps…as long as we three can stay awake tonight. Do you think we could?" He smiled, and the lines around his sightless cracked marble blue eyes danced, and I liked him then, very much. Joe gave him a quick impulsive hug, then disappeared into our little house to light the fire and make a comfortable chair beside it for his father.

I liked that Joe was so affectionate toward his father. I liked it very much. I was wistful, myself, that I was not yet allowed to be. I wondered if I would, if he would ever know me for who I was. If it ever could be.

Thinking all this in a confused sort of tangle, I didn't follow Joe. Instead I went to the god, and sat at his feet. He put his hand on my hair and twined it idly with long, gnarled fingers that must have once been the beautifully molded white hands that so captivated my mother as a young girl.

"If you are Joe's father," I murmured, still hoping there was a way to make him and Joe understand, "then you must be…"

"A very foolish man," he sighed. "Yes. A wandering solitary, who threw love away when he had it and pushed away the power he traded it for instead." He bent his head and laughed that soft laugh of his. "But alive, you know. Very much alive."

I was silent at that. But in my heart I agreed.

He smiled. "A beauty of your own," he said, comparing me in his memories to…who? "And a strength, too, if I'm not mistaken." He gave a chuckle. "You'll be a daughter to me, will you then? I never had one, you know. It was a pleasure I've often missed."

I opened my mouth to speak, then thought the better of it.

Joe came up to us and took our father's hand, leading him toward the house, and Conor Barr sighed with contentment and said, "Let's eat and drink together, and I'll tell you of my adventures. Then, my dear son, tell me of yours."

Joe laughed, lashed his tail about, and led him to the house. I followed them inside.

We ate simply and bountifully that night, and drank the deep red wine that magically appeared in bottles in the cupboards over the little iron sink where we washed our wooden dishes. And the fire blazed up like a companion, and never once needed to be fed, as if our words were all it needed to burn, as if its warmth was its contribution to our gathering there together.

But there was something that nagged at me, warned me of dangers to come. My fears and premonitions increased through the night until they piled up so high that the tower fell down and buried my young girl's hopes underneath.

Young girl's hopes are fated to be buried. It's what grows from that compost that is the final flowering fruit. But I didn't know that then.

There was something strange about seeing the two men together. For the man…the god…who sat there with us, drinking and eating slowly, who told us of his adventures climbing mountains, crossing deserts, traversing great stretches of the wild wood of fairy tale, that man was definitely Conor Barr.

But Conor Barr had been eighteen years old when I was born, and nineteen when Joe was. He wouldn't be a day more than forty now.

The man sitting there with us now, making Joe laugh at a particularly pungent description of some courtier they had both known, was older than that—much older. His hands were gnarled, the backs covered with ropy veins. His hair was silver and his skull shone pinkly through its thinning on the top. This man was seventy years old at the least. I looked at him more narrowly, trying to make out a clue to the mystery. And as I sat there puzzling, I noticed something else. The cobwebs I had seen at the foot of the meadow had moved up as the sun set down. If you looked at the window, you could even see one clinging to the cloudy pane there in the early evening dark.

Leef saw it too. He looked at me, and, curling his tail around his eyes, lay down with a sigh.

The magic was over, I realized later. We had feasted on it, and it was almost gone. That kind of magic, young love magic—Joe and I had almost outgrown it. It was time to move on.

But now Joe was explaining to our father how he had come to be there.

71

He had never told me this story before, and of course, his telling the story now meant it was the beginning of the end of this part of our story. I listened, half-feeling the disaster that was coming. There are many things you can only learn by sorrow, and that, to my sorrow, I was learning now.

"I was out hunting," Joe said, leaning forward. Hunting? I thought, startled. Could this be the same Joe who was so kind to Leef and Grete, so clumsy in catching a hare, so grateful that the magic food that appeared required no effort on his part. Hunting?

I began to have a hazy thought, an understanding of how my life had been one of women. Women teachers, women companions—all excepting Will. In my mind I stood on a cliff, wondering what was in the chasm beneath, covered by the mist.

Hunting?

"But what I was hunting for, I can't remember," Joe said, looking more thoughtful than I had seen him before—marvelously thoughtless Joe, whose whole world existed in whatever was right in front of him, never the past or the future. I had noticed this difference between us: when I looked at time I saw an endless line, while he saw a vivid exclamation point and nothing more. "Sometimes I wake up in the night and know I've forgotten, but still the memory doesn't come back."

This startled me. I, too, woke in the night trying to remember. Why had we never spoken of this together?

I must have looked some of what I thought. But Joe didn't see this look. He was busy poking at a log in our woodstove with a stick, making it blaze up one last time before it consumed itself and died.

"I was out hunting for...something. I don't know what. In that forest of dead trees, the forest that goes on and on for miles at the end of the marshland, that never burns because of the bog underneath it that got left after the Great Flood. I knew I shouldn't have gone on, hadn't our scientists told us there was nothing there? Nothing to be seen, no life, nothing but dead wood."

Joe struck at the fire with a sudden violent jab and then went on.

"But I wanted to go on. So I did."

He drove a car there, he said, but it soon bogged down in the sand, and he abandoned it, walking on. He had a toy dog with him for company, a robot dog of the kind the rich hunt with in Megalopolis. And the dog ran ahead of him until it was just out of sight. Joe followed behind.

"So I didn't watch where I was going for a while, which I know was a mistake. And as I got in deeper, it was like the trees behind me closed up the path as soon as I'd made it. I went farther and farther. By now I'd lost the dog. I whistled, but there was nothing but dead quiet. It was getting dark, and I had no idea where I was. The branches above me got thicker, all dead and covered with a dry gray moss. I could barely see the sky. What I could see was clouded over, too, so there wasn't a star to be seen as night came on, or the Moon Itself, or even the False Moon to guide me.

"I shimmied up one of those dead smooth silver-barked trees, hoping to get sight of where I was from up above. It was a good choice, because when I got up higher, I saw I was near the edge of a clearing, one that shone weirdly in the twilight, as if the False Moon had managed to shine through the branches of the dead trees after all.

"Well, it would have been a clearing, anyway, if it hadn't been strung with a web, its cords thick as my arm, a web that was growing even while I watched. My eyes started to get used to that weird silver light, and I could actually see the web grow."

I shuddered at this. For I knew that the web growing in our meadow there was of the same kind.

I remembered all this soon after, when I entered the Dead Wood myself in fruitless search for him and for the happiness that I should have known could not be recovered. I saw a different Dead Wood than Joe. By then I understood that we could never see the world in the same way, that indeed it was wrong to hope for that. I still was angry, and angry with him, poor Joe, for that hard fact. It took many years for me to understand that this was the point of love, not that two people think and feel as one, but that they think and feel as two, and that the joining of the two different visions leads to a new vision of the whole.

To a new symbol.

But I didn't understand that then, at eighteen years old, just hovering on the edge of my own advance out again into the cold of the world. Out into the cold of my own heart. For as I sat there by the fire, a chill fell over my heart, a cold anger. Rage. Resentment. Envy. There was a whole world out there that Joe and Conor knew, that I was excluded from, that they talked about easily between themselves. Two men together. That's what it was. No women allowed. It made me angry.

It made me angry that Conor did not know me as his daughter, and that Joe did not know me as his sister. And me the elder! That's how silly I was that night. For now I know how little it matters, what acknowledgments, what tributes others give. All that matters is that we love. That's the truth of it.

But that night I was angry. I was angry that to both of them I was unknown.

My world was unknown to them. As I listened to Joe tell of his trip into the Dead Wood, and watched his gleaming face, I thought, "He never told me this!" He had never told me because I would not have heard it the way he meant it, and because life in the Bower of Bliss was only half a life to him, not a whole, and he lived in it to please me.

He had to be doing, Joe. He had to be searching, questing, no matter what problems, what destructions might arise. Realizing this, I felt a fury I had never experienced, like a bucking horse that I hung onto for dear life.

And the cobwebs grew at the windowpane. They were my cobwebs, I realized with horror. My clutching fingers, holding on to Joe.

Who was Joe looking for in the Dead Wood that day? Not me. Not a person at all.

He wasn't looking at me now. He was looking at Conor. Our father, who he had known his whole life, who had been stolen from me by him and his mother, a father who did not know me at all. And as Joe looked at our father, he was happy. He was known. Like a child who comes in out of the rain to a parent waiting for him by a warm fire. "I remember now," he said, for being with his father restored his memory, just as being with me, his love, had made him lose it, lose who he was. "I know what I was looking for when I looked into the clearing, Father. I was looking for the Key."

I hated him when he said that. I wanted him to have been looking for me.

It was only now that I realized Joe had never asked me about who I was or where I came from.

As I brooded on this, I could feel that strange rage grow.

The Key, I thought angrily to myself. The Key that was my quest, not his; he was looking for the Key. And doubtless (I continued to think, adding fuel to a fire that would shortly rage out of control) he was thinking I... we...our love had interrupted that search. What about me? Hadn't I given up my own search for it to be with him?

All of this was very silly, of course. But it may be that these kinds of feelings have a purpose: to end things that must end and to suggest new things to come after.

Certainly new things came now. Anger at Joe and my father, for one.

I had never had a father. I had never had a brother or a lover. Now I had all three, in the Bower of Bliss, a relationship that they ignored. They ignored all the work that had gone into the Bower, all the comforts, all the happiness. I could feel their restlessness, I could feel Joe yearning to leave in search of the Key.

The Key. I was supposed to search for the Key. What had I given up?

If I had not taken up my own quest, there must be someone else to blame. Who better to blame than the loved one closest by? For I could feel him searching for someone to blame on his own account, and I could feel the cold wind of his blame blow hard on my cheek and pass by.

Leef watched us both anxiously, his little furred head turning side to side.

Joe talked proudly now of his time in the Dead Wood. He talked in a way I found peculiarly repellent. He seemed to me to preen, to strut a little, and to boast.

"Of course, I saw Death there in the clearing. She is everywhere, just as Grandmother always said, but this was her land, the Dead Wood, who else did I think I was going to see? She was there, sitting in the midst of a group of hideous hags, each one swinging from a seat of cobwebs there. And she was the most awful and hideous of them all."

"Don't be stupid," I said sharply—I think the only time I had spoken so in the Bower, and both Conor and Joe looked at me in sudden amazement. I continued. "Death is a beautiful woman, not hideous at all."

They were silent, wondering. They looked at me, and then turned away. They had no way to understand the words that I had just said, so it was as if they had never heard.

Now my secret was that I had indeed seen Death before. I had my own vivid memories of her from that winter's afternoon, when my mother had run into the Great Hall where I played with my dolls, went to meet the stranger she thought was the god in front of me now. But my mother found, instead, Death. Death stood behind Will and stepped out from behind him to lead Lily away. I was the only one who saw them, saw her, saw Death, and saw, also, that my mother knew her, and loved her—feared her, but trusted her, too. I saw them walk out of the Great Hall, hand in hand.

So when I heard Joe describe Death that night, I was angry. Or rather, angrier.

Then came the worst of all. Joe telling our father now what he heard Death say.

"She looked at me. She knew I was there!" He was excited now, rocking back and forth clutching his knees to his chest and restlessly pushing his hair back with one hand. "Death herself, and she knew me! And listen… this is important…this is what she said: 'Boy you are now, man you will be. When you grow a serpent's tail and lie with a lizard by a Wall of Fire.'"

He leaned back now, eyes gleaming. "Kind of old-fashioned, that kind of thing. But I liked it. I knew the minute I heard her that I was on to something. So that's what I need to find. A Wall of Fire."

"But, Joe," I blurted. "It's been there all along, the Wall of Fire." For there it was, right outside the window, glowing as it had since we'd first arrived, Star on guard beside it.

He didn't hear me. I didn't realize that then. I thought he pretended not to.

"Isn't that cool?" he said, grinning boyishly toward Conor. "Wouldn't that be cool? To have a tail like a snake, and lie with a lizard by a Wall of Fire?"

"But, Joe," I said again. Leef cheeped unhappily.

"On my quest, I mean," Joe said, still to Conor, as if I wasn't there—so I thought. Of course I was there to him. Of course what Joe wanted was for me to admire him. But I didn't know. I was too young. When you are that young, Love is lacking.

"If Death said it, that's what I'm heading for. A Wall of Fire and a snake's tail." He shook his head. "But here I am instead." He shook his head again. "Good to see you, Dad."

That was when I couldn't hide it from myself any longer, couldn't push the knowledge away from me so that I could live here in bliss in the Bower.

Joe didn't see the cobwebs curling up the meadow toward us, tapping eerily at the window behind his head.

He didn't see the Wall of Fire.

He didn't see the strangeness of how old our father, Conor, had become… far older than his chronological years.

He didn't see his own serpent's tail.

Worst of all, he couldn't see…didn't see…hadn't seen…my lizard half. Joe didn't know me. I didn't know him.

But I loved him. And he loved me. Didn't he? Didn't I? Didn't we?

The cobwebs crept closer to the window, writhing round the frame.

I was afraid now. I was mortally afraid. Was everything I had assumed up until that moment a lie? How much of what I saw was true and how much my own comfortable lie?

Joe's anger. His vanity. His wishing to be the center of it all. These things, kept at bay these three years but never lost, roared back from somewhere, somewhere I had seen them and hidden them away again.

My anger. My vanity. My wishing to be the center of it all. My longing to be alone and be off on my own adventure. My need to understand my lizard half, where it had come from, what it was meant for. My need to find the Key.

My doubts. My doubts of my own vision. My doubts of my own strength. My doubts due to Love.

The cobwebs reached in the glass, shattering a pane onto the floor of the cottage. My lizard tail lashed. My heart cried out, "I wish it! I wish I'd never loved at all!" But something stopped me.

For it wasn't true that I wished I hadn't loved. I loved Joe, and that could not be regretted, although that love was the first love of a young girl, which is sharp and sweet and shallow, until it's deepened by Trouble and Time.

I was silent in my confusion. I grasped at a simple reason for my silence. For the pain that now took my breath away.

I thought it was my love for him. But I was deluded—although the delusion was explicable, even forgivable. For it wasn't my love for him that kept me silent and caused the pain. It was my fear of losing his love for me.

Which is a very different thing, indeed. A very different thing.

That took me many years to learn. That fear of losing love is the disaster. To give in to a loved one truly from love is something that takes so much strength and wisdom…oh! so much! And I was still far from earning that strength, that wisdom.

Instead, I temporized. Not to put too nice a name on it, I lied to myself. I told myself I must have been mistaken. If he hadn't seen what I did, maybe

I had seen wrong? Or maybe there was some kind of middle ground…it was understandable, I told myself. It was too much to see. It was a girl's vision, not a man's. Was that it?

Didn't it become a princess, a queen, to yield? Wasn't it arrogance to think I knew best, that I saw more clearly than those who I loved?

Of course it was, I argued to myself. So I grit my teeth, and stood up, my lizard tail lashing to belie my cozening words, and I went over and kissed Joe on the forehead. And I said, "I love you." It wasn't a lie in itself. But it wasn't what I meant to say. I meant to cry out, "How can you love me if you can't see me?" But I didn't ask that of him. I had no faith. I didn't believe he could see me. Worse, I didn't believe that if he could, he would love me still. And I was willing to give up his knowing who I was for his love. Even if that love was only for a shadow on the wall.

It was a mistake. It took me many years and much painful journeying to realize just how and why. But the effect of my mistake was immediate.

It was Joe who became a shadow. He began to disappear. Right there. To my horror, I could see him fade away right before me and my father.

"It was like waking up from a dream," he told me later, as we held hands and walked together on the Road of the Dead. For Joe was dead then, and the dead see more clearly…if they want to, anyway. And Joe certainly did. As we walked our last walk together on this world, he saw me clearly. And he loved me. I had no doubt of it then.

"All at once, it was as if none of it had really happened. Not meeting you in the wood, not Grete, not Leef, not living with you those years, not Father appearing.

"It all began to turn into a kind of mist, like a dream, or some voices you hear from too far away to make out what they're saying. You and Dad faded away. Funnily, the last thing I could see in focus was Leef. He must have climbed onto your shoulder, and he stared at me with those round, deep eyes of his, as if he knew what was happening, but there was nothing he could do about it.

"And then it all got smaller and smaller: the picture of all of you blurred, like an image seen through the barrel of a telescope as you shut the lens down, and then the image went black, and I woke at the edge of the Dead Wood. Men there were searching for me, calling my name; Grandmother had sent them when I didn't come back. I'd come down to the Ruined Surface to see my mother, and I was supposed to join Grandmother at the ship to go back to the False Moon, and when I didn't show…

"No one seemed to think it was at all strange that I'd been gone three years, or that I'd aged since I'd been gone, and since they didn't worry about it, soon I didn't either…"

Here he laughed ruefully and passed a translucent hand over his brown hair. "It was as if the last three years had never happened at all. Though every night I would wake with a start—remember I told you about that? Every night, sure I'd lost something really valuable to me."

I looked at him. In Death he was dearer to me even than he had been in Life. A terrible thing. And I knew I was dearer to him then, too.

"Back there at the Crossroads," he continued, for that was where we met this side of Death, at the Crossroads where we waited for our fates, "back there when you came, it all came back to me, all in a rush." He looked at me with a tenderness the younger Joe had found difficult, and shook his head. "But all too late." And I could see through him now, for we were beginning the downhill climb to the harbor where the boat lay to take him away.

"Not too late," I said then, and I surprised myself as well as Joe with the firmness of my voice. I squeezed his hand and felt my palm pass through his, for our time was running out fast.

"It was not too late," I said firmly, "for hasn't Death given us an hour of real love, an hour never before given between one who's dead and one who's alive?"

At this he grinned his wide, lopsided grin, and folded me in his transparent arms. The embrace felt like a breeze coming in the open window at night during the start of spring.

But he was silent, then, for he could speak no more. In this world, our time had run out.

I stood there on the shore, watching him board, watching Death greet him, watching her give the order for the ship to cast off. And I stood there a long time, even after Death joined me, watching the white sails shrink into the distance and disappear over a horizon no one alive could name. I still stood there thinking, until she took my arm and pulled me gently away. I shook off what thoughts I had then that clung to a past I couldn't change, and turned and began the long walk with Death back to the crossroads that led to home.

But that was all seven years later. And I was a different person that day, the Lizard Princess no more.

On my side, that night, as Joe faded from sight and disappeared, it was as if the lights shining on a play went out, as in a giant theater. One by one, the familiar objects around me disappeared as well. First the big bed faded into the wall, then the wall faded and was gone, and there was only forest beyond.

Then the woodstove we had sat around so comfortably lost all its warm color, turning silver and black, like the negative of a picture, then splintering, shattering and dissolving as if the negative had melted into the flow of Time.

Then the jars I had filled with food for the winter vanished, their jewel colors fading out.

The other three walls fell and shriveled, and all that was left was the lintel and the standing wooden door.

And outside the door of the cottage was a serpent's tail, as if Joe had shed it when he fled.

It was a shining, moonless, starry night above; and the cobwebs swept up the meadow, so that it appeared to be shrouded in a fog. Grete neighed nervously. Leef, wide-eyed, sat on my shoulder as I stood at the open door. Then that door, too, faded away and was gone.

There was nothing left of the Bower of Bliss. Beside us, running into the mountains of the west, the Wall of Fire still burned, and Star stood before it, silent, guarding it with her sword of flame.

My father stood behind me. After a moment, I heard him give a deep, sad sigh. I turned, and I could see he looked young again—tired and worn, but not old. In a moment, I knew the man I had seen before—that Joe had not seen; he must have seen Conor in this form all along—was my father in the years to come. And that this meant I would know him in the years to come, and that lifted my heart, just a little.

"Is he gone?" Conor asked, his hands held sightlessly before him.

"Yes," I said sadly. "He's gone."

Conor sighed. "And you?" he said gently. "What will you do?"

"I'll find him." And I believed it then. I believed that was the sum of my desire: to find Joe and find again what we had.

I had thought it was Joe I was searching for. But I know now I was searching for the Key.

"Father," I said, and he didn't protest. He thought of me as the bride of his son, and that was enough. "Father, let me send you to a safer place."

"What could be safer than this, daughter?" he said, and I yearned to tell him the truth—but where would I begin?

I whistled for Grete, and then, leading my father to the flat tree stump where Joe had split our wood, helped him mount, closing his hands firmly on her mane.

Her nostrils flaring, Grete dipped her head to mine. I whispered in her ear the way that Clare the Rider had taught me, and Grete snorted her understanding and waited for the first command.

"Father," I said. "I have a journey to make. Grete will take you home."

Conor contemplated this from the horse's back. "And will I see you again?" he said.

"Yes," I promised. For I knew it was true. Though I knew, from my vision, that when we did meet again, we would both be much older. I know now it was a happy meeting, for he was able to hold his grandson, then, in his arms. And I was able to tell him the truth. Then it was the truth, for I had learned by then how to discern what was true from what was half-true…which is often more destructive than an out-and-out lie.

We met again, as in my dream, on the bench under the spreading tree at the home of Amalia and Francis, where I had gone to bear my child, Joe's and my child, the only child conceived, so far as I know, on the Road of the Dead. And my father lives there now, in a solitary hut Francis built for him just out of sight of the Small House. The people of Ventis and Amaurote call him 'the Hermit', and they often go to him for advice. He lives there now, an old wise man. A god. My father.

But all that came much later. Now I clasped my father's arm for the last time, spoke the word to Grete, and stood away as she leapt up and was gone.

We were alone, Leef and I, by the Wall of Fire. Waiting, still, for our orders, and to know what it was we were meant to do next. For I knew that if you wait in silence and true faith, your path opens itself up and beckons you on.

So I waited for my instructions. I waited to know my itinerary for the Voyage Out.

That first night out, I lay down on the springy grass next to the Wall of Fire, which emanated an encompassing warmth, as if it were an enormous stone hearth.

This was comforting. I could spread out there on the turf, and with a start, I realized I had always been somewhat cramped there in our wide bed in the Bower of Bliss. Joe's habit had been to move as far over to my side of the bed as he could, arms held out to hold me, head nuzzling my neck, and I had never, in all that time, been able to reclaim my half.

Now I could. Was the cost, then, loneliness? I wondered as I fell into a deep, dark sleep. Still, I knew I had to find Joe no matter what. And I had to find the Key.

I had no dreams that night. Instead, I blessedly slept.

Part V: The Centaur and the Mermaids

I slept until the black sky just before dawn, when both moons had sunk down and the stars wheeled. It was then I heard a 'click' and a 'push' and a thoughtful 'bang,' as if a door had opened and then quietly shut.

I sat up suddenly. What door? Leef was already awake, and he was staring down the Wall of Fire to the west.

"What was it?" I said, ruffling my hair, but he didn't answer. He left me, walking along the wall cautiously.

All the cobwebs were gone, now, as if dissolved by the night, and I saw something move in the woods at the end of the meadow.

Leef looked over his shoulder at me. I scrambled up after him.

Walking quietly along the Wall of Fire, side by side with Leef, I held my fingers out to the wall, and felt its warmth slide through them.

Then I blinked. In the middle of the Wall was now a Door. One I had never seen before, though this hardly should have surprised me, given how blind I knew I was to so much else. A wide Door, looking like old carved and gilded wood, but made of fire. No handle, no doorknob. Just a keyhole.

Of course I looked through the keyhole. And saw…ah, it makes me sigh even now to remember what I saw. It was Arcadia reborn, as if she had become what I had always hoped she would. Green and growing and filled with life, with new stories that flowed in a colorful stream through the landscape, like a living river. Home. That was what it looked like through that keyhole. Home.

I know it now for what it was, for what it is: the Domain of Life, where all stories, all symbols come from. For I have been on the other side of the Door, and I have opened the Door with the Key.

I can't describe what I felt. The sight filled me with hope that I could find it again, and filled me with despair at the thought that I might not have the strength to find the Key that would open the Door.

I knew the Key I looked for was the Key to that Door.

But who had opened it? For I knew that's what had woken me—someone opening and shutting that door behind them.

I peered down the meadow into the woods, for now the dawn was starting in the east, and the light was a dim silvery gray, and the stars took their leave, one by one. There was something…someone standing in the woods under the biggest of the fir trees. Then it moved, and I saw it was a horse. A sudden worry went through me—had Grete lost my father in some accident and come back to me?

"Grete?" I called out softly. There was a quiet snorting and I could see the horse paw at the ground. Leef gave me a look, and I bent down so he could run up my arm to my shoulder. He whispered in my ear.

"Not Grete," he breathed. "Not a horse."

Startled, I looked at him, but he stared intently at the form under the tree.

The light grew. The sun came a quarter way, over the mountains behind us, and lit a passage down the meadow to the trees. That was when I could see him clearly, standing there, noble in the dawn light.

A centaur. The centaur. The centaur who was rumored to live in the far north of the Samanthans, where no Arcadian had ever gone. He had been seen, it was said, by some children who had gotten lost on a summer's day and a summer's night. He had found them, spoken to them gently, and then sent them home. They had come back full of the story, and the sheer joy of the meeting. But it had been hard to believe them. Aspern Grayling had been furious when the rumor went round Arcadia in a flash—it was what he called the kind of superstition that kept us 'a backwater'…although what was wrong with being a backwater was never made completely clear to me.

But the children hadn't been fantasizing, or woolgathering, or lying, for here he was now. The centaur. I was dazzled. Half-man and half-horse. The best, the most virtuous, of both. You could see the wisdom on his face as he drew near.

He made his way toward us now, limping slightly, I saw, on his left side back leg.

I made my way toward him quickly. It felt unseemly to let him approach me. As if he were some kind of king I owed fealty. Not the kind of king who rules, mind you. The kind of king who leads.

"Master," I said quietly as we came face to face, and I bowed my head.

When I looked up, to my surprise, I saw there were tears in his eyes. They were tears, I was sure, of joy, not of sorrow. And the joy was in seeing me.

We stood there a moment in silence. I was moved, but by what? I couldn't see, not even in the dawning of the light there in the meadow. I was moved by a memory so deep that I couldn't find it again. But it was a memory so strong and vivid that the feeling of it, even if not the thought, could fight its way up into my heart.

He shook his head gently. "Friend. Not Master at all, Snow."

We turned together, and walked east along the Wall of Fire. I was worried by his words.

"You know me, then?" I said tentatively, and gave a nervous half-laugh. "Little did I realize I was on such terms with such noble company."

He looked at me with a half-sad, half-amused expression, and I caught a swift look that flashed between the centaur and Leef before they both looked away.

"Don't you remember, then?" he said.

I shook my head.

Half man and half horse. The best, the most virtuous, of both.

"You chose to come to this side," he said. "Don't you remember that?"

Leef gave a heavy sigh in my ear, and when I looked over at him on my shoulder, I saw the lemur and the centaur commune again, wordlessly.

"No," I said. "I don't remember."

We walked on. I dared now to put my hand on the centaur's glossy chestnut shoulder. As I did, he leaned his head toward me, as Grete might have done to show affection.

"You said that all this world was in need of was the tiniest bit of kindness and of courtesy. Of Love," he said. We walked on, and I hardly noticed when we left the meadow and continued along a forest path next to the Wall of Fire. "You were angry when none of us agreed. That was what you said, Snow. You really don't remember this?"

He paused, because now we had come to a crossroads. One path led up to the Wall of Fire. The other dove back into the woods. Looking at me curiously, as if he waited for me to choose, the centaur continued. "Star said it was more than that." He laughed as if the memory amused him. "But you were always so stubborn."

He smiled at me. I could feel, through the palm of my hand, the throbbing of an artery in his side. And he stopped, waiting, the way Grete did when she waited to know which way I would choose to go.

Without thinking, I said, "Choose the way for me, Storm." And he tossed his head with delight, whinnying. Leef sat up on my shoulder and gazed at me.

"What?" I said, startled, as Storm whinnied again triumphantly and turned us down the left hand path away from the Wall of Fire.

"I never told you my name," the centaur said. "I never said my name was Storm."

In sheer exuberance, he cantered on ahead of us, tail held high, silver hooves flashing in the light that now streamed through the trees, a warm gold light.

The path we walked along wound and wound; it went south, then north, then west…always west. At first it was wide enough for us to walk side by side, but after an hour or so, it straightened and tightened and rose, back and forth, north/south, north/south, winding up. But always winding west.

The sun rose overhead and began to dip down in front of us. I was tired, though I thought it impolite to show this. Storm saw, though. And the centaur, still as fresh as he had been at dawn, offered to let me climb on his back.

Thankful, I did. He bent his forelegs, and I pulled myself wearily up, Leef jumping down before me.

We walked on.

"Storm," I said, and then I hesitated. I had been silently thinking over my questions all that time. But now the questions overflowed, and I couldn't help speaking. "Storm, did you know my mother?"

I couldn't see his face, but I could feel him. I could feel him give a sigh that I couldn't interpret—there was both joy and sorrow in it.

"Oh yes," he said. "I knew Lily. In many forms."

"Ah," I said. I remained silent as long as I could manage it.

"And do you," I said tentatively, "know Joe?"

At that he stopped, and turned his head, peering at me kindly.

"Joe?" he said doubtfully. "No. I don't think I know the name." And turned again and kept on.

"Because," I said, "I'm looking for Joe."

He walked on in meditative silence.

"I've lost him," I said helplessly. I didn't know what else to say. And the words seemed to be escaping from me like birds let loose from a cage.

"I think he's in the Dead Wood," I said, not knowing what or where the Dead Wood might be.

"Ah," he said this time. "I can get you to the Dead Wood. If that is where you want to go, Sophia."

It was the first time he had called me 'Sophia'. I noted that. But I didn't know what to make of it.

"All right then," he said briskly. "Now that I know where we want to go, we can pick up the pace a bit." And he warned me to hold on.

He ran.

Glorious gallop. Never to be forgotten. Straight up and out of the forest and over a rocky outcrop and then…spread out below…at the foot of the steep mountain where we had gone through the rocky pass…never before seen…

The sea.

The centaur wheeled up as we came over the pass and stopped, as if to let me take in my first sight.

I was moved. I had never seen it before, the green blue, white-tipped, ever-moving expanse of it. But I knew it as if I had. I recognized it. It had been home. It had been the most beautiful, the most timeless, and the most loved of homes on my world.

How could this be? I wondered in a swirl of wordless thoughts. How could home be all the feelings I had, for Arcadia, for the garden on the other side of the Wall of Fire, and now for this turquoise ocean, shining silver as the sun headed down in the west above it?

"She loved it, too," the centaur said, and I knew he meant Lily. And Leef stared straight down at the sea, and I knew it was true of Leef, of something deep inside him that was larger than the lemur body he found himself in now—that he had always loved the sea.

It's no wonder it took me such a long time to be able to see in Megalopolis with the same eyes I see in Arcadia. I know now that entering the Dead Wood was an early exercise in half-blinding myself to living things; for unless one does half-blind oneself in this way, it is nearly impossible to see things as the Megalopolitans do. Their sight has been trained, over time, to see only the abstract, to see only the sign rather than the living thing itself. This has had tremendous value for them in terms of building their really astonishing technology, but it blinds them to much else. As a blinkered horse will go faster without knowing the landscape she travels in—so Megalopolis.

For how could I bear to see what I did see that day if I had spent my life in Megalopolis? How could I have come down the mountains on the back of a centaur, and seen the mermaids rise in the sea?

This is what Aspern Grayling can never understand. How can it be worthwhile to trade clear sight for the illusions of power? How can that be? But of course, he thinks what I see are illusions, the product of a diseased mind.

But to see the mermaids rise up out of a turquoise sea, to see them greet me as the daughter of one they had loved—no. This was not disease. This was fact, but a fact renewed, reborn, a different realm of fact than the constricted gray room where Megalopolis dwells.

A larger world.

I have lived sixty years, and I have seen marvels. I have seen the exquisite garden of TreMega on the False Moon. I have seen many things greater than that, and filled with more true feeling. But of all of these, the memory that can never be erased is the feeling of seeing the mermaids rise out of what was once our true home.

How did I know this? I didn't know it. I felt it. Like a white light, all the way through. Like a light that lit up all that I could see, for miles around, showing up detail and color and delight that had been hidden in shadow before.

In that white light was a freedom I had never yet known, but that is with me still. I have nurtured and protected that freedom through many adventures and hardships. Sometimes, strangely, it was the hardships that nurtured and protected that freedom the most.

This is something Aspern Grayling will never understand. Not because he can't. But because he won't. You have to be willing to take the hard way in order to win this freedom. You have to be willing to accept—oh! all the way through!—that you are something small and fragile, and yet you have to have the faith—all the way through!—that somewhere is protection beyond your control. Aspern won't accept. Aspern won't give in. Aspern won't give up. He won't take the hard way, and freedom is forever just outside of his grasp. He hates those of us who hold it so lightly. His envy would, if it could, destroy the world.

That threat is part of my own Hard Way, too.

But making my hard way through the Dead Wood prepared me for the harsher, tighter world where Aspern lives and breathes, the world of Megalopolis, of the imperium that demands each human being sacrifice her or himself for its grandeur. I needed to survive, and the need to survive, I discovered, brings all the vital functions down to their lowest pulse. It's a necessary conservation. When you are in extremity, every perception is the eye's—and the mind's—most basic possibility.

Seeing the mermaids that day, before I made my harsh journey across the Dead Wood, gave me more than survival. It gave me life itself, as if the sight...the feeling...had spread out a safe, beloved, spring green meadow around me and Leef in all directions. One filled with animals that roared with the joy of being, and flowers whose scents alone were food enough.

There they were, as if I had known them all along. In a way I had, for it had long been a favorite childhood bedtime story that my nurse, Kim the Kind, never tired of telling me, of the day that she and my mother and another girl named Phoebe walked into the sea and feasted with the mermaids.

It was where my mother found the Key. I remembered that now, and my heart leapt.

"Oh!" I said. "Oh, oh! Storm! May we go to them? Can we go to them?"

Storm turned his head, inclining his neck regally and smiled. "Of course, Snow," he said softly. "They've been waiting for you all along."

The mermaids had been waiting for me?

We trotted down the path of white rock, right to the pale gold sand of the cove where emerald-green seaweed made patterns on the bright blue sea. The mermaids waited there—some sitting coiled and silent on silvery rocks dripping with dark green, and some floating lazily on the spiraling currents in the little bay.

Beached on the sands beside the bay was a small skiff of teak and brass, with a cunning cushion of rose-colored silk in its middle, and at its bow, a brass ring through which was threaded a golden silk rope. A boat fit for a princess. For a Lizard Princess.

Storm stopped now on the beach, his front hoof pawing down. Now that we no longer moved so swiftly, his limp was pronounced. His back left hoof, I saw, dragged in the sand.

Something warned me not to ask about this. Instead, I awkwardly dismounted, shaking my lizard's tail out behind me, and stomping rather ungracefully to get the circulation going again in my cold-blooded feet.

That was when I saw her rise up out of the sea. A real mermaid. She walked toward me with her hands held out in welcome. A welcome I could feel all the way across the sand.

Was this the same mermaid that my nurse had so often described as having given her, my mother and Phoebe, the friend they left behind them there, a similar welcome? She was an emerald-faced mermaid with golden hair and purple-black legs colored like winter seaweed, on which she walked in stately fashion…for as Kim had never tired of telling me, it is a mistake to think that mermaids have a fish's tail, a misperception that comes from the fact that every mermaid is born knowing how to put her legs together to use as a rudder, a blessing in the navigation of oceans the wide world over.

She was silent, as are all mermaids, and her mouth was a silvery crescent upturned. She held her hands out to me, and I, ungainly on my lizard's feet, lurched forward to take hold of them. When I did, I felt a surge of sisterhood, of belonging, the like of which I had never felt before.

My lizard's legs and tail, I realized, made me kin to the mermaid. What we shared was a mingling of warm blood and cold.

I held my kinswoman's hands in mine and tears came to my eyes. I turned to Leef, wanting someone close to me to share my joy, and saw, to my surprise, that he and the centaur stood together down at the edge of the shore, and that they and the mermaids gazed at each other in a deep and pregnant silence. A silence that meant they knew each other from long ago. A silence that surrounded a reunion that brought joy to both sides.

Wondering at this, but unable to make anything of it, I found my voice, though it sounded harsh to me, as if it hadn't been used in a very long time. "Thank you for this welcome. I've long wanted to know you."

The silent answer came back, "And we you."

I cleared my throat. "I have been told many stories of the time my mother and my nurse were among you, and that it was from you that my mother took the Key." I felt, rather than said, my question, "And do you have it still?"

"No," came back the silent, sadness-tinged answer. "We do not have the Key, nor do we know where it can be found."

"Oh," I said. My next question was silent, as I scanned the faces of the mermaids floating in the bay before me. "Where is the friend of my mother, the girl called Phoebe, who walked with Lily and Kim into the sea and to the Mermaids' Deep, and was left behind by them?"

A light seemed to glow in the mermaid's face, and I recognized this as a mermaid smile. She turned slightly and inclined her head toward the beach. I blinked, for I didn't understand. It seemed to me that in her gaze she meant Leef, my lemur, who looked sheepish now, and pushed irritably at the sand.

Then Leef looked up at me, and his eyes were the eyes of a mermaid, the eyes of a girl from the Moon Itself, the eyes of a comrade-in-arms. Good eyes. Old eyes. They were half-laughing, half-apologizing, and I knew with a start what was meant by their look.

The mermaid turned now, holding my hand in her own, and led me down to the skiff. Leef skittered across the strand and hopped in. I stepped in and sat on the little cushioned bench gingerly, trying it on for size.

"But wait!" I said, for the mermaid looked purposeful, as if she were about to push us off. I jumped awkwardly from the little boat onto the wet sand, and ran back to Storm, burying my face in his shoulder. His arms held me tight, and he kissed me on the head.

Would I see him again? I knew I would. I have seen him, and in that form, even in the face of Aspern Grayling's insistence that no centaurs roam in the far reaches of the north. For I have been back to the northernmost Samanthans in search of the Door in the Wall of Fire, and I have seen Storm again and had many private conversations with him about what has been and what will be. And those conversations have added so much to my small store of understanding, that small store that gives rise to the name they so inaccurately call me: "The Wise." For which of us is truly wise alone? If we are wise, we are wise together. And those who love are never truly parted.

Still, it was hard to say goodbye that day. As it is so often hard to say goodbye to those one loves. So very hard.

The mermaids tugged on the silken rope, and pulled the skiff out to sea. A breeze rustled past, and Leef curled up against my thigh, sleeping in the sun as we skimmed the water lightly.

You might have thought I would have looked at him differently now, now that I had seen a glimpse of who he really was. But oh! The day was beautiful and warm, the sea was soft and blue-green, the breeze was cool, the scents from the ancient evergreen trees that ran all the way down the mountains to the edge of the sea were alive, and I was a human being, glad to be there at that time, on that world, feeling those things.

It is why we become human, we creatures of other worlds and other realities. To feel these things. And these things cannot be felt without being in this body, which seeks to survive. And to survive in this body, one has to forget many things. Many important things. But as a crystal glass can only hold so much wine without overflowing, so we can only hold so much sight.

Though we can, I have found, grow to hold more. Unlike the glass. We can, painfully, grow to hold more joy.

I think now that it was my lizard half that enabled me to see things my human half was ill prepared for. And I know…I knew then…that it was my lizard half, not my human, that helped me now to survive.

It was my lizard half that recognized my kin. Even where it would have seemed impossible. For the body doesn't lie about what it knows, and my body was a new mixture of sensation and knowledge, striving to join the disparate parts together into a larger whole.

The Dead Wood taught me that. The Dead Wood that almost killed the human in me, but fell back in the face of my lizard nature.

My lizard and my human nature both rejoiced as the mermaids pulled the skiff along beside the coast, where the Donatees run down to the ocean, and the waves break against their tall trees and raspberry bushes. My lizard and my human nature felt all the way through how much I owed to the mermaids, my cousins, my ancestors who still lived in harmony with the sea.

I gave myself up to the moment, and gave myself up to the only perception of Leef I had had until then: the loving lemur who had come into my life, watching me, guarding me, keeping me company when every other company failed. My guardian animal.

It was enough. It was enough for Leef, too. He grunted with contentment as we sailed along, hugging the coast, heading south for the edges of a half-destroyed Megalopolis, what we call now the Ruined Surface, once it was washed away in the Great Flood that happened right before my birth. The poor lived there now, the workers, the caregivers for the rich who, for whatever reason, could not restore their health on the False Moon—for the False Moon, no matter its technical magnificence and cold beauties, is a harsher place than its Megalopolitan boosters will admit.

But still Megalopolis insists on blinding itself to the harshness, the insalubrity, the actual toxicity of the False Moon, insists on its wonders and the wonders those who live there will find as they make their way farther and farther into the universe—that is, farther and farther away from all that makes us human and that gives us human joy.

It was human joy I felt fully that day as we skimmed the surface of the sea, in search of my lost love and in search of the Key. It was the last time I would feel such joy for many years.

The beauties of that coastline I have mentioned, and indeed, have written about elsewhere. I have written also of how, as one nears the edge of Megalopolis, the trees begin to shrink, to stunt, and the blossoms on the lush rhododendron bushes disappear. The breeze turns hot, the waves choppy and gray.

This is the approach from the north to the Dead Wood. Soon, the trees, the bushes, the flowering plants falter, then disappear altogether, and the land is a desert of bare reddish-brown hills. Only when one looks more closely does one sees a sprinkling of plants—spiny brown crowns, seemingly dead. It is only when one lands and investigates further that one can see the plants live without roots—for the only moisture they need is the gray fog that blows in from the sea.

That gray fog covered us now, and the skiff moved more slowly as the mermaids found the going harder. Leef sat up, alarmed, and dank drops fell from my skin onto the floor of the little boat. Leef lapped up a bit, experimentally, and shook his head. I ran a finger across my uncomfortably dampened throat and tasted. Brackish. Not good.

It was then the bottom of the skiff ran aground. The fog deepened until we couldn't see more than an inch in front of our faces. As it opened, I saw we had come ashore.

The mermaids had been left behind in the sea.

Part VI: In The Dead Wood

Not good.

I lumbered out of the skiff where it lay rocking on a bed of sharp gray rocks which hurt even the tough lizard skin of my feet, as I held out my arms for Leef to run up to my shoulder. We made a painful way to the rocky beach ahead.

We turned and peered into the fog. I couldn't see the ocean, but I did make a small jump of surprise looking back at our boat. There on the little bench was a lumpy cloth bag. I plunged back and grabbed it. Just in time: a juddering wave lifted the boat out of reach, back to the sea where the fog swallowed it up. I knew I had seen the mermaids for the last time. This was their last gift to me. Without opening the bag, I slung it across my chest by its strap and felt heartened by its weight.

I knew we needed to go south. For south past the Dead Wood were the outskirts of the Ruined Surface of Megalopolis, and surely Joe was to be found there? Turning to the brownish red dust of the hills, Leef clinging to my neck, I walked on. The rocks underneath cut at my feet, until they gradually lessened, leaving nothing but a floor of fine gray dust. The Dead Trees towered up over the trail. And we walked on, and into the Dead Wood.

I don't know how to describe the horror of that place. Everything was dead—everything. For miles in all directions, a horrible sameness, no change, no sound, no life. It had stretched out before me, a barrier to where I wanted to go, and with the sea behind me, and the mermaid sailors gone, I had no choice but to plunge through.

How far did it extend? There would have to be an end to it. So I plunged into the Dead Wood, with Leef scampering, worried, at my side.

It was easy going at first, if all you cared about was the road underfoot. What was left of the trees—silver, gray, sickly white, bleached, lifeless—didn't stand in our way. There was no underbrush, no careless branches growing across the path. Underfoot, in all directions, was a powdery gray sand, like pulverized bone, that, while smooth to walk on, also floated in the air. By the end of the day, both Leef and I were covered with the fine stuff—in our hair, on our skin, under our nails.

There was no water. We were careful to keep the sea to our right as we walked. There was no sound in the Dead Wood, and it was heartening to hear, even in the distance, the thundering of the surf. No seabirds, though. The whole time we spent toiling across the Dead Wood, the sea was the only living sound. There were no birds in the wood, no animals, no living thing of any kind.

Except for me, the Lizard Princess. And her lemur, Leef. He never complained, not when we lay down in that horrible dust at night, utterly exhausted by the inexorable sameness that surrounded us. We looked up at the sky, hoping to see the Moon Itself and the stars, but nothing could be seen but black. Black at night, gray in the day. As if that miserable gray dust formed a permanent cloud overhead.

There was no food of course. Dazed, I had forgotten the mermaids' gift, until Leef tugged at the bag when I sat, momentarily despairing, lost in the sameness of the wood. Opening it, I found a honey cake, and a flask—oh blessing!—of precious fresh water. Even tiny portions of both proved to be enough to hearten us, me and Leef, whether because there was magic in them, or because the memory of the mermaids' care for us was nourishment as well.

But as we went on, the problem was water. The lack of water, except the small amount in the flask.

After three days of walking, I realized I had been too hopeful. How could the Dead Wood go on very far? Even if it did, there had to be rivers running down the Donatees to the east, snowmelt that must run down to the sea. I'd been confident we'd cross a river very soon. So I'd let myself drink enough to satisfy thirst, those first three days in the wood. My lizard half stood us in good stead here; we needed far less water than if I had been fully human. And of course my lizard legs could carry us farther than the mere princess could ever have managed on her own.

I could carry Leef, too, who by this third day was nearly fainting as he went, and not just for lack of food and drink, but at the sheer horror of the sameness of it all. The bleached, uniform, dead, gray sameness. That was the hardest thing to bear.

We ran out of water on the fourth day, and our pace slowed frighteningly. Even my lizard strength had begun to fade, and Leef, now clinging to the empty bag slung across my chest, his fur dull, would every so often give a mewing cry. That sound was the hardest, the worst, for I knew he would never have allowed himself to complain, unless he was so far gone he couldn't help himself.

Unless he was dying.

I knew he was dying.

I knew I would die, too, if we didn't see the end of the Wood soon. But there it stretched, farther and farther ahead, and behind us, five days' walk. We would never last five more days, I knew. Leef couldn't. I knew I couldn't either.

That night, in the same total, dreary blackness, we sank down to sleep. I tried to plan. But all I could think of was the dryness inside my mouth, and how I could hardly breathe through the clogging gray dust that filled my throat and nostrils. I drifted into a dream, where Leef and I were home again in my big bed in the Tower, the windows opened wide to a spring night, the air cool and wet and green, the night birds singing, the…

All at once I was awake. Dawn. I could see the gray light even with my eyes shut. Leef was already awake. In my ear, he breathed faintly but urgently, "She's here. She's here." And opening my eyes, I saw, standing there in the Dead Wood, beautiful, slender, strong and tall, Death herself. Hands on hips, elegant arms akimbo, she looked about scornfully. Then she looked at us, shaking her head in a contained fury.

"Dead Wood," she snapped, as I sat wearily up and gazed on her beautiful and terrible face. "This place has nothing to do with me. It needs a new name—or I do."

Hope entered me now, as if Death had brought her along as a friend. And Leef, too, had a little brightness in his dying eye.

Death sighed. She shook her head again and held out one slender, ivory-colored hand to help me up. Had she come for us then? Obedient, fearful, half-hopeful, at the end of my strength, and now reenergized by Death, I clasped her hand and let her pull me up.

"Get out of this horrible place," she said, shuddering. I was amazed to see that even Death loathed the Dead Wood. "They call it the Dead Wood, but it's far worse than that, far worse than anything I could ever create. Go, go…walk to the sea."

With that, her hand let go of mine, and she faded away into the silvery dead trees, her mocking laugh echoing back—mocking the Wood, not us the Living, mocking the lifelessness that pretended to a relationship, a true relationship, with Death.

What Death meant was this: there is an end from which there is no rebirth, and this end is a vastly different thing from Death and her works. But we, poor perceivers, in our ignorance have confounded the two, not even having a separate name for the Final End. For the Dead Wood was the home of that Final End. From the Dead Wood would come no more green shoots, no new spring, no rebirth…and it was this version of death

Death herself.

that Death treated with such scorn. This was not her Death. This was not the Death eternally partnered with Life.

The horror of the Dead Wood was just this. That it was the End from which there could be no Beginning. It was the Final End. And I can see now, so many years later, it is this Final End that threatens to overrun the whole of Megalopolis. And after her, Arcadia.

That day, unseeing, I followed Death's advice. We turned west. It took us a day to get to the sea. We came out of the Lifeless Forest onto gray shale, and Leef, whose eyes, even dimmed as they were by then were still sharper than mine, spotted an estuary, a river…something, something that ran to the sea, wide across the shale and sharp rocks and sands to the south. Holding him closely to me, I hurried as fast as I could, though I seemed to myself to move in slow motion, as if against a strong wind.

At dusk we reached it. A marsh. A fetid, poisonous-looking, soggy marsh, which stretched as far as my eyes could see. To the east, then, and the north, the Lifeless Forest. To the west, the sea. To the south, the marsh. I collapsed next to it, too tired to cry, as Leef crawled hopefully toward its edge, recoiling at the smell of it. There was nothing there for us—nothing. I don't remember any more than that thought. Nothing. Then I must have fainted, for I remember nothing more of that day.

I would have died there if I hadn't understood I had kin at either side of the Dead Wood. If I hadn't been able to recognize those of my own kind, if I had shrunk away from those I had affinity for, pushing them away, not recognizing their kindness and relationship to me. I would have died.

Easy to see one's kinship to mermaids. Although it shows the wisdom of the mermaids that they were able to see their kinship to me.

It was Leef who brought me back to myself. Where I had the strange advantage of my tough half-lizard hide, he was all tender, fragile mammal. He was all loving animal too, adding to his vulnerability, since the energy of love, so our Arcadian physicists tell us, goes out to meet others in trust. If it finds no response, it disappears into the sad and meaningless void, until the creature who generates it in hope wears down, leaving only the spirit. The physical nature wastes away.

So it was for Leef. In his distress, his energy poured out of him, pouring down a sand hole there at the edge of that poisonous marsh.

But I was there too, near the void and unconscious, lost to any potential beauties of the world. It was Leef's love that poured into me as it poured out of him. It poured down and down and down through the layers of dark despair and deathly unconsciousness where I lay buried. Like a shining hook on a silver wire, it sought me out and caught me—I grasped it—just as I was about to slip away into a stream of nothingness.

It caught me. I held it. I remember that first, inchoate struggle between dark and light, and some kind of strange, indefinable marriage between the two as Leef's love pulled me, bit by patient bit, upward. Leef's love for me found my love for him and drew it upward, away from the kind of death for which we have no precise descriptive word: the death of the spirit. The death of hope. The death of joy.

These are the deaths that Death, furious, wanted no part of, and these were the deaths that afflicted me now, drew me on, the deaths that formed the darkness in which I sank, by the marsh, farther and farther to the black, muddy, fathomless bottom.

But Leef's hook caught me. I caught it and climbed it and it held me. It tugged me up to the smallest remembrance, which I grabbed hold of in my desperation, to use as a brief respite in my long climb back to consciousness and pain.

It was this memory:

Of Leef. Of his beauty and his vulnerability. Of how if I sank and sank and sank, he would sink too. How I was his protector no less than he was mine, and how my own love for him had tied me firmly to the hook of his love for me, giving me the strength to swim back upward, guided by the silver line that connected us, back to my fate, which was tied to his. Tied through love.

This is something Aspern Grayling has yet to understand. That these ties are real, are real physical forces—that they are often stronger than any force of arms. I've had many opportunities to test the strength of that assertion. This was one of those times.

I rose back up through the muck and mire of my own despair, searching in the dark for that little animal who was loyal to the end, and who loved so much. I felt him first, cradled in my arms, his fur matted, his heart beating fainter and fainter, and my alarm gave me a last jolt of needed energy. That enabled me to open my eyes, bleary, confused, but knowing my goal: if there was a way to save Leef, I had to find it.

But who was 'I', I wondered? For I was not yet back to myself.

Opening my eyes, for a moment I felt I had fallen back into a dream. For in the murk of what passed for twilight in that desolate place, bending over me and the lemur, were three creatures, black against a dim gray sky.

Later, I was to discover that the creatures were covered in spots of dull gold light, as if stars had been shaken over them through a heavenly sieve. But on the Dead Wood side of the Marsh those stars were extinguished. So the big animals with their enigmatic, oval, neckless heads stood shiny, smooth, and black before me, their tails twitching just enough to show that they were alive.

Had I screamed and pushed them away, they would have fled, for they had, as I found later, much reason to be shy of humankind. But I was half-lizard, and that drew them, and that told me what I needed to know. Kin, my lizard half told me. Brothers, sisters. A part of me as much as the mermaids had been. My lizard half knew this, and that knowledge spread to my human half as well.

I struggled to sit up. Leef moaned faintly from my lap. At this, the creature directly in front of me, the largest of the group, bent toward us in response, and while my human half wanted to shrink back, my lizard half knew—this creature was not a threat, but was offering me sympathy.

I saw a crest on the creature's head as it inclined forward, a kind of crown that topped a dorsal ridge running all the way up from its tail. Trying to shake myself back to full self-possession and failing, I thought dreamily, "The Queen. The Queen is here."

At this the animal nodded, as if in satisfaction, and I realized I must have spoken aloud. This brought me—my faculties—up farther from the murk, and another thought occurred to me: "Can they help Leef?"

At that thought, the smallest of the creatures nimbly darted forward and lay a webbed front foot onto Leef, holding it there for a short time, until the lemur stirred groggily and—oh blessed moment!—opened his eyes.

The shock of this helped restore my lost faculties, and I was now, though very weak, more firmly myself than I had been in some days. The smaller creature was close enough that I could look into her eyes (for I knew without a doubt it was a 'she', though how I knew I have yet to understand), and in those eyes I saw an understanding. A kinship—not just to my lizard half, but to my human half. With a start, I thought, "These are cousins. Sisters. Brothers. Friends." At which the creatures nodded vigorously, holding out their webbed front feet as if in greeting.

It was my lizard half that had recognized them, and my lizard half had called them. But it was my human half that reached out to them, now, in love.

The small creature held out her front foot again, and I, suddenly understanding, held out my right hand and took her foot in greeting. And I kept hold of it as the Queen (as I now thought, correctly as it turned out, of the largest of the creatures) silently directed the third, a plump, amiable boy of their kind with a less developed dorsal fin, to lie flat and take me onto his back. Leef climbed wearily onto my shirt and I opened the bag still slung there, into which he gratefully sank, and then I grabbed hold of the dorsal fin, first gently out of fear of hurting him, but then, encouraged by his joyful laugh, which kindly mocked me for doubting his strength, I took a firmer grip. And the creatures slid in the marsh water and began to swim across, with Leef and I on the boy's back.

A few years later, in one of the myriad museums of the False Moon, I saw, nailed to an exhibit wall, a hide of one of the creatures, even in death a velvet black with gold sprinkles and swirls haphazardly spread like a galaxy of stars. It was in a dusty, little-visited corner of the place, and the flyspecked placard beside it proclaimed a long, scientific name I couldn't pronounce, and said the animal it represented "has been long extinct, once hunted for its hide and use as fertilizer." I could scarcely bear to look on it, and Leef and I never returned.

Part VII: On The Ruined Surface

As we swam across the marsh, the water beneath us and the sky above began to glow with a faint blue-green light. It was only then that I realized the sky and the water in the Dead Wood had been black, then the same gray color as the fine dust of its ground. The gray that was the only color we saw the whole endless time we crossed that foul place. But now, clinging to the back of the creature—salamander? newt? friend—the world around us began slowly to come back to life.

Not as much life as I was used to. Not as much life as I would have liked. But still—life.

I knew when we crossed into fresher water, water that might be safely drunk, for it turned below me into a clear, sweet, silver blue. And I saw pictures in it as we swam, as if they pushed their way to the surface, pictures of trees and flowers and animals of all kinds, as I had seen in the Bower of Bliss. Not so riotous, not so joyful as there, but even here, in the middle of the marsh on the edges of Megalopolis, a multiplicity of life, of story.

We were out of the Dead Wood.

The day lightened as we swam, and the small creature swimming swiftly beside her brother flipped one of her black-clawed forelegs against the water so that it splashed onto us. And Leef, opening his dull eyes, smelled

109

the water as it splashed up, opened his mouth and drank.

It wasn't the clear, crisp water of an Arcadian stream. But it was fresh, and it revived us. I can still remember its taste.

I didn't know it then, but there was not much fresh water in that marsh, just this blue green strip that the creatures kept to, which came rushing down from the pure snowmelt of the Donatees. For as we came in sight of the opposite shore, the very edge of Megalopolis, the water again turned, not gray, but the fetid green of a dying sea. The three creatures stopped there, and, swimming in circles, seemed to confer. The Queen looked at me, kindly as I thought. With trepidation I looked down and saw that the water was shallow here, what there was of it pushing its way sluggishly through the algae. I could stand. I realized they could go no farther without danger to themselves, so, grateful, I slid from the back of my guardian, into slimy water that rose up to my waist.

We shook hands, or forelegs, solemnly, and it cost me as much of a pang to leave the three as it had cost me to leave the mermaids. With all my heart I thanked them, and with all their hearts they received my thanks before turning to swim away.

Turning toward Megalopolis, carrying Leef, I trudged through the edges of the Marsh, where it struggled to live. I could feel that struggle, though it looked like it was dying. This was harsh going. As I tore through the masses of water weeds, some dead, some dying, but some, miraculously, fighting their way back to life, I felt my heart tear a little, too. When things are dead, completely dead, the sorrow stays the same. But when there is a hint that life might still be there, the sorrow of that tears at the soul.

On the other side of the Marsh, where we emerged across from the Dead Wood, the land wasn't much better. It was alive, that's true—just. But the terror of walking there was worse. The landscape itself seemed to groan as Leef and I went, as if in pain…and a dead thing has no pain. To hear it cry out like that, and to be unable to go to its aid, was almost unbearable, until we became hardened, as are all who manage to live without going mad in Megalopolis, hardened to the sound. It would be unbearable if it wasn't that all in Megalopolis had to bear it. And now Leef and I were learning to bear it as well.

The land was dying, that was clear. It wasn't yet the Dead Wood, but if nothing was done, it would be soon. And we were all the same world, Arcadia and this land of the Dead Wood. What happened here would happen there.

What then, could be done?

Years later, I asked this same question of Star as we sat in our Council of Two, discussing matters of High State, "Why, if it is true what you say, and I and countless of my fellows here have been born and reborn in a multiplicity of forms, then why have we not all, by now, combined what we have learned, and solved the problem of the Dead Wood?" But Star only put her forefinger to her mouth in the universal sign of silence, and I knew what she said was that we would never know, for it was our job to toil in the dark. For it is in the dark where new forms are born.

That day, as Leef and I trudged along toward the haze of smoke rising from a human settlement of some kind, I felt the dread pang of the old forms dying. He said quietly, "Look." I stopped a moment. At my lizard feet were piles of dead bees, husks, thousands of them in small bee cairns all around us.

My human feet could not have borne walking through those exquisite corpses. Any more than the Sophy I had once been, who had died, I think, in the Dead Wood—any more than she, tenderhearted, deluded girl, could have let Will the Murderer lose a game of chess when it meant so much to him.

These thoughts passed through me as I scanned the landscape and saw more of the velvet black and gold bees. Dead, and worse, much worse, dying. To see them dying in this way was almost more than I could bear, and yet I summoned up the determination to trudge onwards.

111

Bees have a special meaning in Arcadia, and particularly for me, Arcadia's queen. For in the Little Meadow, above the Small House, on the outskirts of the pretty town of Ventis, in the Arcadian foothills of the Donatees, are the hives that belong to the domain of Amalia Todhunter and Francis Flight, my godparents and the foster family of Walter Todhunter.

Amalia, as her name indicates, descends from a family who had much to do with foxes, the gray ones that keep our fields free of pesties of all kinds. "Hunter" is a misleading term here; unlike the names of Megalopolis, many Arcadian names prize a symbolic over a practical meaning. "Todhunter," in our land, refers to people who study the ways of foxes in order to understand more of the ways of our dogs, and, indeed, our fellows. The Todhunters have always been known for their ability to heal domestic animals, and Amalia has inherited this ability to a spectacular degree—which is why, even now in her honored old age, the Small House is a riot of pets: dogs, cats, mice, tortoises, parrots, an owl…and of course, a fox, whose ears flop like a puppy's, and who follows her wherever she goes.

But it's the Flights I mean to speak about now. Francis Flight, husband of Amalia, is one of the Donatees Flights: famous beekeepers. The Little Meadow is the most famous Bee Garden in all of Arcadia. And as Arcadia is known for the quality and sweetness of its honey, this is a very real form of fame.

The Bee Garden of the Little Meadow holds about a hundred hives, sometimes more, sometimes less, depending on the year and the mood of the bees. These bees make what we call the Queen's Honey, for they feed on the highest mountain flowers of the Donatees, and on the flowers of mountain herbs, as well as the lush clover from the easternmost fields stretching out from the prosperous vine-growing town of Amaurote. It's this feed, and the warmth of the hollow of the Little Meadow, combined, I am certain, with the character of their guardians (and Devindra has students working hard to prove the physical truth of this), that produces this most prized of honeys.

Like all expert beekeepers, Francis and Amalia have calm, easy-going temperaments. They love their bees, and the Little Meadow has always seemed to me to be filled with sunlight, even on the gloomiest days—the very opposite of the ruin of Megalopolis, always gloomy and in shadows even on the sunniest day. Their Bee Garden is a true garden, so different from what Leef and I were nearing—what the people of Megalopolis call the 'bee yards'.

We had neared the bee yards over the corpses of discarded bees, huge complexes meant to produce honey on an industrial scale: cold, gray, harsh, and now empty. The bees had all but died out in Megalopolis by the time Leef and I arrived on its shores. And I was later told by the people living nearby that the bees had been of a particularly fierce and angry strain. All the workers in the bee yards, in the heyday of the honey factories, had been forced to wear full protective clothing, morning to night, against the vicious stings of their charges.

The bees tended by Francis and Amalia, though, always seemed to me to be particularly calm and even-tempered, as much so as their guardians. I often played in the Little Meadow under the shadow of the hives, while my mother, the queen, gossiped in the cottage with Amalia. I was never stung, no, not once, not even when I ventured a finger into a honeycomb where the bees flew to and fro.

What I remember is warm breeze, sunlight, happy droning, and flowers. Then after my mother died, I lived there a full year before Devindra had stabilized the Regency and brought me home to Mumford, and the Queen's House by the side of the Juliet River.

But I always thought of the Small House as my other home. I was not the only child of Arcadia who did. There were so many fostered there over the years, and I made many valuable friends my own age when I stopped there after my mother's death—valuable because they were not the friends I would have made had Michaeli, the Lord High Chancellor, and Aspern Grayling had their way. They would have kept me trapped in a ghetto of princehood, as a precious artifact is trapped by its guardians. But Devindra was stronger than they were then, and it was easy, for a while at least, to let her have her own way.

So I grew strong as a child, tended along with the bees.

It was not so easy by the time I completed my quest. The days of the Lizard Princess had come to an end and those of Queen Sophia had begun. I returned to be queen. It was not so easy then. I had learned, during the days of my quest, and particularly in the hard days I speak of now on the Ruined Surface of Megalopolis, to take good care. It was to the Small House I journeyed in secret on my return, and at the Small House where I left the future of Arcadia in the beekeepers' care. It was instinct that took me to the home of Amalia Todhunter and Francis Flight. My own best instinct. I remembered their compact, comfortable cottage in its well-tended garden; I remembered their happiness as a couple. It was a pleasant place for a child, a stable place—a place of healing.

I never heard an angry word between Francis and Amalia—never. When I commented on this, in the days when they gave me refuge before I moved from the time of the Lizard Princess to the reign of Sophia, Francis laughed and said laconically: "Anger doesn't go with bees." This trait was of immense value to me. When I was a child, almost a young woman, on one spring visit to the Small House, I watched them sit for a moment, hands entwined, under the enormous oak tree, and the thought passed through my mind that if I ever had a child, this was what I would want for him.

It was and is a great good place, the Small House by the Bee Garden in the Little Meadow. A place to grow a great good future. Or at least the hope of one.

All of this, protected and proved by the bees.

A living Bee Garden. Utterly unlike the bee yards that Leef and I made our way through now, through the rustle of the dead and dying bees of Megalopolis.

In Arcadia, we know that the night holds two kinds of sleep. The first is the lightest, and one wakes from it, in the still of the night, refreshed and thinking about the days before and the days to come, before falling into the second sleep, which is the sleep of dreams. Those two parts of sleep are like a smooth stone skimming across the surface of a clear lake, skipping across for the first part, then sinking to the bottom surrounded by dreams.

But in Megalopolis, sleep, when it comes—and there it comes only in fits and starts—is like a rock rolling down a cracked and dried-out riverbed, rolling down to a sea that receded long ago.

I could never sleep properly in Megalopolis, neither on the Ruined Surface nor on the False Moon. I would fall asleep as normal, as if I were back in my Tower Room in Arcadia, or in the Bower of Bliss with Joe, but within an hour, I would wake, clawing at the air, grief-stricken with nameless loss, calling out 'No!' while Leef shifted uneasily at my side.

More: I was aware of my lizard half there, as I had never been before. It hurt. My right thigh would throb at night with the pressure of my blood turning from warm to cold. My back cried out with the hardship of dragging a tail behind it. My leather feet pulled at my legs, my scales chafed, I could never truly settle. Night after night in Megalopolis it was always the same.

Then there was the breathing. The air was different there from anywhere else I had ever been. Thinner, with an undercurrent of a subtle poison I could sense faintly, just below the threshold of consciousness. A poison that made me fearful and uneasy as I breathed it in and out—and not just me, but Leef, too. Every night felt like a battle, a losing battle with a powerful enemy, a battle to keep myself and Leef safe.

Here was another oddity. In Megalopolis, on the Ruined Surface, I had such dreams as make me shudder now to remember them. Black dreams. Dreams of explosions killing innocents, of earthquakes, of enormous waves of water like the one that destroyed the Great City in the year of my own birth. I would wake gasping for breath, and a black thing, like some dark hand clutching my heart, would squeeze me inside, and I would feel it trying to drag my heart down, down, down. I grappled with it, confused, baffled—what was it? What did it mean?

Everything was so fragile there, in Megalopolis. It was as if in some kind of mass hysteria, the people there built and built and built, throwing a building up higher and higher, raising it continually closer to the sky, rather than putting any thought into securing its foundations. Until it was as high as the heavens, flashing lights and emitting loud, imperious noises far above the place from which it had sprung.

And yet—there had been joy, I would tell myself sternly in my days there. There could be joy again. Though that seemed impossible to me, that time I spent in the Great City and on the False Moon.

The terrible sadness I felt as we crossed the boundaries and made our way to the miserable settlements left at the outskirts of the Ruined Surface was not just a sadness, but also a sickness. I'd heard about this sickness. Its official name in the clinics of the Great City is Generalized Atmospheric Grief. But it was popularly known, among the straggling, struggling populace where I made my first home those days, as the Daily Despair. The symptoms of the Daily Despair are plain: on waking, one feels oneself pressed down upon by a curious weight, like a heavy load of wet feathers. These push against the torso of the sufferer, with special weight on the chest right above the heart. This feeling of pressure is accompanied by varying feelings of grief...varying according to the personality and history of the sufferer, making this a very difficult illness to treat.

Although the weight typically lifts throughout the waking day, the sense of loss, of grief, of mourning, commonly remains, interfering with the ability to feel commonplace pleasures. A meal, a drink with friends, the touch of a loved one, all become muted, dragged down by this dreaded and all-too-common virus.

A sufferer from Daily Despair doesn't say, "I caught it." More commonly they say, "It caught me."

Leef and I entered Megalopolis. And the Daily Despair caught me,

116

right away.

I felt it as we walked toward the smoky horizon where the settlements of the Ruined Surface began. We were walking through a scraggly copse of the kind that passes for a forest there. I felt a lack, and the creeping of an unfamiliar despair.

"The trees," I said to Leef. "The trees here don't talk."

We both stopped and listened. Leef looked at me, concerned, and leapt lightly off my shoulder onto the stony ground. He ran from tree to tree, stopping for a moment beneath each one, gazing up into its branches.

These were all the same kind of tree, a type of evergreen, though straggly, sparse and sullen-looking. At one particularly misshapen specimen, Leef chattered in a low, hopeful tone. I heard nothing. But it was clearly different with him, for he paused as if listening, nodded, chattered again, listened again. Then he reached out gently and touched the tree's bark, patting it once as if in farewell. And he came back sadly to me.

"What is it?" I said, alarmed.

"They're all gone," Leef said as he tugged at my leg to be picked up again. "The Nature Spirits. They've all gone away."

Now, I have never seen nor heard a Nature Spirit, but I have heard the grasses, and the flowers, and the trees speak—beautiful dialects, of which one can only understand the kernel, rather than the words. The meaning. The content, rather than the form, as it were. Leef had always assured me that it was the Nature Spirits who spoke through them, and that he could hear them more clearly than I could, even seeing them in certain lights.

"Who was that you spoke with, then?"

We walked on. Leef sat mournfully curled on my shoulder.

"She wouldn't say. All she told me was that when the others left, she was too sad to move on. So she stayed."

"Will she die?" I asked, afraid.

He hesitated, and then gave a tiny shrug. "I don't think a Nature Spirit can die. I think she'll just fade away." He brooded over this, and I asked no more. That was when I saw the smoke in the distance and knew we must be at the edge of a settlement—even though the city of Megalopolis had been cut to pieces by the Great Flood, on its outskirts inhabitants who survived and who had lacked the resources to flee to the False Moon gathered together into these casual slums on higher ground. It was one of those I searched for now. We were tired and lonely and hungry and wanted the companionship of our own kind.

Later, when we found our way to the False Moon, it was harder to find our own kind. On the False Moon, there weren't many of what are called the 'Lower People', that is, the descendants of the Megalopolitans who were left behind on the world after the Great Flood, those who hadn't had the money or the connections—for a lucky few were servants to the Upper People, and so survived the deluge along with their masters—to fly to the settlements on the False Moon.

These Lower People were mainly from the same stock as the Megalopolitan women and children who had fled over the Ceres Mountains ahead of the Flood, right before the disaster, driven by an instinct and a fear that had warned them aright.

It was during that flight that I was born. So many of the Lower People left in the slums clinging to what hillocks remained after the waters receded resembled the advisors and protectors of my childhood, those who had made their way to Arcadia with my mother, Lily. There were the dark-skinned, black-haired hawknoses of the Marsh People, from which my dear Devindra had come. And then there were the enormous slanted eyes and golden-brown skin of the ancestors of my nurse, Kim the Kind, and of my friend, Clare the Rider.

The people there had changed, though, since the days my friends had fled their part of the world. These people were not as those I had known, and knew. They were a people like the weather on the Ruined Surface—extreme, rough, even violent. In one day there you can have a scorching sun, hailstones as big as a child's fist, wind that blows old people down hills with its relentless force. The people matched this atmosphere, being changeable, unpredictable, violent…and shy.

Surprisingly, they were shy. Or perhaps not surprisingly at all. The circumstances of their environment probably had forced a response that most, in their hearts, despised. Most then hid their true natures in their hearts, protecting them until a better, warmer, calmer day.

Of course, there were the other methods of protection against a harsh, cruel, and violent fate that the weaker of the Lower People chose. To spend even a small amount of time in Megalopolis is to understand the use, and the overuse, of drugs and stimulants of every kind. The daily reality there is too sharp, too shiny, too harsh to take easily without aid of some kind. Without the aid of a strong heart and hope—any amount of hope no matter how small—it is impossible. With the Daily Despair rampant, drug treatment presented itself as an absolute necessity, whether prescribed by a doctor or by the sufferers themselves. This was not only true of the Lower People, for the Upper People were forced, from time to time, to return to the Ruined Surface when struck by disease of any kind. The False Moon did not allow for healing. Only the earth could aid with that, as I found when I sought my Joe's mother, Rowena, in one of the clinics for the rich that are established on the Ruined Surface below. Drug treatment was, and is, a necessary evil in Megalopolis.

This treatment has the unintended side effect of making all of the difficulties involved with living on the Ruined Surface far worse than if the medication had never taken place at all. As our Arcadian scientists have long held, there is a use for pain, even a need for it, both in the microcosm, to let the body know that something is wrong, that something needs to be changed, and in the macrocosm as well. For every individual has their place in the body of the community, and when individuals are in pain, they are signaling to that body that something is wrong. They are calling for restorative action of some kind. The more bodies signaling this, the more acute the pain, the more pressing the need for change, the louder the call for a creative response.

But the more the parts of the community are drugged…anaesthetized… against the pain that would rightly be theirs if they stood —if they could stand, if they were allowed to stand—healthy and firm in their own interaction with their world, if they are invalided out, as it were, of the battle to make life better, more human for all, then the Body Politic will stagger on, drowsy, unthinking, unfeeling, unconscious, from useless activity to hopeless end. Like a lumbering, brainless golem, not knowing itself, its world, or what it does in and to that world.

So Megalopolis. So the people I now found myself among.

I learned much from my time on the Ruined Surface. Mostly I learned that a people barely surviving have no time for Love. I learned that Love is not enough in dealing with people who think that if they are to survive, it is either them or you.

I learned that they, these people so corrupted and worn by the harshness of their life, were more to be pitied than to be blamed. But I learned—oh, important lesson!—that compassion should never mean weakness, lest it fail in its true mission, which is a human mission, and so never fruitful outside of the many contradictions of the human race. And, feeling the edges of this compassion, as it were, with the tips of my fingers, at first I, from habit and ignorance both, sought to pull the whole fabric nearer to me, to drape myself in it, to protect myself, and those others, from my own hot anger and my own cold fear.

Until I learned a lesson past this: which is that sometimes the only way to show Love is to drop the fabric and let anger and fear show, in all their naked Power. I learned that on the Ruined Surface of Megalopolis.

I had little doubt of being able to defend myself against aggression in this foul-looking, foul-smelling place. Though I was a young woman raised in the safety of Arcadia, I was also the Lizard Princess, who had crossed the Dead Wood…and who, long before that, had watched her mother murdered before her own eyes. My mother's murderer had been my teacher these long years, his very curse giving me a reptile's strength and a reptile's cunning. Was it not those gifts that enabled me to survive this far?

It was Will's teachings, also, that began to teach me a queen's cunning. When you learn a game like chess, and play it every week with a tutor bent on teaching you the meaning of every move, not through words (for words can confuse, and words can lie), but through action, which, if rightly observed can never tell anything but hard truths about the actor… then you learn.

So I learned the truth about Will, who had murdered my mother. I learned he led me on to make mistakes in my own moves so that I would recognize, in burning shame, my own faults—those faults that lead to errors of judgment, and from there, to fatal errors of action.

I learned that vanity could be turned easily to account by a canny opponent. I learned that pride always goes before fall. I learned that there are extremities where planning ahead is of no avail, where you have to grit your teeth and make painful, careful decision after painful, careful decision with no promise of salvation, hoping against hope to crawl your way, inch by inch, out of a likely fatal hole. I learned how there are times where only planning would save you, far-seeing and cunningly hidden by an endless patience, where you would have to swallow defeat after defeat, keeping always that goal of a final victory in sight.

I learned all this. It took years, but I learned it. And I learned, slowly enough, that it was by this teaching that Will the Murderer hoped to make atonement for his mistakes, his ignorance, and his fatal actions.

There was one last lesson I had not yet learned, when, out of Love, he laid his curse upon me. I had not yet learned the lesson that turned me into the Lizard Princess and sent me on my way. I had not yet learned that misplaced mercy can destroy everything that's been painfully won by cunning and strength…and Love. Yes. I had yet to learn the difference between the prizes won by Love, and the prizes won by Power, and the necessity of striving past these for the ends won by a marriage of both. And it was this lesson Will had sought to teach me.

It was that last lesson I was learning now, there on the outskirts of the Ruined Surface of the Great Empire that is Megalopolis. But before I learned it, I needed to learn that in a quest for power, there will be no mercy shown us from the other side. As long as I had scorn, and no pity, for that side, I had great confidence in my own strength. But my weakness, as Will knew, was that I loved easily and well, and that I thought I could spend that Love on those who didn't feel the same.

But I was learning those lesson. Living in that filthy, degraded slum in the far reaches of the Ruined Surface, beside the foulness of the Marsh, I needed those lessons now.

It was strange to me then that the Megalopolitans I met never seemed to notice my lizard legs and feet and tail. One foul night by the Marsh, I was attacked by a man who, judging from his eccentric gait and jerky movements, must have been on one of the many drugs available in that part of the world. He grabbed me as I made my way back from an errand done in exchange for a small pallet for me and Leef. He tried to put his forearm around my neck and pull me down, as several of the dull denizens of that street looked on, uncaring.

By this time, though, I had learned the use of my reptile's tail and, without a thought, neatly looped it around his throat, pulling him backward until he hit the pavement and was knocked unconscious—all in a flash, without even disturbing Leef, who had lain curled up in the pouch slung across my chest. But who now crawled out and stared.

"What will you do now?" he whispered. For he didn't know, he couldn't predict, the last few weeks living hand to mouth had changed me so.

I considered this. I considered the body of my attacker and how to deal with him now. There was no hope of help from any kind of police force. The police of Megalopolis had long ago become nothing more than a private security system for the rich.

But I questioned the wisdom of just leaving him there. If he attacked me, there would have been others he had preyed on as well.

While I pondered this, a small crowd of women gathered around us. They must have been attracted by the groans of the man as he struggled back to consciousness. There were five or six of them, and one whose name I even knew, who had exchanged greetings and small favors with me before. She lived in the cellar of my boarding house (although that is too grand a name for the wreck of a house which we all shared). I met her regularly at the never-emptied trashcans in the back. She, like me, made attempts at keeping our mutual home clean and ensuring no useable object escaped detection and salvage.

Her name was Deb and she was a little thing, but strong, as she showed now in the ferocity with which she kicked the groaning man in the ribs.

"Gently now, Deb," I said without thinking as I reached out and pulled her back.

"Why?" she asked as a sudden look of fear darkened her face. "Will he hurt me?"

I looked at her as she shrank back against my shoulder, clearly less afraid of me than of the broken man on the ground.

"Has he hurt you before?" I asked as more people, mostly women, but children, also, and one toothless, limping old man, emerged from a gathering mist, gazing openmouthed at me as if waiting for some miracle to occur. They looked down at the groaning man, and their expressions were unmistakable: simple hatred. The loathing of the preyed-upon for their tormentor. And when they looked up at me: simple hope.

A small child, a girl not more than ten years old, with hair even more carroty red than my own, appeared at my knees, grabbing hold of my shirt, as if for protection.

"He hurt me," she said softly. No one said another word.

It was settled in my mind, then, in that instant.

"Go get a pillow," I said to her. When she looked back at me, eyes wide, without answering, I said, "Do you know what that is?" She nodded. "Don't be scared, then. I won't let him hurt anyone. But get me a pillow, as quick as you can."

At that, she smiled, a dim smile like a half-moon shining behind a fog, and was gone as quickly as she'd come.

A moment later, there she was by my side, holding a vile looking piece of fabric and flattened fluff that must have once been a pillow someone would have wanted on their bed, but which now—well, it would serve the purpose I had for it.

The man groaned again. I knew I had to act quickly. Taking the square from the child, I laid it on his face and, putting one lizard clawed foot atop, pressed down with all my weight.

As I did, I looked swiftly around the gathered crowd to see if there was any protest, any objection showing on any face. But there was nothing. There was sternness in one face, grim satisfaction in two or three, intent attention in another. But no regret. No protest. No plea for mercy. No horror.

The body under my foot shuddered. I pressed harder until it struggled briefly and was finally still. Then I peeled the pillow off the man's face and looked at him; for all that he had meant violence toward me and toward these others, still, he was a man. But there had been no help for it. No good paths, all the choices were bad.

The women, behind me, still silent, began dragging the body away to some unknown dark burial, rifling his pockets for what money he had on him that would do them some good now that it could do him no good any longer. I walked away, heavyhearted at doing wrong, yet still accepting the wrong as the best choice available to me.

This was a moment I remembered often later, on dark days, the kind of dark days that inevitably come to every queen. The decision I made that night was one that laid the foundation for my future life, and the future of those I had in my care.

But I was heavyhearted as any real queen should be at decisions so taken. And my steps were slow. So slow that at first I didn't notice an odd fact: the claws of my lizard feet had shortened and tightened, and my tail curled and slashed now, less like that of a lizard, and more like that of a cat.

It was indeed days before I completely took in this strange change in my build. But right away I did see a change in my status in the neighborhood. The women and children now acted as if I had been their friend for years. The men, at least all those past boyhood, avoided me, without malice it must be said, but still with an unmistakable, though elaborately masked, fear. Unmistakable, too, was how the women rejoiced to see this fear, as if they now had a champion they could finally claim as their own.

At first I found this a burden almost too much to bear, but as time went on it became more and more endurable, even cause for a quiet satisfaction, until, inevitably, it turned into a part of myself, and I was able to go on.

The Marsh hadn't always been this way, dying, poisonous, home to a degraded tribe. My own dear Devindra had told me many stories of the place when I was a child, for the Marsh was from where she and her folk had originally sprung. "From the days, Sophy, when it was a vale—hence my name, you see." It had been a vale, a valley—"the biggest, widest meadow you can imagine, Sophy, so my mother told me, though she had never seen it in her day either, no, not her mother or her grandmother either." Those were the early days of Megalopolis's exploration underground. The mild earthquakes this caused widened the rift already made by the winter runoff from the Donatees, which now filled the valley with a marsh.

"And so my ancestresses," Devindra continued, spinning a bedtime story I loved to hear, "who were resourceful by nature and by necessity, turned to fishing for their livelihood. With that, and kitchen gardens, my people supported themselves—not grandly, of course, but in a sturdy, independent, careful sort of way."

That is, until the inevitable happened, and Megalopolis, bloated, outgrew its boundaries, spreading in all directions over whatever peaceful communities would put up the least fight.

"Gradually, Sophy, the industries they built fouled the Marsh, and their new methods of fishing left nothing behind, and the air sickened, and the water was poisoned, and the men of my grandfather's generation left to find work, leaving the women behind. And how were the women to survive, except by servicing, in whatever way was required, the Megalopolitan laboratories and schools? For those sprang up on the ruined land, both because it was cheap to build there, and because it offered a unique opportunity to study what should not, in the future, be done to a living community."

Devindra's much-loved mother, Tilly, was a washerwoman. And to be a 'washerwoman' in the Marsh, as Devindra explained when she judged me old enough to understand, meant to take care of the needs of the technicians and the scientists in the nearby facilities, in whatever way they demanded…and could pay for.

I didn't at first understand. I didn't understand the concept of prostitution. How could I, without careful thought and study? I had no experience of such a thing. There was no such thing…there is no such thing…in Arcadia. Why would there be? There is enough in Arcadia for everyone to have a decent, if not luxurious, quality of life, and those who want luxuries can usually find them in a less degrading and painful way. Arcadians hate, above all else, to be treated as objects, and so it would be unheard of for anyone to choose being an object as a way to make a living. The closest I could come to the idea was the example of a handful of women and men who had married much richer people than they were, apparently without much affection. But these unfortunates, and their spouses, were greatly pitied by the rest of us as being incapable (some people are) of one of life's greatest joys: a marriage of lovers. We aspired to the Ideal, but of course it wasn't always possible for one reason or another, and so there were many variants on the attempt. But not prostitution, as Devindra tried to explain it to me. No, there was nothing like that.

It was the women of the Marsh, Devindra among them, and their children who made up the bulk of the refugees from Megalopolis the night that Lily fled with them over the Ceres Mountains.

"We had been uneasy for days, myself and my neighbors, we could feel some kind of shift in the atmosphere," Devindra said. "What was it? At first, each of us thought the dread and the deep desire to get away were strictly personal, a physical manifestation of some psychic unease. But then, as the unease among us grew, we talked about it, shared our experience, and found our neighbors felt the same, as ourselves.

"Our animals were restless, too. And then, mind, we had the reputation, the women of the Marsh, of being mildly psychic. In fact, I once wrote a research paper on the subject, tying psychic powers to early trauma, the suffering working to develop a faculty that all humans possess, but in normal circumstances seldom need.

"In each one of us there was a growing panic, a panic that paralleled a tightening and groaning of the earth under the tortures she had received— tortures that demanded catastrophic release. Like animals fleeing some disaster, a fire or an earthquake or a flood, we fled what turned out to be all three. That was how we came to our new home in Arcadia."

Their old home became a flooded, poisoned, fetid lake that receded into a poisoned fetid bog. It took years for the sea to help the Marsh reassert itself, even if feebly. It was in this version of the Marsh where I now lived. Where I now found one of my greatest loves. For it was in the Marsh that Susan lived, experimenting with new strains of rice that she had bred herself, with the hope that they would be easily grown, harvested, and shared. Susan, who lived and coaxed the Marsh itself back into life.

Part VIII: SUSAN

I still well remember the first time I saw Susan—for 'Susan' she was to me from the first, as she was to all the wretched inhabitants of the women and children's quarter in the Marshland. Susan, who had been Commander Susan B. Riggs in the days of the Great Megalopolitan Invasion of Arcadia, the occupation that had brought my own mother to Megalopolis and to her fated love for my father.

Susan, who had known my mother. Known Lily, as she was when just a girl, before tempered by time into a queen.

Susan, who had reached the highest position that a young woman of Megalopolis, lacking family and protectors, without property, without those wiles that lead a person —and not just a woman, either—to trade portions of themselves for prestige or gain. The highest such a girl, a woman, in that great imperial city could hope to achieve.

She had been a commander in the invading force, as I've said. As such, she was part of a great Megalopolitan experiment, a cautious one, but a risk for them all the same: placing women in positions of obvious masculine command so that the people meant to be commanded were fooled and cowed by the sex of their conquerors into disbelieving they had been conquered at all…but would feel nurtured, empathized with, even loved by their new masters. And so be less inclined to rebel.

Susan, as Commander Susan B. Riggs, had excelled at this kind of sleight of hand, all the more so because she was perfectly unconscious of performing the trick. In truth, she had been fooled by the trick that had been played on her by her own masters: she believed she was considered as 'good' as a man in her profession, and she was proud of her rise in it.

It was only later, when doubt set in, that she found ways to secretly scour the records of her employment. Only later that her illusions were smashed.

"That one, anyway," she said to me, much later, over mugs of the whiskey-spiked mint and honey tea we drank together at twilight, on the little ramada outside the square cottage she'd built with her own hands by the side of one of the many arms of the Marsh. She held up a finger. "One down," she said cheerfully. "Who knows how many more to go?" And she laughed, throwing her magnificent head back as she did, her undyed blonde and silver hair unruly like a lion's mane, and her Megalopolitan teeth as straight and white as they had been when she was a girl.

Still holding her illusions, "holding them dear, Sophy," she said, laughing (for I was shortly Sophy to her as she was Susan to me), she rose in rank to General, and not just General on the ground, but General in the Counsels to the Council of Four, the only woman to be so named, the only woman with that kind of power. "Though that doesn't count Livia, of course, who runs them all, and how she managed that I'm sure we'd all like to know."

She didn't know that Livia was my grandmother. Not then. She didn't know that Lily was my mother, though I was to tell her later, and, after she got over the initial shock, and the brief fear that she had revealed too much too soon in the name of sisterhood, she told me many stories of them both, stories I've told elsewhere and still think of, taking them out like bolts of cloth and running my hand over them, in the night when I wake briefly between the first and second sleeps.

It was Susan who found me Rowena. And it was Susan who sent me, finally, to Livia. Without Susan, I would never have found my way. I would never have found the Key.

The first time I saw her was from far away, from behind, and her lanky, still beautiful soldier's body was silhouetted by the setting sun. The little girl who brought me to find her pointed, as we stood on the crazy quilt of planks set out over the sideways oozing of the Marshlands, and said, "There is Susan." Said it proudly and fondly, for my friend-to-be was 'Susan' to them all in the Poorer Quarter, to them all but especially to the younger girls who admired her with a tender ferocity that boded well for their own futures. It bodes well, to have a model such as Susan to lead a girl through the complexities of her own life.

Susan's gold-edged silhouette, even from a distance, expressed competence and discipline. But the flexibility of her movements, as she stooped and sprang up again at the edge of the Marsh, illuminated by the setting sun, promised tolerance and kindness, too. Flexible she was, though she complained humorously to me in the days we lived together in her little cottage of a growing arthritis in her knees. "Like an old horse," she said, snorting with that husky laugh of hers. For I loved Susan, and she loved me, and if I could have chosen a grandmother, it would have been her, not Livia.

But we don't choose these things ourselves. On reflection, that's all for the best.

The little girl who had led me to this edge of the Long Finger of the Marsh scampered away once her duty was, to her mind, fulfilled—she had brought one of her heroines out to meet another, greater one, and now she would run home to announce her mission completed to her mother, sisters, and aunts. So I picked my way carefully over the rotting, algae-covered planks, and, as I got closer, I saw the tall, slender woman was bending over small shoots planted there in the Marshland.

She was in her late forties then, and lanky—lanky in a beautiful, useful way. Her eyes were a cracked marble blue, very like Livia's, I found, when I finally met my grandmother on the False Moon, but in Susan's case set in an efficiently tanned face, surrounded by that mane of silver-gold hair. Her arms were tanned, too, freckled and dark, but only up to where she would always push her shirt-sleeves, past the elbow and nearly up to the shoulder.

Her upper arms, and the tender, hidden parts of her body were a tranquil white, the veins pulsing blue here and there. In the bath (a double-sized one she had built herself with stones, and heated by the sun), the tan lines on her ankles, her neck, and her arms should have been awkward, but instead, strangely charmed the viewer—me, the viewer who often bathed with her, which was strange, because Susan was one of the handful of Megalopolitans who saw my lizard half for what it was. It didn't repel her, even from the first; it amused her, even attracted her, and we shared everything there—board, bath, bed—for a while.

I owe so much to Susan. I learned so much just from watching her own private, joyful battles. She was trying to bring the Marsh back to life. And this, as I found out soon enough, was one battle she was finally winning.

The first lesson she taught me was that nothing done in a hurry is of any lasting use.

"The opposite of the way I was taught, the way they taught me, Sophy," she said in her wry way, pushing the gray blonde tendrils that always escaped from their worn clasp out of her eyes. By 'they', she meant her superiors in the imperial armed forces.

"In Megalopolis," she said, "it's always 'bigger, better, faster', but if you're paying attention, soon enough you realize that's a self-defeating lie. You wake up in the morning with that lesson in you, and you're wound up so tight there's no room for any new idea—for any idea of any other way of being—to grow. Morning to night, it's run run run...no question why or where, right? It's run run run...right into a wall, Sophy. Right into a wall."

This was one of our first nights together, a night where we did nothing but sit on her little porch, watching the Marsh. There were many nights like that with Susan.

"I like to watch it come back alive," she said simply. She meant the Marsh. And it did come back alive—I could see it rising from a death-in-life even in the time I spent there…could smell the gassy toxins recede, could smell the green, thick smell of the healthy Marsh, could even smell an intimation of home, of my own Ceres Marsh where the Juliet River runs down underground from Arcadia, heading for the Donatees and the Sea.

We could hear frogs croak at dusk. We could see a lone hawk circle and dive. "That means mice, maybe even small fish," Susan would say with dreamy triumph later, as we dozed in her bed and fell asleep in the rough, lavender-scented linen sheets.

I would dream of a place where Time was a friend, not a foe, where everything moved in a quiet, joyful dance. When I woke, I knew that place I had been was Arcadia. But an Arcadia not yet born, one it was my own task to create.

Then there was the day she told me how she found which side she should be fighting on…and for what.

"To be more human," Susan murmured that day. "To be more human than we are or have yet been…that's our real battle."

She said this one evening as, in the cool dusk, I helped her plant another small marsh field of rice starts, a kind of brown hybrid rice she was experimenting with that she hoped would be of a type to reseed itself and spring up in nooks and crannies where normally no rice would be expected. Much as I suspect she hoped the values she lived would reseed themselves, too.

"And what does that mean, then, Susan?" I asked. "To be more human?" I laughed. "More human than I am, certainly."

She looked at me affectionately, for that was Susan's way; she had an affectionate relationship with all around her, plants, animals, sky, Marsh, people…

"It's possible that a half-lizard, half-girl is already more human than most people," she said. "For to be more human is to be more than we are now. More…and less."

At this she looked contemplatively out over the Long Finger of the Marsh to the southwest. As the sun set to one side, all orange, green, and rose, it was as if the light coaxed the landscape into accommodating itself to her vision of its future: lush rather than fetid, fertile rather than barren, fresh rather than salt. You could see its latent beauty, the beauty that Susan had toiled singlehandedly to bring back to it. And you could see she was, against the mightiest of odds, winning in her battle, and that the fight was carried on in joy rather than pain. For Susan knew that efforts made in joy move farther and faster. For joy is self-creating, self-generating, self-sustaining, and even the efforts of one person using her own joy as energy can create a cascade of effects far past what can be achieved by any number of miserably toiling, resentful, half-dead hearts.

"I've thought about it a lot, Sophy," she said. "Since I was in the service, in the Great Occupation of Arcadia—what we in Megalopolis called the 'Peace Mission Before the Great Flood'. I learned a lot, during my assignment there, and it's no exaggeration to say it changed my life."

She laughed softly to herself…at herself, and waved her arms wide. "It's to be seen whether that was for the good or not, eh?" And then she stretched and gave an 'oof,' and suggested we go back inside and have a glass of wine.

As we walked, in the companionable silence of two women who have shared a day's work well done and now will share the comfort of shared food and drink, I found I was holding my breath with suspense. For I had already guessed what was coming next in the story Susan had to tell. I had to remind myself to breathe. And come next it did, when I was curled up on my own little chair by the open window, with Leef on my lap, as Susan lifted her glass in a small gesture of cheer, and continued her tale.

"Well, it was an invasion I was a part of, of course. We could lie about it all we wanted, to ourselves and to our victims, but Invasion and Occupation was what it was. Ugly words, eh? And if there was one thing the Megalopolitan military tried to avoid, it was overt ugliness. We of the military had learned the benefits of charm, of the slick exterior hiding the corrupt intention. Of the attractions of charm allied with a goodly dose of power. It's the power that forces the victim to the desired end, after they have been seduced by the charm."

I had seen Aspern Grayling use the same technique, the same charm, for his own purpose, to his own scale, in his own way. Was to see him use it many times in the future, as well.

"So we were charming. We learned, in early training, that the marketing of Megalopolis was more than half the battle—it was practically the whole of it. Get 'em in one direction with the charm, and they think, 'Why should we fight?' Get 'em in the other direction with superior firepower—you don't even need to use it, nine times out of ten, just carelessly show what you could do if you weren't so damn charming, and then they think, 'Even if we fought, we could never win.' Get 'em coming and going, that's what my mentors drummed into us…but the charm offensive, that was the key. And it never failed. Not with all the communities that used to exist autonomously outside the city limits. We swallowed every one of those up by charming the hell out of them. Especially charming their young. Swallowed 'em one after another, and fast, under the direction of the Council of Four. And of Livia, of course.

"Have I told you about Livia? Maybe some other time. She's a story in herself."

Yes, I thought. Please tell me about Livia. My grandmother. Yes. But Susan went on with her tale.

"No, the charm offensive never failed. The charm of our art, of our fashion, of our style—all of it superior to the rustic backwardness of the communities on our outskirts…at least, that was our story. And with over a third of our military budget going to marketing, we could get our story across, crush the timid stories of the rural places that scarcely understood the value of selling themselves…hell, our charm was like some kind of tentacled monster reaching out in all directions, clamping down on local cultures, strangling them, and gathering in the corpses.

"All the communities fell, one after another, in twenty years. This all happened after I joined the military at the age of sixteen. I lived in one of those little communities, Sophy. That was where I grew up."

At this, Susan pointed out the window dead south, where the last streaks of light now topped a blackened expanse of Marsh. And she reached out to top off both our glasses with a bit more wine.

"Sandela, it was called. Pretty place. About fifteen thousand souls. Of course, it's all under water now."

Then she was silent, thinking about her old home, as the sun set with finality, and the sky darkened and the stars began to come out one by one. It was a warm night, and we sat there watching in silence, forgetting the food laid out for our supper on the table.

I held my breath. I knew we would come to it soon. And then, there it was.

"Did I say all the communities, Sophy?" she asked briskly. "Well, all but one." I could only just make out the glitter of her eyes in the dimness, for we had yet to light the lanterns. She shook her head. "And that one was called Arcadia."

At this I gave a helpless little jump.

"Do you know it?" she said, looking at me searchingly in the dim light, but the moons were not yet up, and I could wrap myself in the shadows while I collected myself.

"I've heard of it," I said as noncommittally as I could manage. "In my travels."

"Ah, well, then," she said. "Then you know there are peculiar stories about the place, primitive myths that somehow have made it into our time, like a newt or an axolotl, leftovers from a bygone age that ordered things in a different way from ours, in…" and here I could hear, rather than see, the wryness of her accompanying smile, "…in the sophistication of our technology and science. For it's said that Arcadia is surrounded by mountains, one range of which is impassable…"

Not completely, I thought.

"…and the other unknown to man…"

Not totally, I thought.

"…and that the green, river-riven valley that is present-day Arcadia was once a slum section of Megalopolis itself. And it's said that it became itself after a huge seismic event that transformed it overnight—in Christmas season, it's said—from a horrible little ghetto to a necklace of villages protected from us, from Megalopolis, on all sides by mountains that sprang up that same night."

Her voice now changed, as if it was the voice of a storyteller from long ago, as if the story told Susan rather than the other way around.

Now this was not a completely strange story to me, though I never knew the whole story of Arcadia, until I found the book where it was hidden, in the bowels of the Great Library, tilting on the dusty shelves where the least valued stories were to be found. Stories for children, fairy tales, forgotten there on the False Moon.

"And it's further said," she continued, "that this cataclysmic event was brought about by one disgusting, lowly, horrible little boy who realized who he really was, realized who she really was, and, claiming herself, refused to join with the powerful forces that had made her land a blasted waste. And that one act changed her world forever."

She was silent again, and I knew what she meant to say: that this was her hope. That the act of even one person could change the world.

"I've heard that story, Susan," I said humbly. For it was true. Bits and pieces were told to us as children's stories in Arcadia. It was a legend, a myth…less grand than that, a fairy tale. Something to be forgotten as we grew old. I had, till Susan spoke, almost forgotten it myself.

And yet there was something in it of the utmost familiarity to me. Of intimacy. As if it were the story of myself, forgotten. Or the story of one much loved.

"Sheer superstition, of course," she said, now briskly, the strange prophetic quality dismissed now from her voice.

"Yes," I murmured in return. "Stories for children. Fairy tales…," but my voice trailed off uncertainly.

Susan looked at me sharply. There was something there. Something in me, something in her, something between us, that demanded attention. But it hadn't yet emerged. We were both searching for it.

"I think," she said, "that I had my first hint of what I mean—of what being truly human means—from a little girl. Well, she wasn't so little, really. A teenager. Not much younger than you, Sophy. But with a lot of spine to her, if you know what I mean. Like you, in fact."

And then she told me a story of my mother.

I've told that story elsewhere, the one Susan told me that night. Of how she was in charge of a school meant to reeducate the young of Arcadia, and how the first lesson that school hoped to inculcate was the idea that we should work hard today to enjoy tomorrow—a lesson it's difficult to teach a true Arcadian, for why, one would ask, is it not preferable to work hard today and enjoy today at the same time?

Lily, my mother, rebelled. A beautiful rebellion, as Susan put it. "I can still see her, those eyes of hers sending out sparks, and sparks, too, when she stamped one of her perfect little feet, sparks like wings. 'I won't!' she said. 'Who cares for you? Who are you to tell me what I should do with my life, what I should think, what I should feel?' At least, Sophy," so Susan went on, "if that wasn't exactly what she said, that was the gist of it. And the gist…the seed…the kernel….What she said stuck with me and grew without my even knowing it."

Which is, I have learned in my travels and in my time as queen, the sign of a real truth: once uttered aloud, it bursts into seeds that scatter, and they grow in every nook and cranny, unsuspected, robust, no matter how hard anyone—an empire, say—seeks to weed them out.

It was that way with Lily's rebellion: her outburst stuck with Susan and grew like a seed.

"Until it was bigger than I was, bigger than anything I'd known before. That little girl, when she said, 'No. I don't agree. No more tomorrows. Today!', which was rank heresy that I was meant to stamp out—it was as if a bolt of lightning struck me."

As if on cue, the two Moons now rose outside—the Moon Itself, rose-gold and glowing, which I silently asked to bless Susan and me, and that night we shared. Then the False Moon beside it, what we in Arcadia call the Phony Moon, white-gold, glittering in the sky, outshining its progenitor. It was the Phony Moon most people saw when they looked at the sky. And they were blind to the Moon Itself.

It was to the Phony Moon that all the riches of Megalopolis had gone.

My mother had danced on the Phony Moon...the False Moon...in her time, with my father. And it was on the False Moon that she saw him kiss Rowena, Joe's mother, and announce their marriage, even though he loved Lily, my mother, and not his affianced bride. It was on the Moon Itself that my mother met Star the Angel, my own Star, and the Moon Itself was where my mother learned her task was to find the Key and bring it back to Arcadia. Bring it back she did; but it disappeared from Arcadia at her death, for Arcadia was not as it should be. And I realized I would have to journey to those moons to find it for myself.

All this ran through my mind as Susan and I sat under the rising of the two moons, both so full so you could feel a double, contradictory pull that made Leef click his teeth nervously and knead his short claws on my shoulder till I had to steady him with one hand to make him stop.

"Goddess help me, I had no idea what she had done to me. I thought the feeling of being struck meant I was under attack, and I had been trained to meet attack with superior force. So I had the girl sent away to the Children's Mine. I wasn't being cruel, I misguidedly thought. The children there were well fed and well cared for, and they enjoyed having productive jobs, so I told myself anyway. I didn't want to hurt her. I just wanted that throb that went through me, that power that felt greater than mine (for what right had this skinny little black-haired thing to challenge the Empire's power with her own?), I just wanted it gone."

A lump had formed in my throat and tears filmed my eyes. All I could do was nod.

Susan, musing under the light of the Two Moons, didn't see. "Lily," she murmured to herself. "That was her name. Lily. She was famous after I knew her, a celebrity in East New York, and then she was a queen. Queen of that beautiful green Arcadia."

"She was my mother," I said. Was I doing right or wrong to reveal myself to Susan? "And I am her daughter, the Lizard Princess. So tell me, Susan, all that you remember of her. For she died when I was very small."

As I said that, a sadness came over me that was like a silver burning cloak, tightening around my throat and heart.

Susan looked at me in the moonlight, tears shining in her beautiful cracked marble eyes to match my own. She said gravely, "I see."

After that, we were both quiet, hesitant. The evening star shone over the Marsh, shining hard to take its place beside the Moons, the star that we Arcadians call the Goddess Star, and that Megalopolitans have named 303zed. Many years later Susan, in exile, took her own hard journey and found me reigning, to her delight, in the heart of Arcadia. I welcomed her in her old age with an honorable retirement in Mumford, our capital, and a position at Juliet College from where she could dispense her wisdom to our eager young. She often says how she thought of me and that night every time she watched the rising of the Goddess Star.

We watch it ourselves, now, on the evenings we spend together in the Queen's Garden.

Then, Susan stood. She hesitated a moment, then made an obvious decision and held out her hand.

I took her hand. And followed her gratefully to bed.

It couldn't last, though, my staying there, so warm and happy, with Susan by the Marsh. For the Lizard Princess was not all of me, and all of me was what I had to become.

Months went by, good months, as we worked to bring the Marsh back to

Susan, musing under the light of the Two Moons, didn't see.

life. Months where I learned much and understood more about myself and about the world around me. Months that brought a strange peace to me. I didn't flee from the lizard part of myself any longer.

I had so much to be grateful to Susan for. There were so many parts of my story that she gave me, open-handed, never minding that they made me grow away from her. It was not that Susan was kind. Susan was practical. She considered this the higher kindness. "Any idiot can see that it is more practical to be kind than cruel," she would say. "Virtue generally is more practical, giving better and longer-lasting results. Although being virtuous," she warned, "does not mean being stupid, Sophy."

In the days that followed my first confession, she coaxed my story out of me, all of it up till then: life, loves, goals, adventures. When she had it, she set her practical mind to solving my problem—finding Joe, and finding the Key.

Strange that she never asked the meaning of the Key. She seemed to understand it without being told, which was the way of her. Less strange, perhaps, was her concern that I find Joe. "He's bound to be on the False Moon with your grandmother," she said flatly. "You'll have to go there." There was no possessiveness about Susan; she loved with open hands, and what came to her came freely, and was not just allowed to go on its way, but aided—given, you might say, a bag lunch and a cloak for the road.

It was time to go. I had known it for some time.

One sweltering night on the Marsh, I got up from Susan's bed and walked on my lizard feet to the edge of the sluggish water where it stretched out to the sea. The False Moon rose up full, coin-sized, the Moon Itself was a mere sliver beside it. But there was enough moonshine to light up the land and seascape below.

I stood there, tail flickering restlessly, hands folded protectively over my breasts, though what I was protecting them from was unknown. I stood there catching a welcome, fugitive night breeze, my mind wandering untethered from the day, watching the moonlight play across the sea.

That was when I saw them. Angels, in the distance, flying toward me from the sea—white and silver and gray. How many? Four, five, seven?

My heart filled and swelled, and I found myself lifting up on my lizard toes, stretching my arms open, as if I could fly up to meet them.

Closer and closer they came, their wings flapping almost noiselessly, and as they flew over, I saw Star among them.

"Take me with you!" my heart cried out in yearning.

They flew on overhead, and I, half-lizard, could not follow. But as they went, one silver feather floated down to me, and I snatched it from the air before it touched the ground.

I went back to bed, but Susan never stirred. I never told her what I had seen, what I had felt. I knew it meant it was time to go. I lay awake waiting for the sun to rise, to see if my memory of the angels' flight overhead changed in the light of the day. It didn't change. If anything, the reality of it grew stronger with the passing hours.

But it was no reality to Susan. To Susan who I loved. For Susan was of Megalopolis. And in Megalopolis there is no such thing as an angel, except in the old folk stories passed down, mother to daughter, by the Marsh.

Then, one evening, Susan mused, as she sometimes did, on these wonder tales of the Marsh—for she had always found such tales fascinating. "Who is to say that these stories of angels and demons and gods are not more important than is usually recognized? Could they be a metaphor for some larger truth?"

I took a deep breath. Could I tell her what I had seen? "S-susan," I stammered, "couldn't it be...wouldn't it be possible...that a person could see an angel?" She stared. I plunged recklessly on. "Or a demon, or a god. Not just in imagination, Susan, but in truth."

At first she laughed uncertainly, as if I'd made a sophisticated joke. That was a horrible moment. Then, seeing I was serious, looked at me with wary astonishment. Almost heartbroken, the way I had been on knowing

Joe would never see me for who or what I was, I said, "Susan, it is me. I see these things. Not just in imagination, but in truth."

Bemused, she shook her head.

We aren't speaking the same language, I thought to myself in my misery. Still I ventured on, insistent. "It's been proved, Susan. Many worlds occupy the same space as ours, and communication between them..."

"Would you like some more wine, Sophy?" Susan said abruptly, pushing her hair back from her face and her chair from the table. She gave me a pitying look that pierced me to the heart, then stirred me to indignation. So I'm an idiot, am I? I thought to myself. A superstitious savage? I brooded over a glass of wine, then had another, and when we went, silent, to bed that night, slept on the far edge, clutching at it as to the railing of a ship, the only thin protector between me and a roiling sea.

It was time for me to go.

It was time for me to go, for Susan's words reminded me, like a slap on the face, of Aspern Grayling, who, along with Megalopolis, scorns those stories Arcadia holds most dear.

For Aspern is determined to end my reign, and, in ending it, to put a stop to the kind of governance I, and any belonging to me, would legitimately bring. For Aspern believes in man becoming like gods (not woman; he is very clear on that, I fear), in the great ruler who will dominate a people for their own glory and prosperity. And Aspern further believes that the transcendent end justifies the meanest of means.

We are locked in a battle of wills, Aspern and I, against my own will, over how Arcadia is to grow. And while this battle continues, no one close to me is truly safe. I think of this often on the nights when I remember all I have lost in that cause.

I think of Aspern, also, as I stare at the False Moon, that shines so dimly and garishly in the night sky, always full, while the Moon Itself waxes and wanes as it has always done—hidden from the blind by the False Moon's glare, hidden from the view of any who believe we can improve on Nature herself. What blasphemy to me, who was the Lizard Princess. What a glorious goal to Aspern Grayling.

Always full, the False Moon, and neither 'he' nor 'she' do we call it, but 'it', for the False Moon is not alive; it is a dead shell and it cannot generate life any more than a mechanical nightingale is capable of laying and hatching a real egg.

It cannot sustain life. I learned that later to my great sorrow. They knew it already, they, the rich who had built the False Moon, but they kept it a mighty secret. One could only live on the False Moon by all sorts of mechanical and technical stratagems. Plants, to grow, had to be genetically modified, and even then they never grew so well as on the world below. Animals sickened and died. Humans—true humans, of human ancestry, with no intermingling of strange genes and experiments—could only stand the atmosphere there for so long, before they gasped for breath, desperately heading back to the world below to breathe in the real air there. Fouled it might have been, the air on the Ruined Surface, but it was still real air that humans had breathed for hundreds of thousands of years. Real water, real earth. These things, it became clear to the scientists of Megalopolis (though they kept this a close secret), were necessary to life itself. But in their arrogance, they refused to give in. Megalopolis kept up the pretense that the False Moon was a paradise—but when its inhabitants sickened, they were sent to hospitals on the ground.

These hospitals, though, were only for the very rich. For the servants of the False Moon there was no return home. But this, as so much else, was a great secret.

It was in such a hospital that Rowena Pomfret Barr now lived, semi-permanently as it happened, for the many drugs she had taken over the course of her life—to achieve beauty, to avoid sadness, to avoid discomfort, to avoid pain—had weakened her so far that she could only survive on the False Moon for days at a time.

As I say, this was a great secret. I had no idea of it. Neither did Susan. Our idea then was to get me to the False Moon, and to my grandmother Livia. This was a perfectly reasonable course of action, given that I was trying to find Joe and to find the Key, and who would know more where they were hid than Livia?

"The only way to get there," Susan said to me seriously as we sat under the False Moon's light, "is to be very rich, or to be hired by the very rich. Well, we know which path you'll have to take."

We had quickly discarded the idea of sending word to my grandmother of who I was, and how I wished to see her. Lily, my mother, had been the enemy of Megalopolis, and this was my inheritance, my legacy, also. It was dangerous to tell of my coming; who knew what agents lurked waiting for some reward to be had from my capture?

"The one most likely opportunity you'll have is that they'll be looking for a nanny again. It's something of a joke down here how many times the word goes out that Livia's nursery needs a nanny. I don't know why, but that's a position they're always looking to fill."

Livia's nursery? I looked startled. "Children?" I asked.

Leef cheeped quietly, staring off the porch down at the Marsh. Following his look, I saw a grass-green snake swallowing a toad whole. The little legs waved helplessly in the air as the bigger creature swallowed it down. I looked away.

Susan sighed. "If you can call them that. Creatures raised out of cells, in test tubes…dishes, actually. Neither father nor mother, born of the cloning of a cell, poor little bastards. The rumor is she thinks she's raising a super race, meant to have all the strengths and none of the frailties of our own poor human bodies."

I must have looked as horrified as I felt. The idea of it—of robbing children of their birthright—took my breath away. Leef stirred on my lap as the snake, replete, slunk away into the reeds of the Marsh, and my lemur hid his head in the crook of my arm.

Such wickedness we neither of us had conceived of. Until that moment.

Surely, I thought shuddering, it must be impossible that such evil would ever come to Arcadia. But that was before I discovered the secrets of Aspern Grayling, and his creation, what Aspern calls the New Man, Pavo Vale. Born from Merope, but not of Merope. The child of Aspern alone, the child without a mother, the child destined to attempt the destruction of Arcadia.

But then was still the time of the Lizard Princess, and the Great Trouble of Arcadia, the Great Confrontation, was still years away.

Sure enough, when Susan and I went to the weekly market the next day, and to the tattered notice board where what few jobs there were would be listed (and always with an anxious crowd of young people jostling for position around under it, staring up hopefully for the sign of the decent work that never came), there was a burly, well-fed functionary, sporting the heavy boots that showed him to be an inhabitant of the False Moon (for no one went barefoot there). He put up a card that said: "Caregiver for the Lady Livia's nursery. Must be eagle-eyed, swift-footed, intelligent, and sturdy. Salary commensurate with experience." But when he put the sign up and stared out at the crowd, all he got back were blank stares. And one or two shouts of derision.

"As if," snorted one young woman clutching a baby to her chest and turning away.

"What happened to the last one then? When was it she went up with you? Just last week? Livia eat her herself, or maybe those monsters of hers did?"

There was a murmur of unease at those words, and the crowd knit closer together, as if a herd of sheep had heard a wild dog howl.

I found myself saying, "I'll go. I need the work. And I love children, too."

The functionary was more annoyed by the hoots of laughter from the crowd ("she'll find out, won't she?") than interested in me. All he did was motion me to follow him. I felt a warm kiss on my neck, but when I turned to say goodbye, Susan was already gone, melted into the crowd.

I followed the functionary as meekly as I could, Leef hidden in the bag the mermaids gave me, slung over my chest, and my eyes darting to and fro in the hope of seeing Susan one last time. But it was years and years…a lifetime for us both…before I was to see my Susan again.

Part IX: ROWENA

It was because of Susan that I found Rowena. And how different Rowena was from Susan! Though she must have been at least ten years younger, she looked twice as old—the overuse of anti-aging drugs in the early years of their development had backfired, and Rowena's face and body had ricocheted from a seemingly permanent nineteen to a quickly deteriorating seventy. Every day I visited her in what they now called the Great House on the Ruined Surface, Time had marched ever more rapidly across her person. The doctors had done everything to stop it, but were helpless in the face of her disease.

She looked permanently frightened behind her mask of fine wrinkles. As well she might be, given how quickly the disaster with that early use of experimental drugs was frogmarching her to the grave.

I pitied her from the bottom of my heart, though I disliked her. She was the mother of my Joe, after all. But how different from Susan, who I esteemed for her upright dignity and depth of character!

But I was mistaken. Not in my assessment of Susan B. Riggs, but in my careless denigration of Rowena Pomfret Barr. For Rowena, in spite of her silliness and her petulance, her rudeness and her almost magisterial self-involvement, had a life force all her own. More: she was responsible for much that was good in her son, my Joe. For she, too, had a steely determination when it came to getting what she wanted, even if her goals were foolish. And she was, at bottom, kinder than my grandmother Livia.

Joe inherited both her determination and her kindness, and I am grateful to Rowena, now, when I see those valuable traits surfacing again in our son. I retrospectively thank her for them, and apologize for any slights I might have shown her in our time together.

If I had known, at that time, that this querulous, vain, silly old woman was responsible for my own mother's death, would I have done anything differently? Possibly. I was still the Lizard Princess then, and fresh from my grim determination in the Poorer Quarter—I had not yet learned how and when to apply that determination. I might have killed her if I had known. No one would have been the wiser, none, at least, who would have cared, for as far as I could see she was disliked by all who surrounded her, her servants, her nurses, her security guards, everyone. Rowena was especially hated by the young, and in particular, young women. In her envy of their youth, she treated most young women she met with contempt, even cruelty.

If I had killed her then, knowing, as I know now, that it was Rowena who had plotted, who found Will, a starving poet, and half-seducing, half-praising him, built up a dream castle where Lily was the tyrant witch, and Will the only one who could free all Arcadia from her spell—if I had known that then, I would never have been able to see her for what she truly was. For how many talents must Rowena have had to accomplish all this! How much strength hidden under that silly, vain exterior! She gave Will the money and the direction and set him marching—her revenge on my mother for being the only woman my father had ever truly loved.

No, if I had killed her as I had the evil man in the Poorer Quarter, I would never have known Rowena for what she was. I would never have known she was also kind.

I had been, until then, on the outskirts of the Ruined Surface, but now Leef and I drew near to its heart. If the slums beside the Marsh had been grim, this was terrible. You could feel the corrosion, the corruption, the despairing desolation that emanated from it. It was as if we entered a fetid sea, stung repeatedly in the face by fouled water.

There was mud everywhere, for the Great Flood eighteen years before had left its awful trace. But this wasn't the mud of the Marsh. There was no hope of renewal in the sludge under our feet as we walked, wearily, beside a stone road that had been recently built, reclaimed painfully from the general decay. We walked off the road, because it was the territory of the enormous machines that, on vicious-looking treaded rollers, made their way heavily to the quarter of the Ruined Surface where the rich still had their houses, where they lived when they descended to the world they had ruined.

East New York, it had been called, though the name was half-forgotten now. Where my mother had loved my father. The place where I was conceived.

The Daily Despair descended now on my chest like a clamp, and I realized it had lifted completely in my time with Susan on the Marsh: she had found the way to fight it off and protect all those within her influence. But as we moved more deeply into the Ruined Surface of Megalopolis, the familiar, dull pain returned. A kind of permanent mourning for all that had been lost. All around me mourned. And seethed with a helpless rage that expressed itself, I was told, in periodic riots, when no person unprotected by the rich people's police force was safe.

The sky burned orange-gray, the mud stuck achingly to my lizard feet. We passed hovels inside which flickered the huge screens every Megalopolitan house was furnished with. The watchers hurled vile oaths in thick voices, and we heard the sound of breaking glass and the occasional slap and cry. I followed the servant down the broad boulevard where my father had ridden years before, my mother behind on her horse, as he brought her to his people. The curious mob had stood by, secretly loathing them even as it cheered and looked on. I had heard the story of that ride many times. But this was no bedtime story I walked through now.

We walked silently, no crowd to cheer us on, just the occasional embarrassed scuttling of a functionary or two. The streets were still. It was the stillness of abandonment, of a place where even the smallest animals had fled. And there at the end of our walk was the Great House.

It was a haunted mansion.

I saw the room where my mother and my father had clung to each other, where they had lived together for a short, sweet and sorrowful time. I saw the corridors that she slipped through with Kim, the night they both fled over the mountains to Arcadia.

I saw the tower where she stood with Livia, my grandmother, where Lily first saw clearly the difference between the False Moon and the Moon Itself.

It was what they once had called the Villa in East New York. It had been the grandest, the most enviable, the richest of all the houses—I cannot call it a home—on our world. Before the Great Deluge, it was Livia's fortress, she who controlled the powerful Council of Four.

When the Great Flood came, the mansion was abandoned, many of its treasures left behind in the haste and confusion. The building itself flooded up to the top step of the tower stairs; I could see the green, algae-covered watermark when I stayed there, so briefly. What riches remained were looted by anyone brave enough to attempt it once the waters receded, before the police force returned. What was left was stolen by the police who guarded it.

But it was a symbol still. It had been a symbol of great wealth, great power, of what the Megalopolitans called 'Full World Dominance.' It had been a symbol of oppression to those in the Marsh, and of terror to those too weak to withstand the punishments it handed out. The Council of Four, egged on by Livia, decided they could not leave it derelict, unmanned, falling down.

They rightly felt it too much of a metaphor for comfort.

But what could be done? The very ground the house stood on was unstable for years after the Great Earthquake. Water from the sea had poured into fissures in the earth, and any new buildings sank or swayed or cracked. The old ones, too.

From this the Great House was not exempt. It sank and swayed and cracked. The boulevard and gardens around it became a sea of mud. But if it was ever to reclaim its prestige, the House needed to rise up once again, inhabited, guarded, with sights and sounds pouring from its every orifice before an admiring, envious, and cowed populace.

Hence Rowena. For it was in this decayed grandeur that Rowena was housed, along with her wardrobe, her jewels, and her attendants: her stylists, her designers, her masseurs, her hairdressers, her manicurists, her nurses. And most important of all, her publicists. For Rowena, by birth, was suited for the greatest of roles, the highest position that Megalopolis could provide. She was the flower of many generations of the wealthiest of the wealthy of Megalopolis, which was why she had been destined to marry my father, a prince of that great city, and destined also to give birth to the heir to it all, Piers Josephus Pomfret Barr. My own dear Joe.

Joe, who refused an easy inheritance, all show and no substance. Joe, whose greatest desire was to save the world. Joe, who wanted to be a hero, never knowing that the very desire negated the possibility of reaching the goal. But a noble mistake, oh, Joe!

My own dear Joe.

It was Rowena, I learned, who had been chosen to bear the first fruits of a Great Experiment. For in their endless war against Death, Megalopolitan scientists had begun to perfect a system of parthenogenesis: that is, the birth of a child who has only one parent. Lily and Devindra had outlawed this idea, back when the science of it was only a rumor. They had been horrified at what it meant—yet another foolish attempt to subordinate Nature to our own foolish whims. "Energy we could be putting into becoming more human," Devindra warned me once, "needs to go to the right places. The right research. The right experiments. The right outcome. Energy that goes into making us less human is greatly to be feared. And must be transmuted to a greater good."

Aspern Grayling did not agree. Aspern Grayling fights against the very idea of the human. As does Megalopolis. To be human is to enjoy and to live, to suffer and to die, for there is no joy without suffering, and no life without death. But Aspern and his fellows in Megalopolis are blind to that fact. They would triumph, they say, over Death. They do not understand that there is no triumph over Death. For Death is a partner in what it means to be completely human.

And Pavo Vale, the son of Aspern and Aspern alone—he is, Aspern never tires of proclaiming, more than human. But to be more than human is to be a monster. There are limits that Megalopolis refuses to understand. And so the half-children, as we call them, continue to be born.

Rowena had been chosen—had volunteered, in her vanity ("what articles, what movies, they made about me! I was the star of the hour!")—to be the vessel for such children. Not the mother. Never the mother. Though she hated being pregnant ("how it ruins the figure! Ruins your life! How it makes you look so old, well, look at me, just look!"), Livia coaxed her, flattered her, bribed her, for who would offer better publicity for the Great Experiment than Rowena? The gossip magazines of Megalopolis adored her, churning out turgid prose and silly, lying pictures about her chic and her beauty even after the Great Deluge.

Who indeed?

Then there was her deep well of spite that served my grandmother's purposes so completely. Rowena's hatred of my father, her husband Conor Barr, and of their son, my Joe. Hearing her talk endlessly as I kept her company in her lavish, verdigris-encrusted room—for no matter how hard the poor staff tried, it could never keep up with the damage that the damp below did to the rococo edgings of her suite—I could tell that she still yearned for one of the three children she bore to love her and her alone.

It didn't happen that way, of course. These children, born as they are of the cells of a single parent, are always lacking in some vital function, some vital force necessary for life; no scientist has yet been able to solve that problem. Of the three, two died, one immediately, one a month after its birth, and in this they were exactly like the triplets that Devindra's daughter Merope bore to Aspern Grayling during the years of the Lizard Princess. Of Aspern's three children, only Pavo Vale survived.

Rowena's third child, Gilda, was born without guile. She was always a weak, faint thing, though loveable; she was as appealing as the shadow of a rose. But she was the wrong child to love Rowena, for Rowena loved no one but herself, and such a person can never be truly loved. No one can even pretend to love such a person, except the cunning, the wary, and the guileful. So Gilda had been taken up to the False Moon to live, treasured by all but the mother who bore her and now petulantly rejected her. It was Gilda they sought a governess for now. Rowena, still living a pretense of responsibility for a child she had no connection to or feeling for, insisted on interviewing the candidates herself. So it was to her service I headed now.

When I first saw her, she was a sleeping beauty.

They brought me to her the morning after I arrived. "She's always a trial after her first meal, better to see her before," a nurse said. "Always going on about how much she weighs, how she's getting fat…it drives the rest of us mad, I can tell you." The nurse, I discovered later, was, like the rest of the household staff, chosen for her stocky build. Rowena couldn't bear to have anyone near her thinner than herself.

It was lucky for me, the nurse said, that I was unlikely to be perceived as much competition to the madam. "Be glad you're no beauty queen," she advised me matter-of-factly. I liked her, and asked her name, but she refused to tell me. "Better not to get attached," she said cryptically. So instead I asked why being no beauty was a matter of luck.

She was a sleeping beauty.

"Keep you out of trouble," she said, as we walked down an endless corridor toward Rowena's rooms. Before I could ask what 'trouble' might be, we were there. The nurse threw open a huge double door, pushed me encouragingly inside, and shut it after me with an infinitesimal click, one that spoke of temper tantrums thrown at noises and interruptions of all kinds.

So this was Rowena. Though she was good enough to me. I didn't like her—no one did. But I had cause to be grateful to her, just the same.

She was asleep as I walked silently on the deep pile carpet toward the canopied bed, the surface covered with silk and lace…and webs. Silvery webs hanging everywhere, climbing up the carved mahogany bedposts, curling on the velvet cushions propped behind web-covered linen.

Covering her body, covering her face, covering her hair. Webs everywhere.

Leef cheeped faintly in awe. We had seen these webs before. But never like this. I shivered, though, to think of the similarity.

Rowena's bosom rose and fell under a veil of web; her white hands curled into claws around gathered strands, her mouth was barely visible as she breathed through them where they parted.

Her hair, as silvery as the filaments, lay in around her. Her beautiful hair.

I caught my breath. Surely this couldn't be normal? But the nurse had said nothing, had not bothered to come inside to check on her patient. Who was I to question the strange arrangements of the Great House?

That was when she whimpered. A childish whimper, like that of a bewildered little girl who has fallen and hurt herself with no one around to help. I walked swiftly to the bed, gathering the webs up as I went, pulling them away from her.

They rose toward me as easily as a spider's web comes when you walk through one by accident in the corner of a disused summerhouse. They leapt to meet me, almost, and I spun the strands as they came into a silver ball. I spun and I spun, clearing the vision in front of me, and I saw to my horror that they issued from Rowena herself. The webs threw themselves out from her body, growing from her very pores.

Was this her illness? Was this what she had retreated to the Great House to cure?

I cleared away what I learned later was the night's growth, always the same every morning, left there by the nurses until they brought in the first meal of the day, for that was their way of defying Rowena. The nurse who led me to Rowena's room had probably forgotten about the strangeness of these webs, how they would strike a newcomer. Either that, or she had deliberately omitted to mention them, in order to initiate me into the mysteries of the House.

The webs clung together into a ball, so light that at a breath from me, it rolled across the room and came to rest against a mildewed wall. Suddenly Rowena's china-blue eyes opened. They were round like a doll's, and fringed by black velvet lashes. She looked at me in silence.

"You're young," she said finally, accusingly, in the voice of a little girl..

"Yes."

"But not beautiful," she said. There was satisfaction in her tone.

"No."

Her eyes flickered up and down with increasing excitement. "Your hands are too big," she said happily. "And your skin too brown and freckled."

"All of this is true," I agreed.

Those china doll eyes widened as she scanned my lizard half. But I couldn't tell—did she see it? I think now that she did, and that she understood what it meant, maybe more than I did, but that this understanding came to her True Self. The one buried beneath the webs and illusions, though, could no longer commune with that deeper soul.

She stretched luxuriously. "Where is my tea?" she demanded, and the double doors flung open soundlessly. Three retainers entered silently with a table, a teapot hung over a spirit lamp, a pitcher of cream and a white china bowl on which lay a puddle of gold honey. Silently, one made the cup and stirred it with a spoon, handing it to me, and I handed it to Rowena.

She gave a sigh of satisfaction and, lying back on the linen and velvet pillows, began to drink. The servitors left as silently as they had arrived.

We sat in silence, and I marveled at the myriad lines running all across her ruined, still beautiful, white face. She had aged dramatically, and the many treatments and drugs had wrecked her looks and her health; yet she maintained the airs and graces of a Beauty. More, a Beauty still the spoiled child of her world. This was no woman to have as a mother.

"I like you," she said unexpectedly, and her smile deepened the cracks on her face. She held out her cup for another helping of tea. I poured it, preparing it the way I had seen, and silently handed it back.

She looked at me contemplatively. So she had taken a liking to me? I didn't know why.

The nurse came in the room, giving the ball of web a contemptuous look as she headed toward the bed. "And how are we this morning?" she asked in that bright, hard voice that carers put on when they dislike their charges.

Rowena didn't answer. She pointed pettishly to me instead. "I like her," she said in her high, whining voice.

"Do you then?" the nurse said indifferently as she bustled about the bed, taking her patient's temperature, twitching the bedclothes back into place. "Why is that? You never liked any of them before."

Who was 'them'? I wondered, but I didn't ask.

"I like her," Rowena repeated, as if she had said something clever. "She's nice." She repeated this again petulantly, as if in hope of annoying the nurse, and in this I'm quite sure she succeeded. "Nice. Not like you lot." The nurse gave a snort, gathered up the balled web and carried it out the door.

Rowena cried after her, "She listens," as the doors shut soundlessly, and we were alone again.

She looked at me expectantly. "You do listen, don't you?"

"Yes," I said.

And I did.

"Do you have children? No? Well, don't. They spoil your life. Take my word for it."

The petulant look returned to Rowena's face, and I thought of Joe, and had difficulty holding back my contempt.

Every morning that Leef and I were there, in that Great House, I would go to Rowena's room; the door would open to me as if in recognition and silently close behind. Every morning the webs draped the bed, covering her body like white mold, grown anew every night as if fed by the damp. Every morning I would unravel the strands, bundling them up for the indifferent nurses to collect later. And every morning I would make Rowena her tea.

That tea smelled like no other tea I have ever known, brackish and constricted. It was a strange color, too: purplish black, like the seaweed we had sailed through, on our way to the Dead Wood. I never had a taste of it myself, nor was any ever offered me.

Nothing was offered me but Rowena's nonstop plaints, from the moment she woke to the moment her eyes shut—click! like a doll's—and she fell into a deep slumber, undisturbed until the morning came again.

As I said, the nurses took a liking to me; I had taken some of the burden of Rowena's endless complaining away from them. They brought me good food and drink at intervals when they did their duty by their patient, rolling their eyes at her monologue, which they must have heard many times before.

They had heard it, but—as Rowena said—never listened to it. Rowena was a sleeping beauty who needed that listening…a real listening…before she could awake from her doll-like daze. Before she could go on.

I have wondered since if I did her any favors by releasing her from that nocturnal web of frustration, resentment, anger and despair. I know now that a person truly listened to has been given the possibility of finding their True Self, and that this is the start for anyone of either the Beginning or the End.

As I listened, every night the webs grew scanter, though at first the difference was too small to easily observe. As time went on, though, it was clear that the web Rowena created each night was indeed dissipating. Even the nurses began to look at me with a kind of superstitious awe.

But that was later. First, I needed patience, to listen to the high, thin whining of the start of her tale, until it settled into an aggrieved murmur. Patience as the murmur rose in volume but lowered in tension into a straightforward narrative…and then, ultimately, as the narrative deepened, fragmented, and fell silent.

Then emerged again. As a question.

But by the time I left, that question was unanswered. I never heard what happened after that, though listening one evening as the invisible servant on the False Moon that I had become, I heard the news of Rowena's death. It was spoken of coldly, without interest, just as a fact in some other dry recitation of facts of a kind that made up the conversation between officials there. I never learned how she had died, whether in one of the riots that periodically swept the Ruined Surface, or of disease, or decay, or by her own hand.

What I did know was that before she died, she caught a glimpse of her True Self. But I never learned whether that glimpse was fatal or fertile.

But I had listened to her story. The same story, over and over, herself the victim or the star, but always the center. I grew weary of the sameness of the tale. I grew weary—desperately so—of life in the Great House.

I had walked through many difficult landscapes on my way to this place—through the Hidden Pass at the unexplored northern end of the Donatees, through the Dead Wood, through the outskirts of the Ruined Surface. Down the Ruined Boulevard on my way to the Great House. But never was I as glad of my lizard half as I was in the House itself. For the floors there, stretching, winding innumerable miles, distances that brought on the curses of Rowena's slaves, had never been properly cleaned after the Great Disaster. The corridors in the servants' quarters were a mass of rubble, broken wire, and shards of glass, all carelessly kicked aside rather than swept away, awaiting some cleanup that never came. Wading through this mess, I found my lizard skin invaluable.

Leef, more tender than I, rode always on my shoulder, his tail curling around my neck, or in the mermaids' bag, which I wore crosswise across my chest. There were almost no other animals in the Great House—no bats, no mice, no insects even. All that remained on the surface was a family of chameleons, tough enough to hide there, blending in with the rotten wainscoting at the foot of the broken-down bed to which I'd been assigned. This was where they lived. They seemed as relieved to have found Leef and myself as we were to have found them.

I think about them from time to time. And chameleons, in Arcadia, now enjoy the Queen's protection. That's the least I can do for the memory of that friendly little family, the only friends that Leef and I found in that cold, cold place.

At least, they were our only friends until the story changed. And help arrived in the most unlooked-for form.

It was in the third month of my listening that Rowena gave me the gift I needed in order to move on in my quest. For I knew what that quest entailed. I had seen the angels overhead, and I had remembered. I was to find the Key and bring it back to Arcadia.

If I was to be allowed to find Joe as well, that would be good for me. But it was not my job. It was my desire, but it was not what I was born to do.

Chafing now to be off, I listened to Rowena. Endless listening. Every day, she would take me through the events of her life. The resentments, the frustrations, the raging anger she felt because of the limitations imposed by her great beauty, her great wealth, and her great position.

It's odd to say that, I know. My Joe would undoubtedly have said sarcastically, "Her problems? Great problems, those!" But Joe didn't understand that those great potential gifts caused nothing but heartache and misery to an as-yet-unformed nature. She had been born silly and playful, and she could have been a charming companion had she not been taught at an early age that most companionship was beneath her.

"I was so beautiful. I was, I was! The most beautiful child born in our family, and our family was one of the most elite, I assure you, so this meant I was the most beautiful child in Megalopolis. I had everything. Everything. People adored me. Papa particularly adored me. He showed me off whenever there was a great dinner party. I would come down in one of my beautiful frocks, made specially for me by the most exclusive seamstresses—hundreds of them worked to make my clothes, night and day, and I almost never wore the same dress twice. I don't know what happened to the ones I threw off onto the floor every night, for they were gone the next morning, and a new, even more beautiful one would be hanging there to replace it."

And yet, when she said the word, repeating it, 'everything,' she looked so very, very sad.

By the second month, I had heard the story of her life. Her fortunate birth. Her pampered childhood. Her glorious debut ("there was not a debutante of the decade who could touch me, not my couture, not my maquillage, not my retinue, not the grace of my dancing—they all said so, all the tabloids said so, everyone, everything!"). Her engagement to my father. ("Of course he adored me. He was thrilled to be chosen by my father to be my husband. I was chased after by all the notable young men, you can be sure. Everyone. Everything!") Her wedding ("The most astonishing social event in Megalopolitan history. Everyone said so. Everything was of the most choice, the most perfect! Everything!"). Her married life ("Everything of the most perfect. My child, Piers Josephus Pomfret Barr, noble name!, the heir to two of the most powerful families in the world! Everyone said I was a beautiful mother. We were a perfect family. We had everything.").

But the story would stop there. It was from the nurses that I heard the gossip of Conor's abandonment of her ("Who could have stood living with her even as long as he did, poor guy...and him so dishy, I was in love with his picture when I was a girl, weren't you, oh yes, we all were, he was everyone's fantasy prince all right, I never saw him in the flesh, but he always looked so cool in those glossy magazines..."), and of her narcissistic rage ("Always throwing tantrums, that one, can't have been pleasant for her kid, I understood he took off sometime after, not a looker like his dad, didn't hear much about him on the news, did you? No, I was more into the father than the son..."). They told me of how she had been chosen, on the False Moon, to be the first woman to bear children born of the cells of one person. No one knew who the sole parent was of these strange children ("Though we all guessed, didn't we? Well, it must have been Livia, her so into herself, and who else could have gotten Missy to risk ruining her precious figure one more time? For ruin it she did, and her looks, between the three kids born and all those beauty pills she swallowed all the time, took her right over the edge, you've seen, there's nothing left but a wrinkled hag who can't do for herself at all, can't walk even, have you seen her try to walk? Can't do it, not on those tiny feet of hers, not the way they bound them to make them fit the size shoe she was so crazy about, ask her about her shoe size if you want to be bored from here to the Moon Itself, go on, I dare you.").

She did tell me about her shoe size, as a matter of fact, in the first month I listened to her. Ordered me to lift the silken comforter and look at her feet. "The ivory perfection of them! I had the finest surgeons at work to make them exactly the size that Daddy thought was most perfect for a woman's foot. And they were perfect, both of them!" Poor, mangled feet. Misshapen, crushed, hurt. I pretended to admire them, of course.

By the second month, though, the story began again, in a different way.

"Of course I was a girl, and they didn't want a girl, Daddy didn't, and Mother didn't either, but why would they? It's the boys who have their way with the world, except for Livia, of course, but she's the exception who proves the rule, wouldn't you say? And the boys are afraid of her, I wouldn't want that, no, I want the boys to admire me, and admire me they did, which was second best to being one, but the best you could do as a woman, because it was a triumph, really, to have them admire one rather than having one admire them, the way all the other women were forced to do. Daddy taught me that; I was meant to be adored, he always said, though of course, it was me who adored Daddy rather than the other way round, well, I mean, that was only right, he was the man. Wasn't it?"

That second month, a note of doubt ran through her narrative like a breeze. "I think my husband adored me. Of course he did. I know he thought a bit about some other girl from before me, but that's the way men are, isn't it, not like us, they play the field, don't they, and it's not always the most beautiful, the most brilliant, the most perfectly turned-out that they turn to when they want a plaything, though of course a wife is an entirely different matter, there you're expected to keep up the value of the family, and that I did, for my value was beyond compare. My value was everything. Wasn't it?"

It was in the third month, though, that the anger began to erupt from below. The words of her story seemed to scatter here and there, fleeing the fire of her rage.

"It wasn't right, the way they kept me hemmed in, the way they bribed me by telling me I was so beautiful, who cares about being beautiful if you can't be loved? Who does? I'm asking you, answer me, who cares about being beautiful if you can't…if you can't…if you can't…"

Here she gasped for breath, she choked, and I saw, from where I always sat patiently by her side, I saw with great alarm a ball of web forming now in her mouth, pushing her petulant lips aside, choking her, strangling her. I leapt up and pulled it from her mouth, holding it, pulling what was left of the thread from her throat, and her eyes gave me a mute "thank you." She had never said those words to anyone in her life and didn't say them now. But her eyes didn't lie.

Who cares about being anything, indeed, if you can't love?

She grasped my hand now, though she had so little strength that it was like a bird brushing my palm. Then she struggled to get up. Alarmed, I tried to stop her, but, frail as she was, she shook me off and stood, for the first time since I had known her, on her own two mangled feet.

From the depths of the Great House, at that moment, came a tremendous roar. For the staff of the Great House, along with the rest of the decaying quarter, had abandoned their normal duties that day to stare at the fake battles Megalopolis periodically broadcast to the general population, on one of the many screens I had indifferently noted were still alive, even on the Ruined Surface. I assumed one of these battles were what prompted the roar now, though whether it was of approval or despair I couldn't tell.

Aspern Grayling lectures often on one of his pet hobbyhorses: the value of organized sport. While I am myself as bored as it is possible to be by any kind of competitive game (had I even noticed how much it was a feature of everyday life and conversation in the Great House and the surrounding environs?), as a queen I have had to admit its importance to the polity. The playing fields, as Aspern points out, are training grounds for our citizen militias, which we do not need for aggressive purposes but for a vigorous defense. It was all very well to be a peace-loving country, so my reasoning went after my days as the Lizard Princess, but every peace-loving individual had better be able to defend that position when attacked. So much I thought we had learned from the Megalopolitan takeover in my mother's time, the one that led to her becoming our first queen.

That I was wrong about that I know now, too, as about so much else. But you do the best you can with what you truly believe and with what you know. And so as queen, I have greatly encouraged sport, though not for those children who dislike it, or are indifferent to it—for those we suggest leisure occupations more congenial to their temperaments. But for those with overflowing high spirits, and a love of group play, plenty of opportunities to exercise their passions are provided for…and several of our best militia captains have come out of these village games. While our best general, oddly enough, is a young woman passionate about astronomy. Our theory was to use the talents of the children we nurtured both for our mutual growth and our mutual defense.

Susan and I talk seriously of this, and with Devindra too, for it is not clear that this is the ideal way forward. But where we are on firm ground is in seeing how we differ in our Arcadian games from those of Megalopolis.

Where we are different from Megalopolis is in our dislike of competition as such—of competition where there is a winner and a loser. What we have discovered, as Devindra never tires of recounting, what our scientists have proven, is that competition reduces the chance of a happy outcome, either for the individual or, curiously enough, for the group. No one, they have found, truly loves to best her or his fellow at some task. Winning leaves feelings of unease, of guilt and unhappiness, for we yearn for connection rather than competition.

So we Arcadians believe. Most of us, anyway. Aspern Grayling, and his followers, who believe in what he calls the 'New Man'—not the 'New Woman' or even the 'New Human', but the 'New Man'—insist that humans are meant to be ruled by a superior force, and the man who proves his superior force in competition is also proving his worthiness to be that ruler.

Needless to say, Sophia is not the New Ruler that Aspern has in mind. Pavo Vale is his choice. The boy born of a father alone.

I did think about Aspern, to my surprise even as I worried about the fate of Rowena, as I stood in that dark doorway of the staff's room, watching the servants all sit slack-jawed, staring at an enormous screen where enormous, anonymous men ran at each other again and again in some competition mysterious…and useless…to my eye. I thought of Aspern and his fawning admiration, his envy and covetousness, of Megalopolitan ways, and I felt, truth to tell, slightly sick to my stomach.

None of them noticed me. Their attention was too taken up by the enigmatic formations on the screen. Rowena had been right. "It will be hours," she said tensely, "before they come out again." I believed her now, and retreated back through the hallways the way I had come, back to her rooms—passing between the banks of gray webbing drawn from her body in the months I had been listening to her in the Great Room of the Great House.

Those balls of sticky webbing reached to the ceiling on either side.

She was still out of bed when I returned, halfway to the door, wrapped now in a swan's down and velvet coat, her long white hair foaming out to her knees behind her, her tiny bound feet hobbling forward in their thin-soled red satin slippers. "Hurry," she whispered when she saw me, and I moved toward her in time to catch her as she lurched forward, unfamiliar as she was with walking on her own. It was like having a willow switch brush you as you walk through the marsh reeds at twilight. As we moved, her figure gained weight as she gained confidence that she could move—that she could exist, even—outside of that enormous, stifling bed of hers. And Leef, who to my surprise appeared not to dislike her after all, perched on my shoulder whispering encouragement to her.

She nodded as she listened to him, and I thought of how much she had changed since my first sight of her, and of how wise Devindra had been when she taught me what she said was a Law of All the Universes: that confession is good for the soul.

I had thought Rowena soulless. But I had been wrong. It wasn't that. It was that what soul she was born with had been trapped, restricted, wrapped in a muffling web of triviality, vanity, self-love. She had a soul, and it had been set free of the cotton wool of that mindless wrapping. After years of imprisonment, though, it was timid: fearful and cautious. It could not simply expand now; it had to feel its way.

We felt our way now. She led me down the corridors and then up, up, up a tower, up the uneven flagstones of a winding stair on which could still be seen the fragments of a carpet now faded to the color of dried blood. We emerged at the top into the night air. The ruins of the formerly great city stretched out before us in all directions. The sight pulled at my heart, bringing tears to my eyes, for here was destruction that need never have happened, disaster caused by heedlessness, blindness, greed. Ruins caused by human failure, human attempts to become more than human, and so falling far below what could have been. Becoming, in their nervous urge to be more, far less than they ever needed to have been. Ruins reflected in the ruin of Rowena's beauty, in the ruin of the woman who stood beside me now.

"I know who you are," she said quietly. And I started. It was not at what she said, though that was startling enough. It was how she said it: quietly, with resignation. The voice of an adult who has learned, rather than that of the child she had been who refused every difficult lesson.

I turned to face her in the double moonlight, for both moons were full. The False Moon, of course, was always so, but the Moon Itself shone that night with the full force of her enlightening mystery.

"You're her daughter, aren't you? Hers...and his." This last said sadly, with none of the spite, the vituperation, the childish malignancy that had gone before. Fascinated by the shift, and half-admiring in spite of myself, I nodded.

Should I have felt in danger? No. I was in no danger with this woman. For she was a woman now, she who faced me, not a child, though I doubted she could maintain so much knowledge for long in a frame so ill-suited, so ill-trained to contain it.

Rowena shivered as a cold air current flowed by, and she pulled her swan's down wrapper tight across her chest. "I've seen your portrait," she said dully. "We have spies, you know, in your land, though it makes me sick at heart to think of it now. Do you know I have a son?"

All I could do was nod. "Yes," I managed finally to say, my throat dry.

"Your brother," she said in an indifferent, gray tone. There was silence again, except for a series of groans and shouts and shrieks that came up from the streets. I noticed these now, though they must have been going on for some time.

"Where...where is he now?" I managed to get out, riding the words hard to make them slow down, sound casual, hide the leaping of my heart.

She shrugged. "He hates me, you know." And this was a statement, not a complaint. Certainly not a plea for the sympathy I, in any case, could not at that moment have given. "I think he has gone to your grandmother on the Phony Moon."

The Phony Moon. She called it that. Pronouncing the words with the same scorn we Arcadians gave it, too.

"You should know him," she said quietly. "For all the wrongs I've done, that I believe would make it right."

What did she mean? I still do not know. The doll-like creature she had been was no longer speaking; this was a woman whose depths were unknown. The doll had lacked a heart. And it was a heart these words sprang from now.

"When you find Joe," she said, as if it was a foregone conclusion, "tell him…tell him I did love him. Would you do that for me, please?"

She looked at me searchingly. I nodded. Of course I nodded.

She sighed and looked again over the streets. Fires flared in the distance, and the shouts and shrieks and screams grew louder.

"You know where the ships wait?" she said, pointing to a tower on a rise nearby, a port built after the Great Disaster for the convenience of the comings and goings at the Great House. I nodded, for I had been careful to find from where the ships left for the False Moon, pondering my own inevitable journey there. "Go now, then," she urged. "Tell them you're the nursemaid I've sent to Livia for the half-children. They know. They've been expecting you this week and more."

"Tomorrow then, I will…"

"Not tomorrow. Today. Tonight. Now. Go now." She spoke with a strange urgency, all the stranger coming from she who had been so languid before. The fires seemed to dance and come nearer, as the shouts from below grew louder. "Down the stairs. I'll watch until you're gone."

Leef gave an encouraging cheep in my ear and I began to obey…and then turned, and wrapping my arms around her frail body, hugged her for the first and last time. "Be kind to my little Gilda," she whispered to

169

me. "For the poor little girl never had a mother worth the name." Another shout, louder this time, came up from the street, and she pushed me away with surprising force, sending me flying down the stairs as quickly as my lizard legs would allow, onto the ruined street.

The smell of smoke was heavy there. The shouts came nearer. I looked up and in the moonlight saw a foaming mass of white blonde hair, and a slim white hand raised to wave goodbye.

Hurrying up the street, I turned into an alley that led to the ship port. All around me were murmurings, thoughtless and angry, full of an increasing, contagious rage; the walls seemed to seethe with it. I looked back and saw lights streaming down the main street toward the Great House. Shuddering without understanding the meaning of what I saw, I turned back on my way and ran the last mile to my destination.

I got there, to the port, just in time—a small ship, the day's supply transport, was about to leave. Rowena had taken care (how? when? she must have told them weeks ago they were to expect me, but how had she known?), and there was no trouble about my passage or my passport.

"You're expected," said the pilot, a young tough-looking woman. She was, I thought, a degraded version of what Susan must have been in her days rising up in the ranks of the Megalopolitan military. "Lucky for you to pick tonight," she continued, laughing unpleasantly. Pointing, she waited to see me strap myself into the lone passenger seat, Leef tucked into the bag slung across my chest, and then she made her way to her own controls and managed her take off. Animals meant to be slaughtered on the False Moon cackled and squealed from the hold.

"The mob's going for the Great House again," she informed me, seeming to be inordinately amused by the thought of it. I must have looked appalled. "Oh, don't worry. Happens every so often, especially when their team doesn't win. They get fed up, get drunk, get into the street, kill every one of their own kind they can find, then take over the Great House and drink it dry before the cops get there—which they never do, of course, until every one of the locals working there is dead. Saves on wages, and there's never a shortage of more needing the jobs. Lucky for you you're on the way out." She spat to the side, "Never seems to hurt the richies hanging out there; the mob doesn't believe in massacring above its station, lucky for them." She laughed again, ending in a fit of coughing. Then she set her instruments and pulled back on the throttle. We juddered and rose, and I could see the dancing lights below converge on the Great House.

As the ship rose farther and farther, I looked down at the muddy brown blight that was Megalopolis. There, at the northwest tip of the Ruined Surface, were the four mountain ranges circling a green and pleasant land. Arcadia. My heart leapt up, even under its sodden mound of grief, and I swore then that if I had anything to do with it, that mud would never spill over the mountains into my world.

But first I needed to live and work in TreMega, the false heart of the False Moon, and learn what false life really meant—how it meant living without Death, and how false death was what the Dead Wood had meant itself. After that...then I could find the Key.

Part X: To The Moons

The False Moon was a triumph of technology. But TreMega, its capital built for the Megalopolitan elite, was more than that. It was a triumph of technique. Not just of science and engineering, but of aesthetics, as well. The dome that protected it, mimicking to perfection a sky seen from the world below, was made of tiny living beings, a specially created polymer that could reflect the smallest change in controls at the Main Center.

It was an exquisite world, the most exquisite I have ever seen. Like a jewel box. Everything there was formed as if by the images from an ideal memory: trees, flowers, birds…every variety that could be remembered. All of these imitated to perfection a life they lacked. So perfectly, in fact, that it made you wonder if they weren't truly alive. I'm ashamed to admit that I wondered if my grandmother Livia hadn't been right when, at the top of the tower in the Villa of East New York, she told my mother Lily that Megalopolitans had become like gods.

TreMega was their creation. It and all that…"lived"…in it. Those trees, those flowers, those plants, those birds, all "lived" their lives according to algorithms written by Megalopolitan engineers, with ever-changing variations in color, both beautiful and subtle, in their ripening and in their aging. The behavior of the originals of these creations was factored into the equations, so that all around us on TreMega, in its unfathomable luxury,

Life as Beautiful Illusion danced a continuous dance.

There were four seasons under the dome. Each one was perfection. Winter in its sheer crystal winterness, spring in its leaping green springiness, summer in its openhearted summerness, fall in its abundant, generous fallness. Each season was far more perfect, more continuously pleasant, more suited to what humans have believed, in error or otherwise, that we are suited for, than the flawed, unpredictable, uncertain seasons of the world below. My Arcadian seasons, for example, which I longed for, every glorious and false day on TreMega, these were the actual seasons the false ones had been modeled upon. For in their quest for a world of perfection, Megalopolitan technicians had closely studied those quarters on the world below, and had been able to make nimble adjustments where the originals were found to be not quite satisfactory.

The winter's snow on TreMega was whiter, more sparkling, fresher, than it had ever been at home. The spring breezes were more delightfully, enticingly cool. The summer days more invitingly heated, and the autumn nights more enjoyably, permanently crisp. The colors were delicate, artful, delightful. The environment, taken as a whole, was a jewel without flaw.

And it was all completely dead.

There were no real children on the False Moon, for it was discovered that they didn't thrive there. By "real," of course, I mean born of two parents, a mother and a father, not sprung from the cells of one, as in the parthenogenesis Megalopolis now proposed as the breeding ground of the future—the children I had been brought to the False Moon to care for.

It was thought to be yet another defect of "real" children (or "organic" children, as they were sometimes called, half-jokingly), that, brought to the False Moon, where all was structured as perfectly as science and technology, joined to unlimited funds, could achieve, they failed to grow strong. Instead these children invariably sickened. A form of anorexia took hold of most of them, where the only nourishment they could hold down was actual dirt that had been brought at great expense from the edges of the Marsh below to add nutrients to the crushed precious stones that made up the soil of the False Moon. Real children had an almost diabolical knack (the words were the Council of Four's, not mine) for finding the stockpiled mounds of this earth and scooping it into their mouths by the handful.

But there was more. Aside from this "disgusting" habit (again, the words belong to the Council), all these children would drink was water that had been taken from transparent cisterns laid out under the light of the Moon Itself. This made no sense to the science of the day. Attempts were made to try coaxing the children to drink other water—water, for example, cured by the rays of artificial light—but the children recoiled from it, some with horrified expressions. This was inexplicable to the technicians who experimented with solutions. The two kinds of water, they explained to their masters, were, for all intents and purposes, identical.

"There are no nutrients in moonlight; it's absurd, ridiculous, unnatural," sputtered Aspern Grayling. And his highest insult: "Unscientific!" This on one of his periodic trips to the False Moon to confer, traitorously, with the Council of Four and their scientists. I heard him. I saw him, traitor that he was.

But he didn't see me.

Curious, that. Although no more than I have discovered: what you don't expect to find, you don't see. "It had to be believed to be seen," as someone once so rightly said.

Now you would think a nursery maid almost six feet tall, with a full head of fiery red hair, who moved on sturdy lizard feet, and was followed by a slashing lizard tail—you would have thought that, even if Aspern didn't recognize me as the womanly version of a child he had known her entire life, he would have noticed the nursery maid of the precious half-children (for that was what they called them, poor lambs) of the Council of Four.

That he didn't was a tribute to the invisibility of servants. Especially the invisibility of servants who minister, without honor, to the most basic of human needs. I have noticed this time and time again in my travels and

I saw him, traitor that he was.

in my studies of other worlds: when the truly necessary arts—say, the preparation and service of food, the cleaning of human wastes, even the care of children—are given over to the lower ranks of society, those who hold that care are invisible to those they help.

Why is that? My own theory—for Devindra and I have spent long hours discussing this very question—is that the blind elite feels shame in their inmost being, in their True Selves, for abandoning responsibility for their own care. And shame and guilt in those who disbelieve in the possibility of either turn into anger, even rage, at those victims they have blindly abused. That rage takes an aggressive form of denying the victims value, even existence. And so the guilty ones literally cannot see.

Be that as it may, it was definitely true that Aspern Grayling could not see me. There I was, shepherding the seven half-children who were my charges, by the Perfect Lake of TreMega. He was there with a delegation from the Council of Four, who were charged with escorting him in his renegade fact-finding mission. Yet he never showed, by even a slight furrowing of the brow, that the sight of me caused him any thought at all. Many were the times, as he conferred traitorously with the enemies of Arcadia, that I passed by him on those perfect streets, on my way to or from the Great Nursery. Many were the times that I stood, silent in the shadows, as the half-children slept, while he observed them and took notes, holding forth in that arrogant, silver-voiced way of his to everyone nearby about his beliefs, his hatreds, and, most of all, his betrayal.

For betrayal it was, his purpose on the False Moon of Megalopolis. Betrayal of everything Arcadia was, and is, and struggles to become. Treachery deep and double-dyed. He meant to imitate Megalopolis in many things, but the worst of these was in the creation of Arcadian half-children. They would have one father, Aspern boasted in the nursery as I listened unobserved. And their father would be Aspern himself, like a god, or a king. "I will have nothing but sons," he laughed, and the technicians laughed with him. "Sons who will be good allies to Megalopolis. Princes in their own right, brilliant, rich, and handsome as a day in TreMega." Sons born with the servile connivance of Devindra's daughter, Merope Vale. She who had so little self-worth that the highest prize she could imagine was to be the mindless vessel of the little princelings of Aspern Grayling.

Livia, my grandmother, told me many things there on the False Moon, in the dark afternoons we spent fencing with each other, after she recognized me for who I was. Those afternoons were when the rest of the False Moon slept uneasily after the excesses of their luncheon, for what else did they have to do there but eat and drink and then diet and purge?

She told me about Merope.

"You know she's always hated you," Grandmother said, her eyes gleaming with amusement. "Oh, yes, I know. I have spies everywhere. Not a sparrow falls in your little Arcadia without my knowing of it."

Livia cackled at this quietly to herself.

I knew Merope hated me. And yet our mothers had loved each other so well. It was Merope that Devindra had carried inside her, over the winter mountains, not yet born while her mother knelt beside mine as she gave birth to me. It was Merope who was the first child of the refugees born in Mumford, our capital, raised with me as our mothers spent long days and nights together working to bring Arcadia back from the terrors and instabilities of the Occupation. I had been fascinated by their work. In the court of Lily the Silent, children were not just allowed underfoot, they were positively encouraged, patted absently as the adults went about their tasks. "Let them learn that way," my mother often said. "It's easy to learn when you watch the ones you love."

She was right about me. I loved her and Devindra, and I learned almost all I knew from watching them. I entered enthusiastically into their plans and experiments, as wholeheartedly as a child could. I strove to be like them.

Merope, though, was different. It was only later in my experience of life that I had a glimmer of understanding why. Merope did not love my mother. She did not love me. She did not even love Devindra, the mother who had suffered so much to bring her into the world.

That people like this exist is a hard truth. For there are those who choose, for no reason any can see, the seductions of Power over Love. And those who make that choice suffer. And because they suffer, they hate.

It was true what Livia told me on the False Moon. From the start, Merope had hated us all.

"Where is my father?" Those were the first words Merope spoke. She had kept stubbornly silent all throughout her childhood, worrying the nurse she shared with me, Kim the Kind. Kim, who coaxed goodness from her charges rather than enforcing it, was helpless in the face of Merope's precocious, aggressive silence. For Merope was fiercely strong-willed, as her mother's daughter would be, and her father's too, if the truth was known about him. Roderick Corman was his name, a name that is still uttered in hushed tones of respect in the academic common rooms of Megalopolis. Roderick Corman, who believed his genius gave him the right to many pleasures denied 'lesser' men: including ruining the lives of any beautiful young students who came his way.

Devindra had been the most brilliant, as well as the most beautiful, with her silky black hair, her eagle stare, her gilded brown skin. What a delight it must have been to the Professor to have the power to ruin such a perfect object. For not only did he seduce her, and abandon her, but he stole her work and presented it as his own, meaning to ruin her soul.

Aspern Grayling, unsurprisingly, is a great admirer of his work.

But Devindra refused to be ruined. Devindra walked out of Megalopolis with the other women and children of the Marsh. And it was a grace to Arcadia that she did so, although a curse to Arcadia the day Merope was born. For without Merope's connivance, Pavo Vale would never have been born. Pavo Vale, who his father worships: "The New Man, the most brilliant prince of the dreams of Megalopolis."

So boasts Aspern Grayling.

The idea of the Handsome Prince was often in my mind in those days, as pondering Aspern's boast, I shepherded those poor little half-children on the False Moon. Of them, my favorite was also my special charge, the one child left of the three who had been born to Rowena. Curiously, that waif-like, sweetly brainless girl was addicted to stories about princes— Handsome Prince fights dragon, Handsome Prince saves maiden… Handsome Prince…Handsome Prince…Handsome Prince…. I must have read hundreds of such tales aloud to her. This was Gilda, poor thing. I had such a fondness for her, the way you would for a doll you swore was alive, walking and talking while everyone else slept—alive, and yearning to become fully human. These children yearned for that, so that it was painful to watch them, to be open to them, for there was always some piece missing in their make-up. Not even the genius of Megalopolitan geneticists had been able to compensate for that defect. The technology had not yet advanced far enough to make a thoroughly healthy child from only one parent.

As we know now in Arcadia, it fails still, even now, almost fifty years later. Even Aspern Grayling's sons, born to Merope Vale, triplets as is usual in these cases, suffered the inevitable defect of their creation. Lionel was born without a brain, and died at once. Marcian, without a heart, lived only a few days longer. And Pavo, who lives even now, strutting and boasting like his father who proclaims him to be the "New Man," destined to rule over all, even Pavo who looks and sounds like the most human of them all—Pavo was born without a soul.

But Gilda's lack was of another kind. I never knew the secret of her parentage, though she reminded me strongly of Rowena. She was as beautiful as Rowena, even as a little girl, not more than eight years old when I had the care of her. She was a fragile, pale gold maiden of the moon, with long fingers, neck, legs, and a thin, waning face. She was clever with her hands. She could mend almost anything. To her despair, though, being rich, privileged, and the hope of Megalopolitan science, she was never allowed to do work considered beneath her station. Only servants mended. I took pity on her when no one else was about and gave her my own tasks to do. This delighted her. She could spend hours darning rents in fabric with such exquisite stitches that they were more precious after her work than before. She was clever that way.

She was beautiful. But she had no joy. She had been born with every other human attribute; she even possessed a soul, the first born in a clone, which made her all the more precious to Livia and to the Council of Four. But that soul was small and cramped and tortured by its lack of space. Its lack of joy.

Gilda sought joy everywhere, feeling its loss without knowing what it was. She looked for it in everything, as a baby animal looks for milk without knowing what milk means until it is gratefully found. She never found joy, poor Gilda, though she never stopped looking. And where she looked, mainly, were in those stories, old and new, collected from more than one world, of the Handsome Prince and his saving of the Princess. She was the princess. But she had no joy of it.

Watching her, I thought of my own father. Conor Barr: so handsome, so privileged, so rich. And of how he had let the rare joy he and my mother shared—a gift!—flow prodigally through his careless fingers. I thought about my Joe, so funny-looking, so earnest, so heroic even in his awkwardness—not a Handsome Prince at all. He was more like another kind of boy in a fairy tale, the one who is regarded as the hopeless fool of the family, and he, like that boy, had won me. We had not wasted our joy, neither could it be taken away from us in our separation.

We lost much, it is true, but we never lost that joy. I never lost it. I can feel it even now, take it out at will, wearing it like a warm coat all these years later, long after I walked my last walk with Joe on the Road of the Dead.

No one can give you that joy. It is a gift that comes from a source so mysterious it must be hidden in the source of life itself. No one can take

She was beautiful. But she had no joy.

it away. It has to be accepted, and nurtured, between two willing partners. Once created, once called up and strengthened, it can never be destroyed.

But of this, my poor, dear Gilda was not capable. So she spent her time—morning, noon, and night—dreaming of a Prince she believed could bring joy to her, to she who had none.

She is dead now, Gilda. Her beauty, her pliability, her value as a scientific breakthrough, all these conspired to give her a high value as a wife. She married brilliantly: a rich, well-connected, dashingly handsome son of one of the Council of Four. But he, having been raised after the time of the Great Disaster, in the sterility of TreMega on the False Moon, he had no joy either, for he was a half-child himself. He had meant to find his joy in his marriage to Gilda, but she, once married to her Handsome Prince, woke painfully from her dream of joy to find neither of them had it to give or to receive.

The knowledge of that ultimate lack was too much for her, poor, weak little thing, and she drowned herself in the ornamental Lake in TreMega, the same Lake beside which she had often played as a child. Gilda walked out onto the ice on a winter's day, all alone, and fell through to the chill water below. Because even in a mechanical world, even when the ice is manmade from manmade water, the ice is sometimes thin, and there is danger. If there is not always Joy in an unnatural world, there is always danger. There is always Death. As we pursue Joy, it runs farther and farther away, leaving those who chase after it in a more fearful landscape than at the start.

Poor Gilda. She had, as they say, everything money could buy, and nothing she, as even a part-human, could really desire. Our Arcadian scientists, who look at our world through a different lens than do the Megalopolitan, have found out why. The discovery came to them, as does so much else, in the fairy tales they have proved hold all the secrets of the human universe. These tales tell us that our true desires come from our bodies, and that money can never be a desire that comes from the body—only from the less important mind that can see what money might buy for the body. And of course, money can be a disease, a cancer, that runs amok through a human life, outgrows its usefulness, begins to be thought of as something valuable in its own right.

But in its own right it has no value. The value is in the things it can buy. Time. Comfort. Sustenance. Once these have been purchased, what then is it good for? Nothing but to be a permanent worry to those who seek to hold onto it too tightly.

It is in these discoveries…in this understanding…that economic policy of Arcadia is born. So different from the system of Megalopolis!

Poor Gilda was a victim of that latter system. Money had made her, with a hope of immortality for those who spent freely on the experiment that was my poor little girl. Money controlled her. For where could she go, poor half-creature, living in a false garden on a False Moon, without it? And money promised her all it could never give, a cruel lie. Those promises: Health. Companionship. Joy. For she had none of these until I came to her as nurse, and Leef and I managed to be companions to her for a time. But ever after, that was all she had—what we could give for the short time we lived with her. It was never enough. It might have been enough for a whole human child, but it was never enough for Gilda.

"Sophy, tell me a story," she would say, and it was always the story of the Handsome Prince that she wanted to hear. I could have told her true stories, about a prince who was handsome, but a failure in love, or a prince who was funny-looking but valiant in his heart, and who loved truly, and who was fated to fail, nobly, in his quest. I could have told her that was a true Happy Ever After story, for a true love never goes away once it's brought into the world, and a true quest, even failed, reverberates in ways that cannot be predicted down the years.

But my Gilda didn't want to hear those stories, and I, to amuse her, ransacked the libraries of the False Moon looking for the ones that would please her. And that was how I stumbled on the overlooked, completely forgotten, silly story of a snotty little boy. And that was—thanks to Gilda—how I discovered the secret of how Arcadia, my Arcadia, was born. Although I am ashamed to admit it took me a long time—too long—before I understood the meaning of it.

I ransacked those libraries for Gilda's pleasure, but that was really just an excuse. In what free time I had, it was my own deepest joy, insofar as joy was possible to me in that airless place, to explore the many storage areas of knowledge on the False Moon. "Library" here is a bit of a misnomer. In Arcadia, a library is a gathering place for readers and for books, meant to encourage discovery, a place of warmth and reasonable comfort, with good light to read and write by. Our technical libraries are really no different in that respect from our more general collections, and it was decided long ago that our knowledge contained in all our stories needs to be available in physical form somewhere in Arcadia. We have other forms of conveying information, of course—screens of a smaller sort than one sees in Megalopolis, and small devices that play Arcadian voices reading from the text. But these are for specialized use. For serious reading (and that word 'serious' includes, to the Arcadian mind, reading for entertainment and relaxation, as well as information), Arcadians need an actual physical book. This book means something far more than the information conveyed by the words inside. Its meaning is also contained in the paper it is printed on, where the paper came from, which tree, who bound the book, who designed it. More than this, Arcadians believe each book also contains energies from each and every person who has read and contemplated its contents. There is an interaction between reader and book. Our scientists have proved this: they have shown that the energy of a book, and the story within it, changes, intensifies, deepens with use. The older, the more handled, the more read, the more loved the individual artifact, the more valuable the book.

This could not be a greater contrast to how Megalopolis looks at its own books. For example, a new book is far more valued there than an old, something that utterly perplexed me as I made my first forays into the deserted stacks of ancient volumes. And then, many Megalopolitan 'books' aren't books at all in the Arcadian sense. They are simply ways to efficiently convey information, whether as a virtual file on a screen or as a galley printed and meant for one or two disposable uses, taken from the enormous bulk of data controlled centrally by the Council of Four.

I was very interested in this system, for I could see the advantages it had over our more cumbersome Arcadian one. Information could be shared more quickly this way; innovation could happen at speed—if speed was what was wanted. Altogether, it was a more nimble and ingenious system, though it manifestly lacked what I thought of as one of our great Arcadian virtues: stability. And as my explorations of Megalopolitan knowledge increased, I found that, vast and intricate as it was, it almost entirely lacked the most highly valued quality of my world.

Wisdom.

For Knowledge is knowing about things, and, Goddess knows, no world could possibly know more about things than Megalopolis.

But Wisdom is knowing the true use of that Knowledge. And in this area, Megalopolis utterly fails.

To learn all this, I read—read a lot—of the books, of the information stored in the warrens of the libraries of the False Moon. Read constantly while Gilda and the other half-children played desultorily by the False Lake of TreMega, or while they slept. For they needed too much sleep, the poor things, half-children that they were.

The libraries had been brought up to the False Moon before the Great Deluge of the surface of Megalopolis—more proof of my grandmother's sagacity and foresight. She had clearly foreseen disaster, perhaps even had a hand in the engineering of it, and acted vigorously to protect the Megalopolitan storehouse of knowledge.

"Technology fails," she said to me one evening, in the time after she acknowledged who and what I was, and she said it with that smile I remember with a shudder: that smile that expressed perfect contempt. "But the written word," she continued suavely, "if protected from water, air, fire, never."

Livia had set herself the task of protecting the books of Megalopolis. And it was my sole joy in my sojourn there on the False Moon that she had.

It was also my education. There, alone, lowly, friendless on the False Moon, I completed that education begun by my mother and Devindra Vale— or at least, I completed the education of the Lizard Princess. That of Queen Sophia had yet to commence, and has yet to end—if indeed, it ever does.

In the Greater and Lesser Libraries of the False Moon, a seeming infinity of books stretched out on an eternity of bookshelves, interrupted here and there by the occasional disused carrel. For no one but myself ever appeared there, and many was the time I could hear muffled laughter and music, and the sound of dancing overhead, from one of the echoing ballrooms where the haute bourgeoisie and royalty of Megalopolis wiled away their time.

I learned many things in that library, many things still so present to me today that, as I drowse, of a hot afternoon, under the Queen's Tree in the Queen's Garden, I can read their words clearly with my mind's eye. I made my discoveries in the most forgotten part of that vast accumulation of knowledge that is the Greater Library of the False Moon, in the dust-covered Children's Section, where no one but me had ventured for years. I was moved by a curiosity to see what had fed these bloodless people I had fallen in with, and a compassion for the child I had the care of. Gilda was hungry for so many human things not easily available on that False Moon, things unacknowledged there as necessary for survival. Affection. The love of animals. The smell of real flowers. And, of course, stories.

Stories I could give Gilda, and I fed her as many as I could remember and imagine. When I ran out of those of my own invention, I took myself to that forgotten nook of the library and brought back armloads of nutrients for the poor child: fairy tales and animal stories, childishly imagined histories and legends of her famous ancestors.

These, I thought foolishly, I read only for the child's benefit. I found more 'serious' stuff for myself, not understanding the different forms that real truth might take.

The books I read were many and weighty, by the finest minds Megalopolis could boast. But there were enormous blind spots in their vision. Men and women were allied in agreement on certain principles…certain values… that were so basic to their thought as to never be questioned.

These thinkers had a rock-solid belief in the inexorable march of Megalopolitan excellence, which allowed no contradictory evidence to get in its way. It was with mixed feelings, to say the least, that I read passing references to the improvement of life for the peasantry who lived on the margins of Megalopolitan society, to the good that had been done, the moral and economic progress, the growth. I knew from Devindra of the tragedy of the Marsh, how it had once been a beautiful valley with a river flowing through it to a sea teeming with fish, until Megalopolis's demand for continual growth dammed the river, poisoned the ocean, and flooded the valley, leaving nothing but the sterile, fetid marsh that my own dear Susan was intent on bringing back to life.

No mention of this in any of the weighty intellectual tomes by the Megapolitan elite. None of the stories of privation, enslavement or exile of the Marsh people were found in any of the books that I queasily devoured. Nothing in the biographies of the scientists who had worked in the massive complexes built on the ruined marshland of the women who gave birth to their unacknowledged children (Tilly Vale! Mother of my own dear Devindra!). No hint of these facts in the arch and curiously light novels representative of the period. Nothing in the cultural treatises of the day, the pontifications about Megalopolis and its inevitable triumphant future.

No. No mention of the Marsh, or of the women and children there who scrabbled for life. No mention of how, when the first faint tremors of the Great Deluge began to emanate from that vast scientific fortress where

187

the Great Earthquake was born, the women and children of the Marsh had known what it meant in their bones, and, grabbing what possessions were at hand, fled into the mountains, right through the heart of the Great City on the very night of my father's ill-fated wedding to Rowena. The women and children who fled past what was then called the Villa in East New York, and what I had known as the Great House, fleeing as they were jeered at by drunken revelers. Devindra had been among those who fled, and my own dear Clare the Rider.

They were joined in their flight by my mother Lily, and my nurse, Kim the Kind. And it was in the winter mountains as they fled that I was born. It was when they were safely in the winter mountains that the Great Deluge overcame the city below.

But in the many books I read that had been written in the run-up to that time, there was not a hint, not a whisper, not a word of the coming of the Great Deluge. In fact, you could, if you looked, reduce the meaning of every one of those books to this simple formula, this bedrock belief about the history of Megalopolis: "Things were bad. Then they got better. Soon they will be perfect."

Wrong, of course. As wrong as a combination of blindness, arrogance, and smugness can be.

Saying this, I condemn my own blindness, arrogance, and smugness, as well.

My grandmother was not backward in convicting me, and all Arcadia, of the same.

"What arrogance!" she said one day in her anger at my resistance to her own point of view. "To say we are close-minded, when it is your tiny Arcadia that closes itself off from the greater world. And not just literally, with your four encircling mountain ranges, but metaphorically, too. Provincial, self-satisfied, inward-looking. How can you call us blind when you can see nothing but a reflection of yourself?"

Her eyes flashed. "We surround you on three sides! And above! We grow out. And yet you have the audacity to accuse us of being frozen, arrogant, destructive. Explain yourself, my girl! Explain yourself!"

She worked herself into a fury now. She drummed her staff heavily on the floor, clutching it till her knuckles gleamed from across the room.

I chose my next words with care.

"I think, Grandmother," I said slowly, "that it is true what you say. We are small. We are local. We are inward-looking. And we do strive to protect ourselves.

"But I reject that we are arrogant. The difference between Arcadia and Megalopolis, in fact, is this: we know that we do not know. More, we know there is much we cannot know.

"That is the burden we carry, as cheerfully as we can. That is the yoke that Megalopolis casts off. What that means is this: we strive to know our limits. And we are anxious only for the greatest amount of happiness for all within those limits. We wish for happiness even for Megalopolis, Grandmother."

"Arrogance," she muttered again. "Sheer arrogance."

"Is it, Grandmother?" I asked. "Then let me ask you this. We in Arcadia, bemused as we are at how you choose to live, never seek to force you to live as we do. But you in Megalopolis never stop trying to force the whole world into your image—by force, if seduction fails.

"Why is this, Grandmother? Surely such restless aggression is the sign of a bad conscience? Could it be that deep down, you doubt that you are right?"

And yet, I know she was right, my grandmother. My somewhat priggish lecture was arrogance. For who was I to lecture Megalopolis and the people who lived and strove there?

For I, as well as they, thought that what I knew, or rather, what I thought I knew, was all there was. I had forgotten any memories that told me otherwise.

On the False Moon, though, they all came back. And I was forced to rebuild my understanding to include those memories, those forgotten stories, to let in all the reality that I could bear.

We Arcadians are fond of saying that our days are filled with so much activity, so much bustle and community life, that these keep us from the most valuable part of ourselves: the spring of our own deep thoughts. It is this spring that refreshes us for the work of our day, and which we consider a precious treasure. And so we value dreams.

Not so in Megalopolis. Not so on the False Moon. There, anything, any time, not concerned with the harsh acquisitiveness and forward movement of the daylight hours was considered time wasted. And as a result, there is no refreshment there in dreams. In Megalopolis, it is considered a sign of weakness to dream.

I never slept well in Megalopolis, far less in the beautiful manmade settings of the False Moon. Not even with Leef beside me. Leef, who had lain peacefully, his head nestled against my arm, during the quiet Time Between the Sleeps, in Arcadia. In Megalopolis, on the False Moon, he was restless, anxious, always alert, never still.

As was I. At first, down below on the Ruined Surface, I had thought my sleeplessness was caused by the poor conditions around me, although I noticed with gratitude that my sleep was sweet and powerful in Susan's small home by the edge of the Marsh. And of course, there was never any real rest in the Great House. Even later, when I found myself housed in a luxury unimaginable to my stolid Arcadian fellows, in the villas of the False Moon, I slept badly, tossing and turning. Was it the lack of fresh air? Some contamination of the soil? The odd distance from the sun? It was none of these things. It was simply this: the place had cut itself off in from everything that makes us human, from the spring from which all our life comes. How could it dream of any reality that would fulfill that life and make it better?

There were other things I to which I was fatally blind. I never noticed until it was too late that there were no living animals on the False

Moon. There were, after all, a plethora of animal simulacra, created by Megalopolitan scientists: squirrels, geese, cats, dogs, even mice. But all of these were experiments rather than living beings. For Megalopolis had discovered that, no matter what care they took, whatever living beings other than humans they transported to the False Moon would sicken with a mysterious wasting illness and die.

"Of course the advantage of all this," my grandmother coolly noted in the time of our talks, after she had discovered the identity of the Lizard Princess behind the costume of the nursery maid, "was that no harmful animals could be brought by accident to the False Moon. This means no plague rats, no poisonous spiders, no germs. Nothing not utterly under the control of man could thrive here, which was a tremendous satisfaction not just to the Council of Four, but to all of us. Imagine! You never have to worry about some large furry bug dropping from the ceiling onto your neck. I for one was thrilled!"

"But," I said, and Grandmother that time raised an admonitory finger, for she had already warned me, laughing, that I began all too many of my sentences with that word. "But," I persisted, "our Arcadian scientists know that the human body contains colonies of bacteria that work in partnership with our body to help us survive. We have never been able to tell what you call 'good' germs from 'bad,' so we tend to leave them all in peace unless some problem arises. How do those animals, small as they are, survive?"

Livia looked at me with distaste, as often happened when I asked a question she was either unwilling to answer…or incapable. "That," she said, dismissing me for that day, "is a great mystery."

I know now it was no mystery to her. She knew that even those bacteria were struggling to survive, because the links between them and the rest of the natural world had been severed by the experiment of bringing everything under the control of man. And I know now that was why Megalopolis was desperate to find the Key. For the Key is what connects us all to All, and whoever holds it can feel the living pulse throughout the many worlds, and feel their own place within it. The Megalopolitan hope was to own the Key and dominate it, as they had dominated so much else, for their own ends. To build a new world in their own way. Why they should wish to do such a thing was beyond me in those days, though now, after years of Aspern Grayling's opposition to everything I regard as reasonable and just, I begin to have an idea.

But I understood none of this then. My blindness was absolute, and I didn't even see the moment when my grandmother, the great Livia, began to take notice of me. She alone of all the self-involved elite of the False Moon had seen Leef, seen that he was a living being, not a simulacrum, and pondered what it meant. She noted my lizard half and began to understand its meaning, too. I had thought myself safe from exposure. I had thought to reveal myself to her in my own time, not hers. There were many human beings with unusual mutations among the domestics of the False Moon, due to the various experiments and industrial accidents of Megalopolis.

Grandmother was not blind to my appearance, and once I caught sight of that, I knew there would be a reckoning soon. I half-dreaded, half-welcomed it. I had been scouting this new world as an anonymous servant, hoping to hear word of Joe, for no one in the upper classes bothered with discretion around those of us they thought beneath contempt.

But there was no word of him, or his doings. He was nowhere on the False Moon. If he had been there, I had missed him.

When did Livia realize her other grandchild, the Lizard Princess, was right there under her nose? Not right away, I'm certain, though later she pretended she had "known all along." It was impossible for Livia to admit to any weakness, and I say that with a certain rueful fondness, for I often see much of my grandmother in me.

Pride and blindness, yes, we have them both, Grandmother and me. They go together. Aspern Grayling shares these traits in full; it's no wonder he admires Livia above all other human beings. The two of them would meet whenever Aspern came to the False Moon with the intention of betraying Arcadia. The two of them walked the beautiful grounds of TreMega around its False Lake, deep in conversation, her white-streaked red head held high, his overlarge skull nodding from between hunched shoulders as he listened intently to her counsel.

I was there all along, there at the little glade that served as a play area for the half-children, tending them as I did every day in my job. But neither Livia nor Aspern paid me any mind. Neither of them saw me. As a servant I was invisible to them.

That invisibility surely saved me those first few months. True, I had the brown skin of my mother, rather than the pale ivory skin of my father and grandmother, but that would not ordinarily have camouflaged me had my grandmother been able to see me not as an object or an appliance, but as a fellow human being. For I have her height, and her strength of build, her unruly crown of red, wiry hair, and her eagle-like beak of a nose. I was her granddaughter all right, to any who had eyes to see it.

She did see it, too. Eventually.

What was it, though, that finally alerted my grandmother that her descendant was actually present before her, privy to her domestic secrets in that way of all slaves, that way fruitlessly denied by all slave owners? What was it that made her look up, wide-eyed, and see me, a result, an intimate result, of her own life, her own choices, her own dreams?

I think it was Leef.

It was a game Leef and I played with Gilda that first alerted my grandmother to who I truly was. The hide and seek game. Leef had taken a liking to the ghostly little girl in my charge, for she had seen him following me and looked at him with longing. Leef found this impossible to resist.

That was Gilda's charm. Unlike the other half-children we knew on the False Moon (and certainly unlike Pavo Vale, Aspern Grayling's half-child on the world below) she seemed, by instinct, to feel her lack. The other half-children were marked by a spurious, and unattractive, feeling of superiority to others around them—to all other beings, in fact, except those in power above them. These children frequently whined over the smallest injury, complained about the slightest discomfort: in short, they were a nightmare for any servant below them in the hierarchy of the False Moon.

Gilda, though, was not like that. And it was her total lack of nasty self-entitlement (for I can call it nothing else) that doomed her. It sometimes happens with these half-children that the half they are missing is the aggressive, narcissistic half, a half we all need to survive. Gilda was one of these unfortunates. She was all yearning love, all gentleness, all sweetness.

Her gentleness and sweetness made us love her. Leef would lie awake at night inventing games for her to play. He had been charmed, the first time she had noticed him: she had looked carefully around to make sure we were not overheard by the playground bullies, and asked me cautiously, "May I pet your doggie?" She knew of "doggies" from the books I had read to her. Although there was no shortage of dog simulacra on the False Moon, she somehow sensed that the "doggies" she heard about in stories were of a different breed. Somehow she sensed that Leef was alive.

Leef was charmed by this recognition, and, bowing invitingly in front of her, let her fondle his head in wonder. Gilda did this timidly at first, as if afraid of what might come of it. But then Leef set his mind to thinking of games for her to play—"the kind of games that will make her strong," was his fond and futile hope.

I entered into these plans enthusiastically. He taught her tag, and hopscotch, and ring around the rosy—all games she was delighted to play with Leef and me, away from the jeers of her fellow half-children, who would have called her "babyish," their ultimate insult.

But it was hide and seek that she liked the best.

My fault that we were caught out, of course. The best place for us to play this game was in a little walled garden right beneath the window of Livia's sitting room. A charming place, that garden, even in its extreme artificiality. In fact, I think that was its charm. It was my grandmother's own conceit, and it made no pretense at imitating nature. Unlike the rest of the inventions of the False Moon.

In Livia's Garden, trees were made of ebony and emeralds. Enormous flower bushes made of velvet and satin were imbued with exquisitely scented perfumes. The grass was a soft carpet of cunningly mingled shades of gold and green. The benches were ivory. The fruit hanging from the polished limbs of the trees were of ruby, amethyst, and topaz.

It should have been vulgar. It should have been coarse and gross like so much else on the False Moon. But my grandmother's fine taste had made it a thing of such original beauty that even I, who was born with an instinctive dislike of the artificial, found pleasure and solace when I walked there.

Gilda loved it. Color trickled into her pale cheeks the moment we opened the door (made of old silver and lace) and shut it romantically behind us. It was our private domain (for I, as a privileged servant and caregiver to the children, held the little brass key), and Gilda felt safe there.

There were so many hiding places among the folds of soft fabric and the shimmering curtains of fine metals in Grandmother's Garden! Gilda and I would hold hands over each other's eyes and count to ten while Leef found somewhere to hide. Then, with a timid squeal of delight, Gilda would begin her hunt. I pretended to hunt as well, finding real pleasure in watching her search. She would run from a sleek brown-black tree to a fall of sapphire that imitated a brook, peering under corduroy rocks and parting velveteen bushes, until—oh, joy!—she discovered Leef nestling there. Their happiness at the mutual discovery was a delight to see, and the three of us would laugh, embracing each other and rolling on the warm, soft, velvet grass.

I was laughing while hugging Gilda in one arm, and Leef in the other, lying on my back under a ruby and jade pomegranate tree, when I saw Livia in the window looking down at us. Something in the way she looked stopped my laughter. I hurriedly stood, brushed off my clothes, and, scooping Leef and Gilda up, let us all out of the garden.

But Leef, creeping onto my shoulder, looked backward. When I cast a worried look behind me, I saw his eyes had met Livia's. And held them. She knew then that he was no simulacrum, that he was a living being. And

I braced myself for the call that I knew would shortly come, bathing Gilda and putting her to bed with a silent kiss. Leaving Leef curled up under her hand, I was ready when the servant appeared with the inevitable summons.

Part XI: LIVIA

The servant ushered me into her rooms, and backed out bowing. He was afraid of her. Everyone was afraid of her.

She stood there, ramrod straight, staring at me. She closed her eyes briefly, as if remembering something or someone, then, opening them, stared again.

"Sit down," she said.

"I'd rather stand."

"Hmph," she said. And then, "Where's the rat?"

"He's a lemur."

"Rat, lemur," she shrugged. "What's the difference? The point it, he's alive."

"Yes."

"She had one, too, you know. Did you know that? An animal... companion. A dog. He was gone before you were born, of course. He looked at me one night the same way as this one did just now."

I was silent at that. It didn't seem to call for a response.

"She was your mother, wasn't she? Lily, I mean."

I was still. She looked at me more reflectively now.

"Yes, I see it. You have my height, my hair, my beak of a nose. But her coloring. Brown. She was very brown. Not like the other one."

By which she must have meant Rowena.

"But those feet!" she said, pointing. "Those never came from our side of the family." Here she gave a snort of laughter.

I answered this, though I was pretty sure by now that she knew more about it than I did.

"A curse," I suggested.

She gave a sharp laugh again. "A curse!" she said. "Fine curse that sets you on your true way. We should all be so lucky to be so cursed." She sat on the open-backed bench set against the window, and grasped one of the dragon's head armrests with both hands, leaning back against the glass.

"I do wish you would sit down," she complained.

This time I obeyed, sitting on a turquoise velvet hassock at her feet, looking up at her.

"Wasn't it a curse?" I asked, intensely interested now.

"A curse, Missy, comes from those who hate you and wish you ill. Your…er…costume for let's not call it deformity, shall we?…has all the signs of being the work of someone who cared very much what would happen to you."

I thought of Will the Murderer, who has become, since the time of the Lizard Princess, Wilder the Bard, the historian of Arcadia, and I knew she was right. Will would never wish me harm.

But here was the mystery: what gift had he intended?

"If you want a good curse, my girl, you come to me." She gave another one of her short laughs.

"Do you hate me then?" I asked, more curious than frightened.

She shrugged. "Hate, love…it's all the same to me. I left those opposites behind me long ago. There is only one opposition left to me, Missy. Only one goal."

In spite of my silent vow to myself before I entered her rooms that nothing she said or did would frighten me, this made me catch my breath. For I knew what she meant. And it quite rightly frightened me.

She watched closely, and gave a small nod of satisfaction. "And what is that goal? Drat it, I've forgotten your name. What did she call you, that mother of yours?"

"Sophia."

"Ah yes. Princess Sophia of Arcadia. Known throughout the universes by her secret name: Snow."

Now I did shiver in earnest. What did she mean, my "secret name"? What did she mean, "known throughout the universes"? And how had she known that childish nickname of mine?

"Don't look like that. I knew far more than anyone ever takes me for— more important, I remember far more. But tell me: what is your guess? What is my goal?"

I was silent again, struggling with my own terror at the enormity of the answer that came to me, like a bubble rising up from the depths.

"The One. You are in opposition to the One." I looked around myself in horror lest someone else had heard.

Her cracked marble blue eyes shot sparks of satisfaction, and her thin mouth (so like my father's, so unlike the generously crooked one of Joe's, or the wide one of my mother's, the mouth I have inherited) gave a tight little smile.

"That's right," she said. "Your grandmother, my dear, is not just a common witch. She is the Devil himself. How does that strike you, eh?"

I couldn't answer. It had come too suddenly, this truth, like a jolt of a too strong drug injected into my innocent system, like a lightning bolt that struck the top of my head. It wasn't as if I fainted, more as if all the nerves in my human and lizard bodies went into overload with the terrifying information.

I must have toppled over onto the floor. All I remember about the end of that first meeting is a flash of light, like an illumination from within, blinding me. For a while after that, I knew nothing more.

It wasn't fear that made me faint. No, even though my grandmother is, it's true, a most fearsome being. It wasn't terror. It was an electric surge of recognition that simply overloaded my body, causing it to collapse, focusing all its energy inward to parse the information received.

What information? That part of my ancestry was the Devil. And not just mine alone. But Joe's as well.

We don't really have a strong tradition of the Devil in Arcadia. By which I mean, an idea of a Being that exists solely for evil and destructive purposes, hating humankind, hating the One from which everything is continuously born. Our beliefs are milder, softer. Tragedy is a fact of life to us, something to be mourned; it is not the sign of Evil in the universe. Death is powerful, but she is not our enemy. We are frightened of her, but we recognize, in our everyday lives and in our communal gatherings, that our fear is only our own weakness, our own partial blindness.

In Arcadia, the Devil would not be thought identical with Death. These are separate entities. The Devil in Arcadian theology tends to be a figure of fun. Children dress up in silly costumes representing him on our festival of The Devas, which celebrates the nature spirits who act in partnership with us to bring the harvest. This festival, one of my favorites, takes place on the first full moon after the autumn equinox, when the first chill of winter reminds us to be merry, and to gather up what we can for winter.

Even then, though, the Devil is not regarded as a cause of crop blight, or livestock death, or difficulties in life of any kind. These are part and parcel of our year; we do our best to allow for them and to make sure that they don't fall disproportionately on one family or another. No, the Devil, in Arcadia, is an almost forgotten bogey used to frighten children. Though he doesn't frighten them. And this is a fatal Arcadian flaw.

For I know he should. He should frighten them very much, children and adults.

In Arcadia, we don't accept that Evil exists, and this is our blindness, our own form of arrogance and vanity. Evil, to an Arcadian, is simply the absence of Good. But I know that this is wrong, even cowardly, a denial of an enormous fact of the universes. Our denial labels us as children still, even though we think of ourselves as adults, for it is similar to the way a child thinks hiding her head in the bedclothes will change a danger that threatens her from without.

In Megalopolis, things are differently arranged. I will not say better arranged—my own opinion is that they could hardly be worse. Still, there are things we Arcadians could learn from that great empire.

In Megalopolis, Death is the enemy. Even more than the Devil…at least, when she is separated from him in the Megalopolitan mind. More often, though, Death is confused there with Evil, and much valuable energy is wasted in futile battles with her in this guise. To Arcadians, this is as if you were to attack a country potentially your ally, mistaking its strength for enmity, while your true enemy, pretending to be your friend, wreaks havoc from within.

Nevertheless, while the Megalopolitan image of Death is, in the Arcadian view, not just wrong, but potentially ruinous, its concept of a principle of active Evil opposed to active Good is one we can learn from. As long as we learn creatively. Only if we can transform the symbol into another larger, more generous one.

As for the symbol of the Devil, it was embodied here in the form of my grandmother. I found it particularly horrible that the Devil should have taken the form of a woman. To have the Devil now appear as one of my own sex, let alone my ancestress, was awful. That she was a woman and my own grandmother!

But what were the possibilities for women in Megalopolis? I thought of poor Rowena, her character as constricted as her bound waist and feet. The servants, the slaves. The preyed-upon girls of the Ruined Surface. Susan, my noble Susan, patiently, step by difficult step, trying to find another way.

Livia triumphing, isolated, over all.

"When you tell people your lies," I said wonderingly in one of those dialogues—those duels—we had after that first meeting, "how can you be sure they will believe them?" For she had lectured me that evening on a ruler's duties. The main obligation, she said, of a ruler to the ruled is to tell them the lies that will make it easier to rule.

Grandmother looked at me sideways with malicious smugness, and sipped at her tea. She seemed to be waiting for me to say more, but I had already learned that to blunder into one of Grandmother's silences was to admit weakness. After a while, a brief shadow of annoyance crossed her face, and she said, "You're missing one piece."

I looked my question rather than asked it, and at that she laughed straight out as if acknowledging a hit. And I must say that Livia, my grandmother, was fearfully engaging in those moments where she seemed to float above the rest of us, buoyed by her lighthearted, malicious charm.

She threw up her hands and laughed, as if to say, "You've won that battle, Granddaughter, well done!" And she said reflectively, "A person, a people, a country, a world will believe any lie you tell them, under one condition."

I arched an eyebrow in inquiry, but by now I knew what was coming. So when she arched her eyebrow to match mine, I threw up my hands in mock defeat, and said, "I know. You can tell any lie and have it believed if the person…the people…the country…the world you tell the lie to want to believe it's true."

Livia beamed at me. "You are much more like me than you know," she said confidingly. "Your father could never have reached that kind of subtlety on his own."

"And my mother?"

"Ah. Lily. (Did you know she wasn't always Lily? No? Well, we'll hold that story for another time.) No, your mother was too good, too true…too good to be true, if you like…to imagine an answer such as the one you've given. No, your mother believed in absolute innocence; that was her flaw. She had come from a place that believed in absolute guilt, and so she rejected that and went too far in the opposing direction. For Lily herself was not as innocent as she believed."

At this, Grandmother stood up and stretched, rubbing her lower back, looking out of the star window, for we talked, this evening, in the inner chamber of her rooms, where no one else was allowed. This was the only window I had seen on the whole of the False Moon that looked out onto the unimproved lands, the desolate reality, and past that, to the star-ridden sky, that a viewer inevitably yearned toward, past the nullity of the landscape beyond the False Front of the False Moon. From here there was a view of the Moon Itself, shining across the faint sight of a strange silvery gleam. And the view beyond the Moon Itself was such as you could have nowhere else on the False Moon. Of the universe stretching out into eternity, of stars near and far, of comets streaking, worlds dying thousands of years before we were able to see their light.

Livia claimed dominion over it all. But I...I was not so sure.

She looked out toward the bright bursts of light in the dark sky. "You see those stars, Sophy?" I went and stood beside her, and she put her arm around my waist. I didn't resist—she was my grandmother, after all, even if she was also the Devil Himself. I had known her long enough to know there was much truth in what she said. I was indeed like her. More like her, I was forced to admit, than like my beautiful, idealistic mother, or my feckless, charming and affectionate father.

"I see those stars, Grandmother," I said, and I put my arms affectionately around her thin waist in return.

"Your mother could only see those stars. Lily couldn't see the darkness they rose out of. She couldn't see they would have no light without the darkness behind them."

I nodded, for I saw the truth in what she said.

I know now that it was a half-truth, but this has taken me a lifetime to discover. The other half is this: if the entirety of the sky were flooded with light, there would be no need for the stars to shine. But this is not a young woman's thought.

"Everything is a partnership, Sophy," my grandmother said thoughtfully, and I started in amazement to hear it—this sentence I had heard so often from my mother, and from Devindra, too. "The partnership of woman and man, of truth and fiction, of the darkness and the stars."

But then she went on. "Most people are too dull, too stupid, too ignorant to understand this. The universe as it truly is, that is beyond them, and will be beyond them to the end of time."

At this her face darkened, and her eyes shone like angry stars. "That is what She will never understand. She believes a creature as contemptible as man can raise his consciousness up to where he sees reality as it really is."

I didn't have to ask who Livia meant by "She." I knew this inadequate word was meant to encompass the One, who is neither "He" nor "She," but both, in an eternal dance that we, so blind, can only see one half of at a time.

"You can't lie to them about just anything," Grandmother said absently, returning to her original topic. "It has to be something the fools want to believe. But if you stick to that—to lies they wish were true—you can make people do just about anything you want."

"What if what I want, Grandmother," I said softly, "is that the others should work with me to understand the truth of things? And working together, to learn how to restore the world to the garden I believe that it once was."

I took my arm from her waist and reached out to touch the star window's glass.

Livia looked at me, eyes narrowing, and gave her magnificent head a toss. "What do you think, Granddaughter?" she said, her voice harshly contemptuous. "Do you think the little fools you live among could ever achieve such a...," here she sneered, "lofty goal?"

"I think that we have no deep desire that cannot, after many lifetimes, be fulfilled. And my deepest desire, Grandmother, is this...." Here I took a deep breath, for I knew what the inevitable response would be. "My wish is for the world to be the garden it can be. Not as it was (and I don't know what it was, if it ever was such a thing), but the garden it could be, tended by ourselves fully conscious of our methods and our goals."

She stared at me then, and the malignant cloud that had been gathering around her as I spoke flowed into her eyes. I knew she hated me in that moment (and what a thing to be hated by the Devil!), she who had been so proud of me a few moments before. I shuddered, but then defiance straightened my back. Was I not the Lizard Princess, whose warm blood mingled with cold?

"And what goal is that, granddaughter?" she said dryly.

"Joy."

At this, I heard a timid scratching at the door, and I went and opened it. Leef scampered in. I bent down and he swarmed up my arm, staring with his round eyes at Livia, who he had always seen more clearly than I.

"Joy," she spat contemptuously. "What a stupid, piddling goal for a granddaughter of mine to have."

She turned on her heel and stalked to the opposite side of the room, where a wall lay curtained. She pulled the shade, and revealed the False Moon's False Front—that sterile, airless pleasure ground with its inhabitants grimly giving themselves up to lifeless pleasures.

"Joy," she repeated with a kind of glittering relish. "You think any of those"—she pointed as she spat the word—"understand the first part of what you mean by that word?"

We stood and looked out at the doomed landscape, at the laughter on faces that was nothing but a contorted imitation of the real thing, at the misplaced gestures meant to indicate enjoyment, at the artificial aids set to mimic a fool's idea of a 'good time.'

The three of us watched all this in silence, a silence like a challenge from the universe itself to the three of us: Livia. Leef. And the Lizard Princess.

"Well, granddaughter?" Livia said, and her tone was a threat.

Leef cried out in distress.

"Joy," I said firmly. "Life that knows Death. Death that follows Life. Seasons felt in depth. Changes flowing in and out again. Joy."

And Leef spoke now in his small, squeaky, determined voice, "Who can tell the dancer from the dance?" he said quietly, and I knew by the strangeness of his tone that he quoted poetry from another world.

"If this is so," Livia said dreadfully. "Then we are enemies, you and I."

"No, Grandmother," I said firmly, for I knew I spoke the truth. "Not enemies. Friends. Partners. Family."

But she shook her head, her eyes bleary, her shoulders stooped, and she said, "No. Not as long as your heart is set on a fool's project."

I didn't give up. "Really, is that what you want, Grandmother? Do we have to be enemies?" I ignored the frightened cheeps of Leef, who clearly thought me wrong to give her the last word in this argument.

Maybe I was wrong. But I wanted to be sure. I wanted to know that I'd left no tactic untried. This was my arrogance, my vanity. It amuses me to think of it now: that in my youth, as the Lizard Princess, I thought it possible for me to bring joy into the world. For this is not something that can be done by a single hero, or even a string of heroes, one after the other. This is only something that can be done by the heartfelt wish of every human being. In a world so often mean, ignorant, and heartless, how is this to be achieved? Maybe the most that can be achieved is for those who love joy to practice it, in and out of season. And maybe that was why I insisted on reaching out now to my grandmother…my family.

She looked at me with a rapidly aging ferocity—this change to her features from a collected elegance to malevolent decrepitude was perhaps the most frightening sight I had experienced on the surface of the False Moon.

I looked at her, and my fright dissolved, and transformed into a kind of pity. How lonely for grandmother, I thought, in a sudden rush of true feeling. That she would push her own granddaughter away—the only person, perhaps, in the immensity of the universe, to understand what she had to say. What she was.

It was that pity I felt for her that changed everything. But not at first.

She whispered, "Yes. It must be so."

I let her have the last word, then. And I turned, Leef clinging to my shoulder, and walked out the door. As I went, I heard her hiss behind me, "Enemiessss...enemies...sssssss...."

Frantic, in my ear, Leef said, "Don't turn around."

But I had no need to turn to get one last glimpse, that first evening we spent together as grandmother and granddaughter (for despite what we both thought, there were to be many more). There was a mirror on the other side of the door, and in that mirror I could see Livia transform into an enormous, coiling, emerald-green snake.

"I come by my heritage honestly," I said to Leef as we walked down the corridor. My heart was strangely lightened, my step firm, and it seemed to me that many things that had been obscure would become clear to me now.

Livia was not only my enemy. We were kin, she and I.

She was my grandmother. In this form, and who knew in how many others? When we met again, in the false daylight of the False Moon, she saw I understood this, and I saw, by the intelligent cruelty of her eye, that she understood it too.

No one else could pierce that understanding, that bond between us. No one else could see what we could see in each other: we two, the Snake Queen and the Lizard Princess.

This bond was a comfort, not a menace. I was no longer alone. Even with Joe I had felt a barrier, over which he could not see clearly into my soul.

But with Grandmother there was no such barrier. Like called to like, whether she and I liked it or not. I could see she was everything I hated and had been taught to hate: she was power-mad, the world to her was an object only fit for her manipulation. I could see she would shrink from no cruelty, no torture, no separation of mother from child, no misbegotten act, from nothing in order to have her own way. She was everything I had learned not to be.

And yet, in that realization, I felt neither afraid nor horrified.

No. To my surprise, I felt nothing but exhilaration. Now I knew from where had come my lizard half. It was an honorable descent. For the first time since that fatal moment back in my childish home in Arcadia (how far away! how long ago it seemed!), that moment when I had let Will the Murderer win a game I should have won myself in fair play, I felt at peace. More peaceful, even, than I had felt with Joe in the Enchanted Wood and the Bower of Bliss. More than with Susan by the Marsh.

As with Joe and with Susan, now with Livia I knew, in my heart, that my time on the False Moon was running out.

I looked thoughtfully at her when we met as she walked with the Council of Four around the False Lake, conferring on the policies of state, while I shepherded my brood of half-children in the other direction. She looked back, with a sharp, unblinking eye.

I laughed out loud.

"Who was that?" one of the Council said in a high-pitched voice. Livia said something in a low tone, and called to a servant, who followed me and the children until we came to the small play area, where he quietly told me that Livia hoped to see me in her rooms that night. I nodded. For now that I knew it was time for me to move on, I would strangely cherish those moments we spent together: she haranguing me; my taking in all that she had to give me, Devil or no.

A profound difficulty now confronted me. As Grandmother became more and more open about the intense interest she felt in the obscure marshland nanny, I watched my image change in the eyes of those around me. When I was nothing but a shadow, a simulacrum (and Leef along with me), whose only function was to serve, no one noticed me. But it was plain to everyone around me that Grandmother, she who scorned the highest of the high, she who had the Council of Four at her beck and call, had taken an interest in me. The walks we took together in the Jeweled Garden, her arm resting on mine; the questions she asked intently, attending to my answers—all of this was observed by her inferiors.

This was very dangerous. It is far more dangerous to be an object of envy, as I was fast becoming, than to be one of scorn.

My time was running out there on the False Moon. I had wasted time. I hadn't found word of either Joe or the Key, though I tried to coax news of them both out of Livia.

"Where is Joe, do you know?" I asked one evening in a casual voice. For to show how much I cared about the answer more would have been to give her another hold on me.

She looked at me craftily and took another sip of tea.

"Joe? Hhmmm. Let's see. Of course he's your brother, you'll want to meet him, won't you? I'm afraid he's not here. He never liked the False Moon, more fool him. I believe he's off on a quest." She gave me a long, satirical stare. "I believe he has gone in search of the Key." This was said blandly. It was the first mention of the Key between us.

I wasn't fooled by her tone. And I told her so.

Her face darkened and her open hand clenched slowly shut. "Don't be impertinent, Missy." She said, in a voice of forced casualness that told me more about its importance than anything else might have, "We need it of course."

"Why?" I asked, and she looked annoyed.

"For our survival," she snapped. "If you must know." And with that, she rang for one of her frightened servants to escort me back to my room. She refused to say anything more that night.

But she had said more than she meant to. And in my anxiety about the time I saw slipping away from me there on the False Moon, so had I. Our meetings had shaken us, the affection we grudgingly felt for each other, and a bridge of feeling sprang up between us. I felt...open to her. She was my grandmother. I came from the same river as she. Her traits, her fate, flowed into mine.

Because I was open to her, I now realize at the start of my own old age, I flowed back into her as well. And this was to have strange repercussions later on.

I was a mass of inchoate feeling, conflicted and confused. Who was I? Who did I love? What was I meant to do? I know now that when this happens—when one day you know quite plainly who you are and what you are meant for, and then it hides itself away again—this means you are on the verge of another discovery that will send you plunging on to your goal.

I said good night to Livia. She made no attempt to embrace me, which was strange, for it had become our custom to put our arms stiffly around each other in greeting and in parting. She stood there, leaning on her ebony cane, her back to the vast window that framed the stars outside the False Moon, her eyes gleaming in the dark.

Neither of us, having acknowledged each other, would ever be the same again. For that is the way of it when you open yourself to someone and they to you. The boundaries shift, the river changes course, the familiar landscape disappears and returns in a new form.

We were connected. It was the image of the Key that, rising up between us, brought us together again.

With Leef curled up against my arm, I lay, that night, open-eyed, feeling I would never sleep again, electrified as I was by the connection. It was in this state that I passed into the kind of sleep where the sleeper falsely believes herself to be wide awake.

I dreamed. They were dreams of real places, with real friends and enemies, even if unknown to me in waking life. I dreamed—it was as if I were there, but wrapped in a cloud of unknowing, so that all outlines were blurred, and all sound muted.

It was a desert I stood in, in that dream. A parched, howling place, where some horrible deed had recently taken place, some massacre of innocents. There was a feeling of dread all around me, but mingled with an opposing feeling of strong determination that the fear be met. My body felt heavy, my arms reached to the ground, and one of them tapped at it, pushing dust away in a cloud. There was a heaviness between my eyes.

Livia was there. Livia—but, at the same time, not Livia at all. Livia in another guise, in the form of a young man, beautiful, arrogant, angry. With her same blue eyes.

Lily, my mother, was there, but a younger Lily than I had known, a girl. Like me, not yet a queen.

A voice said, "Father of Lies, Father of Lies from the beginning." I knew that voice, but from where? It was the voice of the Centaur, and I tried to turn my head to greet him—something odd about my neck making the maneuver difficult—but the speaker stepped forward, and I saw, not the Centaur, but, of all things, a silly plush-stuffed bear.

Then I heard myself say this:

"There have been times when the Weak have conquered the Strong, oh Prince! There have been many such times." I grabbed at the ground again with one hand, and something glittered there, as if all my fingers had fused and turned to silver. Like hooves. As if my hands were silver hooves.

I must have cried out in my sleep, for Leef, weak as he was—for he had been weakening steadily there on the False Moon—tapped me gently on the chest till I woke. When he saw he'd woken me, he looked into my eyes by the light of the full Moon Itself, then curled gently up against my shoulder and fell back to sleep himself.

As for me, I lay awake till the False Dawn, pondering my dream.

It was only later that day I realized why it was familiar, when I read to Gilda from a children's book I had found in the library. The one that was her favorite.

I had discovered it originally in the dustiest reaches of the children's library, a silly tale of an ugly, snotty little boy. It looked unpromising, but nevertheless I brought it, in a stack of others, back to the nursery to let

Gilda choose. To my surprise, out of all the other books, she lit upon that one. It was leather and gilt bound, the gold tarnished, the leather torn.

It was her favorite book. She had come to know it by heart. "Snotty Saves the Day." Horrible title, I thought, but Gilda was entranced by it, by Snotty's falling down a rabbit hole, by his meeting with the pony—the unicorn, rather!—named Snowflake, his demi-god status with an army of Gnomes, his capture by a Teddy Bear Army, his discovery of who he truly was.

I found this last the only truly moving portion of what otherwise seemed a fairly childish book. Snotty (how I hated that name) discovers who he truly is…and that discovery changes his world.

I would read, watching Gilda for the first signs of drowsiness; once she had fallen into peaceful sleep, I would quietly close the book and steal away. I sometimes caught Leef looking at me sharply from behind his hooded eyes, which had lately, to my great worry, begun to film and darken. Seeing my look, he would turn away and pretend to busy himself: performing a somersault, which he found harder and harder to do as time went on, or eating an apple, which he did with less and less relish.

During one evening's bedtime story, as I droned through the familiar part where Snotty realizes he has always been, not a snotty little boy, but a loving little girl, something tugged furiously at me. Gilda had by now fallen softly asleep, and my own voice slowed as I read aloud, "Snotty cried. She cried and cried. Sobs poured out of her. Her face twisted and quivered, and her nose ran with snot. She choked. She gagged. And still…" My voice faltered. I looked up. Leef, weaker than he had been that morning, stared at me, unblinking.

I started the sentence anew. I could feel him willing it.

"And still Lily cried."

I shut the book and stared back at my lemur. "My mother," I murmured. Closing his eyes as if with relief from some long held pain, he nodded.

I looked down at the book in my hands and knew, in a flash, that I held my mother's very history. More. My own.

212

"My mother," I said again softly. And after a moment, Leef opened his eyes and said, in his quiet way, "Yes, Snow."

Snow. I was Snow. And Star, the angel....

I looked back at the page. Snotty realizes who he is while holding the Key, it said. The Key! Why had I never noticed the Key in this story before? What did it mean?

It rushed on me suddenly, overwhelming, a whole new world, a whole new system, a whole new way of seeing. I put the book down, bent over Gilda, brushing her hair out of her closed eyes, kissing her forehead, and then, leaving the fairy tale behind, I lifted the weak, tired Leef onto my shoulder, my mind a roar of confusion, my legs buckling beneath me.

I went back to my own room, barely able to walk, and collapsed on the bed, immediately falling asleep like one exhausted, or drugged, or deathly ill.

And dreamed again.

This time, I was a unicorn battling a dragon. The dragon, triumphant, took off my horn with a slash of its claw. I screamed in agony, and the dragon's eyes gleamed in triumph, and its eyes were the eyes of my grandmother. Of Livia.

I heard her voice in my sleep.

"What you need to understand, Sophia, is that your strength comes from me. Not from your mother. What energies you need, they are mine to give."

I was no longer a unicorn with a dragon. I was myself again, swimming in a river of sleep, clutching at her words.

The more she spoke, the larger her words became, and the smaller the room, as I drifted along the tide of sleep. No swimming away, I told myself, groggy, bemused. No swimming away.

"You are me, Sophia, little as you might like it. Your goals are twined with mine. And your—our—children will inherit. Not just the earth, Sophia. But the Moon and the Stars and the Sun itself."

How did I have the power to withstand her, my grandmother? Somehow I did. Somehow what she said made me hook my arms stubbornly around a passing tree trunk as I drifted down the stream of sleep, drifting on her words. I hung on for dear life and let the words drift by.

"No," I said sleepily. "No."

With that, I pulled myself out of the rushing, seemingly inevitable, stream of her words, panting, onto the dream beneath the tree that had saved me. I gazed up at it. It was green and lively, although beautifully gnarled, and hanging heavily from its branches were apples shining golden in the sun. In gratitude, I sank deeper into that sleep where I was vividly aware of just two things: my grandmother told the truth in telling a lie, and I had taken that lie, and changed it into a new truth. By virtue of the tree and my dream,

As I lay there, one of the apples ripened and fell—plop—into my right hand. I grasped it. Pulled my arm heavily up, lifting it laboriously to my mouth, and took one crisp, juice-filled bite. I swallowed. Smiled. And tasting it, I knew who I was.

And recognized in a children's story the history of my much-loved land.

A unicorn's history that was my own. A snotty little boy's history that was the story of my own dear mother. A story of her discovery of who she truly was, of her transformation, and, through that, of the transformation of a part of Megalopolis into Arcadia.

And beyond that?

At that, my arm fell back and I fell even deeper into the world of dreams, as if into an endless hole, and when I woke, the whole world—all the worlds—had changed for me. And would never be the same again.

When I woke up, I saw more clearly than before. And what I saw was this: that Leef was dying.

Part XII: THE MOON ITSELF

I write this sitting under the Queen's Tree in autumn. A leaf falls on the page, and I look up at my companion, that green tree that gives the golden fruit we call the Queen's Apples, and I smile, reaching out to lightly touch its trunk.

If it weren't for the comfort and companionship of that tree, it would be too difficult to speak now of Leef. How I miss him, my dearest friend in a lifetime that has been blessed with many a dear friend, so many of whom had passed away into the river of time. Of all those I have known, it was Leef, the lemur, who saw me the clearest and who, I believe, loved me the best.

And I loved him.

It was that love that helped him survive as long as he did on the False Moon. I discovered later—too late! too late!—that the reason living animals from our world could not survive in its atmosphere was simply this: on our world there exists an intimate and complex web of connection, an invisible root system that covers all the planet, connecting every living thing upon it, not only to each other, but to the dead in the past and the unborn in the future.

Megalopolitan scientists deny the existence of this web. More than deny it. Read their papers on the subject—Aspern Grayling is always insisting

I do so, so I'm well familiar with their thinking. Through all their narrow arguments there squeaks an unmistakable cry of anguish: if such a web exists, surely our entanglement in it means that we are unfree? That we can never escape our bonds? That we can never, ever, transcend Death?

And it's true: we cannot. Our Arcadian scientists have discovered that truth. Artists of both lands have, of course, understood this from the start of time. As has anyone who has ever touched the Key.

But without this web of connection, animals brought to the False Moon from the world below could not live. Without this series of veins through which we all receive the nourishment from our world appropriate to our natures, they faded and died.

Humans had this trouble as well, even if it went unidentified, for the insistence that it was impossible made it all the more impossible to see. But it was not so extreme with us. It was human will that had brought us all to the False Moon, and this shared goal, this common, fiercely held belief, tied us all together, giving us just enough nourishment to hang on.

Not all, though. Megalopolitan scientists were well aware that there was a peculiar wasting disease that quickly struck certain temperaments—usually those inward-looking souls who delighted in ideas and creative works of all kinds. Painters did not thrive on the False Moon. Poets—the few who ventured there (for most were too impoverished to even attempt the journey without a patronage that rendered their poetry mute)—died almost immediately. Sculptors and architects did slightly better.

They called this the Fading Sickness. Eventually, it was seen, it would affect all who lived on the False Moon. And the Key was seen as the antidote to this. Hence its importance to their world.

As for me, I never felt well on the False Moon. Unfamiliar aches and pains, an occasional gasping for a clear breath that never came, the only stabbing headaches I have ever experienced before or since…these became such an everyday reality that I soon forgot what real health felt like.

Leef also suffered, and far, far more. I know now it was our connection that kept us both in what health we had, and I see why Livia and the

216

Council of Four were convinced the Key would save them all—that Key which embodies the connection of all that Is. What feeling Leef and I had for each other was a version in miniature of the whole feeling held in the Key, as a matchlight is a version, in miniature, of the Sun itself. That feeling danced back and forth between us like a strong flame…though without a fire from which to renew itself, that flame flickered, dimmed, and eventually died.

It happened so quickly. (But when is the end of any great friendship as slow as we might wish it to be?) I was taken unawares. Leef was quiet about his sufferings until it was too late, and yet, what could I have done if I had known? Once there, on the Phony Moon, we had no way back: servants who came there were never allowed, by order of the Council of Four, to return home, lest they tell the world below of the secrets held above.

So when Leef sickened, his eyes silently conveyed the awful truth: that he was moving away from me quickly, and no matter how desperately I reached, I could not hold him back and keep him with me.

We saw this, and, two prisoners, despaired.

It was when Leef was dying that I understood that I had to flee my grandmother and the False Moon, in whatever way I could. Unbearable as was the thought of my dear friend leaving me forever (was it truly forever?), more painful still was the knowledge that on the False Moon he would be treated after death as an object: disposable, outworn, useless.

He looked at me, his eyes dimming, his once beautiful gray-brown fur matted and patchy, a slight painful pant causing his sides to heave and subside. Here on the False Moon, he would be tossed aside like trash, for where could I bury him? There was no depth, no compost, no layers of the past where he could be laid to rest. There could be no funeral pyre to release his body back to the sky, for there was no real fire allowed on the Phony Moon.

"Don't worry," Leef whispered. "Don't worry, dear, dear Sophy."

I was frantic. Frantic with distress at my helplessness, at the clumsy ineptitude of my lizard feet, at my complete inability to find a way out. It was, in my bleak imagining, as if I confronted an enormous gray stone wall, towering and smooth, through which I knew we must pass in order to be saved, but on which could be seen no hint of a door: no seam, no latch, no keyhole.

Leef's eyes grew dimmer by the hour. I held him, helpless, in my arms, and, stroking his pelt, murmured useless, inarticulate sounds of comfort. I looked with aimless unseeing eyes out the grimy window of my room. I paced through endless corridors, holding him, instinctively keeping on the move, to stave off the final rest.

I found myself walking the corridors outside Livia's rooms. I was allowed; the servants had seen me often enough there. They left me to myself. I frightened them, I with my lizard feet and the prestige of my grandmother's regard for me. I gazed out the round windows, coming upon the one next to my grandmother's rooms.

That was when I saw it. That flash of silver to the left, toward the unseen Moon Itself.

The evening packet must have landed and sent a particle of reflective light down, slantwise, to shine for a brief moment off a bridge that was not supposed to be there.

Driven by an unnamed instinct, I stood as tall as I could, carefully cradling Leef in my arms as he began to cheep faintly. I stood and stared and saw the silver gleam broaden and resolve into a shape.

The shape of a bridge. A silver bridge.

In that dim light, I could see it was the silver bridge that led to the Moon Itself.

What fear I felt spurred me on rather than trapping me there. For the fear of Leef dying on the False Moon was greater than any fear I might have of the unknown. There was a bridge, it led away, we would flee across it, we would take our chances on what we would find on the other side. We would take our chances on the Moon Itself, that Moon that had always been our friend from afar.

When we walked across that Silver Bridge, sparks flew from the connection still between Leef and me, there on that wild and cold crossing. We swayed on that Bridge between the False and the Real, and what fear I had helped rather than hindered our flight. We needed that aid, for the crossing was difficult. No one had ventured it in ages, and the flooring fell beneath our feet into the vastness of the space below.

I tried not to look down and stepped as quickly as I dared.

We climbed up the Silver Bridge, and the stars hung heavily about us, some shooting past, falling into the depths of the sky. And the world lay below—our beautiful world that had been ruined by not just the arrogance of Megalopolis, but by Arcadia's blindness as well, so that only a tiny portion remained unscathed—a world iron-colored, iron and bronze, but pure white to the north…. Leef and I stopped a moment, catching hold of the silver railing of the swaying bridge. We gazed down to see our dear Arcadia, green and deep blue and loamy brown, with pure white snow atop the peaks of the sacred Donatees.

My heart rose up in me. Arcadia glowed with the colors of earth: dark red and green-blue and silver and the gold of harvest. "Home," I thought, and Leef, weak as he was, echoed the thought in my ear. "Home," he breathed.

As far away from home as we were, there on the Silver Bridge to the Moon Itself, it felt close enough to touch. On a wave of that feeling, as if it picked us up gently and rolled us to a safer shore, Leef and I hurried across the Silver Bridge to the Moon Itself.

Did I wonder why there were no more crossings from the False Moon to the Moon Itself in my day? For I knew my mother had made the same crossing before me. It had been a favorite story of my childhood. It was only later that Devindra told me that crossing had been led by Livia, when she and the Council of Four meant to force my mother to find them the Key. I had never thought of that before. Livia certainly never mentioned the Moon Itself in any of our talks, and I don't believe this was meant to hide its meaning from me. I believe a fog of forgetfulness had settled on the False Moon, enveloping all of its inhabitants, even Grandmother, in a cloud of unknowing. What was outside that cloud remained hidden until it chose to reveal itself.

It had chosen to reveal itself to me now.

At the end of the Silver Bridge was a gate. And at the gate was an angel, standing as silently as had Star before the Wall of Fire in the northernmost Samanthans. A sentry, sword in hand.

But this was not Star. This was a more severe angel, separated from all human, all animal, concerns—pure abstraction. Cold, pure, partaking of neither Life nor Death, but only of Eternity, she…he…it…stared at us with cold, clear, unseeing eyes…or, rather, eyes that saw so far past us, down the echoing, innumerable corridors of Time, that we two were nothing more than a floating mote at the corner of the angel's eye.

This being who guarded the gate to the Moon Itself swept open the barrier, and stood, stone-like—although nothing could be further from stone than the fire-like substance of which this creature was made—as we passed by.

I felt chilled to the bone as we passed. For this was one of the cold angels, a breed distant and sharp-edged; they burn with a feeling of ice, and there is much good done in all the worlds by their work. I know that now.

But I am human—all the more human for my years spent as the Lizard Princess—and I cannot bear their glacial purity, their clean, cold anger, their chill vitality. I cannot bear it past the point where I can bear it.

They are for other beings than I.

I can worship them. But I cannot love them.

That night, they had come to take Leef away from me. Not that I knew that with my head. But my heart felt it, and beat painfully, slowly, in my chest.

The Moon Itself glowed to meet us in the light of a million stars. I stepped onto its silver dust, alert, in pain, not knowing where I was to go or what I was to do. Leef whispered a direction, and I turned toward a beautiful pavilion, one of the few truly beautiful structures Megalopolis ever created. It glowed like a lone jewel there in the midst of the glowing craters, perfectly preserved in the thin, cold, diamond-hard air.

"Go there," he said. And I obeyed.

As we neared the door, Leef whispered again, so faintly that I had to stop and pull him from the satchel up to my shoulder so he could speak into my ear.

"I want…I would like to come back as a tree, Sophy. One that flowers in spring and has fruit in the summer, dropping its leaves in the fall, and bare in the snow. A tree like that."

I thought he was joking, a little, just to give us both some heart. So I laughed, trying to cheer him up, for I still didn't allow myself to believe that he was dying there on the Moon Itself. I said, "Why not a star, Leef? Look at them all, so beautiful. Wouldn't you like to be one of them?"

He shook his head lovingly but with a great weariness. "No, Sophy," he whispered. "If I were a star, I could only be with you at night. A star lives so much longer than your human life. It would be so long till we could be together again. No. I would rather be a tree. As you get older, Sophy, you won't want to travel. We can be together for the whole of your life, that way."

I write this now, as I've said, under what we call the Queen's Tree, an apple tree that flowers earlier and longer, and bears the apples that are prized as a gift from the queen. Rosy pink and gold, those apples. And at their core, a star.

That tree grows in the most beautiful spot in all Arcadia, beside a stream rising from the spring that gives water to the Queen's House. The tree is the pride of the Queen's Garden, and I sit under it every afternoon that I can. Is it Leef? I will never know for sure in this life. But I love the tree for itself, and my plan is to be buried among its roots. When it falls, as it must in time, it will fall on top of my grave.

I know now that this is not the only life I have had, or will have. I know that, and I remember what I had forgotten countless times before. I know this because I keep the Key. The Key will not let the holder forget what Is. Not if she or he truly wishes to know.

But for all this knowledge, there is no lightening of the terrible grief that comes with the parting at death. There was no lightening of my feeling there, on the Moon Itself, as Leef inexorably slipped away from me. How could it be otherwise? A human…an animal…is half body, and that body can only know and take in what a body can. The spirit is helpless to aid it in going farther than that. Yet it's the wisdom gained in the body, wisdom gained through suffering and grief fully accepted and fully lived, that enlarges the spirit and gains the spirit's gratitude for the shared partnership. This is a great mystery. But I know the truth of it.

And though I have known Leef through many lives, and will know him through many more, many more forms, sexes, relationships, this knowledge did not help one fraction of the grief we shared when we parted forever in these forms, that night on the Moon Itself.

First, though, before the final parting, came his last gift to me. He led me to the pavilion where I was the first to look on the Book of the Key since my mother before me. For since then, the Abstract Angels have arrived to guard it from the sight of those who would use it for ill. For Power rather than Love…though both those words have a different meaning for the High Angels, far different in intensity and in purity than our own.

I know this. I was an angel myself. I saw it in the Book. Once seen, it was never to be forgotten.

Never an angel like they are, though. A lower form of angel, one who is created to feel and think rather than to simply, austerely, supremely be. They are my fellows, but they know and see far past what I have ever known and seen into Eternity. They cannot feel Compassion, for they see how everything that happens fits into the pattern that is the dance of all the worlds. Pity is beneath them. They cannot be called into another life than the one they have lived since the beginning of Time.

I, though, have tumbled through Time like a child somersaulting down a grassy hill. Angel, fairy-tale creature, princess, lizard…I had been them all, and doubtless more besides. It was all there, my entire history and the history of all that Is, in the beautifully illuminated book that I stood before now. I turned its pages in wonder. I had been these all, all working toward the same Goal, all searching for the same Grail, all straining after…what? I strained every nerve now to grasp it, to grasp who and what I had been. I held it for a moment, lost it again, and in straining, I forgot, also, for the moment, the friend who had brought me to this time, this place.

I saw all this in the Book of the Key, and I gasped as I worked to understand it. My adventures as the Lizard Princess had brought me to this point. But it was my grief for the coming death of my friend, Leef, the tears that clouded my eyes, that in the end, moved me toward a clearer sight. For as I turned the pages and saw moving pictures of myself, a child with Lily, a girl with Joe, a woman with Susan, I saw a picture of myself with Leef, and, crying out, turned from the Book to see him anew.

How could I? How could I have forgotten him?

Through the arched doorway, I saw him. He had dragged himself painfully out onto the starlit surface of the Moon Itself, and he tilted his dying face upward. I ran out toward him calling his name. Then I stopped, held back from movement by awe. For they were overhead in the hundreds, my fellows who I recognized only in fitful flickerings now. Angels. Abstract Angels come to take Leef's body back to earth, and his spirit away with them. Not from a human compassion, which they are far beyond, but because they are incapable of acting in any way other than in harmony with the Right.

223

In a flash of agony, I saw the truth of my life. For in that life, I have a choice, a choice the Abstract Angels can never face through the miracle of their own perfection. I can choose, or I can refuse, the Right. And in choosing the Right, I enrich it. I enrich the meaning of the universe through the use of my free will. And that is the meaning of being human. That is the meaning of being animal. That is the meaning of grief, of suffering, of death freely accepted.

That is the meaning of my love for Leef and his love for me. I saw it in a flash. And in that flash he looked a sad goodbye, as the coldest and highest of the angels landed sternly, swooping him up in its arms, and flew off, followed by its fellows.

Oh, my heart was full as I watched the angels, now that I recognized them as my fellows, as I watched them depart, voices raised in a song as pure and harsh and sparkling as ice on a mountain glacier. I knew in my grief not just where I belonged, but why I had been sent here, where I did not belong: to join what had fallen asunder. To join the animal and the human, and to join them with the angels by sharing what understanding and wisdom I could.

They seemed to sternly call to me, in sounds so cold, so high-pitched it was almost impossible to hear what was said. Yet I know what they sang. "Come with us. Your work is undone. Come with us. Complete your work and die to be born with us again."

I cannot tell you what this call was like, except to say I felt it—chill, stern, determined—in my inner human core, as if a flame of ice rose up from between my lizard legs, up, up, up, through my human heart to my human eyes.

I silently answered from my heart. "How? How can I come with you? You see my form. You see its limits. Why call me if to join you is impossible in this life?"

I felt anguish as I answered. I felt grief for the death of my friend, and suffering at the thought that my answer would displease the creatures soaring above. That they would abandon me, leave me here on the Moon Itself all alone.

And yet, they were almost too much for me, and my anguish was mingled with a craven hope that they would pass on, and just let me be.

Then I saw her.

Heard her first before I saw her. Sound before sight. Her clear, beloved voice like the warmth beside a fire, so different from the chill abstractions of her fellows.

Star. My own dear guardian angel, Star. I had thought she was left behind above Arcadia, high in the Samanthans, guarding the Wall of Fire. Foolish thought, for wasn't she an angel, and cannot an angel go anywhere in the worlds?

But Star was the only one of the angels who, to my knowledge, had ever ventured onto our world in that form. She told me that story when I was a small child. The story of how she looked down at our world and seen something there, a green sprout in the mass of gray—"for Megalopolis covered the world then, Snow"—and had made it her project to coax that shoot, and nurture it, and help it grow.

Her fellows had tried to talk her away from her dream, but an angel's dream is an unstoppable force, moving forward in its own organic way, colliding with or overcoming obstacles as circumstance demands.

So Star had come to Megalopolis: a hideous, undifferentiated mass of men and women scrambling to climb over their fellows in desperation to retreat from the encroachment of its hideous sameness. To escape the draining of joy, the miasma of anxiety, caused by that very fight, the screams of triumph and defeat covering the world like a dank fog.

"I found the one child on which the future turned, Snow, and that was the ugliest, smallest, snottiest child on the entire world."

It was my mother Star found, when Lily was still a miserable little rat of a boy living off scraps and criminal leavings. It was that little boy Star

My own dear guardian angel, Star.

guided till he remembered who he really was. He was Lily. The first queen of Arcadia, the beautiful country raised up in the midst of Megalopolis in that one moment of recognition.

I had heard the story, though I hadn't believed it was literally true, of course. And then I found a book detailing the same story on the shelves of the children's library on the False Moon. I had read through it, sitting by the artificial fire that warmed the schoolroom, long hours after Gilda slept peacefully in her swan-shaped bed, and I had thought and thought and thought again as I read it to her, over and over again.

Then I knew: one person knowing who they truly are can change the world.

Now I heard Star's beloved voice call out warm through the glacial high-pitched tones of her fellows. "And who are you, Snow?"

Maybe it was the thin air of the Moon Itself. Maybe it was the starlight that danced and shone at my feet, darting like fireflies in the Queen's Garden at night. Images...memories...again began to dart in my mind. A unicorn without a horn. A small child sleeping in her beautiful mother's arms, arms that smelled of roses. An angel...

An angel flying high, side by side, with Star, feeling her distress, loving her, believing in her, following her counsel.

An angel named Snow.

My name.

"Just so," came Star's voice like a melody. "My younger sister, my beauty, my fierce white Snow."

It was too much. Not, I believe, for my spirit, but for my physical nature in this lifetime. Too much for the human sinew and veins, too much for the reptile scales and leather skin...too much. Feeling flooded me. I was nearly overcome by Joy itself. But instead I drew myself up, and lifted my arms to be taken, and in a moment, a cold wind whistled across my face.

And yet, I was warm.

Folded in the arms of Star, I was carried by her from the Moon Itself, down, down, back to my world, to Sophia's world, the world of the Lizard

Princess. In my satchel, I still held the small children's book I had taken from Gilda's room. I had read there of another journey Star had taken once, holding my mother in this same way as she brought her to her new world, the world that had become Arcadia, the world that she would someday lead and die in leading.

I was, I knew then, both my mother's daughter and my guardian angel's sister, and many more beings besides. For now, though, as the Lizard Princess, I had one goal and one alone: to bring the Key back to Arcadia and there to live out my life as Sophia, the queen of Arcadia they call the Wise.

I leaned against the breast of my sister, Star, and, silently offering up a prayer to the One, gave myself up to my Fate.

We flew to the Road of the Dead. And that was where Star left me.

Part XIII: ON THE ROAD OF THE DEAD

In all that time, I never once thought of Joe.

Now is the time to talk of Joe. I miss him now in my old age, for he never returned as I believe Leef did, in any form. As I walked with him on the Road of the Dead, and saw him set sail on the ship to the Faraway Land, I knew that was where I will find him when this form of my own life ends.

What I miss is, perhaps, not so much Joe himself: the tousled, earnest, idealistic, energetic boy I first loved as a girl, and then the heroic, anxious, frightened and brave young man I was to meet now, at the Crossroads of the Road of the Dead. Those two versions of Joe I've already had. What I miss is the river our two life streams never made. Looking at Francis Flight and Amalia Todhunter, I have seen what such a long joining can mean, and what it can bring. I see in them how passion deepens to love, how differences join and form a third way. I have seen the sweetness that comes from their knowledge of each other through the years, the days, hours, moments spent side by side. The many changes that no one knows but those two. Finally, the death that sees them both slip off, one waiting for the other to catch up, the movement into the universe of two portions of life melded into one larger whole.

That is what I miss. Wistfully I think, "Will he know me then?" Because now I am sixty, and we were so young when we parted. I look for him in our child, but all I can see in Walter is Walter. That, I know, is for the best.

We were always different. It was the differences between us that led us to our different fates, for our motives came out of our very selves. For his motive was a noble, flaring pride, while mine was a workmanlike, sad duty.

It was as if we faced each other. On his side, all the heroes of past ages and worlds stretched out behind him, all those supernaturally brave, intelligent, worthy heroes. On my side, the many, many people who supported heroes in their quests. Without them no triumph would have been possible: the mothers, the sisters, the lovers, the wives, even the cooks, cleaners, and laundresses. On his side, a struggle for supremacy over evil, which means a struggle for supremacy, for this struggle cannot end with a final victory, but must reassert itself time and time again. On my side, a stubborn, painful widening of vision, with the faith that a clearer sight would produce a clearer act. On my side there is no triumph, for to triumph is to beat down another side that will inevitably rise up again. On my side there is mitigation, negotiation, inspection, creation. But there is no triumph.

What is a hero without triumph? What is a hero without an enemy vanquished? What is a hero without someone to award him his laurels? What is a hero without a people to rule, or even to refuse to rule?

What is a prince? What is a king?

All of this I saw when I met Joe again. All of this I knew, in my heart, would mean that we would, in this lifetime, inevitably part. For all that I had the illusion of forgetting him on my journeys as the Lizard Princess, of course I had not: how could I? We were two halves of the same whole, and without him, I can never be more, I can never be complete. I can work, though, for the right, for the safety, for the inevitability of the two halves joined, whole once more, no one side in shadow, glowing in mutually creative wisdom.

And in doing so, making the earth itself and our life on it complete.

It had been ten long years since I left Arcadia. Now I stood at the Crossroads of the Road of the Dead. It stretched out, a white stone path, away from a spreading oak tree.

Death was there, standing elegantly as she does, waiting for me as Star set me gently on the ground.

"So this must be the Road of the Dead," I murmured to Leef, then remembered, with a sharp pang, that Leef was no longer there.

Moving forward, I meant to offer Death a respectful greeting. But we were interrupted by the sound of a blaring horn.

Crossing the white stone path was a wide road paved with the kind of grubby tarmac used in Megalopolis, the sort that has buckled and caved, melting in the hot sun, cracking in the ice. A jarring sound, as if it came from Megalopolis.

What had the great city to do with this place? Didn't it believe that it had locked the door forever to the Road of the Dead?

Next was the sight of the huge, open vehicle that made the sound. A loud, juddering, lavender metallic and fake leather thing, the kind that once covered Megalopolitan roads, but was now only the possession of the wealthy.

I had never paid them much mind myself. And the arrogant young men who usually drove them never paid me much mind in return. For the few rich young men of Megalopolis looked for young women of Rowena's sort: blonde, fragile, empty-headed. The type of woman that I had grown into was not for them. Even without the awkwardness of my lizard half.

It was a young aristocrat of that type who drove the horrid thing. I could see that even from far away. He wore a wide-brimmed hat, and the light glinted off a silver charm on the brim.

The…thing…came closer, clanking and screeching as it skidded to a stop on the white rocks of the path.

And Joe leapt out.

When he leapt, my heart leapt too, leaping up to meet him, in a sudden, painful surge of joy. "Joe," I said, but not loud enough. He didn't see me. Instead he headed straight for Death.

"You have it, don't you," he said accusing her. Accusing Death! The audacity of it took my breath away. "You have the Key."

"Joe," I said, more urgently. This time he heard. He turned and stared. He raised up a hand—a hand to protect me from Death.

It had been ten years since we had last seen each other. He was still the same fresh-hearted boy, now man, who leapt first and then asked "How far?" The passionate determination on his face showed that his years searching Megalopolis for the Key had ripened rather than ruined him.

"Sophy, keep back!" he said in that voice that used to make me bristle back in our days together in the Bower of Bliss, for who was he to command me? Now it fell on me like a rock, crushing my heart. I was helpless to tell him how foolish that was. Instead, I left it to Death.

"Don't be stupid," Death said sharply. "Sophia and I are old friends— older than you'll ever know. She has nothing to fear from me."

I stepped forward. I saw Joe's guilty look that meant he had forgotten me in his quest. I wanted to reassure him that I had forgotten him, too. But that it didn't matter in the end, for we belonged together, we two.

I hoped he would reach out and pull me to him as I went. But I didn't stop. Instead I moved forward toward Death, and kissed her on the cheek.

Death looked at us both and gave a quiet sigh. Her elegant fingers tapped her slender neck, "So," she said. "You have arrived at the same time on the same quest."

"Yes," I said, looking at Joe. He still made no move toward me, and he looked angry. I knew that expression. It didn't mean anger with me. It meant anger with himself for feeling fear.

"It's my quest," he said now, in a fury. "Nothing to do with Sophy."

Now I was angry myself. "Hah!" I said. How quickly the emotion changed. Wasn't he the person I loved most in the world? Weren't we confronted by Death? But my anger didn't surprise me. It felt like the most natural thing in the world.

There was a smile in Death's eyes as she observed all this, even if her mouth stayed grave. She was much amused by the two of us, though Joe was blind to that.

"Ah," she said, "I see."

A shudder of fear went through me. Not of Death. But of Joe's idea of himself as a hero. I saw that Joe thought the goal was to defy and conquer Death.

You can never conquer Death. You should never even try. That line is the limit of our capacity, a boundary around the garden that could be. And isn't our goal not to cross that boundary, but to cultivate the land inside?

In my alarm, my anger died down as quickly as it had flared up. I ran clumsily back to him and took his arm, for the first time in ten years. "Joe," I said, and I tried to pull him back from where he stood.

Instead of coming with me, he pushed me away. That hurt. But I couldn't help admiring every part of his tall, rangy body as it issued a foolish challenge. How brave! How deluded! Blind, yes, but beautiful, too, and for a moment, I lost myself again in admiration of him, wanting with all my heart to help him in whatever quest he chose for himself, no matter how doomed.

I knew in my heart, though, that he didn't have the strength it takes to be a real hero. For a real hero is one who needs no one to admire her or him.

So I despaired.

He stood there issuing a challenge to the goddess, who looked amused at his presumption.

"Ah," she said good-humoredly. "I'll make you a wager."

At that, I felt a thin wisp of hope. There are many tales, in both Megalopolis and Arcadia, of a hero contesting with Death. When she loses, in these stories, Death always pays her debts.

If there was to be a wager, I had a chance to help Joe win—to save us both. For in my despair I thought, what was left for me if Death took him away?

Both of us, I strongly suspected, were doomed to win, not our hopes, but something else. Something that would benefit someone else entirely.

So be it, I thought to myself. Because I knew that was my best chance: to give in and put my will to work in support of my fate. No matter how far that fate was from my hope.

But Joe, I knew, would never give in.

How could he help it? For Joe was himself, but like us all, he was what his environment made of him. He was born in Megalopolis. And the land of his birth raised him to fight hard to be the center of all eyes. For that was, and is, the height of achievement for a Megalopolitan boy. For they think—those rulers of three quarters of our earth and a moon besides—that it is this discipline that made them great.

If great they are. As if great is what humans are meant to be.

We in Arcadia take a different view. We try, and we encourage our children to try, to not be great. But instead to be ourselves.

I knew Joe could not help but be himself.

So I waited.

"This has nothing to do with Sophia," Joe said tensely. I could see how this amused Death even more. How was it that Joe couldn't see how playfully Death spoke to him, couldn't see how trivial she thought his defiance?

"Oh no," Death said. "It's not for you to say what Sophia will or will not do here." She glanced sideways at me, and Joe looked at me, too. But I didn't speak.

"Here then," Death said, coaxingly, as if offering a child a toy. "See those caskets here?"

As she said that, we did indeed see them. Three small containers on the ground, under the shade of the ancient oak. They hadn't been there a moment ago. But Death, playful as she is even in her terrible awesomeness, had pulled back a curtain to a fairy-tale world and invited us to enter.

"Yes, we see them," Joe said, staring intently. He didn't notice that he had answered for me.

"I wonder," Death murmured. I looked at her sharply, but she did not return my look.

"Three caskets," he said, entering into the spirit of the tale that Death had made. "One of gold, one of silver, one of brass." At this, he looked sheepish and gave something sounding suspiciously like a snort.

I looked up with hope at that. Was he beginning to see? Because if he saw, we could walk out together, leaving triumph behind, and leaving Death to chortle to herself and wait for another day to walk with us on the Road of the Dead.

But the moment slipped away.

"Traditional," Joe said, in a scornful tone. "Every school child in Megalopolis knows this game."

I was silent. I knew I had to be. It was his moment. To try to save him from it would only make him hate me for taking it away from him. What would our life be like after, resting on a secret hate?

"What do they know?" Death asked blandly. "All those schoolchildren in Megalopolis."

"They know that, in the story, Death puts the question of three caskets to the hero. If he chooses rightly, he wins his boon."

This is not the way the story goes in Arcadia.

"And wrongly?" Death said. "What about then?"

"The penalty, of course, is to go with Death," Joe said, impatient. "But," and here he drew himself up proudly. Too proudly. "But the true hero does not choose wrongly."

"Joe," I said, and tugged at his shirt. For in the Arcadian version of the tale, there is no true hero, only a trio of girls who decide not to choose, but instead sit down on the grass and ask Death to tell them a story. And Death, charmed, does so, giving them each a gift to take back to each one of their small towns. In the Arcadian version, the three girls live long and happy lives, and smile to see Death enter when she finally comes to take them away.

Arcadian fairy tales are ill thought of in Megalopolis.

"Joe," I said again, more urgently. But either he ignored me, or didn't hear. Oh, Joe! He was sure he was a True Hero. About that, I would not like to disagree. I loved the True Hero in him. That was, if I can call it that without arrogance, my own small tragedy.

Here is my secret thought: that he was the Last Hero of our world. And with the Last Hero, the story has to change. From that moment on there would be no more Real Heroes in the world that held both Arcadia and Megalopolis. That world would call for a new kind of story, a different one than the tale of the Hero overcoming Death.

A new story, too, than the one of the three virgins befriending her.

A third story. One that hadn't been written yet.

I shivered then, I shiver still, at the thought of the immensity of the task. A new story to write for the world.

"Choose then," Death suggested, her eyes narrowing to sparkling slits. They flashed between us. Her amusement grew.

Watching her, I stepped beside Joe. In his eagerness, he had moved away from me, forward, closer to Death. Shuddering, timid, but with a dawning understanding of what was needed now, I put a hand on my own True Hero's arm.

"We'll choose together," I said firmly. "We'll make the choice together. After that, you can take us both, or let us both go." I nodded fiercely. "Together," I repeated.

I was wrong, though. Joe turned and looked at me, amazed. I didn't see this at first. I was busy looking at Death, gauging her reaction, and I could have sworn she looked pleased. But Joe, in his agitation, once more didn't see.

"No," he said. "No!" he shouted. And he shook my hand away from his arm.

Tears come to my sixty-year-old eyes, remembering that moment and the pain I felt, all over my half-woman, half-lizard body at the rejection.

"Sophy," he said rapidly. "This is too important for us to take a chance like that. You see that, too. If you let me choose first and I'm wrong, you'll have one more chance."

And if you choose first and choose right, I thought to myself, you'll have all the glory of the hero. It was a moment of sad illumination.

Looking into Joe's young, clear, intense eyes, I saw that he knew nothing of this. Any motive other than the most purely heroic was buried so deep inside of him that he couldn't see.

He was the Last Hero. His deepest wish was to be the Hero who saved the world. But deeper, even, than that wish were others that it did not become a Hero to have. Joe knew that they didn't belong to him. For wasn't he a Hero, born and bred?

"Joe," I said, as calmly and persuasively as I could, but with little hope of being attended to. "Let me choose with you. Surely you must see that the two of us could choose more wisely than just one of us alone?"

He looked at me with a smile of great tenderness. He took me in his arms and kissed me, there before Death. A cold wind blew—but Joe didn't feel the chill.

I knew then that I'd failed.

After his kiss, without waiting to see if I agreed, he stepped up to the caskets under the oak tree.

A gentle breeze now replaced the wind. Light dappled the caskets below, shining through the branches of the oak as they moved in the breeze.

Now light, now dark, now light again.

Now dark again.

The brass casket gleamed.

"Not brass," Joe said. "For the Key wouldn't be hid in cheap metal, no matter how strong."

I was amazed at his confidence. Would I have passed over one of the caskets so easily?

The breeze passed through again. The branches shifted. The brass fell into shadow.

The silver now gleamed, sunlight glancing off its polished surface.

"Silver," Joe said, "is the color of the moon. But the moon takes its light from the sun. The Key wouldn't hide in a casket like that."

The silver now disappeared into the shadow of the tree.

So Death dramatized the story. Even in my despair, I appreciated the fairy-tale finesse.

A bird appeared now, in the crown of the oak, and sang—a beautiful, mournful, full-throated song. It sang and sang and sang, and Joe, taking the song for an omen of his success, looked up at it gratefully, the sun shining full on his face. The sun shone full on the golden casket, too.

Seeing this, I was afraid.

I knew he would choose unwisely. That his choice would be fatally wrong. Was I to leave him to his fate?

The young Sophia, in the days before the long years of the Lizard Princess, would not have hesitated. She would have done whatever it took to stop him. But I was the Lizard Princess now, who would one day be queen. I had learned to keep silent when I needed to, no matter what the cost.

I had learned in the ugly suburbs what had to be done.

I had learned in the Marsh what silences had to be kept.

I had learned at the Great House on the Ruined Surface when to leave things alone.

I had learned on the False Moon how to suffer in silence.

I had learned on the Moon Itself who I was. And I learned this in the death of a friend.

Was I to throw away this hard-won wisdom now?

My life and Joe's. That was the trouble. Not just my life. But I saw there, at the Crossroads on the Road of the Dead, the path I had to take to truly be a queen. And I was still and let him go, bravely and foolishly, to his own fate.

Joe was triumphant now. He reached for the gold casket. I held my breath, for I knew in my heart that the Key was not there.

He reached for it, and a terrifying screech filled the air. He dropped the casket, and we both looked up.

To see the Dragon, as it screeched again, and dove toward me, murder in its red-rimmed eyes, glittering green and gold claws reaching for my heart.

The Dragon, she…he…it…. I remembered it now, with a sharp stab of pain. The creature I had battled in another life, on another world. In that life, on that world, the Dragon had won.

"Sophy, no!" Joe shouted, and dove toward me. He grabbed me, pushing me over, covering me, and in that moment, unable to stop its momentum, the Dragon sunk its talons into him, pulling him from me.

I cried out, reaching out for him, grabbing his hands, pulling him back. The Dragon shrieked again, this time in agonized failure, dropping Joe, its unintended prey. His body knocked the breath from me, as I clutched at it, crying.

A hero. He was a real hero now. And he was dead.

Joe was dead.

Death stood staring at us as if learning from the sight. As if Death had any wisdom to gain! I have often pondered that moment since, but can make nothing of it.

At the time, though, all I felt was a sharp agony, and a dull lack of understanding. For Joe, who I held in my weak human arms and with my strong lizard legs, was dead. Dead, I repeated to myself dully. There was no time to understand this awful fact, as the Dragon knocked us over together. I tore my lizard feet on the rocks I had braced myself against. The dragon swiped at me with a claw, and I felt my tail rip in half.

Another moan, and I saw, beside me on the ground, not the Dragon, but my grandmother—our grandmother—Livia. Who wrung her hands and cried at the sight of us.

"It was you I wanted, Sophia," she cried. "Not my grandson." She turned, enraged, toward Death. "Let him go," she shouted. "A mistake! It was she who was supposed to walk with you on the Road of the Dead."

"So she will," said Death mildly. And then, more sternly, "Sister, leave. You have played your part. Go back until the story calls for you again."

"Sister"? I thought. "Sister"?

Crying tears of fury now, she came to me, Livia, my grandmother, and I saw her change, rapidly, from form to form—from grandmother to Dragon to beautiful young man, and into many other forms I am frightened to name. I knew she hated me, and I knew I was no match for her. But I knew I had Death to protect me.

Turning Dragon once again, she snatched Joe's body from me, lifting it up into the sky and disappearing into a cloud.

When Joe was gone—for he was gone—all the sadness and terrors and wounds of the last ten years, the years of the Lizard Princess, caught up with me, as if I had been trying, fruitlessly, to outrun them all this time. My mutilated tail and two ripped toenails throbbed. A thin, sour spittle made me clench my teeth. The soles of my leathery feet hurt now with a thousand tiny cuts that must have happened on the Moon Itself, but which I had been unable to feel.

Until now.

Then there was my heart. We say 'my heart sank,' and the meaning is that the heart gives up, like an exhausted child, and refuses to move. Mine did this now. My body sank, too. The simplest action would now take enormous quantities of the energy that leached out from me, as if it were running out of my heels and my toes.

All I wanted, at that moment, was to choose the most useless casket, and follow Joe on the Road of the Dead. Or, better yet, walk with him, side by side.

I saw her change, rapidly, from form to form—

I was alone with Death.

Who sighed.

Jumping to my lizard feet, I lumbered over to the caskets. "Let me choose!" I shouted.

Death said nothing. She swept an arm in the direction of the caskets as if to say, "Be my guest."

Scornfully I picked up the brass casket and shook it onto the ground.

But nothing happened. Death looked modestly away.

Angry now, I picked up the silver casket and peered inside.

Nothing.

I turned to Death. But still she made no move.

Now I turned to the gold, exaggerating every movement in my grief, as if I performed a magician's cheap trick.

For now I suspected the truth.

Opening the casket, I proved it. Empty. There was nothing there.

Turning to her, I shouted, "I knew it was a trick all along. I knew there was no Key in those caskets. There was no way for him to choose rightly. Every choice meant Death!"

She looked at me mildly. "This is true. It was his time, the end of the hero's time. Not a bad fate for a hero. To be the last."

Death sighed again. I stared at her, and at the spreading benignity of the oak. A glint shone there, between its two great branches, above the bole, half-hidden in the moss and fallen leaves. Walking toward it—it was calling to me as surely as if it had called my name out loud—I could see its form, mysterious, under the green and brown and gray.

The Key. The Key where it had been carried by the bird that sang in the tree, after my mother had dropped it on her own walk down the Road of the Dead.

Waiting for me.

I looked questioningly at Death. "You yearned for different things,

Sophia," she said. "He yearned to win, to triumph over life. He yearned for What Might Be."

"And I?"

"You yearned to find yourself." She sighed one more time. "You and Joe: two sides of a single whole. Now," she said, more sternly, "grasp the Key. Take hold of your Self and What Is."

What choice did I have? Indeed, I wanted none. This had been my quest, to discover myself...in Joe, in Susan, in Livia, even in Rowena. For no true good could be accomplished without that knowledge.

I walked forward to where the Key waited for me, and reaching out, took hold of it.

When I took hold of the Key, a lightning flash went through me. My adventures as the Lizard Princess had enlarged and strengthened the container into which this force now poured. What I know now—and only grasped instinctively then, as I grasped the Key—is that the cold blood of my lizard half had mingled now with the warm blood of my princess half, the whole of it sheltered in my soul. What was left was a queen. It was as a queen, not a princess, that I grasped the Key.

What awakened in me were many things that cannot be said, for the words for them have not yet been born. But then came an understanding of the common origin of all that lives. Nothing could ever be seen the same way again, now that I understood.

As I did, the landscape shifted and changed.

I was standing in the center of all the worlds, under the Tree of Life. For it was in the Tree of Life, on the Crossroads of the Road of the Dead, that the bird sang.

All the many roads, all the many lives that could be lived, all the many worlds, stretched out like spokes of a wheel from that center. Looking down one, I could see a life where Joe had lived, where he and I were happy, surrounded by grandchildren. Down another, where he had also lived, querulous, miserable, angry at never having achieved a hero's task.

And there were other worlds as well. There were worlds in as much danger as ours, questing worlds, worlds on the edge of defeat. There were worlds that had learned wisdom, fruitful worlds, worlds of fullness and delight.

From one of these worlds now, down one of these roads, a figure walked toward me. She walked toward me. For it was undoubtedly a she.

"Sister," I whispered. For here was a mystery.

Standing before me now was a lizard, staring at me with yellow hooded eyes. Standing upright, facing me squarely, on a pair of human legs: beautiful, spare, well-formed, as would belong to a princess.

We stared at each other, then fell together in an embrace. I hugged the Princess Lizard as if she were a dear companion, missing from my life for a long time. As indeed I think she was.

When we embraced, another transformation took place. My lizard half transformed again, and there I was, Queen Sophia, fully human. What was left of my lizard half were a pair of curious shoes, bright green where my lizard skin had been green-gray, round-toed and wedge-heeled where my feet had been horny talons. I found I could walk great distances, over any obstacles, in those shoes. These shoes I wear today for my walkabouts in Arcadia.

And the Princess Lizard was restored, as well, complete again in her lizard nature. She saluted me, turned, and walked back to her world down her road.

I watched her go, shifting from foot to foot, feeling the novelty of my legs, now returned to a body that perhaps knew more now about their use.

Then I heard someone call my name.

"Sophy."

I turned on my newly human heel. And there, at the head of the long, wide Road of the Dead that leads from the Crossroads of All the Worlds, stood Joe.

He called to me again.

"Sophy," he said.

I went to him gladly.

As I went to Joe, I passed by two figures standing on either side of the Road. On one side, Death. On the other, Livia—for she had returned. If she had ever been away.

I reached Joe and held out my hand, which he took. Another mystery. He was dead, of that there was no doubt, and yet his hand felt as warm and smooth and solid as it ever had in our days in the Bower of Bliss.

"I can do that for you," Livia whispered, hissing, from her side of the Road. "I can conquer Death and wrest Joe from it, and send the two of you together back down the Road of Life. And you'll rule together over All That Is. How could that be otherwise, my own grandchildren?"

I looked at Death. She smiled at me, and looked away, in feigned indifference, I thought.

I looked at Joe, who smiled at me with the same smile of Death. He showed no eagerness to take Livia's gift. In fact, he showed no sign of having heard Livia at all. Instead, he gave my hand a tug, and I understood him to mean he wanted us to walk together as long as we could, as long as it was allowed, along the Road of the Dead. To the harbor where the ship waited that would take him away to the Faraway Land.

That was what Joe wanted now.

"Choose!" Livia hissed. I faced her then.

"Goodbye, Grandmother," I said. "I do not think we will ever meet again in this lifetime. Though we will hear of each other often enough, you and I."

I turned back toward Joe and didn't bother to look at her again, though I know that behind me, she was gone. And if I have ever deserved what they call me—'the Wise'—it was for my refusal of the Devil's bargain at that moment.

Joe and I walked together on the Road of the Dead, hand in hand, in love, at peace, through waves of warm eternity that eddied and flowed around us. The air caressed us, carrying the most wonderful of smells. I still remember them. Ripe strawberries. Rain. Seaweed. Cedar trees in the sun. And the sounds were of a landscape content with itself. Water rushed and spilled. Birds sang. Bees hummed.

It was as if we swam, lazy, through liquid golden honey.

We said many things to each other that had never been said before, but that had always been there, waiting to be said. And I stored up these words like summer food stored against a threatened endless winter.

It was summer as we walked, as it always is on the Road of the Dead. As I was entering the summer of my life, as Joe was leaving the summer of his. We met there.

We climbed the last hill, and I clung to his arm, for I knew—we both knew—the end of the road was near. At the top, under a tree, we gazed down together at a harbor that opened out to an endless blue-green sea. A ship waited there for Joe. We sat together, on the soft moss under the tree, holding hands, looking into each other's eyes for the last time in this life.

We kissed.

That was when the miracle happened. A miracle of kindness, for Death is not cruel, as people say. She does her duty according to her lights, but she takes no pleasure in any suffering it causes…though neither does she feel shame. She has it in her to be kind. Who else would have more opportunity, would see more places where kindness might dwell? She had said we were friends, after all.

So now a curtain of pale green leaves sprang up around us, waving in the breeze, smelling sweetly of mown grass, hiding us from sight. Joe pulled me to him one last time, and we loved each other there, under the tree that marks the way to the harbor of Death. And it was sweet.

Part XIV: In The Domain Of Life

I watched him walk down the hill alone, and I watched him board the ship. I saw a small body scamper to meet him. I knew it was Leef, and I waved a forlorn goodbye as the ship cast off. Joe and Leef leaned over the edge of the boat, watching me, until it was no more than a white speck in that endless sea. Then it was gone.

When I turned back, Death appeared at my side. She walked with me, recounting many stories of my mother, and of the Key, which hung, heavy, rose-gold and ornate, in the bag slung across my chest.

Death taught me uses of the Key. She did this with few words. She told me the truth about it. And she told me about the enemies of the Key, who know full well what it is and what it can provide, but who, in their arrogance, believe the Key to be wrong, harmful to the worlds, and who are determined that it must be hidden, or, better, used for their own ends and then destroyed.

"They believe that humankind can't bear the truth," Death said. "And they are not the first to believe so, in this world you return to or any other."

She told me all this as we walked. It was well that it was so, for the walk back on the Road of the Dead was unutterably dreary. What had been the green and pleasant landscape it meandered through on the way to the harbor turned, in the opposing direction, into a negative of itself: ash-gray

247

and black. For it was never meant to be viewed from this angle.

Each step away from the harbor was made with greater and ever greater difficulty. All the gravity pulled toward the Land of the Dead, the Faraway Land, and to walk away from it was a task indeed.

Still, I did it. There were moments where I longed to sit or even lie and rest along the road. But Death warned me not to stop until I reached the oak tree at the Crossroads of the Worlds, and I obeyed.

Even after she kissed me and left, sending me on my lonely way, I obeyed. I was able to walk on, for I carried the Key. More than the Key. Something weighed on me as well. But the weight of this unknown thing— this treasure—was not difficult to carry. It felt, rather, as if it lifted me up above the grief that weighed me down. What it was, though, I had not yet guessed.

I had a growing feeling that I carried something else away, something precious, something hidden. Something unheard of on the Road of the Dead.

When I reached the Crossroads, I had no difficulty finding the road that led back to Arcadia. Death had left her staff leaning against the old oak tree, and I took hold of it, thinking it would be a help on the long walk to come.

I have it still. "The Queen's Staff," we call it, and no one has ever been able to identify the wood it's made of, a petrified kind of wood, black and gold and scarlet-streaked, harder than granite and just the right height.

It was the staff that led me along the road back to Arcadia. I stood there at the crossroads of the innumerable roads of the innumerable worlds, but only one road said 'Home.'

The road to home stretched out through a green and velvet landscape that looked sharper and more beautiful than any landscape I could remember having seen.

Now it was a fact that, roughly since the year of my mother's death, the landscape in our world had flattened. Scientists of both Arcadia and Megalopolis had noted this, unable to account for its cause. What had been clear and three-dimensional before appeared as flat as a painted surface, or a moving picture on a wall. There were people who had a memory of the depth of it before, and even I, who had been so young at the time, could recall the vivid look of the thing that we had somehow lost. Our world had lost a dimension, as if it lost a scent of flowers in winter, the fragrance still lingering in memory, but impossible to describe to any who had never smelled it on a summer breeze.

Devindra and her colleagues in Arcadia proved the dimension was gone. Though no one noticed its absence in everyday life, which went on as it always had. Even I paid the loss no attention. Devindra tried to explain the importance of it to me. She explained how she and her team had made precise measurements, but the facts went out of my head as soon as they entered. I had nowhere in my mind to hang them. The way things were then seemed to me to have always been so. And this was true not just of me, but of everyone in Megalopolis and Arcadia.

She observed this sadly, and said it was inevitable. That all that was left of what had been was memory. And memory changes and shifts.

I now held the Key, and the whole of the landscape surrounding me, stretching out at the Crossroads of the Road of the Dead to infinity, snapped back into place. Depth reached out in all directions, everywhere, toward everything. Toward every reality, and, more importantly, toward every fantasy as well. Like a child's toy, where you pull a string and the entire picture leaps to attention.

It was the Key that restored the lost dimension. The Key was the thread that pulled it back into place. The thread that tied us invisibly, one by one, together.

I looked on the renewal of the world, whose enchantment was all the stronger for having been created from the old, with a fresh delight. If you have stood before a scene washed by the rain and lit by sudden sunlight, a scene once suffused with a dull haze, and witnessed its change into something sparkling, green and new—if you have seen your field, your forest, your home transform itself before you—you will know what I felt there, under the tree.

I walked on, carried effortlessly by my lizard-green boots, striding with the aid of Death's Staff, through a landscape alive in every detail and corner. And I knew what I walked through was the Domain of Life, where symbols rose up from a source so mysterious it must be, I knew, the source of life itself.

As I walked, breathing deeply, symbols formed themselves around me on either side. They were no longer abstract. They were real. They were the emerald green, ebony-veined leaves above me. They were the red-brown dirt at my feet. They were the living beings of all kinds, bounding across the fields: the etched fluff of the rabbit, the tenacious chatter of the squirrel, the sharp redness of the fox.

It was all there, and I with it. And there, in the center of it all, stood Life herself. It all came from her, as water springing with eternal generosity from a fountain. I walked by reverently, and saw her mystery, saw her three aspects, the maiden, the matron, and the crone, saw them join back into one. A sight never to be forgotten, a sight seldom granted to those living this one life.

A rising joy spilled up and out of my heart, melting as it went the grief that I still carried from the Road of the Dead. The grief washed away, and left in its place was my knowledge of Home. That I was Home, and that I had brought back to my world what it needed. That my quest as the Lizard Princess was complete.

Almost.

Nearly.

Not quite.

There was one more symbol waiting to be born.

Ahead lay the far side of the Wall of Fire, the other side of the Bower of Bliss, at the northernmost reaches of the Samanthans, where Star stood, waiting for me, at the Door I had been unable to open at the start of my quest.

I walked to it now, the world deepening and singing around me, and, holding the Key, fitted it into the lock of the Door in the Wall of Fire, and turned it.

I opened the Door, walked through, and heard it shut softly behind me.

The centaur waited for me on the other side. He kneeled, and I gratefully mounted on his back.

We rode back through the Samanthans, through her high mountain passes, past her juncture with the Donatees, where the two ranges join together and point toward a hidden path to the sea. We rode down and down to the foothills, and we spoke of many things, though this is not the place to say what those things were. For I held the Key now, and many more things were clear to me than had been before. I knew myself. I knew myself in relation to the centaur, in relation to the land we walked across, in relation to Arcadia, in ways that had been muddy and crooked to me before.

This was not a joyful vision. This was a heavy burden at first, as if I had been weighted down with tools and forced to carry them overland to finish a necessary project. Yet there was joy in this, too, as there is always joy mingled with anxious fear in the face of a task that needs completion. Joy that it has been given, and hope it will be achieved, and then...there's the fear that one will not have the strength.

"But why would the One give a task that couldn't be done?" the centaur asked as we cantered across a meadow of wildflowers. For it was spring. And the air smelled sweet. It smelled of home. I sighed with weariness, but also with relief, and joy at our comradeship. I hugged him around the chest, burying my face in his back where the horse's body joined the tanned human skin. I was tired, but I gained strength from him, from his nearness and familiarity, from knowing what we had meant to each other in our many other lives.

As we went on, spring bloomed all around us, the air heavy with promise, the trees budding new leaves, new birth everywhere. I felt my kinship to all of it. And as we walked, I realized the new life springing up around me was growing inside me, too.

For Death had spoken the truth when she said she gave me gifts no one else had ever had before me. She had given me a gift with a lavish hand— and not just me, but Arcadia too. For she had allowed me to walk with my own true love on the Road of the Dead, and she had guarded us while we shared one last embrace across a border that no one crossed before us. She gave us to each other, and in doing so, gave our son to me. Not just to me. But to all he would love, and all he would work for, long after my time here is done.

Part XV: Sophia The Wise

The centaur and I parted in the Donatees, over the scattered mountain settlements that climb up them in search of ever-clearer air. Above Amaurote, that beautiful, vine-covered town. Above Ventis, stolid and practical, the land of butter and honey. I will not say what words we exchanged in the leave-taking, for those were private between us. But it was not the last time I would see him, nor the last time I would hug his neck and bury my face in his side. He is the godfather of our son, Joe's and mine, for he came out of the mountains when the baby was born and blessed him, making a bond between them that I knew would be valuable, given the dangers that faced any child of mine in an Arcadia unsettled and unsafe. I knew the centaur would always be there for Walter—for that was the name I chose for our son, a common and unobtrusive one in Arcadia and Megalopolis, another way to hide who he was from those who would steal his True Self from him before the time came for him to claim it for himself.

I sit writing in what we call the Queen's Garden, and I know that while this history of the Lizard Princess is meant for the archives of Arcadia, really it is meant for Walter...for my son, and for the daughter born to Walter and Shiva. Shanti. My granddaughter.

I sit here in the Queen's Garden, by a stream running into the Juliet

River: a stream rising from the spring that gives water so abundantly to the Queen's House before running into the Juliet, down to the Ceres March, under the Donatees, through the edge of the Dead Wood, down to the sea.

I sit here on a wooden chair with a cushion, a wooden stool for my feet, under the spreading branches of Leef's tree in the spring and summer. In the autumn I watch its leaves and apples fall, and in the winter I still rest beneath its bare branches, wrapped up against the cold.

And I write this history for Shanti, my granddaughter, who is innocent of any knowledge of her descent, who knows me not…except as her own dear godmother. Who will be ignorant of her True Self and her True Destiny until she reads these lines, and has her past restored to her.

After the centaur left me, I walked slowly, taking my time. There were houses—farms—scattered here and there along my way, inhabited by those Arcadian souls whose dearest happiness is solitude, and whose greatest virtue is the openhearted hospitality that only the solitary can truly provide.

There was much hospitality shown me on that road. Evening after evening, I was welcomed after my day's journey into a warm house, with an early spring fire blazing in the hearth, and the pick of the last of the winter's stores and the earliest of the spring's crop for a feast to be shared. There was always wine, for we were in easy reach of the luscious wines of Amaurote, or beer, for the mountain folk are famous for what they brew. And afterwards, a white liquor made of flowers or berries, to drink with new friends and toast good night.

I always slept well in these houses, whether on the spare bed of a child gone off to seek her or his fortune in one of Arcadia's towns, or on a pallet laid carefully in front of the fire.

No one knew me. For it had been ten years since I had disappeared, I was told, "on the quest of the Lizard Princess." The songs, the stories, knew it was a quest…but a quest for what, that I never heard in any of the tales told around the household fires of a night.

And always I held the Key. Each day the Key gave me a greater measure than before of a mingled joy and suffering, and each day I found that I was like a vessel that expanded, grew, could hold more and more without spilling a drop.

I grew. And the future grew inside of me. I knew that great secret now that all mothers-to-be hug to themselves: that theirs is the care of the future. And I knew the fear of not caring for it aright.

I hoped the child would be a boy. Arcadia had need of a man as well as a woman, one who would love a woman himself and bring all of his qualities to the marriage. Not in the way of the men at my so-called 'court': Aspern Grayling who despises women, and his son who has no mother. My Lord High Chancellor Michaeli, whose perverse longing for a son has destroyed the happiness of his daughters and granddaughters.

I heard news of these men, and their plots, on my way home through the mountains. All along the way I heard news of Arcadia. Fearful news. The fear in me grew, and I knew that the child I carried needed more than a mother's care, more than the care of someone who was called on to be a queen. I knew that if the child were indeed a son, to raise him in the Queen's House as a prince would be a disaster. I alone, with the women of the Queen's House, would never be enough for his needs. Worse than that, there was danger there for any child of mine.

Aspern Grayling had already openly defied the Queen's Laws, had made experiments in the forbidden, had created a child from his own body, with no mother except the deluded Merope Vale, who carried his doomed children to term, both from love of him and hatred of her mother and me. The whole of Arcadia knew the story of how the first two of the triplets, Marcian and Lionel, had died. And how Pavo Vale, called as he was by his 'mother's' name, in the custom of our people, was growing to manhood in his father's house.

"A likely lad, bigger and stronger than any others you see in Arcadia, but something of a bully, so they say, we don't get much sight of the nobs out here, but you know how news travels, what's your impression, my dear?" For my story was that I was a student at Juliet College, on an expedition to collect mountain flowers and herbs from the other side of the mountains. I had to account for my weary look, and the amount of time I had been away from things. I said I didn't know about Pavo Vale, but that I had sat in on many lectures given by Professor Grayling, and I was sure he was a brilliant man.

"That's what we hear, my dear, brilliant is the word, and all the young men following him now. Glory! That's what we hear him teaching. It's hard for the young, isn't it, without a queen to show Arcadia the way to go. It's understandable, isn't it, that they'd want a stronger hand. And no one in the Queen's House now but women, mainly. Women and Wilder the Bard, of course."

That was the first I'd heard that Will the Murderer, himself transformed in the years of the Lizard Princess, had now become Wilder the Bard. I missed Will. Or Wilder, as I was to call him now. It would be soon enough to go home after my son was born, but when I did, one of the first friends I would go to would be my friend in the tower.

I had so much to tell him.

"What about Michaeli?" I asked cautiously of one of these mountain families that gave me hospitality. A mother, a father, and three children who tumbled constantly like puppies. I'd taken care to find out that Michaeli still lived, and was still the Lord High Chancellor, administrator of all the Queen's business, my mother's biggest mistake, and the bane of my early childhood with his endless lectures on what he considered my 'royal' duty.

How wrong he always was, vain, silly Michaeli, always confusing his own need to be important with a true need to be great.

"Oh," said the mother of the brood, shaking her head while she and I watched her husband and children play tag in the new grass of the meadow. "Of course he left the Queen's House years ago, when our Lizard Princess went away. He could never get on with the women of her house, you know.

256

He always thought the leaders of Arcadia should live in a grander way."

Her husband came into the house, one small laughing daughter clinging to his waist. "And maybe he's right," he said, gently detaching the little girl. "His house is a grand one, and maybe we all share in the 'grand' that way. Maybe that's what we need to protect us from those who would be grander than us."

But his wife shook her head. "Servants," she said. "I don't hold with servants."

"But doesn't the Queen's House have servants?" I asked, knowing the answer, but wanting to hear what she would say.

"Well, of course, but there should be another word for them. You're a scholar. You know the difference. In the Queen's House, people have duties, same as we do here in this house. But there's no ruling one over the other, same as here." Her husband rolled his eyes at this, and she hit him playfully on the arm. "You know what I mean," she insisted. "I don't know how to say it, I didn't do more than two years at Yuan Mei Agricultural College. But we have duties here and we do them, each what is necessary for each to do. But lord it over each other? Never. We don't do that here. Why should it be different with the ones in the Queen's House, or in the Villa of the Lord High Chancellor?"

"Now that's a different matter than our house, dearest," her husband said. But then the other two children ran noisily in, and that was the end of that conversation, for it was time to make the food, and eat and drink, and put the children to bed.

I wanted to spend more time with the wife of the house, getting her advice. She was quite willing, once she knew I was having a child. For she knew much about childbirth and childrearing. So we sat long over the dying fire while she shared what she knew. Her husband, cheerfully and frankly bored by our talk, took himself off to bed. Once she knew he was asleep—his snores shook the little house—she turned to me with a worried look on her fine, open face. "I don't know why, but for the first time in my life, I'm afraid of the future in Arcadia."

She gave me much to think about. The next morning I walked away from their home with my head full of it. I waved goodbye, knowing my son should be raised among people like this, and not where people like Michaeli and Aspern Grayling would have his unformed ear.

For I had seen what happens to a people when one person begins to think her or himself of more value than another. I had seen what happened to Megalopolis. And I knew that it was Livia's plan, hers and Aspern Grayling's, that Arcadia should become such a place. I knew that my son should not be raised there.

No. Amalia Todhunter and Francis Flight, in the Small House, by the Little Meadow, would raise Joe's and my son. And he would have his grandfather close by.

When Walter was born, it was winter, the season of my own birth in the mountains. But how different his birth was from mine. Mine was a pause in flight over the snowy mountains, attended only by women and children and shivering animals, unsheltered from a certain future by necessity. His was all welcome and warmth in the loving household of Amalia Todhunter and Francis Flight, who were to be his foster parents, his grandfather—my father and Joe's—there to receive him, to cut the cord, and to hold him for the first time. All was cheerful. Even the winter snow fell softly, and no wind blew that night, as if to cushion his entry into the form of this life.

"A miracle," my father muttered under his breath, thinking I, drowsy from the birth, wouldn't hear. For it had been the lesson of his long, self-imposed exile from his own land, his own upbringing, that had taught him the hard fact of miracles. Yet still, though he was the Old Hermit now, inside him was the young Conor Barr, the princeling ashamed to admit there were such things as miracles in the world. But what else than a miracle could it have been? Conor's wanderings until he found his children in the Bower of Bliss, his return on Grete to the household of

Francis and Amalia, the small hermitage they built him to await the return of his daughter—for they were sure of it, Francis and Amalia, because they were sure that nothing happened but for the good. It was Francis and Amalia who told Conor the truth about me, a truth, Amalia told me later, he must have suspected, for he showed no surprise.

Then the return of his daughter, and the birth of his grandson. And the promise that he could live the rest of his life out near the child, teaching him what he knew, watching him grow, knowing that the exuberant life that reached up to the sky, like a trained vine heavy with fruit, owed something to him. Not just to his body, but also to his mind, and his heart and spirit, too.

A miracle it truly was. I myself gave thanks silently to the One, and to all who serve the One. I prayed to know what I should do next.

I had known that my son should be born with men to receive him. Men as well as women, who would form his thoughts and his acts in the years to come. It was a bit of a joke among us there, in the Small House, how imperious I became in the days after Walter's birth. "A queen, then, are you?" Francis would tease me, as he had when I was small and my mother brought me there to play in the long grass under the oak tree, to learn what I might from the Small House's example of modest joy.

Francis was right in his mild joking. Every day after the birth, I grew more like a queen. For every day I grew more certain in my mind, and more precise in my orders, about what should be done for my child. Both for him and for me.

The imperiousness that so amused Francis and my father found more understanding in Amalia. She understood, before I did myself, that it held at bay my deep grief at the certainty that I had to leave my child, and return, alone, to the Queen's House. For it had been a place of unresolvable strife since the day I grew my lizard legs and disappeared. "They go back and forth, forth and back, fighting about how the land is to be governed, under what star, and for what result. Best you go back, and lend your strength to the side of the good."

I knew what Amalia meant by 'the side of the good,' for we had no doubt, she and I, of what that would mean. A land of chosen limits. A land meant for the care of all. A land kept alive and green by the partnership of all, rather than the fight for dominance of the few. No, we had no doubt. We had no doubt that what Aspern Grayling calls sentimental and naïve stupidity was the higher truth. But his doctrine, of excellence ruling over mediocrity for the good of all, is a seductive one, especially to the young, and it was this doctrine I wished to keep from my son until he was old enough, and wise enough, to see it for what it was. Let him grow to freely make a choice of his path, rather than risk his being seduced in his weakness by one that he, and the Arcadia with which his destiny was inevitably entwined, would come to regret.

So I knew I had to leave him. Baby that he was, I needed to give him to Amalia and Francis's care, as I had once been left, and return alone to take up my duty as queen. There can be few acts not utterly immoral that are harsher to the spirit of a woman than the need to separate from her own child. But so it had to be.

"It's good you go back," Francis said to me as he sat with Walter and me, in the too few moments we had together as mother and son—for I have kept close touch with my son, and he has known me as a kind fairy godmother, revered by his foster parents, Francis and Amalia. They told him he was the child of their dead daughter, so he never grieved for the mother that he'd lost—except, perhaps, in the depths of his heart, which never forgets the past, no matter how far back the wound was received.

I knew I would wound Walter, but I also knew that Francis was right. I heard the accusation in his courteous understatement. I had left Arcadia too long. I, whose task it was to lead her gently to a daily renewal. For without that, factions form and wrestle in the dark. Evenly matched, they pull each other down into the mud.

It was that mud I needed to keep Walter from now, baby that he was. Like a sick animal, who knows instinctively where to find the herb that will make them well, I, sickened by what I heard on my return of the power

260

struggles taking place in the Queen's House, hurried to the Small House of Francis Flight and Amalia Todhunter, and gave my son into their care.

And I have never regretted it. Sorrowed for it, yes. Wished with a passion that the road could have led elsewhere. But never ever truly regretted it. For I saw the boy, and then the man, that Walter became: open-hearted without imprudence, well-formed without vanity, witty without malice, blessed with all the powers one would wish for one's child. But always allied with that most important virtue of all: with kindness. His curiosity about the people around him, and his generosity to them, have won him respect. And love.

He is a loyal friend, a loving husband, and a caring father to his daughter. The granddaughter I longed for, the child Arcadia will have cause to thank.

All of this would have been lost forever had I brought Walter, in my pride and my selfishness, to the Queen's House, where Aspern and Michaeli would have taught him the arrogance that they call noble pride, the cruelty that they call realism, the narrow-mindedness that they call rational thought, and the self-centeredness they call heroism.

No, I don't regret it. As usual, in suffering there is joy, and in joy there is suffering. Of all the truths that the Lizard Princess found behind the Wall of Fire, that one is the undisputed queen.

My life has been a fairy tale. More: a necklace of fairy tales, each one following the other in a circle, to meet at a clasp formed, finally, by the Crossroads at the Road of the Dead. And this is our battle, Aspern's and mine, the battle for the future of Arcadia. He scorns these tales and the lives they make up, believing in his pride and fear that his life is a straight and narrow line between towering blank walls, leading upward, ever upward to…what would Aspern say? To a triumph over Death, he would say, and at that I can hear Death give a delicate, elegant snort. I can hear her say, as plainly as if she were here beside me now (and perhaps she is, at that), "How does the little man hope to triumph over Death without an equal triumph over Life?" And I can hear the laughter of her sister Life as well, echoing down the mountains from her Domain. Even in these days of turmoil, of threat, of malice, and of rage, her presence lightens everything in Arcadia. It lightens my heart and my spirit.

It is my spirit that has lived these fairy tales. And, oh, how my spirit pities the spirit of Aspern Grayling, which is caged and enslaved in the dark.

All things change. Nothing stays the same. Will the Murderer becomes Wilder the Bard, transmuting his pain and guilt into songs of an Arcadia that was and that is and that can be. Conor Barr starts as a selfish, callow prince, only to end his days in a hermitage in the hills, watching over the grandson who knows him not. Aspern Grayling starts as Andy Dawkins, ambitious child of an Arcadian farm, and meets the tragedy of his family's death at the hands of the Empire with a change in his own story: for his choice was to become strong as the murderers he watched slaughter his mother and father and sisters in the Megalopolitan invasion. His choice was a different one from Will the Murderer's. He chose to become a different man, certainly, but the difference was this: he chose never to be weak again: he would always remain on the side of the strong. He changed his story to one of superiority, power, and rage. And there are many who admire him and that story. Many who would follow him. Many who, in doing so, would strike at what makes Arcadia the hope that she is.

That is the story of my enemy.

And I, Sophia, born to a mother who was a reluctant queen, am no reluctant queen myself, having been the Lizard Princess, who learned in that half cold-blooded, half warm-blooded body what is necessary to lead myself and Arcadia to wisdom. The wisdom is within those symbols that first rise up, then grow old, and die a peaceful death, or stagger on, turned sour, in life-in-death. The saddest time in a land is when people follow those dead symbols, follow them blindly, insisting on their supremacy, arrogantly ignoring a new symbol's right to be born. For new symbols push to be born, and in that painful birth the future is contained.

We can choose our attention. We can choose our future. For—dare I say this?—our future can be, if we choose, one of inevitable misery, an illusion of far sight. Or—and this I do believe, I who have lived many lives to prove the truth of it—it can be, without false sentiment or naïve indulgence, one of radiant, mutual joy.

For joy married truly to suffering, Life joined with Death, is a greater, wilder, more fruitful joy, a more vivid Life, than any other, anywhere else, any place in all the worlds.

But if I know anything, it is that you cannot tell anyone anything they are not ready to hear. And what they are not ready to hear, they are not ready to see. Having written these pages as an offering to the future—and who knows the offering's value?—I will keep my own counsel until I judge the time to be ripe…and hope that some will understand, in time, the meaning of the years of the Lizard Princess.

So I rode home alone through yet another spring, the spring that was to be remembered in the songs of Wilder the Bard as the beginning of the reign of Queen Sophia, who her compatriots call "the Wise"—whether rightly or wrongly, only Time will tell. Devindra greeted me at the gate of the Queen's House, and I saw she knew I had succeeded in my quest, for there were tears in her eyes. And the tear that fell down her cheek was like a round crystal raindrop, newly fallen, spilling off a green leaf in spring.

"No, I do not see her. And what's more, I wouldn't want to see her if I could."

Aspern was looking particularly elegant in his exasperation with me that day we had our final break, the theatrical rupture that he had long meditated and planned. He looked natty, as he always did. The young Andy Dawkins, who I heard from others had been rawboned, messy, and passionate in his days as a student, had been changed utterly, into this composed, swift, brilliant gentleman in the perfectly fitted pearl-gray suit, and the perfectly ironed cream-colored shirt, and the perfectly shined shoes made for him by the artisans of the False Moon during his surreptitious visits there.

He looked, every inch of him, a lord of the elite of the False Moon of Megalopolis. And every time we met—for this was to be the last time—I felt a pang of grief. For I knew that young Andy Dawkins had been forced to hide himself while his family, farmers who resisted to the end the first Megalopolitan occupation, were brutally killed. I knew—did he know? does he know? how much does he know of who he truly is?—where Aspern Grayling had come from. From that moment in time, he was no longer Andy, he was Aspern. He was no longer a Dawkins—his mother's name, in the custom of Arcadia—but a Grayling, the name of his father. And he must have sworn to himself he would learn from the strong what it meant to be strong. To be untouchable. To be unassailable. To be triumphant over Death.

"Angels do not exist," Aspern said flatly, now. "Except in the fantasies of children, or the wildest imagination of a dissolute artist—and you know what I think of them."

He had been trying for years to reinstate punishment for capital crimes, as in the days of the Occupation. Only Devindra's prestige and force of character held him back from arranging for Will the Murderer to be hanged, when I, Will's protector, was gone in the days of the Lizard Princess. Watching Will's transformation, slowly but surely, into Wilder the Bard had simply added fuel to his rage at what he called the "womanish system of justice that is the shame of Arcadia."

"Womanish." An insult, you see. We could never see eye-to-eye, Aspern and I. Hardly a surprise, when I had seen, in my days in Megalopolis, what "mannish" on its own could become.

"The only place else you will find an angel," he said now, looking over his beautiful gold-rimmed spectacles at me, "is in the derangement of an unhealthy mind."

My mind, you see. My unhealthy mind. My derangement.

I sighed.

Star looked at me, both sad and angry. I could see both in the way her wings flapped slowly, disconsolately.

"Which only shows what I have been saying for years: how completely unfit you are to rule this or any other land!"

"Oh," I said. "I don't think I rule here. Not in the way you mean, Aspern."

"Exactly my point. Exactly why I've asked for this meeting today. I have a petition here, asking for your abdication. You say you don't rule, you've never wanted the queenship, never wanted to rule, you've said so yourself many times…"

"What, Aspern?" I asked now, exasperated in spite of myself. Always, I try to stay calm in the face of idiocy, no matter how determined. It was Aspern alone who could try my patience to its limit. And perhaps that was why I grieved so thoroughly when he was gone, and I could no longer speak to him face to face. "What have you forgotten? What is it I say after that?"

"Yes, of course," he said with that look of scorn that frightens so many into agreeing with him—at least to his face. "You constantly say what I constantly hear repeated in the common rooms of the colleges of Otterbridge: you do not rule, you guide." He gave me a look of deep disgust. "As if what a land needs is a guide."

I sighed again. "Well, we'll just have to agree to disagree on that. Because of course you know, Aspern, that I will never abdicate. I will not abandon the responsibility I inherited from my mother—not one jot of it."

He threw up his hands. "Your mother!" he shouted, rolling his eyes. "She believed in angels, too. Angels, unicorns, centaurs, mermaids—she and Professor Vale allowing…encouraging a deluded population to believe in such ridiculous fairy tales. Irresponsible! I give you the benefit of the doubt, I believe you simply use such nonsense to control the discussion, you can't possibly believe any of it yourself, you, an intelligent woman. But I'm calling for a democracy, where each rational man is able to choose for himself, on the Megalopolitan model. This is the future, you can't deny it, you can see it for yourself!"

There was a moment of silence while I turned over possible responses in my head, and in my heart. Aspern, meanwhile, waving the sheaf of paper that presumably made up his petition, looked triumphant, as if he had scored the winning point in a game.

Finally I ventured a question. "You can see Star, correct? Standing beside me?"

Aspern gave her an impatient glance and shrugged. "An illusion. Hallucination. These kinds of visions are common, we know, not just in Arcadia, but in Megalopolis as well. A visual trick generated by a strong personality bent on dominating the minds of those around them."

"Ah," I said. "By strong personality, of course you mean me." I murmured to Star, "I should be flattered, I suppose." But the angel beside me just shook her head.

"You know what this means, we've had these discussions often enough. I defy the entire program you have set out for Arcadia, I defy your superstitious notions, I defy you, the so-called 'Queen Sophia the Wise'."

Oh, he was winding himself up now. He was superb in his own way. And in his own mind, too—there, Aspern always reigns supreme. In his own mind, no one else can touch him. Strange how such confidence can generate a hold on weaker minds. Strange, also, that he accused me of the manipulations he spent his life in perfecting.

He continued to shout, and that was when I knew there were others listening at the door. Others ordered by Aspern, their master, to make a record of this, the 'confrontation' he meant to be the excuse for his final break with our law, his final leap into absolute rebellion and betrayal. "I defy you and the State, for all to hear." At this, he threw open the door to my council room, and, indeed, as I had guessed, showed his followers standing, crowded in the anteroom. Pavo Vale, his son, was at their head.

He repeated his defiance. "I publicly proclaim my opposition to your rule..."

"To my guidance," I corrected mildly.

"I proclaim," he shouted superbly (for when was Aspern anything less than superb?), "I proclaim my belief in a New Age, where a man's strength is his only staff and comfort, and where genius is free to make its own way, untrammeled by law or custom."

"He means his own genius, of course," Star said with an irony that was unusual among her kind. Angels are not usually given to sarcasm.

Aspern glared fiercely at Star. "And I intend," he hissed, "to free us all from superstitions like that one." Here he pointed right at Star. "To free us all to see Reality by our own lights."

I watched some of my fellow Arcadians nod as though they seriously agreed. If they saw Reality by that light, I thought, what they were bound to see would be very dim.

"To lead us from the fog of childish fairy tales into a courageous new world!"

At this, he turned and marched for the door. A wonderful performance, I thought, now detached from the scene, for the result of it was foregone, and in my head I had already started to prepare for the conflict that was to come.

Before he reached the door, and his followers on the other side, he turned back and jabbed an angry forefinger my way. "Remember it!" he announced, and, storming theatrically out, he was no longer a fellow Arcadian I might speak to, reasonably, humorously, as my equal in down-to-earth common sense—which is the equality your true Arcadian prizes above all else.

Aspern had ceased to be a fellow Arcadian, as I knew now he had planned all along. He transformed himself into Archenemy Aspern Grayling. He was now a sworn enemy to me and my land—something almost inconceivable to me, who had laughed at how the Megalopolitans constantly fought among themselves.

"It was inevitable, you know," Star said. "He hates us, we creatures of the One, we beings outside of linear thought, we inhabitants of the tales themselves. He knows you are one of us, Snow. And he hates you most of all."

267

I sighed. I had failed as a human and a mother, I thought. I had failed as a half-lizard, half-princess. Had I failed as a queen? It was too early to tell, for even if the symbols I represented had had their day, as Aspern thought, my duty was not yet complete. I knew this, as the keeper of the Key that Aspern lusted for. I knew my duty was still to come, though my time was short, and I was sad almost to death. Now it was time to do what I dreaded: to add a pair of wings to the form that was and is "Sophia the Wise" and fly into a battle I had hoped against hope to avoid. But a battle I saw now was inevitable, my fate, the reason for my birth in the winter mountains.

So do all the stories come full circle, and clasp again at the crossroads of the worlds, before starting out again. And it will be someone else after me who will take the stories I have left and turn them into something new again. What will that be? I don't know. But I have faith in the future. I have faith in the transformation of forms; I have faith in the wisdom those transformations bring. For was I not the Lizard Princess?

Sitting beneath the apple tree in the Queen's Garden, I make my plans. And I am, for the time being, content to work without anxiety about result, offering up all my effort, all that I was, all that I am, and all that I can still become, to the One, the hidden One, who reigns in the place from where all things are born.

THE END

Afterword by Shanti Vale

ALAN FALLAIZE is an old friend of my dad's, and he's asked me to write some words here—from 'the younger generation', he says. Most of our lives have been filled with nothing but fighting here in Arcadia, over who and what we're meant to be. It's exciting to think I'm writing to another world. You wouldn't know much about us. So I'll try to tell you my story as well as I can.

You wouldn't know what a shock it was to find out that Queen Sophia, who I'd always thought of as kind of a fairy godmother, was actually my dad's mom. I mean, she wasn't the kind of person you would think was anyone's mom. She was a bit apart from the rest of us, and was always worried about us all. It was weird to find out she was actually my grandmother.

It turns out she told Dad years ago that she was his mother. But he kept quiet about it till now. He says there was too much going on—too much fighting. He was worried about us, I mean about me and my mom. He didn't even tell her until he told me.

I'm sure my Dad's reasons were good ones. But I can't help wishing he'd mentioned it a little sooner. I would have liked to have told Queen Sophia I was proud to be her granddaughter. More than that—the news would have gone a long way to making my mom and me feel better about our family. I don't mean my close family, me and mom and dad and granny Devindra. I mean my mom's parents. Her mother was Michaeli's youngest daughter Aurora. But her dad was Pavo Vale.

You wouldn't know what Pavo Vale is like, though I know Godmama…I mean, Grandmother Sophia…tells a little bit about him in this book. We don't like to talk about him much, but I figure now's the time to do it. Dad says it is the right time, and I always take Dad's advice about stuff (or regret it, usually). He says Godmama…I mean, Grandmother, would have wanted it all known, no matter how gross it sounds.

Because it's Pavo Vale, the slug, who's at the head of what they call 'the

Resistance', which is just a cover up for the Megalopolitan power play it really is. He's who they want to put in charge of Arcadia. Which would mean, as my dad points out, Megalopolis would be in charge. Aspern Grayling calls him 'the New Man'. If he's the New Man, I'd take the old type any day.

Pavo Vale married my great aunt Faustina, Aurora's older sister. And then he got Aurora pregnant. She was only a little girl, and she wasn't very stable to start with, at least that's what I hear. High-strung. She had her baby—my mother—and then went down to the Marsh to drown the baby and herself. Lucky for mom (and for me!), granny Devindra guessed what was happening and got there in time to save mom. But not Aurora, poor little sap. And Devindra brought my mom home and raised her as her great-granddaughter, even though there really isn't a blood relationship. Granny always said that isn't what matters anyway.

That's why we're Vales. Not because of that oaf Pavo. He's really only a Grayling, anyway, since he's parthenogenetic. Merope Vale, Granny's awful daughter, just carried him.

I hope you're following this. I know it sounds nuts. But that's my family.

So I mean you can just imagine how my mom and me like to think we're descended from, let's face it, a baby-rapist. But there you go. You can't run away from who you are, can you?

That's why it was such a stunner—such a relief!—to find out Dad is actually the son of Queen Sophia, making her my real, true blood grandmother. I mean, Dad's foster parents, Francis and Amalia, were terrific. I adored them both. Who wouldn't? Everyone did, but Pavo Vale, the creep.

But Queen Sophia was special. My fairy godmama. She took care of me when I was little. Let me play in her room with the Key. She told me stories, especially on winter solstice night, when she'd babysit me so Mom and Dad could go to the Midnight Celebration.

In fact, she told me quite a few of the stories that are in this book.

Those were really special times. When I look back, I know that except for my mother and father, and granny Devindra, I've always loved Queen

Sophia the best. More, in a way, because it was like we chose each other to love. I was always in awe of her. I wanted to be like her. Granny Devindra was a scientist, and I'm not too great at science. Mom is an artist—you should see her drawings, incredible—and me, I can hardly draw a stick figure on a horse.

But Queen Sophia was a storyteller. And, I think, so am I.

When she died, I was only twelve. I miss her more than anything. She left me her library. That was a surprise. I thought maybe it meant she thought I was a storyteller too. Although Dad now says it meant a lot more even than that.

I think it also meant what Alan says. That what he calls 'the younger generation' is going to have to figure out a way past this civil war. That if we're going to do that, we need stories that tell us how and why.

That's what I'm going to do with my life. Hear stories, trade stories, tell stories, and hope we can figure out, with their help, how Arcadia is going to survive.

THREE YOUNG
WOMEN
AND
DEATH

An Arcadian Fairy Tale

. Three young women were friends. One came from Eopolis, the town they call 'the prudent'. One from Paloma, called 'the vain'. The third was from Wrykyn, known as 'abstemious', but this is a joke, for people from Wrykyn are famous for their love of the good life. The three had known each other all their lives, and loved meeting to tell stories and to laugh. What they liked most of all was to laugh. So they met one spring, to tell stories, and to laugh, and to look for mushrooms in a mountain meadow after the warm rains. There they met Death. This was no surprise, for Death was often found with mushrooms sprouting after the warm spring rains. "Here are three caskets," Death said, and there they were: one brass, one silver, one gold. "You may each choose. The one who chooses best may have her heart's desire." The young women knew what Death meant. The two who chose worse would leave with her that day and walk along the Road of the Dead. "You first," Death said to the young woman from Eopolis. But she, prudent, refused to go before her friends. "You then," Death said to the young woman from Paloma. She was silent, for she had a secret wish to be more beautiful than her fellows. Her friends, knowing her thoughts, laughed. She shook her head. "Then you," Death said to the life-loving young woman from Wrykyn. "Surely you will want your heart's desire." But the young woman from Wrykyn said, "My heart's desire is to sit with my friends and hear a story no one has ever heard before." The three young women, knowing each other's thoughts, laughed together. For this was a wish that did not need Death. Still laughing, the young women from Eopolis, Paloma, and Wrykyn fell onto the new meadow grass. Death couldn't help but laugh herself. So good-humored Death sat and told them a story no one had ever heard before. Then she sent them home, each with a gift, though what gifts those were their towns keep secret to this day.

The three young women lived long and happy lives, even when sorrow overtook them, as it must all that lives. And when Death returned, she came for all at once. The three old women walked together on the Road of the Dead telling stories and laughing. For what they liked best was to laugh.

MORE ABOUT THE HISTORY OF ARCADIA SERIES

The HISTORY OF ARCADIA series tells the story of a world that was literally formed by a story, by one person discovering and claiming who she really is . . . and of the subsequent events that led first to a deceptively happy world, then to an inevitably tragic outcome, and finally to a slow rebuilding of the world on foundations more deeply and thoughtfully laid. Each book includes bonus Arcadian legends and fairy tales, and relates how the manuscript crossed the barriers between Arcadia and our own world to arrive at Exterminating Angel Press. The first three novels in the series are *Snotty Saves the Day*, *Lily the Silent*, and *The Lizard Princess*.

Coming soon
Report to Megalopolis:
The History of Arcadia
(November 2016)
In this, the fourth book of the series, Aspern Grayling has his say about Arcadia and its works.

To get an idea,
turn the page...

Extract from the forthcoming book
Report to Megalopolis: The History of Arcadia...

To the Lady Livia
Chief Consultant in Camera to the Council of Four
Chair for Life of the Campaign for Peace in Our Time
Governor General of the False Moon

My dear Livia,

For you know it is the honor of my life that you are, in fact, my dear friend—you who have shown all the worlds their way forward in a universe falling every day more dangerously into torpid entropy. You have had the vision (it's been my privilege to watch you put your vision into action) to know what it is Man must do in order to maintain his necessary dominance over a—let's face facts—terrifyingly unforgiving Natural World.

I've said it often enough in our private conversations: I heartily salute you and all your works, and I endeavor to supplement them with my own undoubtedly poor efforts. Even though you have been kind enough to call those efforts courageous...even heroic. But this was for you to say. Not I.

From my desire to participate in the great project of Megalopolis comes this modest report, paid for by the Megalopolitan Council of Four, for which grant money I am appropriately grateful. Should I gain my goal here, this work will cover all aspects of my native land: that is, ARCADIA. Such a report, as you and I have often discussed, has been needed for many perplexed years by every sector of Megalopolitan government—the ministries of finance and the arts, and, most of all, the military.

I will attempt to present all known information about the land of Arcadia here, in a concise and clear form, excluding no fact that could conceivably be of interest and use to the Megalopolitan mind. And, of course, to Megalopolitan plans for the future.

This is my goal. We'll see if I reach it. Your keen eye will be the judge.

One caveat: I hope to sound good-humored, rather than aggrieved, at the lack of understanding accorded me in my native Arcadia. "No prophet honored in his own land," as you, laughing, have often pointed out. How often have you and I touched on this subject! You've been kind enough to say that those who misunderstand and misinterpret the goals of the Megalopolitan project are more to be pitied than loathed, and I have come to agree with this wise point of view. Of those who deliberately misrepresent what you—what we—tirelessly try to achieve, for the good of all Mankind…well. About them, perhaps the less said the better. Although I will be forced to account for and dissect their opposition to the ideals of Megalopolis in the proper order and at the proper time. That they hate our freedoms is clear. How they mislead others to do so is less apparent.

I will say this here: I cannot help but wonder whether a constant diet of fairy stories such as Arcadia feeds its citizens—stories of centaurs, mermaids, magic spells, and miracles including angelic intervention—has been the downfall of that land. Educationally harmful as such teaching must be, could it be anything but *inevitable* that a populace fed such nonsense should prove so irredeemably stubborn? More than stubborn, *silly*? Nay, even so stupidly stubborn in its naiveté as to be rightly named *wicked*.

For how could it be otherwise than wicked to stand in the way of progress for All, in the name of what I could only call, had I found this thinking on an individual level, the product of a *diseased mind*.

This, then, is Arcadia. Land of fairy stories and wishful thinking. Land, alas, of my own birth. Let us see if, in naming its policies and their history, I can point a way to correct any imbalances found in them in the present day. My plan is to portray them clearly in all their childish idealism.

Along the way, of course, I will suggest important reforms: those reforms that Megalopolis is so well equipped to enforce.

Let us hope, dear friend, that the March of History continues in the rational manner we both honor. And that Megalopolis conquers, as Logic demands that it do.

For the good of All.

Whether they like it or not.

With respect and admiration always,
Your devoted friend and servant,

Aspern Grayling

ACKNOWLEDGEMENTS

Looking at the thanks to's at the end of *Lily the Silent*, the second book in THE HISTORY OF ARCADIA series, I'm struck by how support for *The Lizard Princess* comes from the same bunch of compulsively creative folk. We must be doing something right to work so peacefully together on so many projects. Very Arcadian.

So here are further Arcadian thanks to all the talented people involved: Nate Dorward, John Sutherland, Molly Mikolowski and Nick Liberty at A Literary LIght, everyone at Consortium Book Sales and Distribution, and at Constellation, too.

Alex, Gray, and Pearl are still my best source for love and cups of perfectly brewed tea.

Yet again, none of this could be done without Mike Madrid, who is not only responsible for the very elegant illustrations of *Lily the Silent* and *The Lizard Princess*, but also for EAP's overall book design. Thanks, Doc!

Along with much gratitude to the noble ancestors of visionary fiction: Hans Christian Anderson, J.R.R. Tolkien, C.S. Lewis, Madeleine L'Engle, Octavia E. Butler, and especially, with heartfelt thanks, to Ursula K. LeGuin.

Onward, Arcadia!

Notes